Emma Dally was born in Brixton and educated at St Paul's Girls' School and Oxford University. She has been Literary Editor and Assistant Editor of *Cosmopolitan*, and Deputy Editor of *She*. Since 1995 she has been Editorial Director of book publishing at the National Magazine Company.

Emma is the author of three novels, *Tomorrow's Past*, *The Cry of the Children* and *Remembered Dreams*, and a memoir of her brother John, *Dying Twice: A Sister's Tale*. She lives in North London with her husband and three daughters.

D1189115

By Emma Dally

Fiction
TOMORROW'S PAST
THE CRY OF THE CHILDREN
REMEMBERED DREAMS

Non-fiction
DYING TWICE: A SISTER'S TALE

EMMA DALLY OMNIBUS

Tomorrow's Past
The Cry of the Children

EMMA DALLY

WARNER BOOKS

A *Warner* Book

This omnibus edition first published in Great Britain by Warner Books in 2001

Emma Dally Omnibus Copyright © Emma Dally 2001

Previously published separately:

Tomorrow's Past
First published in Great Britain in 1995 by Little, Brown and Company
Published in 1996 by Warner Books
Copyright © Emma Dally 1995

The Cry of the Children
First published in Great Britain in 1997 by Little, Brown and Company
Published in 1998 by Warner Books
Copyright © Emma Dally 1997

The moral right of the author has been asserted.

A CIP catalogue record for this book
is available from the British Library.

ISBN 0 7515 3177 4

Printed and bound in Great Britain by Mackays of Chatham plc, Chatham, Kent

Warner Books
A Division of
Little, Brown and Company (UK)
Brettenham House
Lancaster Place
London WC2E 7EN

www.littlebrown.co.uk

Tomorrow's Past

To my children,
Rebecca, Alice and Ruth

Part One

CHAPTER 1

❦

A Child is Born

IT WAS A FINE Saturday morning in May, one of those early summer days when the pale blue sky is clear, no clouds can be seen and the sun shines promisingly through a shimmering haze. The air was still crisp with the residue of spring, causing the women on the street to pull their woollen shawls tighter around their shoulders and the men to wonder whether they should still be wearing warm winter vests under their shirts.

Kentish Town Road was busy with shoppers. For those women whose husbands were lucky enough to be in work – and had handed over all or part of Friday night's pay packet – it would be a good meal tonight. Irish stew, perhaps, or steak and kidney pie with lashings of gravy. They might even be able to run to a nice joint of beef for the Sunday roast if they were lucky. For the first few days of the week the food would be relatively abundant. By Friday they would be down to a supper of bread and *dripping*.

Thirty-five years into the twentieth century, Kentish Town was a shabby, run-down part of north London. It had not always been so. One hundred years before, at the beginning of Queen Victoria's reign, it had enjoyed a brief reputation as a fashionable suburb. High on the hill which runs up to Hampstead and Highgate, Kentish Town had offered green fields and fresh clean air to those choking on the filthy grime in London. However, the popularity of the area had rapidly ended with the coming of the Midland Railway in 1864. The railway extension brought its own dirt to pollute the wide streets and tall villas which had once housed wealthy, genteel families and their servants.

These Victorian dwellings still remained, but since that time many of them had turned into run-down terraces and tenements filled with some of the poorest families.

Some were poorer than others. Respectable working-class families, whose men had skills which kept them in work and who were anxious to improve their living standards, lived alongside those for whom life was a struggle in which they were always the losers. Such people lived on the edge of society, barely part of it at all.

Though most of the inhabitants of Kentish Town were working class, many middle-class families still remained there, tied by their roots to the place where, in better days, their parents and grandparents had been born and brought up. Unlike their friends and peers, these families chose to stay living on the hill rather than depart to the more salubrious villas and gardens in Highgate and Hampstead.

But whatever a person's station in life, the community spirit was strong in Kentish Town. It gave everyone a sense of belonging, a support system, even a sense of responsibility – so long as the community's rules and customs were observed in return.

Regardless of the shifting population, the shopkeepers of Kentish Town always knew what their customers could afford. Bob Worth, the butcher, was one. He knew that he would sell more chitterlings, tripe and lambs' hearts than any good steak or lamb chops. But he still had some customers who could spend more on one Sunday joint than another customer could spend on a week's family cooking.

On the day our story begins his shop was busy. Women of all ages were queuing up and chatting as they watched the master butcher at work, cutting up the bloody meat with his choppers and sharp knives, banging loudly on the wooden block in the middle of the shop. Bunches of furry, glass-eyed rabbits were strung upside down across the window front, above a table piled high with fat sausages and chunky pork pies. Mr Worth worked fast, shifting his vast weight from one foot to another. Behind him, from thick metal hooks set into the ceiling, hung heavy beef carcasses waiting to be cut as the orders came in.

Bob Worth was large and square with heavy, thick brows which hung above his eyes like hairy caterpillars. After his size, his most striking feature was his hands which had the tips of several fingers missing. Customers noticing this for the first time would wonder, as Bob handed over their pound of scrag or sweetbreads, whether one of his fingers was included in the package.

Mr Worth lifted his large head and looked over the counter. 'And what can I do for you, Miss Turner?'

A small child stared up at him with bright grey eyes. She was slight and neatly built. With her well-trimmed brown hair, she was noticeably clean and tidy, dressed in a Fair

Isle cardigan over a white blouse, blue serge skirt, white socks and leather sandals.

'I've come to collect the joint my mother ordered yesterday,' the girl said slowly, as though repeating lines she had carefully memorized. A pink blush crept up her neck as she spoke. 'My mother's not feeling well today,' the girl continued. 'She asked me to pick it up for her and says can you put it on the account.'

Mr Worth nodded and wiped his hands on the bloody apron wrapped around his large belly. Hobbling off to the back of the shop, he returned moments later with a bundle wrapped in white paper.

'It's all ready here, Miss Annie,' he said, 'a nice piece of pork. There's a good amount of crackling on it, your mother'll be pleased to see. I'm sorry she's not well. Please send her my best.'

As the girl left the shop, the women in the queue started to shake their heads.

'That Mrs Turner's been quite poorly lately,' said Mrs Rose to the woman behind her. Mrs Rose was a short spindly woman with thinning yellow hair and a liverish complexion to match. Her stooped frame was frail. She looked as if she could barely carry the large wicker basket in the crook of her elbow, already packed with carrots, cabbage and potatoes from the greengrocer next door.

Mrs Jones nodded. 'Yes, she's been quite ill. She's needed the doctor several times. And it's not just that baby she's expecting,' she added darkly. 'I think there's something else, you know . . .'

Mrs Rose dropped her parcel of meat into her basket. 'Well, let's hope she 'as more luck with this baby,' she said. 'She's 'ad a bad time losing those last ones.'

Mrs Jones sniffed. 'Well, bad luck comes to all of us, whatever our station in life,' she muttered. 'Money won't stop you getting ill health.'

'That's true, Pat,' returned Mrs Rose with a warning sharpness in her voice. 'But, you know, them Turners are a decent family, and I wouldn't wish the death of a child on anyone.'

As Mrs Jones was silenced by her friend, little Annie Turner walked up Kentish Town Road clutching the heavy white parcel to her chest. Her freckled face was set in an expression of intense seriousness. She was thrilled that she had been allowed to go to the butcher's on her own that morning, though she was sorry that it was because her mother had not felt up to going herself. Now, at last, her mother considered her old enough to do the errand by herself without being accompanied by Jack or Clara.

Jack was with his friends and Clara had gone with their father that morning to his office at the piano factory in Camden. He had to sort out some papers. Clara always jumped at the chance to go to the factory on Saturday mornings. While her father worked, Clara was allowed to play on the newly finished pianos, freshly tuned and about to be shipped off to the showrooms the following Monday. She liked to be the first person to play a serious tune on any new piano. She liked to make a first impression on the instrument before it made its way into the world. And as far as her father was concerned, the only time Clara could stay out of trouble was when she played the piano.

Annie pushed a stray lock of hair out of her eyes and smiled at the shopkeepers as she passed. She was feeling so pleased with herself that she did not even feel shy as she normally did. She felt so good and strong that when the little worry about her mother rose in her mind, she was able to push it back again for later. She was determined to enjoy herself for now. Feeling quite bold, she waved to the people on the tram as it trundled up the road towards Parliament Hill and Highgate.

Passing the jewellers, Annie stopped to look in at the window. Her mother had warned her not to dawdle but she could not resist having a quick look at the jewellery, especially the engagement rings – diamonds, with rubies, sapphires or emeralds, twinkling in the sunlight.

With a dreamy look on her face she held her left hand out in front of her, her fingers spread, and turned it one way and then the other. Just looking at the rich blue of the sapphires made her feel warm deep inside her.

'He'll be a lucky man what buys one of those rings for you, luv.'

Annie turned to see Mr Hamilton the stationer standing outside his shop. His bald head was shining in the sun. He had lovely big brown eyes and had probably been a very handsome man in his youth, her mother once told her. He was always friendly to Annie, who thought of him as a kind man.

Annie glanced at him and then looked away, wishing that the blush creeping over her cheeks and neck would disappear.

'You need more paper for your drawings, Annie? There's more for you here whenever you want.'

Annie loved to draw. One day she was determined to be a famous artist. Mr Hamilton provided her with scraps of paper and charcoal whenever he had some going. 'Thank you,' she whispered, staring down at her feet. 'I've got plenty for the moment.'

Mr Hamilton nodded. 'That's fine then,' he said, 'but make sure you let me know when you're running out. We got to encourage the next generation, ain't we? You never know, you could be as famous as that Picasso.'

Annie didn't know what he was talking about. She smiled sweetly at him and sidled away up the road towards home.

Annie decided to walk up Leverton Street on her way back. Unlike most of the other houses in the neighbourhood, the houses in the southern end of Leverton Street were in fact small cottages, with two rooms upstairs and two down. A few had two families squeezed into their small space but most of them housed one family. If the family wasn't too large or if finances demanded, the front room was often let out to a lodger to help with the rent.

Annie loved the colours of the Leverton Street houses, the pale blues, soft pinks and primrose yellows. Although mostly sooty and peeling now, they seemed like fairies' homes. She did not know that these pastel hues were first painted on by earlier Irish inhabitants homesick for the Emerald Isle and the small southern towns they had left behind.

When Annie turned into the street it was jumping with life. Some boys were playing football in the cobbled road, while others were standing in a circle passing a cigarette around. The younger girls were skipping and playing hop-scotch, while their older sisters sat on the walls gossiping and giving each other advice about their hairstyles. Occasionally one girl would cast a critical look at one of the boys across the road, lean over and whisper a comment to her friend.

Annie could see Jack and some of his friends from the

grammar school leaning against the wall and swapping cigarette cards. Jack looked away quickly when he saw his little sister. Annie shrugged. Now twelve years old, Jack always disowned her when he was with his pals.

Just then she caught sight of Maudie Sprackling's vast backside in her doorway. Clad in a floral dress, Maudie's bottom wobbled and quivered as she scrubbed at her doorstep with the scouring stone, just as she had been doing when Annie had passed thirty minutes earlier. She was doing it several times a day now.

'Maudie's going mad,' Clara had said only that morning. At ten years of age, Clara knew everything about everyone. 'She's never been the same since her Fred ran off with Connie Smith.'

Annie felt sorry for Maudie. According to Dolly Pritchett, moon-faced Maudie had been unable to have babies and her husband had hated her for not giving him a son. He had run away one night about eighteen months ago with the Smith girl from across the street. It had caused a lot of bad feeling at the time, and some people even blamed Maudie, which Annie couldn't understand. It must have been awful for her to go on living right near the Smiths after that. Annie thought she might have moved away, but she hadn't.

Poor Maudie now stayed at home, eating and getting fat, when she wasn't at her job cleaning for the doctor's family in Highgate. When she wasn't eating, she would get out her scrubbing brush and have a go at her doorstep for hours on end.

'She'll scrub it clean away if she goes on at that rate,' Clara had giggled.

On the other side of the road Mrs Whelan was washing

her front window. Her house was always spotless inside and out. It stood out like a beacon in a street where most of the other houses had not seen a lick of paint for years and buddleia bushes sprouted out of the brickwork. Mrs Whelan liked everything to be clean – she even washed the stucco on the front wall of her house up to shoulder height.

Annie always thought it funny that Mrs Whelan should live next door to the Smith family. With its broken windows and front door falling off its hinges, the Smiths' house was easily the tattiest in the street. Sometimes Mrs Whelan seemed to be itching to give the front of the Smith house a good scrub, too, while she was at it.

Most of the Whelan children were as tight-lipped and proper as their mother, and her husband, a tax inspector, was just a little mouse of a man. He rarely uttered a word. It seemed a miracle that Mrs Whelan had ever produced a daughter like Marie.

Marie was Clara's best friend, and that said a lot about both of them, Annie always thought.

'Hey, Annie!'

Looking up, Annie saw Kitty Challen waving at her.

'Come and 'ave a look at this stag beetle.'

Kitty and her twin sister Betty were poking and prodding at something in the gutter. The hems of their grubby frocks brushed against the dirty cobbles as they crouched in the road.

'Yeah, 'e's a real fighter!' Betty Challen held up the stick with the angry beetle balanced on the end. ''E's got an ugly mug, all right. Looks like Kevin Smith.'

The twins giggled in unison, shaking their blonde heads.

Annie waved. She knew the twins from school and had always been intrigued by their identical looks.

The twins smiled and waved their strange hands. They both had webbing between their fingers and toes, like little frogs. It was because they had been born six weeks too early, Clara had told Annie with great authority.

Annie turned right into Falkland Road and set off for her house. Annie's family lived in one of the tall terraced houses at the end, bang opposite the Methodist church and school. The Turners had the whole house. Annie's father had been born there, as had his father before him. There was lots of space. Everyone had their own bedroom. There was a fine dining room on the ground floor and a large parlour on the first floor next to Frank Turner's study.

Until they died a few years before, Annie's grandparents had lived in these two rooms on the first floor, but when they died, the family spread out freely. The front room on the first floor became the parlour, and then Annie's mother turned the downstairs front room, which was formerly the parlour, into a dining room. 'It's good to have different rooms for different purposes,' she would say.

But the Turner children were aware that theirs was probably the only household north of Leighton Road that had a room solely for eating in. Certainly their living space seemed luxurious compared with what most of their neighbours enjoyed, since Frank, who worked as a clerk in the piano factory in Camden, earned a good enough living to support them all. And although his wife would certainly have liked to follow their friends to the healthier areas of Hampstead or Highgate, Frank Turner wanted to stay where his roots were. 'What was good enough for my father and his father before him is good enough for me. I wouldn't feel at home any place else,' he would say with a light laugh and a sparkle in his fierce blue eyes. 'I'm part of Kentish Town and Kentish Town is part of me.'

When Annie got home she found her mother in the hallway leaning against the piano. A hand supported her back. Her normally serene face was twisted up in pain.

'Annie, put that meat in the ice box,' Grace Turner said weakly. 'The baby's coming. You'll have to run quickly and get Dolly to help. Ask her to get the midwife.'

Annie stared at her mother in horror. Grace Turner was breathing quickly through her mouth like Mr Garcia's horse when it was exhausted. Then her face was screwed up in agony. Annie backed against the door.

Suddenly her mother's face relaxed again. She smiled feebly at her daughter. 'It's all right, love, don't be scared. It's always like this. Now quick, get Dolly, will you?'

Throwing the joint of meat into the ice box in the kitchen, Annie ran down to the corner to Dolly Pritchett's house.

Dolly was peeling potatoes on the table in her kitchen, a huge black cauldron bubbling on the stove behind her. On the floor against the wall, two large baskets of washing waited to be ironed by Dolly and then returned to their owners. Dolly cleaned for Grace Turner five days a week but she also took in washing and ironing for most of the neighbourhood.

Dolly was a vast woman, as wide as a doorway. She had given birth to six children, all of whom had lived, and now they were producing many grandchildren on whom Dolly doted. Her hands and feet were the size of a man's. Her long greasy grey hair was tied up in a bun around her head, and when she walked she swayed from side to side, like Mr Garcia on his way back from the pub.

'Hello, cock,' Dolly said when she saw Annie.

'Mother says the baby's coming and to get the midwife.'

Dolly sniffed. 'We don't need the midwife,' she said. 'Look what happened the last few times the midwife's been. Fat lot of good that did your mother, eh? Besides, the midwife'll be out on her nursings, seeing all the new mums. She probably won't have time to get here.'

Taking off her pinafore, Dolly undid the roller towel from the wall and slung it over her shoulder. 'Come on, then, let's go.' She lumbered out of the house like a moving mountain, with little Annie following behind.

Annie's mother was halfway up the stairs and leaning against the wall. 'It's coming, Dolly,' she gasped. 'I have to get to bed. I hope the midwife'll be here soon.'

Dolly turned to Annie. 'Off you go now, Annie,' said Dolly, giving the girl a pat on the bottom. 'Go out and play. And if you see that father of yours coming home from work, tell him to stay away. He's going to have another mouth to feed by the end of the afternoon. It's quite early by my reckoning but not as much as you was. I'll sort things out here . . .'

Annie watched Dolly help her mother upstairs. She was still hovering in the doorway when Dolly came down again to get a bucket of water from the scullery.

'Off you go, Annie,' called Dolly, lumbering upstairs again. 'Your mum's all right.'

Her mother didn't sound all right at all. Every now and then Annie could hear a howl of misery coming from her parents' bedroom on the second floor. Each time she shuddered. Her mother sounded like an animal.

She sat down on the front doorstep thinking about what

it would be like to have a baby brother or sister. She hoped that this one wasn't going to die like the other two. Annie could just about remember the last time. She could remember her mother sitting in bed and crying. Annie had put her arm around her, as far as it went. She remembered crying but nobody put their arms round her. Nobody seemed to know why those babies died.

The noise from upstairs was beginning to disturb her now. Annie could hear her mother moaning loudly. Then she'd hear Dolly's soothing voice, murmuring to her.

Biting her lip, Annie crept upstairs. She stopped on the landing and peered through the half-open door.

Dolly's huge body blocked much of the view but Annie could see that she was tying the roller towel to the bed rail.

'Pull on this, love,' she was saying. Annie watched as Dolly stroked her mother's back rhythmically up and down .

Her mother was lying on her side on the bed, which was now covered with a mackintosh and newspapers . Annie saw a flash of bare leg. Her mother was breathing loudly and panting. 'Oh dear God,' she groaned. 'Jesus Christ have mercy.'

Annie was astonished. Her mother never swore.

Every now and then Annie's mother let out a low moan and a deep throaty grunt. She was pulling on her roller towel, which was quite taut. Annie watched in awe as the bed rail slowly bent under the strain.

Dolly was bending low over Annie's mother's legs. 'That's it, lass,' she said in a low voice. 'You can push now. Push!'

As her mother let out a low growl which rumbled on,

growing louder and louder until it turned into the most terrifying, blood-curdling scream, Annie shot down the stairs, out of the back door and into the quiet safety of the back garden.

Most of the gardens in Falkland Road were just scrubby bits of open ground, bare patches of hard earth with weeds taking over wherever they could. They were hardly used except for hanging out the washing or keeping a few chickens, as Mr Spratt did next door. Further up the road, Mr Garcia, the rag-and-bone man, kept his old horse in his back garden.

There were few flowers anywhere, for only the hardiest plants could thrive in the filthy London air. And the air in Kentish Town was particularly dirty because of the trains roaring through, belching their black fumes into the sky. It was easy to see why people had to wash their windows all the time – or why they didn't bother. It was a losing battle.

The gardens were divided by low, tumbledown brick walls along which many of the local children liked to scramble. Next door to the Turners, Mr Spratt's chickens scratched around in the dirt and clucked softly, while Marmaduke the cockerel strutted proudly up and down. The chickens weren't laying very well at the moment, Mr Spratt had told Annie the day before. That was too bad, seeing as when Mr Spratt wasn't having one of his 'turns' he was very generous with his chicken eggs. Eating those eggs made up for being woken up by Marmaduke at the crack of dawn.

The Turners' garden was quite different from all the other gardens nearby. The walls were their full height, straight and well pointed, and the garden itself was nicely laid out with a small lawn and narrow borders containing the toughest kinds of shrubs and flowers that could withstand the most difficult growing conditions.

Annie could not bear to think about what was happening to her mother at that moment. Trying to concentrate on the garden and its plants, she pushed past the speckled laurel bush and carefully picked her way round the prickly red berberis which sprawled across the crazy-paving path. Down one side of the lawn, the London Pride was in flower, its tiny pink blooms thrusting stiffly upwards as if competing with the blue bearded irises which had just begun to unfold their soft petals.

At the bottom of the garden was a shed where the gardening tools were kept, and a beautifully crafted wooden hut where Rabbit lived. Annie's father had originally trained as a cabinet maker and had, with loving care, built the hutch for Annie's eighth birthday, the January before. Rabbit was a large black-and-white buck, and he was Annie's friend.

Still fighting back the images of her mother's distress, Annie opened the door of Rabbit's hutch and lifted him out. He never bit her and always seemed pleased to see her.

Annie held Rabbit close and buried her face in his grubby soft fur. His whiskers tickled her bare arms as she held him to her breast. She looked up and around her, at the tall spire of the Methodist church across the road, at the run-down backs of the houses overlooking the gardens. Because it was a Saturday and a fine morning, there was a lot of noise out here as well. Annie could hear people shouting and squabbling through the open windows. Someone was playing an Irish jig on a fiddle and elsewhere a child was screaming.

Annie hugged Rabbit and sighed. She looked up at the

houses in Dunollie Place, which ran at a right-angle up to the gardens. There in the end house, as she had been for the past week, was the little girl staring out of the top floor window. Her sad face peered down at the world below. She had large, widely spaced eyes and short bangs. Annie gave her a little wave but the girl pulled away and disappeared behind the curtain.

Annie sighed. How complicated the world is, she thought. I want to be that girl's friend but she doesn't want to be mine. Yesterday a baby was in Mother's tummy and today it's going to be outside it. Annie suddenly remembered that Dolly had said that the baby was coming early. Did that mean it would also have webbed fingers and toes like the Challen twins? But then why did Dolly say that the baby was not as early as Annie had been? She'd never heard that before. She'd never been told that she had been born early.

There was no holding back those thoughts any longer. The image of her mother writhing in pain flashed before her eyes and the sound of her mother's awful cries rang in her ears. She shuddered again. Well, if that's what having children did, she didn't want to have any, ever . . .

Yet as she thought that, she had in her mind's eye the image of poor Maudie Sprackling scrubbing her doorstep hour after hour just because she didn't have any children. No, Annie didn't want to be like that, either.

CHAPTER 2

❧

The Brooch

THE BABY WAS A little boy named Bobby. He had a crumpled face and tiny black curls squashed flat against his head. He lay in his crib for most of the day. When he was awake, he made strange fluid movements with his hands and sweet snuffling noises through his nose. When he was asleep, he was silent and still. He hardly moved, apart from the slight rising of his chest as he breathed and the gentle pursing of his lips as though he were dreaming of sucking at his mother's soft breast.

Annie loved to sit and watch her baby brother asleep. He was so small and helpless. Then she began to draw him. Hour after hour she would spend trying to capture Bobby's minute features with her stick of charcoal on the paper so kindly supplied by Mr Hamilton. Annie was a naturally talented freehand sketcher, but hours of self-motivated practice had developed the talent she had been born with to an impressive level. Her ability to capture the world on paper was the one thing in her life that Annie felt sure about. She knew she was good at that, if nothing else.

Grace was confined to bed for ten days to recover from the birth. Dressed in a broderie anglaise nightgown, in her younger daughter's eyes she had never seemed prettier. Nor had she seemed so happy, with her skin glowing and eyes sparkling.

Grace was a handsome woman with a strong, slender frame and lean, well-shaped limbs. Her pretty round face was framed with soft, wavy blonde hair which she wore in a short bob. Her eyes were such a dark brown that the pupils were lost in them. Occasionally they gave off a slightly distracted expression, as though her thoughts were elsewhere, but usually they were alert and, like her thoughts, fully focused on her family.

She was always gentle and even-tempered with her family. In those early years, before her circumstances changed, she had endless patience with her children and was always ready to encourage and praise, or listen and advise. Annie loved her dearly.

Grace was regarded as a good mother, even by those who criticized her for appearing stand-offish. She was scrupulously fair to each child – if one had a boiled sweet, the others did too – and she was always available, always there to wipe a salty tear from a red cheek or kiss better a scraped knee. She went out of her way to spend time with her children. As an only child herself, she worried about what it must be like to compete for a parent's attention. She wanted all of her children to feel special in their own right.

During that lying-in period after the birth, Dolly came in every day for several hours. She did her usual cleaning but also the shopping and cooking for the family, teasing Frank good-naturedly when he came in from work, and serving up tea for the family at the kitchen table.

'That baby's the spittin' image of you, when you was a nipper, Mr Turner,' she said, placing on the table a dish of burnt sausages and over-crisp bacon. In spite of their familiarity, Dolly always made it clear that she knew her place in the Turner household. She shuffled back across the room to get the mashed potatoes from the oven. 'I remember those exact same curls when you was born.'

Frank and his children sat around the pine table. Earlier, Frank had opened the window above the sink to let in some cool air. The newly installed black boiler in the corner of the room was very efficient at providing hot water on tap all through the year but it made the kitchen very hot on warmer days.

At the sight of Dolly's lumpy mashed potatoes, Annie's big sister Clara wrinkled her nose and grimaced.

Frank laughed. 'And I've still got those curls, Dolly!'

'Well, you could say that,' returned Dolly with a smirk, 'but there are fewer of them and those that are left have to share yer head with some grey newcomers. Yer dad had the same curls, too.'

Annie raised her eyebrows with interest. She loved to hear about her ancestors. She still had a clear memory of her grandfather sitting by the coal fire in the room upstairs and talking about the old days. She could see the white stubble that had appeared on his chin in the evenings, and the network of blue veins on the backs of his bony white hands, and hear his ancient croaking voice.

'He was a fine man, yer dad, in his heyday,' added Dolly. She stood nearly upright, leaning against the table with a dreamy look in her eye. 'Good folk, they was, yer parents. Always helping people out when they needed it.'

Frank turned to Annie. 'Now, my grandfather, your

great-grandfather, watched this house being built. He remembered the land being cleared and the walls going up. He used to have picnics in the field where our garden is. Imagine that! He could remember when Kentish Town was just a village on a hill three miles out of London, and beyond were woods.'

'My grandfather used to tell me about swimming in the Fleet River as a boy,' chimed in Dolly, not to be outdone. 'He used to catch fish where Anglers Lane is now. That was before it turned into a disgusting sewer where everyone chucked their rubbish.' She nodded and patted Frank on the shoulder. 'You know what I like best about you Turners? It's that you've always stayed here in Kentish Town when you could easily have taken yourselves off to a better place, especially since you've done so well for yourselves.'

Frank laughed. 'Well, who'd ever want to leave old Kentish Town? It's the only place to live, as far as I'm concerned.'

The Turner family had deep roots in Kentish Town. Frank's great-grandfather, Caleb Turner, had come to London in the 1850s. Caleb was the son of a farm labourer in Devon but he had been apprenticed to the village carpenter and went into cabinet making. In the mid-1850s, with his young wife and son, he moved to London in search of work. He found there was a good living to be made in the burgeoning piano-making industry which was centred in Camden. His son followed in his footsteps, as did *his* son, Frank's father. Born in 1898, Frank was also apprenticed to a cabinet maker, and went into employment at the piano factory. But he was an ambitious young man and wanted to do more than his ancestors before him.

He studied hard at night school to pass the necessary exams to be able to move to the management side of the piano-making business.

Frank was not well-travelled so he could not compare his surroundings with many other places, but Kentish Town always seemed to him to represent the diversity of human life. Unlike his wife, he loved the contrasts that were always before his eyes – the rich villas just streets away from the shabbiest hovels, the dirt and filth of the railway just yards from the fertile fields and sweet-smelling woods of Hampstead Heath.

Frank was a sociable man, and a caring one, too. He was not rich but, thanks to his father, he owned the house he lived in and he was certainly richer than most of his neighbours. It was not uncommon for Frank to reach into his pocket to help someone in need. And he had tried to bring up his children to believe in two important rules: to educate oneself to the best of one's abilities, and to help anyone in a less fortunate position than oneself.

Dolly started to pull on a cardigan ready to go home and leave the family to their tea. She had to try hard to get her sleeves over her fat lower arms. 'Mind you, I'm not sure that Mrs Turner always feels that way. I think she'd like to be higher up the hill. Well now, I'm off. Bye, all!'

With that, Dolly lumbered out of the room and down the hall and, as always, slammed the front door so hard on her way out that the whole house shuddered in her wake.

Bobby was an easy baby and settled enough for Grace to get on with her household tasks as she wished. He fed well and slept well. Everyone described him as a 'good' baby, but the label made Grace laugh dismissively. 'How a little baby can be described as good or bad is beyond me,' she would say. 'But I am glad I have an angel,' she always added with a smile.

Soon life at Number Forty-five with the new baby seemed perfectly normal, and Annie could not remember what it had been like before Bobby was born.

One evening, when Bobby was about eight weeks old, the Turners had just finished their tea. Much to the relief of the family, Grace had resumed doing the cooking so they were now spared Dolly's offerings. That night they had eaten a good meal of pork chops and fried potatoes, followed by stewed prunes and custard.

Clara had already washed the dishes and it was Annie's turn to dry them. She handled the plates carefully but her mind was elsewhere, as it so often was when she did routine tasks. Her thoughts were off in a fantasy of colour and form as she conjured up the next picture she wanted to paint with her new poster paints. As she placed the plates and dishes in the cupboards and sideboard, Frank went outside to fill up the coal scuttles for the boiler and fireplaces. After clearing up the cooking pans, Grace had gone upstairs to her bedroom to give Bobby his evening feed. Jack was in the dining room bent over his homework, his schoolbooks spread out across the table, while Clara practised her scales on the piano. She was waiting for her father to join her playing some duets.

Annie went out into the garden to feed Rabbit and when she returned her father and Clara had already launched into a series of lively tunes.

Annie sat on the stairs and listened to the music for a while. She looked at her handsome father with his broad, smiling face under that head of black curls. Beyond him sat Clara with her thick blonde hair falling down her long straight back as her slender fingers moved gracefully over the piano keys. With their short, straight noses and strong chins, their silhouettes were strikingly similar. They were instantly recognizable to any stranger as father and daughter.

The piano notes rose up the stairwell and filled the house. Annie held her chin in her hands and smiled, quietly tapping her foot and nodding her head in time with the music.

Whenever Frank and Clara played, Annie longed to join in and sing joyfully at the top of her voice. But she knew she could not without ruining it for everyone. She was completely tone deaf. It was so unfair that she should be the only one not to be able to sing a note. Her mother had a sweet voice and even Jack, when he could be persuaded to join in, could hold a tune well.

Perhaps Bobby will be the same as me, Annie thought hopefully.

She climbed up the stairs to her parents' bedroom and peered in through the door. Her mother was in the far corner sitting on the low nursing chair. She was wearing a long dark skirt and a soft cotton blouse which, as she was still feeding Bobby, was half-unbuttoned. Grace was trying to write something with one hand, while Bobby, supported by the other arm, nursed quietly at her breast.

She looked up and smiled warmly at Annie, her eyes glowing with maternal love. 'I'm making a list of things we have to do for Bobby's christening,' she said. 'The vicar's coming tomorrow to discuss the arrangements.'

Annie stepped into the room with an eager smile. She loved to plan things. 'Can I help?'

Grace held out her arm. 'Come and sit next to me here and we'll make the list together.'

Annie sat down on the floor next to her mother and leaned against her legs. For a few moments Grace stroked her brown hair absent-mindedly. 'You're a good girl, Annie,' she murmured.

A warm feeling spread through Annie's body. Praise from her mother meant so much to her. It seemed to fill a space inside her and affirm her as a real person. Grace often praised her children, and equally, too, yet Annie never felt as confident as Jack and Clara seemed to be. However hard she tried to dismiss it, she always had a strange nagging feeling deep inside her that she was different.

'Now, perhaps we ought to look at what Bobby will be wearing. I wonder if you can reach the christening gown. It's at the top of the wardrobe.'

Annie leaped up. 'I'll get it!' Going over to the high mahogany wardrobe in the corner, she pulled open the heavy doors. Then she dragged a chair across the room and climbed onto it.

'There's a big white box at the back of the top shelf there. Just bring it down and we'll open it here. Are you sure you're tall enough?'

Annie reached up. She could just see the white cardboard box at the back of the shelf. It was surrounded by parcels wrapped in tissue paper – her mother's best woollen cardigans put away in mothballs for the summer months, along with the precious Fair Isle caps and mittens knitted long ago by her grandmother.

She could barely reach the white box with her outstretched arms. Her fingertips brushed it and the box moved slightly. She lunged at it again and the box fell off the shelf and on to the floor. The long christening gown spilled out of its wrapping of tissue paper and spread over her feet.

'Oh, it's beautiful!' exclaimed Annie, picking up the soft white garment and holding it up in front of her. It was made of the finest silk with delicate smocking across the chest and along the cuffs. It was long, and lined with several cotton layers.

'My mother made that gown twelve years ago when Jack was born. You were the last one to wear it . . .'

Grace's voice had suddenly gone soft. Tears were flooding her dark brown eyes.

Annie walked over and placed her hand on her mother's shoulder. She knew that her mother was thinking about the two babies who never got to wear the gown. 'Bobby'll look very handsome in it,' she said quietly.

'Now, let me clear up this mess.' She started to pick up the cardboard box and the tissue paper the gown was wrapped in. Then she noticed something else. A small object wrapped in tissue paper had also fallen out. She picked it up and opened the paper. 'Oh, Mother, what's this?'

In her open palm lay a large brooch, a circle of diamonds and sapphires set in heavy gold. The gems twinkled as she held them up to the light. 'It's beautiful,' she whispered in awe, holding it out to her mother. 'I didn't know you had anything like this!'

The expression on her mother's face made her stop short. The look of anguish was one Annie would never forget. Grace was frowning, staring at the brooch. Her mouth was open, but no words came out.

'What's the matter, Mother?' asked Annie, suddenly afraid.

'Put it back!' Grace forced out her words in a hoarse whisper. 'Put it back where it was! I don't want to see it!' Her lips had paled. She looked almost frightened. 'Please.'

Annie hastily wrapped up the brooch and reached on tiptoe to put it back on the wardrobe shelf.

By now Grace had collected herself. 'I'm sorry, love,' she said. 'I didn't mean to shout at you.'

'But where is the brooch from? Where did you get it?' Annie felt dizzy with questions.

But her mother was shaking her head. 'It's from another life. It was given to me by someone, by the person my parents used to work for. You know my father was the farm manager for some people in the country. They were always kind to my parents. The lady gave me the brooch.'

'But why did she give it to you? She must have liked you a lot.'

Grace sighed and looked down at the floor. 'She just wanted to give it to me,' she replied vaguely.

'But it's beautiful,' Annie persisted. 'Why don't you ever wear it?'

Grace looked back up at her with an expression Annie had never seen before. She looked as though she were wincing in pain. 'Sometimes you can't take things from one life into another one,' Grace said simply. 'It's too dangerous.' Then she turned to stroke Bobby's head. 'Look, Bobby's going to have curls just like his father's,' she said, making it clear that she was changing the subject.

The baby had finished feeding and fallen asleep with his head back and mouth open in a contented stupor. Grace buttoned up her dress and placed the baby in his crib beside the big brass bed.

'Thank you for getting the gown out for me, Annie,' said Grace. 'Now it's time for you to have a wash and go to bed. You've got school tomorrow.'

As Annie climbed into bed half an hour later, her head was spinning with her mother's words. What did she mean, another life? And why can't you bring things from one life to another? And most of all, why was it dangerous? Dangerous in what way?

She lay in bed thinking of that dazzling jewel and trying to work it all out. By the time she finally drifted into sleep, she had reached the obvious conclusion that her mother must have stolen the brooch from the lady who was her father's boss. Why else would she hide it away?

It was not long before Annie did make friends with the little girl she had seen in the window of the house in Dunollie Place. The very next week, in fact, the girl had turned up at Annie's school in Islip Street. She had come after the register, and Annie had watched as the newcomer, now bright red in the face with embarrassment, was ushered into the classroom. She was thin and gawky, with freckles on her nose, but her long face had a pleasant expression, and Annie was impressed by the thick brown plait which fell straight down her back.

As if sensing Annie's interest in the newcomer, Miss Cole, the teacher, asked Annie to look after the shy little girl and show her round the school. Annie had smiled in the friendliest way she could and patted the hard wooden chair beside her to indicate that the girl, who was called Tilly Banham, should sit down.

In no time, Annie and Tilly were best friends. Annie was Tilly's partner when they had to team up for lessons, and played hopscotch or cat's cradle with her in the playground during break time.

Tilly was a quiet girl and did not often speak unless spoken to. But she was quick and clever at school, and watched everything that went on around her. She was happy to have just one friend in Annie, and Annie, who had been bossed around by her big brother and sister for all her life, appreciated the way Tilly looked up to her for guidance.

Annie told Tilly about her family – her new baby brother, big brother Jack, and sister Clara who was two years ahead at school and who was always getting herself into trouble. Indeed, as if to make the point, that same day Clara was given a double detention for throwing a bucket of water out of the science room window into the playground below. Everyone knew that Clara Turner was the naughtiest girl in the school. But they also knew that she was clever. That helped her get away with behaviour that would have got most of them expelled.

Tilly confided to Annie that she was an only child and her parents had lost all their money when her father's business collapsed six months before. Now her father was out of work. They used to live in a big house in Highgate, she said, but her father's debts had been so big that they had to sell their house and move into rented accommodation in Kentish Town. She hinted that her parents were both unhappy. 'And they don't like having to live in Kentish Town,' she added. 'They think it's a slum.'

Annie sniffed. 'There's nothing wrong with Kentish Town,' she said. 'Lots of people here go way back to the time when it was the countryside. Sometimes I pretend it's still the countryside, too. Lots of nice people live here, you'll see.'

'Oh, I like Kentish Town,' Tilly said hastily. 'And I've met you.'

Annie smiled. 'You'll have to come to my house and meet Rabbit,' she said. 'But in the meantime, I can send you messages from my back garden.' Together, the girls devised a sign language so that they could communicate between their houses.

Annie and Tilly began walking home together from school. Annie was pleased not to have to walk with Clara at the moment because her older sister had recently been in the habit of teasing her by making jokes about how different Annie looked from the rest of the family. Only last week Clara had said that Annie had probably been adopted at birth from an orphanage. For some reason her sister's teasing was much more upsetting than usual.

When she could not bear it any longer, Annie had gone to her father in floods of tears and been relieved by his response.

Frank laughed. 'Nothing ever changes, does it! My older brother used to tease me by telling me that I was a changeling – found under a tree on Hampstead Heath. It drove me wild, even though I knew it couldn't be true. I was the spitting image of my father from the day I was born, so I knew it was nonsense but it still upset me.'

Annie frowned. 'But that's the point. I don't look like anyone.'

Frank smiled and put his arms around her. She loved

the smell of his clothes. 'I think you look rather like my grandmother,' he said. 'Your genes have just skipped two generations, that's all.' Frank ruffled her hair. 'You have to get tougher,' he said, 'and ignore the silly things that Clara says. She's just trying to get you worked up. Older brothers and sisters always do that.'

Annie smiled sheepishly. 'Thank you, Dad. I'll remember that.'

With Tilly as her friend Annie was able to steer clear of Clara after school. They walked home slowly, prolonging their time together and talking over the events of that day at school.

One day the two girls were walking up Kentish Town Road when they saw old Mrs Horder and her son Danny standing outside the baker's shop.

Mrs Horder was a tiny little woman with white hair. She always wore long black dresses, and had done since her husband had died a few years before. Danny was her only child. And he was still like a child even though he was at least twenty years old. He was a big boy and towered over his mother, whose hand he always held when they were out in the street together. He seemed to have little control over his head because it was always flopping about on top of his wide shoulders. His thick tongue hung halfway down his chin and this made him dribble constantly. He could not talk but instead he communicated with a series of grunts and snorts.

Some of the local children thought Danny was scary but Annie was not afraid of him. Her mother had told her that there was something wrong with his mind, which meant that he would never grow up to be able to look after himself. She said it was because Mr and Mrs Horder had been nearly fifty when Danny was born. It was sad, and he needed a lot of looking after, which was even harder for Mrs Horder now that her husband was not around to help any more.

As the girls approached, Mrs Horder waved towards Annie. Danny was grunting and seemed to be pulling away from his mother. 'Oh, Annie, dear, I wonder if you can help me . . . I need to go into the baker's to choose a cake for my neighbour's birthday. Danny is too frightened to go into the shop. Something's upset him and I can't persuade him to come in. Would you stay here with him while I pop inside? He'll be quite happy to stay with you and I won't be a minute.'

Annie smiled. 'Of course, Mrs Horder. We'll just wait until you come out. Hello, Danny.' She smiled at the great hulk of a youth who was staring mournfully at the pavement.

Danny grunted, while Tilly, who had only seen Danny from a distance before, stared at him in wonder. With his thick black hair and coarse features, he reminded her of one of the ogres in the Grimm's fairy tales she had been reading. But since Annie wasn't afraid, she tried not to be either.

Mrs Horder was in the shop for a while. There were few shoppers about as the pair waited outside with their charge. Then Annie noticed two scruffy boys coming up the road towards them. They were not from her school but she recognized them anyway, as members of the Torriano gang, which had been causing some trouble in the neighbourhood recently – stealing washing off the washing lines and tipping dustbins upside-down outside people's front doors. The Torriano gang was a group of boys from Torriano School in Torriano Avenue. They were renowned for their toughness and wild ways. The leader of the gang was Roger Knight, who was twelve, and known as the worst tearaway in the neighbourhood.

The boys had seen her, too, and started nudging each other as they approached.

The bigger one started to jeer. 'Look at the idiot boy, then, yer ought to be in a zoo!'

The other boy laughed and together they began to chant: 'Zoo time for Danny, zoo time for Danny.'

Danny was looking quite distressed. He scowled and shook his head violently, then squealed as he backed away. Annie had to grab him by the arm to stop him stepping back off the kerb into the road.

'Go away! Leave him alone,' she yelled. 'He can't help it!' Her fists were clenched tight as she stood her ground.

Now the boys turned on her.

'Ooh, listen to her, then. Talk posh, don't we? You're a hoity-toity one, you are!'

The bigger boy reached over and lifted Annie's skirt. 'Got clean knickers on, then, have we?'

The boys both roared with laughter as Annie danced around the pavement trying to stop them lifting up her skirt again.

'Go away!' she screamed. She looked around, hoping that a grown-up would come and help.

'Go away!' shouted Tilly. She chewed the knuckle of her thumb and jiggled up and down anxiously.

'Go away,' the boys chimed back at her, circling them menacingly.

Suddenly there was a shout. Looking up, Annie saw her brother Jack running towards them.

'Shove off!' he yelled at the boys. They turned and ran up the road. 'You're all right now,' Jack shouted at Annie as he ran past, 'I'm going to get them!'

Annie watched with wide-eyed admiration as Jack ran up the road after her tormentors. The smaller boy darted off down Holmes Road while the bigger one ran on. Jack followed the bigger boy. With his longer legs, he easily caught up with him and tackled his ankles. The boy fell heavily onto the pavement.

Although she was fifty yards away, Annie could see Jack turn the boy over on his back and pound him hard in the chest. The boy was shouting and begging for mercy, but Jack would not stop. 'This'll teach you to pick on people weaker than you,' he hissed. Grabbing the boy by the ears, he dragged him across to the gutter and rubbed his face in a pile of fresh horse droppings in the road.

Jack then stood up triumphantly. Breathing hard, he tossed back his hair, his face red from the exertion.

He sauntered down to join Annie and Tilly by the baker's shop. Mrs Horder was just emerging with her cake in a large cardboard box.

The boy had got to his feet and stood with his hands on his hips defiantly. He yelled down the road. 'Get yer big brother to help out, eh? Well, we can all play at that game!' Then he shook his fist and ran off up Leighton Road towards Torriano Avenue.

'Who is that boy?' asked Tilly. She was still shaking from the experience.

'That was Ian Knight,' replied Jack. 'His big brother is Roger, you know, the leader of the Torriano gang. I don't suppose we've heard the last of them now.'

Annie frowned. 'Thank's for helping us out, Jack,' she

said quietly, 'but don't you think you might have gone a bit far, rubbing his face in the dirt like that?'

Jack shrugged. 'Probably,' he said. 'Who knows? But he deserved it, so who cares?'

Annie and Tilly walked home in silence, each girl reliving the terrifying excitement of the incident in the high street. Annie's arms were still trembling as she turned over and over in her mind the image of Ian Knight shaking his fist at her and shouting out his threats. It scared her out of her wits. She was proud of her big brother but she was also now frightened of what Ian's big brother might do in revenge.

The Turners were regular church-goers and attended the church in Lupton Street where Bobby and all the children had been christened. The older children also attended Sunday school in the church hall. They went after breakfast for an hour before returning home to get ready to go to church with their parents. Annie rather liked Sunday school because she loved Bible stories, and nowadays she was joined in her group by Tilly, which made it all the more fun. And she loved looking after the little ones as well.

One Sunday on their way to the church, Jack mentioned that he had seen Roger hanging around in Leverton Street.

'That doesn't mean anything,' said Clara. 'His great-aunt lives there. He's probably just visiting her.'

Annie shivered. It scared her even to think of Roger, the leader of the Torriano gang. She did not know what he looked like but his very name conjured up images of demons and monsters. She slipped her hand into Jack's and squeezed it hard.

Sensing his little sister's fears, Jack for once did not push her away. He squeezed her hand back and then awkwardly placed a protective arm around her.

Clara did a cartwheel on the pavement. It was perfectly timed, with her strong legs following on from her carefully positioned arms.

'Oh, Clara,' said Annie, 'don't you care if everyone can see your knickers?'

Clara tossed her blonde curls and snorted. 'No,' she laughed. 'I don't care a bean. I don't care what anyone thinks!'

Later on, at Sunday school, as Father Gregory read the story about Joseph and his coat of many colours, Annie suddenly began to feel nauseous. Sour liquid rose up in her throat and deposited itself in her mouth. She excused herself, and spat out the sourness in the sink. Then Reverend Richardson suggested that she go home early. He was a kind man and sensitive to the ways children thought and behaved. He had been a hero to the Turner children ever since the terrible day when Clara was caught pocketing the money from the collection plate, and he had been so nice about it and not made too much of a fuss.

Annie was relieved to escape from the stuffy church hall and in spite of her queasy stomach she ran all the way home without looking to the left or right. She was terrified that Roger was out there and going to get her.

But she reached her street quite safely and slowed down to walk the last few yards to her house.

Inside, the house was quiet. That was odd. Annie had expected to find her mother in the kitchen, preparing Sunday lunch.

When she went into the kitchen it became clear that her

mother had been preparing the meal. Large peeled potatoes sat covered with water in a saucepan on the stove.
The carrots had been scrubbed and cut into long strips.
They too sat in water ready to be boiled. The meat – a
plump shoulder of lamb – had been placed in the roasting
pan and covered with a blue-and-white checked dishcloth
until it was time to put it in the oven. On the sideboard was
a large prickly pineapple. This was for pudding, cut into
thick slices and served with Carnation milk.

'Mother!' Annie called up the stairs but there was no
reply.

It was creepy. Annie began to climb the stairs up to her
room. As she reached the second floor, she could hear
noises. Her parents were in their bedroom. She continued
up the stairs.

But as she approached, the noises coming from their
room frightened her. There were moans and shouts coming from her father. Peeping through the crack in the
door, she saw a terrifying sight. Her parents were on the
bed. Her mother was lying on her back with her father
right on top of her, completely naked. He was moving up
and down like the dogs in the street when they were
messing around.

Annie stood transfixed by the sight and sounds. She had
never seen her parents without their clothes on. Her
father's white buttocks were moving up and down faster
and faster. He started to mutter in time: 'Oh yes, oh yes.'

Then suddenly he collapsed on top of Annie's mother
with a great groan, his body shuddering for a few moments
until it stopped. He muttered something into Grace's
shoulder. It was hard to make it out but Annie could have
sworn he was saying 'Thank you, thank you.'

Praying that she would not be heard, Annie started to creep downstairs again. In her mind's eye she could see her father's backside and her mother's expressionless face staring up at the ceiling.

She had almost reached the bottom of the stairs when her stomach lurched. The acid rose in her throat. She let out a little moan which was quickly followed by a fountain of vomit arching out over the banisters and splattering all over the wooden floorboards in the hall. Clamping her hand over her mouth, Annie dashed into the scullery and expelled the rest of the vomit into a tin pail.

As she retched into the pail, Annie heard hurried steps on the stairs. Moments later her mother was beside her. Grace was hastily pushing wisps of hair into place.

'Annie, love, are you all right? We didn't hear you come in.'

Grace put her arm around Annie's thin bent shoulders.

Behind her mother, Annie became aware of her father's large form in the doorway. He looked both confused and concerned but Annie was too busy being sick to notice his expression or the dishevelled state of his clothes, pulled on in a hurry. 'When did you get back, love? Are you all right?'

Annie nodded and waved them both away. 'I just came in a few minutes ago,' she lied. 'I just came in and was sick. I'm sorry about the mess, Mum, I'm really sorry.'

Grace hugged her daughter and glanced back at her husband. Thank goodness Annie had not been upstairs. Frank looked as relieved as she was.

Being sick made Annie feel much better. She did not have to go to church with the family and she did not feel like eating any lunch afterwards, but by the late afternoon she felt quite normal again. In fact, she felt well enough to go out into the garden to play with Rabbit.

The minute she stepped outside she knew something was wrong. The door to Rabbit's hutch was open, and the hutch was empty.

'Rabbit!' Annie called, looking frantically around the garden. How could he have escaped?

She found Rabbit behind the shed. He was completely stiff and cold, lying stretched out on the earth. His head had been bashed in, his neck broken.

Annie fell to her knees. Sobbing loudly, she hugged the dead animal to her and rubbed her cheek across his fur. 'Please don't be dead. You can't be dead, you can't be,' she cried. 'Please be alive!' She jumped to her feet and, with a great howl of despair, salty tears pouring down her cheeks, ran to the house cradling the dead rabbit in her arms.

CHAPTER 3

❧

Maudie

GRACE HAD ALWAYS FOUND it difficult to make friends. Ever since Frank had brought her home to Kentish Town, showing her off triumphantly as his beautiful new country bride, she had always felt like an outsider.

An only child, she had been born and brought up in a small village in Sussex, at the bottom of the South Downs. She met Frank at a barn dance in Chichester. They had been introduced by an acquaintance of her parents whose son had invited a friend to stay for the weekend. He was a lad who worked with their son in London. The two young men had planned a week of sailing in Chichester harbour.

With his fierce blue eyes and head of curly black hair, Frank had literally swept the shy Grace off her feet. He monopolized her all evening, giving no one else a chance to dance with her. In no time, Frank Turner had won over Grace's parents, too. He was, everyone agreed, a natural charmer who exuded friendliness and enthusiasm. His zest for life was catching. He collected friends wherever he went, as though people were attracted to such a happy soul in the hope that some of it would rub off on them.

Frank and Grace had a brief, intense courtship, and were married in a tiny Norman church in the next village. After a week's honeymoon in Hampshire, Frank took his bride home.

Grace did not take easily to London. After breathing pure country air all her life, the dirty streets of Kentish Town disturbed her deeply at first. But her devotion to Frank was stronger than her distaste for the crowded environment, and she quickly came to appreciate the fresher air on Hampstead Heath and in Highgate Woods where, before the children came along, the young couple went for long peaceful walks every weekend.

After her solitary country upbringing, and being a self-contained creature by nature, Grace never felt much need to seek out friends of her own. She was quite happy with the company of her husband and children and the brief everyday contact she had with the local people in Kentish Town Road.

It came as a surprise to her, then, to find how much she liked Marion Banham, the mother of Annie's new friend, Tilly. For the first time in her life, Grace discovered the pleasure of sharing a common point of view with someone other than Frank.

Like Grace, Marion was in her mid-thirties, though the many grey hairs on her head made her appear older. The women got to know each other because of the girls, who spent nearly all their time together, and they soon found that there was a strong bond between them.

Marion was a tall, big-boned woman with strong features. She had brown wispy hair, a slender waist and narrow face which seemed at odds with her thickish ankles and plump arms. Ever active, she walked in long strides everywhere she went, as though she had more energy than she could ever use up in a day. She always seemed cheerful and sane, however hard life became for her. She never lost her temper or panicked, and she could always be relied upon to be sensible.

Marion was proud and strong-minded but not a snob, even though she was quite openly unhappy about her predicament. 'It's having to prop up Geoffrey that I find so hard,' she confided to Grace one day. 'He always used to be so certain about everything. Now he doesn't seem to have any sense of himself at all.'

Marion's husband had sunk into a deep gloom and did little except sit in his room all day and read books. Marion coped well, eking out a living for the family by tutoring. She never complained but it was obviously a relief for her to talk openly to her new friend about her problems. And Grace felt flattered that Marion seemed to respect her opinion about the matters they discussed, and that she trusted her enough to confide in her about her sadness at not having another baby.

'It just never happened,' she said wistfully. 'And that means Tilly is all the more precious. Mind you,' she added, 'in the present circumstances, it's probably just as well that we only have one child.'

The women talked about public affairs, too, and gossiped along with the rest of the world about the abdication of Edward VIII and his love for Mrs Wallis Simpson. 'Just imagine, 1936 will be known as the year when three kings reigned – there's George, Edward, and now his brother George.'

'He must love that Mrs Simpson very much to give up the throne for her,' remarked Grace.

Marion sniffed. 'Yes, I wonder if he'll seem like such a catch to her now,' she added drily.

Annie had been pestering her mother for weeks to allow her to take Bobby out. She helped her mother look after the baby as much as she could, feeding him his stewed carrot and scooping it off his chin and spooning it into his mouth again. She soon learned how to change his nappies, deftly folding the material into kite shapes to get the right thickness in the right places. (Her mother explained that it was done differently for girls.) She even managed to push the safety pin through the layers of towelling without pricking the baby once. And she walked around with him just as her mother did, holding the baby so that he could rest on her hip.

She loved to act as Bobby's mother. It made her feel grown-up and responsible. It made her feel like her own mother. She had always observed Grace and imitated her in admiration. She now brushed her hair in a dreamy fashion, just as her mother did, staring out of the window, lost in thought as her head moved up and down until her hair fell thick and sleek down her back. She copied the way her mother ate her food, taking small pieces and chewing slowly for a long time. She even walked like her mother, in short, springing steps, and had the habit of putting an apologetic hand up to her mouth when she laughed unexpectedly loudly.

At home, Grace had always been happy to let Annie help with Bobby. 'You're my extra pair of hands,' she would say. But in spite of Annie's pleas, Grace had never let her take the baby out in the pram on her own. She never gave a reason, simply saying, under pressure from Annie, 'Oh, when you're a little older. You can do it then . . .'

Annie would fall into a hurt and bewildered silence. Why would her mother not trust her with this one task? It was so unfair.

In the end it was Marion Banham who persuaded Grace to allow Annie and Tilly to take Bobby out in his pram. The two girls had both been pleading with her. Annie was desperate to show Bobby off to the street, and to pretend that he was hers. After all, her mother let her bath Bobby and dress him, and change his nappy. Why not let her take him out, too? The answer was always no. Until Marion intervened.

'Go on, Grace,' Marion said, 'let them take the baby out for a while. They're good girls, you can trust them to look after him.' Marion smiled at Grace. 'It'll give you a bit of a break, too. And you can't be tied to Bobby all your life, you know.'

Grace shrugged her shoulders but then nodded. 'Yes, you're right. I'm not sure I'd trust Clara to be responsible, even though she is older. But Annie's always been a sensible girl and Tilly – well, I certainly trust her.'

Annie's eyes widened with excitement as Tilly nudged her in the ribs. 'You mean we can take Bobby out in his pram? Oh, we'll be ever so careful with him, Mother, I promise.'

'Just round the block,' said Grace. 'Not across the road.'

Annie's face dropped. 'Oh, couldn't we take him down to the shops? Can't we do a bit of shopping for you, Mother?'

Grace hesitated. Then she caught a glimpse of Marion's

raised eyebrow. 'Oh, all right, then. But promise me you'll be careful crossing the roads. If you go as far as Fortess Road, you might as well go to the dairy and get me a pint of milk – and a quarter pound of butter, too.'

With the money clinking in her pocket, Annie felt she must be the happiest girl in the world as she and Tilly set off down the road pushing the huge wobbly black pram.

'Let's pretend we're the baby's parents,' said Annie solemnly. 'You can be the father.'

Annie took her friend on a tour of the neighbourhood, up Lady Margaret Road, down Countess Road, up through the top of Leverton Street and then out onto Fortess Road. As they walked, Annie pointed out the landmarks to her, and told her about all the people in the area. She told her about Mr Spratt who lived next door, who loved his chickens and who had never been the same since his wife had died, and the Fenton sisters whose fiancés had both been killed in the Great War and who had never recovered. They lived together and squabbled like children even though they were both older than Annie's parents. Once, Annie's father had found them fighting like tomcats in the hallway. They'd been arguing about who should have the wishbone from a chicken, and he had to pull them apart and calm them down before he felt it was safe to leave them alone.

The girls went to the dairy and bought a bottle of milk and a quarter pound of yellow butter cut off the slab. Clutching the few pennies left over, they went into the sweet shop next door. There, under the tolerant gaze of Mrs Barker, the shopkeeper, they stood for many minutes, agonizing over the rows and rows of sweets laid out on the counter and in the large glass jars on the shelf at the back. There were gumdrops and peardrops, bull's eyes and aniseed balls, long black coils of liquorice and stumpy orange sticks of barley sugar. What a difficult decision it was!

After much deliberation, they made their choice and finally emerged satisfied with a quarter pound of sherbet lemons.

'We have to finish them before we get home,' said Annie, popping one into her mouth. 'We're only allowed to have sweets on Saturday.'

The girls wandered slowly round the streets sucking their boiled sweets and relishing the fizzy sherbet seeping slowly out onto their tongues. 'Next time we'll get gob-stoppers,' said Annie.

Everywhere they went, passers-by stopped to coo at baby Bobby and his chubby red cheeks. At first he sat up in his pram and beamed at every one of his admirers, but he had not had much of a nap that day so by the time the girls turned into Falkland Road again, the little fellow was leaning back sleepily against his pillow, his mouth half-open and his eyelids drooping.

'And there's Mrs Garcia,' whispered Annie, nodding towards a middle-aged woman leaning over her front gate just ahead. She looked rather exotic with thick black hair coiled around her head, and a richly patterned shawl around her shoulders. She had a strong beak of a nose and tanned skin as though she had spent all her life standing against the wind.

'Who's Mrs Garcia?' Tilly whispered as she leant towards her friend.

'She's married to Mr Garcia, the rag-and-bone man,' returned Annie. 'You know, the one with the horse.'

Tilly nodded. She knew the horse. She longed to stroke his velvety nose.

'Mrs Garcia's a nice lady,' explained Annie. 'She ran away with the gypsies when she was little, and she's travelled the world.' She decided not to tell Tilly what Clara said, that Mrs Garcia had never travelled further than Streatham, in south London, where she came from in the first place. It was a mean thing for Clara to say, particularly since it was not true.

As the girls approached, Mrs Garcia looked up and smiled. She had large, friendly black eyes. 'Hello, Annie,' she said. 'And this is your little brother . . .' She peered into the pram at Bobby, who was now lying back fast asleep with his mouth half open. 'What a lovely specimen!' Her laugh was a bit like a witch's cackle. 'Now, I've got something you girls will love,' said Mrs Garcia. 'My cat's had kittens, and they're just beginning to play. Come in and see them. You can leave the pram outside. The baby'll be quite safe.'

Feeling privileged to be invited in, Annie parked the pram against the wall of the house and followed Mrs Garcia and Tilly inside.

The Garcias lived in two rooms on the ground floor of the house. They also had the garden at the back, which Annie could see from the kitchen window was full of the rubbish Mr Garcia collected on his daily rounds. There were rusty old bed frames and huge sheets of corrugated iron leaning against the wall. Broken chairs and tables had been flung into one corner while unidentifiable bits of machinery lay piled up in another.

At the far end of the garden there was a large wooden stable with a roof made of corrugated iron. 'That's where Juniper lives,' explained Mrs Garcia.

She led the girls into the front room. It was dark and crowded, with a double bed in the far corner, shelving, and a table covered with an oriental rug. The atmosphere was claustrophobic with the heavy thick drapes hanging over the windows. A pungent musty smell hung in the air.

'Be very quiet,' whispered Mrs Garcia.

She guided the children over to the corner where a small ginger cat lay in a wooden banana crate. Pushing up at her belly as they suckled and mewled in thin little voices were five kittens of assorted colours.

Tilly dropped to her knees and edged towards the cats as Annie peered at them. It was quite hard for her eyes to adjust to the dim light. Along the mantelpiece there were rows and rows of pots with strange plants growing out of them, and from a couple of hooks screwed into the ceiling were hanging thick bundles of dried herbs.

Tilly was stroking the kittens with great care. 'I really want a kitten,' she said quietly.

'Perhaps your mother will let you have one,' said Annie.

'You can have one of these when they're ready to leave their mother,' said Mrs Garcia.

Tilly shook her plaits sadly. 'Even if my mother said yes, I know that Father won't. He hates animals.'

Annie watched the tiny kittens for several minutes. She was suddenly aware of tears pricking her eyes and an almost overwhelming desire to hold Rabbit. How much she missed her friend! Until now she had not realized just how much she, too, longed to have another pet to love as she had loved her rabbit.

Annie did not want to think about it now, and she certainly did not want to cry in front of Mrs Garcia, so she was relieved when Mrs Garcia got to her feet and shuffled out to the kitchen next door.

A couple of minutes later, Mrs Garcia returned with a plate of ginger biscuits and two mugs of milk. 'I expect you're both hungry,' she said quietly, holding out the tray.

The girls munched their biscuits and sipped their milk.

'Is it true you can look into people's futures?' Annie felt daring to ask the question. 'That's what my sister says.'

Mrs Garcia fixed her dark eyes on Annie and nodded. 'Your sister says quite a lot, as far as I can tell,' she said. 'Some of it nonsense, some of it quite accurate.

'Now,' she said, reaching out to take Annie's wrist, 'let's have a look, shall we?'

She gently turned Annie's hand over, and ran her fingertips over Annie's palm. 'Oh,' she said approvingly, 'you've got some good strong lines here . . .'

Annie stared at her pink palm with interest as Mrs Garcia began to talk about life lines and heart lines. Then Annie made the mistake of looking over at Tilly who was back on the floor playing with the kittens. As Tilly rolled her eyes in mockery, Annie started to giggle. She clasped her hand to her mouth. 'Oh, Mrs Garcia,' she gasped, 'I don't mean to be rude but . . .'

Mrs Garcia smiled benignly. 'It's all right, dear, I'm used to people not taking me seriously . . .'

Annie blushed in shame. 'Oh, but I do take you seriously.'

Mrs Garcia shook her head dismissively. 'I don't care about the mockery. You see, I know people's innermost secrets more than they would like to admit.'

Suddenly fearful, Annie stared at her in silence. Was she joking or not? Mrs Garcia continued. 'For instance, I don't need to read Mrs Whelan's hand to know that she worries about something every minute of the day but never about the things she's really worried about.'

Annie frowned. She could not work that out at all.

'And I don't need to touch your mother's hand to know that she has a lot of troubles to think about.'

Annie shook her head. 'No, you're wrong,' she said. 'My mother's very happy. She was sad for a bit, when she lost the babies, but now she's got Bobby she's all happy again.'

Mrs Garcia nodded. 'Yes, dear,' she said tolerantly. 'But feelings are usually much deeper than that . . .

'Now, what about you, dear?' she said to Tilly. 'Shall we see what your future holds?'

Tilly giggled but got to her feet and held out her hand. Annie sat down next to the kittens and stroked them quietly. Half her mind was thinking about how much she would like to try to paint these tiny mewling creatures with their soft ginger or tabby fur, and the other half pondered Mrs Garcia's peculiar remarks. What did she mean about her mother?

Suddenly there was a loud banging and clattering outside, and they heard the front door opening.

'Oh, there's my young man come home for his tea,' smiled Mrs Garcia.

Annie peered into the hall. There was Mr Garcia, leading his horse, Juniper, through the house to the garden at the back. The leather harness which attached the horse to the flat cart was swinging loosely around its flanks and belly. The cart was parked in the road outside.

'Did you get past the pram all right, then, love?' called Mrs Garcia.

Mr Garcia led the horse past the door and down the

passageway and out towards the back door. 'Pram? There ain't no pram there,' he said matter-of-factly.

As the meaning of his words sank in, Annie gasped and ran to the open front door. There was indeed nothing there. The pram had gone.

She gave a cry and ran to the gate to look out into the street. Up and down she looked but apart from a few people walking along on the pavement, there was no sign of a pram.

She was paralysed with shock. What would her mother say? Who could have stolen Bobby? What if he was hurt? Worse, what if he was dead? What if they never saw him again? Terrifying thoughts ran through her head as she stood frozen to the ground, her legs trembling, unable to decide what to do or where to go.

Tilly, who had run after her, decided for her. 'I'll go that way,' she said, pointing towards the church and the way home, 'and you go that way!' She pushed Annie in the other direction.

Annie started to run. There was an awful buzzing in her ears as the frightening thoughts continued to flood her head. Her heart pounded in time with her running feet.

Reaching Leverton Street, she stopped and looked anxiously up and down. To the left, she saw the Challen twins playing in the road. 'Hey!' She waved and called to them. As she approached, she realized that she was whimpering. 'Please let him be all right, please God, let me find him. I'll always be good, I promise, please just let me find him unharmed . . .'

'Have you seen our pram?' she called to Betty and Kitty Challen. The twins stopped their skipping for a moment to consider but then shook their heads and went back to their game.

At least Annie knew that the pram could not have been taken that way.

She ran north, up the hill towards the shop opposite the Pineapple pub. A man was hanging around outside waiting for the doors to open. 'Have you seen someone pushing a big black pram?' she asked.

The man shook his head. Annie ran on up the road, asking the passers-by. But no one had seen the pram and they generally peered curiously at little Annie Turner, her hands twisting anxiously and her lower lip quivering as she spoke.

Then at last someone could help. 'Yes, I saw a pram, Annie,' said Mrs Patty. 'My eyesight's not too good, you know, so I couldn't see who was pushing it. But as I went into the shop, I saw someone pushing it up that way.' She pointed towards the top of Leverton Street where it curved around towards the church in Lupton Street. 'That must've been about ten minutes ago, I'd say.'

Annie dashed up the hill, her sandals slapping loudly on the pavement.

As she came up to the imposing church on the brow of the hill, to her immense relief she saw the pram in the churchyard. And Bobby was sitting up in it. Thank goodness! He wasn't dead.

The pram was pointing away from Annie so Bobby could not see her as she approached. Sitting on a bench, holding the handle of the pram with one hand and rocking it gently, was Maudie Sprackling. She was talking to Bobby quietly in a soft crooning voice. She was smiling at him and nodding her head, as Bobby stared back at her with an uncertain expression on his face.

'Oh, Maudie!' cried Annie. 'How could you do that?

How could you take Bobby? You scared me to death.'

Maudie jumped to her feet, her big moon face confused and red.

Recognizing his sister's voice, Bobby spun his head round. A second later he began to bawl.

Maudie clenched her fists. 'Oh dear, now look what you've done,' she said faintly. 'He was all right until now.'

Annie ran to the pram. Undoing the straps, she lifted Bobby out and hugged him tight. He immediately stopped wailing and beamed at her and Maudie.

'You mustn't do that, Maudie,' Annie scolded. 'You mustn't take other people's babies and not say where you're going . . .'

To Annie's dismay, Maudie's face suddenly seemed to crumple. She sat down heavily on the bench and began to blubber. 'I'm sorry,' she said. 'I knew it wasn't right but I would never have harmed him. I was going to bring him back soon. It's just that when I saw him there in his pram, I just wanted a little go at pushing him up the road. I've never done that before, you see, and I wanted to see what it was like, to have a little baby in his pram. And he's so good. Even when he woke up, he wasn't afraid. I'm so sorry if I frightened you. I just couldn't help it. It was like someone else was doing it and I was just watching . . .' Tears began to trickle down her pasty face. With her eyes all red and bloodshot, poor, unattractive Maudie looked even more of a sight than usual.

Annie tried to smile. She reached out and gave Maudie a kind pat on the shoulder. 'It's all right, Maudie, I understand.' Inside, she felt sad for Maudie and she wanted to stop the next outburst from her.

But Maudie continued. 'Nobody knows what it's like,'

she moaned, 'to be barren, not to be able to have babies. I don't feel like a woman at all. My Fred left me because I couldn't have a baby. Four years we was married and no baby came. It was this very church that we got married in four years ago. All in white I was, with bridesmaids and confetti. I was slim in those days, too.' She looked down over her heavy body, waving her hands in a gesture of despair. 'Look at me now . . .

'No, I walked up the aisle that day and I was imagining having my first baby christened here. When I walked past the font, I couldn't keep my eyes off it. All I could see in my mind was a baby crying as the holy water dropped on its forehead. I wasn't thinking about the wedding at all.'

Her voice dropped to a whisper. 'He was keen, too. A big family, it was all planned. But then nothing happened according to plan. I couldn't have children and then my husband left me because of it. He ran off with that so-and-so Connie Smith.' She spat out those last few words, her voice trembling with fury. 'Connie didn't hesitate to run off with another woman's man. Not content with any of the other men she'd had in her time, she had to have mine, too.'

Tears of sympathy pricked Annie's eyes as Maudie wailed on. But she did not know what to say. 'I'm sorry,' she mumbled, strapping Bobby back into his pram. 'But I must go or my mother will be wondering where we are.'

Maudie waved her arm at her. 'Yes, you go home,' she said bitterly. 'You don't need to worry about me. Nobody cares about me.'

Annie hesitated as she looked at Maudie's hunched, shapeless frame on the bench. She put her hand in her pocket and pulled out the brown paper bag. 'Would you like a sherbet lemon?' she asked, pushing the bag under Maudie's nose. 'They taste good . . .'

Maudie looked up at her. With its down-turned mouth and red, blotchy skin, her face was a picture of pure misery. But she tried to smile as she took one of the sweets. 'Ta,' she whispered. 'And I am sorry, truly I am.'

Annie turned and pushed the heavy pram out of the churchyard and set off for home.

As she walked down Lady Margaret Road, she began to worry that Tilly might have gone home and told her mother that Bobby was lost But to her immense relief, she spotted her about a hundred yards away, coming up the road towards her.

'Everything's all right,' yelled Annie. 'Bobby's safe.'

As she walked back to the house, Annie felt a surge of happiness fill her chest. After all the fear and panic, the relief was exquisite. She was sure that she knew now what a mother would feel. Her responses had been more than just those of a sister – after all, Clara would have behaved differently. No, she was more like a real mother to a real baby. A smile crept over her face. Never before had she felt so much like her mother. It made her feel extraordinarily alive and purposeful.

CHAPTER 4

❧

Local Boys

ANNIE FIRST LEARNED THAT her mother's general health was seriously worsening on the day Grace could not open the chutney jar.

Before then, Annie had noticed that Grace sometimes had difficulty setting up the ironing board in the kitchen, fumbling for some time as she tried to plug the iron into the adaptor in the light fitting. She had been aware also that her mother was slow to get going in the morning, and occasionally complained about being stiff.

'I'm getting old, that's my problem,' she would say as she hobbled around her room getting dressed. Annie sometimes saw that her mother's feet and ankles were slightly puffy and red. Even though Tilly said that her mother – who was older than Grace – did not seem to suffer from stiffness in the mornings, Annie had never thought there was anything unusual.

One evening the family was eating supper – cold mutton and boiled potatoes – and Grace got out a jar of green tomato chutney to accompany the meat. Picking over her food, Annie noticed that her mother was taking an unusually

long time to open the jar. Grace had not said anything but
persisted in trying to twist the metal top, a frown of frustration on her brow. She was clasping the jar with one hand but
the other hand seemed too weak to get the top to turn.

Clara reached up her hand. 'Let me try, Mother. I can
do it.' With hardly any effort, she unscrewed the lid. It
opened with a whoosh of escaping air, and Clara set it
down in front of her mother.

It was a small incident and nothing was said about it at
the time. But Annie was aware of her father looking
intently at her mother, and her mother was unusually
subdued for the rest of the meal.

A few days later, Annie overheard her parents talking
about Grace's health. Annie had just finished painting a
picture – of the baby Moses being found in the bulrushes
by Pharaoh's daughter – and she was anxious to show off
her efforts to her parents, who were upstairs in the sitting
room.

She could hear them talking as she climbed the stairs
from the half-landing. The tone of her father's voice made
her stop short outside the door.

'Well if you can't even sew without pain,' he was saying,
'then you can't go on ignoring your arthritis. It's affecting
your life in an intolerable way. You've got to find out if
someone can help you. You must go and see a specialist,
someone who knows about these things.' Her father's voice
was firm and concerned.

There was a pause and then Annie heard her mother
saying weakly, 'There's no point. It all costs too much . . .'

'But we can afford to see a specialist,' protested Frank.

'Perhaps a specialist, yes, but you don't know about the
treatment afterwards. I don't want this to ruin our finances,

or to jeopardize the children's futures. I can live with it, Frank . . .'

Annie could hear her father pacing around the room. 'That's quite ridiculous. I *know* things can be done to ease the pain. And if it's really the money you're concerned about, then we should use your brooch to raise the money. We can take it to Fish Brothers. It's obviously worth a lot and we'd easily get enough to cover any major expenses. Then I can pay back the loan.'

Grace's voice was low and plaintive. 'No, Frank, I can't let you do that. I just can't.'

Frank rubbed his eyes wearily. 'But we have the brooch,' he sighed, 'and you never wear it. It sits at the back of that shelf doing nothing. I just think we might as well make use of it when it can help us.'

'I'm sorry, Frank, but I can't. Please let's leave it at that.' Grace turned away, twisting her hands tightly together. 'I'm sorry,' she added quietly. 'I just don't want to use that brooch for anything.'

Frank's voice softened. 'Why not, Grace?' he asked gently. 'I've never understood why you're so peculiar about that brooch. It's a fine piece of jewellery, and it saddens me that you don't wear it, even just in the house, for me . . .'

'No, I'll never wear it,' Grace said, shaking her head.

Frank came over to the sofa where Grace sat and settled down beside her. He took her hand and kissed it. 'I love you, Grace, you know that. I want to help you be in less pain but I don't want to do anything that will make you unhappy.' He paused and then added, 'But I would like to know about the brooch. You've never explained why Camilla Pearson gave you that brooch in the first place, though I've always understood that it was a sign of gratitude towards your parents, or perhaps to make up for her thoughtless behaviour when your mother died. But if that's so, why do you hate it?'

Grace was silent. Her lips were pressed together and she leaned against her husband's chest. 'Please, Frank, I'd rather not talk about it, please don't press me.'

As silence fell, Annie decided to creep on upstairs to her room. She could show them the picture in the morning. Her parents' conversation had revealed that her father knew no more about the brooch than Annie did. Why was her mother so odd about it? What was the story behind it?

A few days later Annie went shopping in Holloway with her mother, Marion and Tilly Banham. Avoiding the noisy, smelly traffic roaring up Camden Road, they took the back route to Jones Brothers where Grace wanted to buy some particularly pretty material. She planned to make some new curtains for the sitting room. Although her arthritis made sewing by hand difficult, she used the sewing machine as much as ever.

It was a long walk, but going to Holloway made a change from Kentish Town Road or Camden Town, Grace's usual shopping areas.

After some successful shopping, when Grace and Marion both found what they had set out to buy, they had tea and cakes in the tearoom. It was good to have a sit-down and rest their legs before setting off home again, and the tea was good, with cucumber sandwiches, scones and butter and deliciously light fairy cakes. Annie and Tilly looked after Bobby who, at two years old, was a bit of a tearaway. He kept grabbing the cakes and stuffing them into his mouth before anyone could stop him.

Well rested, the party set off for home. Bobby was strapped safely into his pram, which Grace pushed as she chatted to Marion about domestic matters. Annie and Tilly followed along behind, playing hopscotch on the pavement as they went, or doing cat's cradle with the elastic that Tilly always carried around with her, just in case.

It was a grey overcast day with a sky that threatened a downpour at any moment. By the time they had reached the final stretch home, walking up Leighton Road, they could feel tiny spots of rain falling.

As they approached Torriano Avenue they could see a man on the corner lurching from side to side. He kept stumbling around in circles. Every now and then he fell to the ground and then picked himself up only to fall over backwards the other way.

Marion turned her head and called quietly, 'Come on, girls, we'll cross here and stay out of that man's way. He's had too much to drink,' she added with distaste.

As the party crossed the road, they noticed Mr Garcia and his horse and cart parked over the other side. Mr Garcia was struggling to haul an old stove onto the cart. Juniper the horse was showing the whites of his eyes and was warily watching the drunken man. Grace pushed the pram out into the road just as a small black car came round the corner phut-phutting and backfiring loudly.

Startled by the noise, Juniper leaped into the air with a great snort. Mr Garcia staggered backwards and the old stove crashed onto his leg. With a yell of pain, he fell to the ground, hugging his leg in agony.

Juniper dashed out into the road and headed off straight in the direction of Bobby's pram. The horse swerved as he reached the pram but as he galloped past, the cart caught the handle of the pram, dragging it violently down the road. A terrified Bobby in the pram held out his arms to his mother and screamed.

Annie watched in horror. It only lasted a few seconds but it seemed much longer. She was certain that Bobby was about to die.

Suddenly a small figure jumped out into the road and grabbed the horse's noseband. It was a boy of about eleven. He hung on tightly to the harness, his legs pulled up under him as he was carried down the road for several yards. Gradually his weight forced to horse to slow down. 'Whoa!' he called in a loud, calm voice, 'Whoa!'

Moments later Juniper clattered to a halt. He stomped his feet, his metal shoes throwing up sparks on the road. His flanks were heaving and his nostrils were still blowing excitely.

The boy stroked the animal's nose. 'Good boy, good boy,' he was saying as the others rushed up. Annie now saw that Bobby's saviour was Tommy Smith, one of the Smiths in Leverton Street. She did not know him well because he went to Torriano school, not hers, but she knew that he was not a member of Roger's gang.

Grace had reached the stricken Bobby and yanked him from his pram. She hugged her baby tight. Tears of relief flowed down her cheeks. 'Thank you, thank you!' she said to Tommy. 'I just thought that was the end.'

'You're such a brave boy!' exclaimed Marion. 'You could have been hurt yourself . . .'

At that moment Mr Garcia hobbled up to take charge

of his horse. His leg was bruised but not broken. It had been a lucky escape all round.

A small crowd had gathered to watch the spectacle of the runaway horse and the baby. Everyone was now singing Tommy's praises.

'How can I repay you?' Grace was overwhelmed with relief and gratitude.

Tommy smiled and shrugged modestly. 'It wasn't nothing,' he said. 'I just did what anyone else would have done.' He smiled, 'And I've always fancied meself as a lion tamer . . .'

Annie stared with admiration at this stocky boy with freckles and straight sandy hair. He had lovely sparkling green eyes, like the sea.

They all walked up the road together, and Annie was pleased when Tommy accepted her mother's invitation to come home for a glass of barley water and a slice of malt bread.

They all sat upstairs in the parlour with Tommy served as the guest of honour and treated as the hero he was. Annie and Tilly sat together in the corner and watched him in wonder. He talked breezily to Grace and Marion with a maturity beyond his eleven years. He was polite and friendly and answered their questions confidently, while at the same time exuding a genuine charm as he complimented them, praising the malt bread which Marion had baked that morning, and admiring Grace's home.

'What a beautiful house,' he said. 'And you have so much room. So many rooms!'

'Well, these houses are bigger than the ones in Leverton Street,' agreed Grace, 'and we certainly have more room than a lot of people might have.'

'You're telling me!' Tommy sniffed at Grace's understatement. 'We don't have no room to sit in like this,' he said. 'All the action goes on in the kitchen, 'cos there are too many people sleeping in the house. All the rooms are bedrooms . . .' He chuckled. 'Of course, there's a bit of to-ing and fro-ing and sometimes there's a bit more space when somebody is away for a bit, but it's never like this . . .' He waved his arm in a wide circle. 'It's wonderful.'

They recounted the events in Leighton Road, and to their surprise Tommy informed them that the drunken man was Roger Knight's father. 'He's down the pub all hours, he is. Roger's always down there to drag him home to make sure he spends the night in his bed and not in the street.'

Annie listened in wonder. Although her father made the occasional trip to the pub, and a bottle of sherry was kept in the cupboard to be offered to visitors, her parents rarely touched alcohol themselves. It really was the demon drink, as she had heard people call it, if it could make someone's father behave like that.

'I'm surprised that Roger can act like a responsible son,' commented Grace. 'He's always struck me as a cruel boy who does not care much for anyone. The way he rampages around with his gang causing trouble for everyone is quite terrible.'

Tommy raised his brows and nodded. 'Yes, he can be very cruel . . .'

'Perhaps someone's been cruel to him,' said Grace, always on a child's side.

'We think he killed my rabbit,' interrupted Annie. 'He broke Rabbit's neck and threw him on the ground.'

'We don't know for certain, Annie,' Grace chided her

gently. 'And we mustn't accuse without any proof. Besides, that was a long time ago now.'

'It was only two years ago, and it must have been Roger,' protested Annie. 'Lots of people saw him hanging around the gardens that day, and Tilly saw him running along our wall . . .'

'That's right,' chimed in Tilly. 'I did.'

Grace raised her finger to her lips. 'Yes, I know, Annie, we all agree that it was likely, but I'm just saying that nobody actually saw Roger kill your rabbit so we can't know for sure.'

Annie frowned. 'Well, I know he did,' she said crossly.

'It wouldn't surprise me,' said Tommy, smiling at Annie. 'I remember Roger being cruel to animals when he was still at my school. He used to pull wings off flies, and once he tried to flush a kitten down the lavatory. He found it in the playground – it was only a few weeks old, and he poured Ajax all over it and pulled the chain. He was sent home for the rest of the week and the whole school had a lecture on being kind to animals.'

'What a horrible story,' said Marion.

'They're all a bit like that, in that family,' added Tommy. 'So if you think my family's bad, you should hear what Roger's family gets up to . . .'

Marion looked at the boy with interest. Relatively new to the area, she was not fully aware of the reputation of the Smith family. 'Is your family bad?' she asked innocently.

Annie glanced at her mother. Then she looked at Tommy. How would he answer?

But Tommy did not seem to be in the slightest bit embarrassed. He grinned, revealing two strong square front teeth. 'The local coppers think so. And I have to admit that my lot don't have much respect for the law, most of 'em. But they're a decent lot, in their way. They'd never hurt no one, even on a job. They've got standards – of a sort. And you'd never find any of them being cruel to animals, not like Roger . . .'

The room was hushed as Tommy spoke. Everyone stared intently at this open, honest boy.

'But your sister hurt Maudie Sprackling when she ran away with Maudie's husband,' Grace said gently.

Tommy thought for a moment. 'That's true,' he said, 'I won't deny that . . . but that was a bit different, I mean, it wasn't just Connie, it takes two, after all . . .'

Grace and Marion nodded.

'That's true,' replied Marion.

'But Connie ain't my sister, anyway,' Tommy continued. 'She's my cousin. My mum died when I was born, so I was adopted by my mum's sister, Jan, who's my aunt. I've always called them Mum and Dad and they've always treated me like they treat the other boys. But I am slightly different,' he added with a touch of pride. 'And I've always felt slightly different, too.'

Tommy Smith was making a big impression on his audience. His politeness and good manners seemed so uncharacteristic of the Smith family they thought they knew. Annie was fascinated by him. He was so confident and so funny. Every now and then he would catch her eye across the room and wink at her, causing her to look away with a blush of embarrassment.

Tommy was still there when Frank came home from work. Annie heard him come in through the front door. He came upstairs and welcomed Marion with genuine pleasure. He was pleased that Grace had Marion as a friend now.

'This is Tommy Smith, Frank.' Grace held out her arm towards Tommy, who had got to his feet and was smiling respectfully at Frank. 'You know the Smiths, from Leverton Street.'

'Good afternoon, sir,' said Tommy.

Frank's reaction was quite strange. The moment the Smiths were mentioned, the smile on Frank's face froze momentarily and then disappeared. He seemed not to hear Grace's account of how Tommy had saved Bobby's life by stopping Mr Garcia's runaway horse. Annie watched her father's face in astonishment. He looked both uncomfortable and angry, with a frown on his brow and his mouth set in a grim straight line.

But he had taken in some of Grace's words. 'I'm extremely grateful to you for saving my son's life,' he said. 'Now, if you'll excuse me, I have some paperwork to do before tea.'

He walked out of the room and shut himself into his study next door.

Annie could not understand her father's reaction any more than Grace could. After Tommy had gone home and they had said their goodbyes to Marion and Tilly, they tackled Frank.

'I was surprised at you, Frank,' Grace chided him, 'being so unfriendly to Tommy Smith. If the children had behaved as you did, they would have been reprimanded.'

Frank had his head buried in the evening paper. He did not look up but he was clearly not reading. 'He's a Smith,' he said flatly. But in spite of his certain tone, he looked uncomfortable.

'So what?' demanded Annie.

'You've never complained about the Smiths before,' said

Grace. 'I thought you liked everyone who lived around here. I thought you all shared a common history, you all went to school together and your parents knew each other, and your grandparents.'

'The Smiths are different,' replied Frank in a low voice. 'I would rather not have anything to do with any of them. They are trouble.'

'But Tommy's different!' exclaimed Annie. 'He's a cousin, he's not a real Smith. His mother died so he was brought up by Mr and Mrs Smith as their son. He calls them Mum and Dad but really they're his uncle and aunt . . .'

'I don't care,' said Frank, folding up his paper. 'It makes no difference to me.'

'But Bobby could have died if Tommy hadn't been there,' said Grace.

'I know, I know,' replied Frank. 'I appreciate his saving Bobby's life – how could I not? But I'd rather not have any dealings with any of that family. It's nothing specific but you can see they're trouble – one of the boys is always in prison for one thing or another. And I decided a long time ago that we shouldn't have much to do with them. I'm happy to be civil to them in the street, but I don't want them in my home.'

'Well, you weren't very civil to Tommy!' shouted Annie.

'That's enough, Annie, don't be rude to your father,' said Grace quietly.

Frank got to his feet. 'I don't want to discuss this any more,' he said. He had to leave the room before anyone noticed how his cheeks were burning with shame.

He climbed the stairs as Grace and Annie shook their heads at Frank's bewildering behaviour.

CHAPTER 5

❧

Sally Brown

CLARA WAS UPSTAIRS IN her room with her best friend
Marie Whelan. The girls were supposed to be rehearsing
their parts for the school play but they had lost interest in
drama and now sat on the bed, swinging their long bare
legs, and discussing their friends and life.

Marie was a thin, gangly girl with a narrow face and
thin lips. Her thick brown hair had never been cut and it
was always tied up in two fat plaits which fell heavily down
her back to her waist. They were like snakes. With her
large, wide hazel eyes, Marie was not unattractive but she
looked quite homely next to Clara.

Clara's looks gave her a presence. Wherever she went
people noticed her. She had sparkling gentian-blue eyes
and wavy blonde hair which, even when tied back, tumbled
down in soft curls. She had strong clean limbs and even
features. Her skin was clear and white, her plump lips the
colour of mulberries. Although only twelve, it was evident
to all that she was going to be a real beauty as an adult.

Marie felt privileged to be Clara Turner's best friend.
Easily dominated, she was happy to be with someone who

always knew what to do next. Clara's bossiness never vexed her. After all, her mother was always telling her what to do, and Marie sometimes worried that, left alone in the world, she would not know what to do with herself.

'Kevin Jones tried to kiss me yesterday,' boasted Clara.

'Well, you're sweet on him, aren't you?' Marie looked mournful. She did not expect anyone to want to kiss her, ever.

'Yes,' said Clara, 'but I told him he had to wait.' She paused. 'I thought I ought to get more practice first.'

'All right,' said Marie, without much enthusiasm.

'Shall we begin?' Clara leaned forward and placed her puckered lips gently on Marie's. She pulled away with a loud 'Mwah!'

Marie frowned. 'I don't think it's done like that,' she said.

Clara looked annoyed. 'Well, let's try again,' she said quickly. 'But this time we should shut our eyes.'

The girls leaned forward with their eyes shut and giggled as they bumped their noses clumsily. They fell backwards on the bed in peals of laughter.

'This isn't going to work.'

'No,' said Marie with a look of relief.

Clara was already bored. 'Let's go out somewhere,' she said. 'Let's see if we can feed Mr Spratt's chickens. That's always good fun.'

Mr Spratt, the old man who lived on the ground floor next door, was happy to have Clara and her young friend help to feed his hens. He had been widowed for many years. He was probably not as ancient as he looked but he was very wizened and people said that he had never quite recovered from the death of his wife. Others said he had gone dotty after being shell-shocked in the Great War. What everyone agreed was that whatever was wrong with him, he had become even dottier after Mrs Spratt's death. Now the only thing he cared about was his large flock of hens.

He loved the birds and he wanted everyone else to love them, too. He knew each hen by name and, in his high rasping voice, would list her habits and foibles like a mother talking about her child.

'Well, that Sandy, now, she's very shy and always waits to eat her food last. But Blackie is a little too forward and has to be fed separately otherwise she pecks the others quite nastily. And that old lady Specky, now she's very fussy about where she lays her eggs. She always has to lay them in the top box in the henhouse, while Titch, there, will never lay inside but insists on finding a spot outside in the run somewhere. I spend hours searching for her eggs, I do, but she enjoys seeing me suffer, I bet. Yes, Marmaduke is a happy boy. And so he should be, surrounded by beautiful women . . .'

The old man chattered on as Clara watched the birds clucking around in the run, a fixed look of concentration in her eyes.

The girls helped Mr Spratt mix meal into a bucket of food scraps from the kitchen. This included discarded eggshells.

'Ugh! They're just cannibals,' declared Clara, 'eating part of themselves!'

Mr Spratt had a pronounced stoop and a stubbly chin which he rubbed with twisted, arthritic hands. 'That may be so,' he chuckled, 'but the calcium is good for making the next lot of eggs. It don't bother them and it don't bother me.'

Mr Spratt had always lived next door. He had two rooms on the ground floor where he had lived with his wife. He had adored his wife, a noisy, flamboyant woman who loved to dress up in all her finery. She never left the house without being well turned out in smart dresses, layers of jewellery, and bright red varnish on her long nails. Clara's mother did not approve of ladies who painted their nails but she had not minded Mrs Spratt. 'She was on the stage, before she married,' Grace would say, as though that excused her next-door neighbour.

But after his wife died, Mr Spratt really had gone to pieces.

People described how sometimes he stood in the garden at night and howled like a dog at the full moon, or how in the early hours of the morning he walked up and down the street ringing a bell. Clara was always watching out for him to have one of his funny turns but the most she had seen was a distracted Mr Spratt walking down the road talking aloud to himself and looking dishevelled and unwashed. But Clara liked him. He seemed to be in his own world, not dependent on anyone else, and he was always friendly towards the Turner family, as well as generous with his fresh orange-yolked eggs which tasted so pungent on the tongue.

'Now you girls wait here,' said Mr Spratt to Clara and Marie. 'I might be able to get a letter into the last post. It would help me if you would dish this out to my darlings . . .' He held up the bucket of mixed meal and scraps. 'Just pour this into that long trough over in the corner there, and then scatter this grain onto the ground.' He pointed to a small sack of grain in the box just inside his back door. 'They've got enough water, you don't need to worry about that.'

Clara took the bucket. 'If you're not back, we'll just climb back home over the wall.'

Mr Spratt went off on his errand while Clara and Marie let themselves into the chicken run. The hens were hungry and clucked hopefully as they circled around the girls' legs.

'Good,' said Clara as she heard the sound of Mr Spratt closing the front door behind him. 'Now we can try something I've been dying to do for a long time. You can hypnotize chickens, you know,' she said. 'Apparently it's easy. I read about it somewhere.'

Marie giggled.

'So now's our chance to try it,' said Clara.

The chickens were so used to being fondled by Mr Spratt and so eager to be fed that it was easy to catch them. Clara dumped the food into the trough and grabbed a big black bird. She handed it to Marie.

'That's Blackie, I think,' said Marie.

'Put it down and hold its head so that its beak just touches the ground,' Clara instructed Marie.

While Marie held the frightened chicken in position, Clara ran her forefinger backwards and forwards around its beak making a large semicircle each time. 'We do this several times,' she said, 'and then you let go.'

She did it five times. Marie let go. The chicken picked up its head and, after a moment's hesitation, it scuttled off, flapping its wings and squawking loudly.

'We can't have done it right.' Clara frowned. 'Let's do another one.'

They picked on six other chickens but the experiment was not a success. Some of the chickens remained rooted to the spot for a couple of seconds but most leaped up complaining loudly and rushed out of reach. Certainly

Marmaduke the cock stayed well out of the way. There was no chance of trying it out on him.

'Perhaps they're the wrong kind of chicken,' suggested Marie.

Clara shrugged. 'Never mind, let's go. I'm bored with this. Let's get something to eat and then go up to Parliament Hill.'

The girls scrambled over the wall and let themselves into the Turners' house from the garden.

Clara found her mother in the kitchen busy bottling pickled onions, marrows and beetroots. The smell of the pickling vinegar made their nostrils curl and tighten.

Grace did the pickling every year and always filled more jars than the family could use themselves. Her mother-in-law had always done this with the idea of then giving the spare jars out to various people in the neighbourhood. For Grace, who found that making contact with the neighbours did not come naturally, it was an acceptable way to remain friendly.

While Grace spooned out the pickled vegetables, Annie sat at the end of the pine kitchen table painting a large picture. She had been hoping to play with Tommy Smith that afternoon. Since the day Tommy had saved Bobby's life, Tommy had become a friend to both Annie and Tilly. They often met up after school and at weekends to go to the library or play jacks. Tommy's serious nature appealed to both girls. Annie's father seemed to have accepted him, too, but he still seemed uneasy in Tommy's presence.

But when Annie called round at Tommy's house in Leverton Street that morning she was told that he was in bed with mumps. 'Came down with it last night,' said Mrs Smith. 'Looks like a hamster today, he does.' So Tommy was not around to play with and neither was Tilly, for she had gone shopping in the West End with her mother.

So Annie had been left with no one to play with but she was not too bothered. She had been wanting to start a big new painting that had been building up in her head for days.

Now the painting was finished. It was of a jungle, full of lions and tigers and brightly coloured birds with long feathers. Annie was very satisfied with it. She had worked hard at it, using every bit of the paper as she had been taught, and being bold with her coloured paints. She was going to give it to her father when he came home from work. She poured the dirty water into the sink and cleared up her poster paints.

When Clara announced that she and Marie were going up to Parliament Hill, Annie was desperate to join them. Having been inside all afternoon, she felt she wanted to get some fresh air and stretch her legs. 'Can I come, too?' she asked eagerly.

Clara frowned. 'Do you have to?'

'Now, be kind, Clara,' her mother chided her. 'Take Annie with you, now. You know she'll be no trouble and she enjoys it so. Here, take some stale bread for the ducks . . .'

Clara and Marie were not delighted to have Annie along, but they were willing to tolerate her trotting behind just so long as she did not interrupt their conversation. And they did not even try to walk too fast for her this time, in the way they used to. Clara actually quite liked Annie nowadays and was stand-offish only when she was with her friends.

It was a warm, sunny afternoon with a fresh southern breeze, a good day to go to the Heath. And there were many other people about, courting couples, dog-walkers, mothers with children, nannies with prams.

The girls ran to the top of the hill to watch the kites dipping and rising in the wind. As usual it was blustery up there. Their hair whipped around their faces and when they shouted at each other, their words seemed to blow away across the Heath. They sat on the grass and looked south over London. They could see St Paul's Cathedral and, far beyond, some hills in the distance.

Tiring of the view, the girls ran halfway down the hill and rolled down the rest. They landed in a dizzy laughing pile at the bottom.

Then Clara started to do cartwheels and handstands, and walked about on her hands, her skirt tucked into her knickers. She had an extraordinary sense of balance and could stay upside-down for ages, until she could no longer stand the pressure in her head.

Annie watched her older sister with pride. Clara was so athletic, so easy with her body, which seemed to do anything she asked of it. She felt ashamed of her own weak and clumsy little frame. The older she got the more she agonized about not being like Clara. For a long time she had assumed (or hoped) that it was just a matter of time before she too would develop the robust physique that Clara enjoyed But as the years passed, she could see that she was merely becoming more like herself – straight and angular. She had been nursing false hopes.

When Clara grew tired of her gymnastics, they wandered on up to Highgate Pond, where they threw lumps of hard bread into the water for the eager ducks.

Clara took off her shoes and socks and wandered out into the mud at the edge of the water. She squealed as the black mud oozed up between her toes. 'Come on, Marie, this is fun!'

Marie shook her head. 'I don't dare,' she called back. 'My mother would die if I got any dirtier.' She looked down at the green streaks where the grass had stained her shirt and white socks. She was already wondering how she would explain those to her mother, who could not abide dirt of any sort.

They wandered on across the Heath, watching the squirrels hopping across the branches of the beech trees and laughing at the pigeons puffing out their feathers in their mating rituals. 'It makes them look just like Mr Worth,' cried Marie.

'Or Maudie,' added Clara with a laugh.

The older girls had stopped treating Annie as a nuisance and they now took it in turns to give her a piggyback. Clara snorted and whinnied in her imitation of a horse.

Now they were getting hungry and set off back home. They decided to stop off at Mr Gunn's on the way, to pick up the groceries for Mrs Turner. She had asked the girls to get some cocoa powder and a bag of rice.

Suddenly the camaraderie Annie had felt with her sister dropped away. In a loud, imperious voice, Clara told Annie to stay outside while she and Marie went into the shop.

Annie obediently did as she was told, leaning against the wall and scuffing her sandals on the pavement. It was always the same, she thought with irritation. Just when she thought that Clara had accepted her, just as she felt equal with her older sister, Clara had to put her in her place. It wasn't fair. She felt tempted to go back home on her own, but she was afraid that might annoy Clara too much. It wasn't worth it.

When they came out of the shop a few minutes later, the older girls were giggling. Despite Annie's pleading, they refused to tell her why. Once again Annie was excluded. She trailed along behind them feeling dispirited.

Clara and Marie kept on giggling and whispering as they walked home. When they reached the house, they went straight upstairs to the attic room Annie and Clara shared. It was clear to Annie that her company was no longer wanted.

Annie sat on the stairs with her chin in her hands and wondered what to do with herself between now and teatime. Usually she would just start another picture but she felt that all her energy had gone in to the jungle picture she had painted earlier in the day. Her parents were downstairs in the sitting room. Grace was sewing a shirt on the old Singer machine and Frank was reading the paper. Annie did not feel like joining them. She did not even feel like playing with Bobby, who was in the sitting room in his playpen.

Suddenly there was a banging on the front door. Annie heard her father go downstairs and talk to someone on the doorstep. She could not tell who it was. But whoever it was, he was angry.

The door closed with a loud slam. Annie could hear her father coming rapidly up the stairs. He walked straight past Annie without even acknowledging her, and went on up to the girls' bedroom. Annie followed on behind to see what was happening. She had never seen her father so angry. His face was the colour of chalk, his jaw set in a look of fury.

'Clara!' he yelled as he pushed Clara's door open. Standing behind him, Annie could see Clara and Marie sitting cross-legged on the bed holding packs of cards in their hands. They were playing Racing Demon. On the paisley eiderdown lay a brown paper bag. It had spilled its contents of sugar biscuits between their crossed legs.

'You little thief!' Frank yanked Clara by the arm and pulled her out of the room. 'You come with me! I shall not have any child of mine growing up to be a criminal!'

Annie flattened herself against the wall as Frank dragged Clara past her. He pulled Clara all the way downstairs and on out into the garden. Moments later, Annie could hear the sound of her father whacking Clara's backside with his leather belt.

She was horrified. He had only ever done that once before, a long time ago when Jack had told a lie about something. It was alarming in any event but Annie was particularly frightened and shocked to see that her father – her lovely warm father – could also do that to a girl. Even at school, it was only the boys who got caned. The most the girls ever got was detention, however naughty they had been.

Slap! Slap! Slap! It sounded as though Frank was hitting Clara very hard. She could hear him muttering angrily but Annie never heard a squeak from her sister.

Then the door slammed and Annie could hear the sound of Clara coming up the stairs again.

Her sister's face was red. She looked straight ahead as she pushed past Annie.

Annie followed her up the stairs. 'Are you all right?' she whispered.

'I'm perfectly all right,' snapped Clara. But her lips were

pinched and Annie could see that she was fighting back tears.

From the bed, Marie stared at her friend in horror.

'Mr Gunn told him we pinched the biscuits,' Clara stated flatly.

Marie shrank away, staring at her friend in horror. 'Oh dear,' she wailed, biting her thumb-nail, 'will your father tell my mother?'

'I don't know,' said Clara.

'I knew we shouldn't have done it,' said Marie in a panicked sort of voice. 'I told you it was dangerous.'

Clara spun around and glared at Marie's frightened face. 'We did it together,' she said firmly. Her throat was tight and her voice sounded squeaky but controlled. 'We did it together and we are equally guilty.'

'It was wrong,' said Marie. 'We shouldn't have done it.' She had begun to cry, terrified of her mother finding out about the incident. She started to mutter a prayer under her breath.

Annie stared at the brown paper bag on the bed. The biscuits were sprinkled with icing sugar and looked delicious. Annie longed to eat one but she did not dare ask for one then. To her surprise, Clara picked up a biscuit and handed it to her. 'You might as well enjoy these while we still have them,' she said. 'And you,' she said, turning to the white-faced Marie, 'should stop blubbing. What we did wrong was to get caught.' She tossed back her thick hair. 'Next time, we'll just be a lot more careful.'

The next morning Grace scrutinized her elder daughter for signs of distress from the beating the day before.

Although she would not tolerate stealing either, Grace had been shocked by the force of Frank's rage and the violence with which he had punished Clara.

But Clara appeared as good-spirited as ever. Whatever she felt under her cheerful demeanour, she certainly was not going to show it to her family. Grace was secretly impressed by Clara's strength. It was something she must have inherited from Frank's side of the family; it certainly did not come from her. Grace felt there was no greater coward in the world than she.

After breakfast, Grace asked Clara and Annie to distribute some of her pickles to various people in the neighbourhood, including Mrs Horder and Mrs Whelan. She handed each girl a wicker basket containing the jars. 'Be careful how you go,' she said.

As the girls left the house, they saw Mr Spratt standing outside his gateway. He looked extremely distressed. He pressed his lips together and pursed them anxiously as he rocked from side to side, shifting his weight from one leg to another. He kept wiping his brow and muttering. Suddenly he raised his left leg and hugged his knee.

'Whatever's the matter, Mr Spratt?' Clara's voice sounded kind. Annie was proud that her big sister could be thoughtful towards a lonely old man.

'Oh dear, oh dear,' wailed Mr Spratt, 'it's me chickens.' His rheumy eyes were wet with tears. 'They've got some horrible disease. They're all dying.'

'Why, what do you mean?' The edge in Clara's voice made Annie glance at her quickly. A red blush was creeping up Clara's neck. Now, that's odd, she thought. Clara only blushed when she was embarrassed. Why ever should Clara be embarrassed because Mr Spratt's chickens were dying?

Annie stared at her sister with narrowed eyes.

'I found six of them,' explained Mr Spratt, 'including my darlings – Whitey, Blackie and Sandy – all of them dead inside the hen house this morning. I can't understand it at all. I've never known chickens drop dead like that, not without being ill first. They was perfectly all right yesterday, they was very well, really.' He clutched Clara's wrist. 'You saw them yesterday, they was all perfectly all right when you went to feed them, wasn't they? They was the spitting image of health.'

Clara nodded. 'Yes,' she said in a muted voice.

'Now I'm afraid they're all going to get whatever it is what's killed them,' continued Mr Spratt plaintively. 'I don't know what I'm going to do . . .'

Annie and Clara left poor Mr Spratt wailing by his gate. Clara remained noticeably subdued as they walked along the road. Finally she said, more to herself than to Annie, 'I wonder how much chickens cost.'

'Why?' Annie glanced suspiciously at her sister.

'Oh, I was just thinking,' said Clara, 'that it would be nice to buy Mr Spratt some new chickens as a present.'

'Why?' Annie was not convinced by Clara's breezy tone of voice.

Clara flicked back her hair. 'Stop asking "why" all the time,' she snapped. 'It's very irritating.' With a hand on her hip, she turned to look at Annie. 'If you must know why, I just thought I might have enough money in my money box to buy some new chickens for him, to be kind. That's all.'

Annie shrugged. She knew for certain now that Clara was somehow responsible for Mr Spratt's dead chickens.

They had reached the corner of Leverton Street where

the girls split up to make their respective deliveries of pickles. 'I'll do the Whelans and the ones down here,' Clara said, crossing the road. 'You do Mrs Horder and the others.'

As Clara ran off to discuss with Marie Whelan how to limit the damage their experimentation had done, Annie walked up to Mrs Horder's house next to the Pineapple pub. She knocked on the door.

Mrs Horder opened it, her bright beady eyes friendly and welcoming. 'Come in, come in, dear.' She showed Annie into the front room. 'We were just having tea, weren't we, Danny . . . ?'

Danny was sitting on the sofa against the wall facing the door. He sat in a great crumpled pile on the cushions, with a large white napkin tucked under his drooping wet chin.

'Here's little Annie Turner, Danny,' said Mrs Horder in a loud voice. 'She's come to visit us. She's brought some pickles her mother made for us. Isn't that kind?'

Danny raised his head and grunted loudly.

'Take a seat, dear, and I'll make a fresh pot of tea,' said Mrs Horder. 'Now you entertain our guest, Danny, dear, while I'm in the kitchen.'

Annie sat down in the chair opposite Danny. 'Hello, Danny,' she said with a smile.

Danny had been holding a piece of sponge cake in his hand. He nodded his head and smiled back at Annie, revealing ugly black stumps of teeth, and rammed the cake into his open mouth. Crumbs cascaded down his front and onto the floor. He snorted and wiped his mouth roughly with the back of his hand and smiled again at Annie.

Annie looked away in embarrassment, and felt relieved

when Mrs Horder returned. In spite of her years, she was a sprightly woman with plenty of energy. 'I made a batch of brandy snaps today,' she said, holding out a tin of sticky golden biscuits. 'They're Danny's favourites. I hope you'll have one.'

Annie munched her brandy snaps and drank a cup of sweet tea while Mrs Horder chatted to her. She seemed like the happiest of people. Annie was impressed by the way Mrs Horder always included Danny in the conversation even though Danny never said a word. He only snorted or smiled in return.

Trying to watch him without appearing to stare, Annie suddenly realized that Danny did not understand most of what was said to him. Sometimes he beamed a smile and giggled, just like her baby brother Bobby did. Yet he was a huge man, and over twenty years old.

Mrs Horder talked to him as if he were both a grown-up and a little boy, ticking him off for picking his nose and reminding him not to slurp his tea. Annie liked her love and kindness but it made her feel uncomfortable as well, though she didn't know exactly why.

When Annie finally left, she felt that Mrs Horder was probably the kindest woman she had ever met. It would be easy to lose patience with Danny, him being so big and clumsy and unable to do anything for himself. But not once did Mrs Horder get impatient with him. She loved Danny as if he were the most perfect being on earth.

'He's a good boy, my Danny,' Mrs Horder whispered as she showed Annie out. 'And he likes you a lot.' She squeezed Annie's arm. 'He's very sensitive to people, you know. He knows who's genuine, and who is not . . .'

Annie delivered the other jars of pickle to the people on

her mother's list and set off back home. As she came near the corner of Falkland Road and Leverton Street she heard a sobbing coming from behind a hedge. Peering into the front garden of the house, she saw Sally Brown sitting on the doorstep. Her face was red and blotchy and her eyes wet with tears.

'Whatever's the matter?' asked Annie.

For as long as Annie could remember, Sally Brown had fascinated her. Sally was six feet tall with thick ginger hair wrapped around her head. She always wore lipstick and tight-fitting flashy clothes, which Annie thought really daring. Although she had lived in the neighbourhood for years, she did not have any friends. No one seemed to have a good word to say for her. If she was mentioned in conversation, people lowered their voices and talked in a secretive way. When Sally walked into a shop to buy some groceries, the women in the shop queues turned their backs on her. Then they would mutter and sneer when she left.

Annie did not know why but she realized early on that people did not approve of Sally Brown, who lived on her own and seemed to have several different gentlemen visitors. She did have some kind of job in the false-teeth factory in Angler's Lane but Annie had also heard people making reference to a night job Sally had as well. Annie did not like to ask. She sensed that enquiring further about Sally Brown was stepping on dangerous ground.

All she did know about Sally was that she was pretty, with a big, round, well-proportioned face. She had dark brown eyes and lovely white teeth which flashed when she laughed. And her laugh was deep and throaty, a lovely abandoned sound that seemed to come from deep inside her.

But Sally was not laughing today. She looked utterly miserable. Her lustrous ginger hair was messy and she stared with dull eyes at the child hovering by her gate.

'Is there anything I can do?' asked Annie.

'No,' replied Sally in a flat voice.

Annie frowned. She did not know what to do. It seemed wrong to walk off and leave Sally crying on the doorstep like that. She plucked up some courage and spoke again.

'What's the matter?' she asked.

Sally shook her head and sighed. 'Oh, it's nothing,' she said. 'Nothing and everything . . .'

Annie continued to stare. She felt rooted to the spot. 'You look a bit sad,' she said quietly. 'Are you sure there's nothing I can do?'

Sally bit her lip and sighed again. 'You're right, love, I am a bit sad.' She shifted to one side and patted the step she was sitting on. 'Come and keep me company for a few minutes – if you've got the time. You're Annie Turner, aren't you?' She smiled wanly at Annie who came over and sat down beside her.

They sat in silence for a few minutes, Annie clutching her empty wicker basket and Sally flicking the laces of her brown boots.

'You're a lucky girl,' Sally said after a long pause. 'You come from a good family. You have parents who are kind to you and want the best out of life for you . . .'

Annie wriggled self-consciously but was flattered by the grown-up way in which Sally spoke to her.

'What do I have?' Sally continued bitterly. 'No one to love and no one to love me. When I was your age, all I wanted to do was grow up and get married. It seemed so simple . . .'

Annie realized that Sally was not really talking to her at all. She was talking out loud to herself.

'But things didn't happen like that,' Sally went on, 'and now I'm twenty years older and still all I want to do is get married. All I want is a kind man I can be a good wife to. Does that seem so unreasonable?' She turned to look at Annie. 'Tell me, does it seem unreasonable?'

Annie shook her head. 'No,' she whispered. She did not know what to say at all. She wanted to escape but she did not know how to take her leave and go. Poor Sally was suffering terribly in her loneliness. It was a feeling Annie had often had herself, especially before she met Tilly, but she had always thought it was something to do with being a child. She never imagined that a grown-up could feel lonely.

But now looking at Sally, it seemed the bigger you were the greater the pain.

'Men don't really like people like me,' Sally said quietly.

Annie bit her lower lip and gave a nod. She was beginning to feel completely out of her depth. 'But you have gentlemen friends,' she declared, trying to sound bright and optimistic.

Sally looked away. 'Mmmm,' she said. Then she fell silent, fiddling with her laces again.

It was getting late. 'My mother will be wondering where I am,' Annie said, getting to her feet and picking up the basket. She backed away.

Sally looked up and waved her hand. 'Thanks for listening,' she said flatly. 'I'm sorry to burden you with my problems.'

'That's all right,' said Annie, smiling kindly at her. 'It was very . . .' She searched for the right word. 'Interesting.'

As Annie set off down the road again she felt upset. It had always seemed that growing up would solve all the problems you had as a child. Being a grown-up meant that you didn't have anyone bossing you around and telling you what to do all the time. Now the future was beginning to look quite different and a lot more complicated.

Poor Sally, Annie thought as she swung the empty basket in the air. Her problems were a bit like Maudie's. They were both lonely. Perhaps they should move in together. Then they would have each other for company and never feel lonely any more.

CHAPTER 6

❧

The Street Party

THE FALKLAND ROAD PARTY was always held on a Saturday in the middle of August. The first street party had taken place nearly twenty years ago to celebrate the ending of the Great War in 1918. It had taken place every year since then, with generation after generation of Kentish Towners taking part. For many it was the highlight of the year.

The party celebrations were spread out over two of Falkland Road's three blocks. All the residents of Falkland Road were invited but other people were welcomed from the neighbouring cross streets. Thus the party took in a large part of the local population. The atmosphere was always one of neighbourliness and good will. Old feuds were forgotten, enemies danced side by side, warring families sat down and ate sandwiches and cake together, and everyone smiled and laughed throughout the afternoon and late into the night.

There was music all day long, from the fiddlers playing Irish jigs to the big singsong around the piano in the evening. The Turners' piano was carried outside by six

strong men and placed in the middle of the street.
Throughout the day, Frank, Jack and Clara took it in
turns to play. At the first street parties, it had been Frank
and his father who played the tunes all day. It was always
understood that the piano entertainment was provided by
the Turner family, and would probably continue to be for
ever after.

All the way down one side of the street trestle tables
were set up. They sagged with the weight of the plates piled
high with food: sausages and pork pies, egg and tinned
salmon sandwiches, and fairy cakes with different coloured
icing. Placed between the plates of sandwiches were large
enamel jugs full of refreshing barley water and pale yellow
lemonade. Barrels of beer were available for all.

A vast copper kettle had been placed at one end of the
street. It was here that Dolly Pritchett brewed up enough
tea to last the day. Her fat face was flushed and sweaty in
the heat of the sun but she remained unfailingly cheerful
throughout the festivities. It was clear to all that she loved
being in charge.

Mrs Garcia had set up a tent outside her house and
pinned a notice to the flap: 'Your fortune or your palm
read by Madam Maria. Tuppence a go.' The tent was
dark inside and draped within and without in richly
coloured shawls with fringed edges. Maria did a brisk
trade all day with people going into the tent laughing and
coming out with rather grave and sometimes even shocked
expressions on their faces. Mrs Garcia looked the part,
with her colourful silk shawls draped around her solid
shoulders and a scarf over her entire head. She sat at a
round table, hunched over the large crystal ball placed in
front of her.

There were always plenty of willing helpers to organize the Falkland Road party but it was Dolly Pritchett and Frank Turner who masterminded the great event each year, just as their parents had before them. It was they who decided how much entertainment was needed, from the magician, jugglers and clowns for the children, to the dancing and plate-spinning for the adults. Months before, Dolly had drawn up a rota of people whose names she had collected earlier, people who would help beforehand and on the day itself. The women volunteers were told how many cakes needed to be baked, how many sausage rolls had to be made and how many sandwiches had to be filled with a specified number of fillings. Dolly also had a list of people she could cajole to cough up a few more shillings for the kitty. This helped to pay for the little extras that made it such a memorable day that people from the area talked about it for the rest of their lives, their eyes glistening with tears when they thought back to those great days.

It was Frank's job to organize the men, arranging for them to collect the long trestle tables and wooden chairs from the church hall and to set them up in place, and to string the bunting (carefully stored in Dolly's kitchen cupboard since last year and the year before that) from house to house to create an open ceiling of fluttering red, white and blue flags.

The children planned their costumes for the fancy-dress parade weeks before – milkmaids, pirates and Robin Hoods – and assembled them from odd bits of material begged from their mothers and grannies and aunts, and bullied their mothers into helping to construct them – the more elaborate, the better. The street party had become something that parents could use to hold over their children's heads in the run-up to the day, with threats of being made to stay in their rooms and miss the party altogether if they did not do as they were told. Yes, the street party was the highlight of the year for everyone involved.

It was an event people planned for months beforehand and talked about for months afterwards. No other street they knew had such a splendid affair and outsiders would wistfully listen to descriptions of it from those who had been there, and hope that they might be lucky enough to be invited next year.

For people from outside the immediate area were not welcome unless they had some link with the area – close relatives who lived in Falkland Road or the relevant cross streets.

Although Tilly would have been allowed to come, she was not there, for she had gone to visit her grandparents that week. Life without Tilly had been rather boring for Annie, but she had spent a lot of time helping her parents get ready for the party.

Early that morning she had been out in the road, holding a plan of the street in her hand and instructing the helpers as to where to place the tables, the piano, and the rope in preparation for the tug of war. She felt very important and she knew that the other children in the street envied her for the authority she had been given by virtue of her status as a Turner. But she made a point of being friendly to everyone so that nobody would think that it had all gone to her head.

It was a shock to see Roger there. Annie spotted him first, walking jauntily down the road. With his head held high and his hands pushed deep into his pockets, he looked very cocky.

'What's Roger doing here?' she asked in dismay. 'Roger doesn't live here . . .'

Dolly was standing nearby. She had another list in her hand and was peering at it to see what else needed to be done. 'Oh, I expect he's here with his Aunt Jane. She lives in Leverton Street and finds it hard to get around now. She said she was going to ask one of her great-nephews to bring her. She always likes to have a young man to escort her, does Jane,' Dolly sniffed. 'She always was like that, even as a young woman.'

Annie was now staring at Roger through narrowed eyes. 'Well, after all he's done to us, he still shouldn't be allowed to come,' she muttered.

As she watched him, Annie could see Roger paying attention to a white-haired old lady sitting on a chair by the pavement. Her ankles were fat and swollen and a walking stick was leaning against her armchair. Annie recognized her wrinkled face and stooped shoulders. She had seen this lady many times in the street, though she had never known that she was Roger's great-aunt.

Roger handed his aunt a cup of lemonade before sauntering off into the crowd. He had grown a lot since Annie had last seen him. Like her brother Jack, he was now fifteen, tall and heavily built. He had thick black hair and a wide forehead above dark hooded eyes. He looked tense. Every now and then he clenched his jaw muscles unconsciously, which gave him a nervy manner as if he were always on the look-out for trouble. He rarely stood still, moving through the crowd, stopping here and there, always glancing quickly around him as he picked food off

the plates and swallowed it quickly. Then he walked over to
the piano where Clara had just started playing some lively
jazz tunes.

In past years Clara had led the gymnastics display – a
group of girls walking on their hands, doing flips, and
performing beautifully controlled body movements. But
this year the display had gone on without her. Suddenly
self-conscious about her changing body, Clara had backed
out at the last minute. Everyone agreed that this was a
great shame, since Clara Turner was the best gymnast
anyone had ever seen, but they were also sympathetic.
They could understand how the girl felt, now that she was
less of a girl, really, and, at thirteen years of age, developing into a woman. She was entitled to be a bit more
modest.

Annie watched closely as Roger sidled up to her sister.
Clara glanced up at Roger as he stood next to the piano
and leaned on the top. To Annie's fury, Clara smiled at
him. How could Clara do that? It wasn't even just a polite
smile either. It was warm and friendly. Didn't she know
who Roger was? Annie scowled.

Dolly had seen the look on Annie's face and squeezed
her shoulder. 'Roger has every right to be here, cock. Now
don't you fret about it . . .'

'But he killed my rabbit,' Annie hissed, thrusting out
her lower lip.

Grace was ladling milk from a churn into jugs. Her
arthritis had not been troubling her much recently, so she
had been able to play an active part in the celebrations
this year. She overheard this exchange. 'Annie, dear, that
was three years ago now. You mustn't hang on to grudges
like this. Everyone's grown up a lot since then.'

Annie scowled again and glared in Roger's direction. 'Well, I'm not going to smile at him. And I don't think anyone else should, either. He's a horrid boy, a bully. He always has been and always will be.'

Grace smiled affectionately at her. 'Just try to enjoy the party, Annie, love. We've been blessed with a beautiful day, so take advantage of it now.'

A big, noisy crowd of people had started dancing. Annie tried to switch her mind off Roger and watch the activities. There was old Mrs Horder dancing with Danny. Mother and son held hands, faced each other and swung their arms in unison. Danny was squealing with delighted laughter, a huge slobbery grin on his wide face. His straight black hair flopped over his forehead. Mrs Horder was tiny but astonishingly agile for someone of her age, pointing her toes as she danced from side to side, her head tilted neatly, her eyes sparkling.

'Danny had better not step on his mother or she'll be squashed in one go,' laughed Frank as he walked past, dragging the thick rope for the tug of war. 'Hey, Annie,' he called, dropping his load and holding out his arms. 'Would you like to dance with your old dad?'

Annie joined her father in the middle of the stretch of road that had become the dance floor. Frank held her in his arms, swinging her round and leading her through steps she didn't know. He manipulated her with such skill and ease that she felt she had been dancing all her life. 'Your mother used to be a great dancer,' Frank shouted at her over the loud, jaunty music. 'She's not up to it any more, which is a shame.' He spun Annie round. 'But you have the rhythm. You're your mother's daughter all right!'

Her father's encouragement gave Annie confidence, and before long she was moving freely to Frank's lead with fluid, graceful movements. As she moved, her heart soared under her budding breasts. I am a woman, she thought. I am eleven years old and a young woman at last!

All around them their friends and neighbours danced. They moved deftly sideways to avoid the Fenton sisters, who were holding each other by the waist and bickering about which direction to go in. They steered clear of Mr and Mrs Smith, too. Although Frank had come to like Tommy and seen what a decent fellow he was, he was still not keen on the parents. In any event, the Smiths had to be avoided because they were such clumsy dancers, taking up a lot of space and barging into other couples without any apologies whatsoever. They also complained constantly about the music and made it quite plain that they did not approve of Clara's choice. 'How about a proper knees-up, then?' they called. 'Let's stop this modern dancing and have a bit of the real thing . . .'

Annie laughed and was surprised to see that her father was relaxed and laughing too.

Later she saw Tommy Smith sitting on a wall. As she waved to him, she felt a twinge in her chest which made her realize how much she was missing Tilly at that moment.

Tommy was still a close friend of the girls. They often all went up to Hampstead Heath together after school, or wandered along the canal from Camden Lock to Islington and back. They were a serious-minded threesome and liked to discuss the books they had borrowed from the library that week. And in their intimacy, Annie had even brought Tommy in on the mysterious existence of her mother's brooch, something she had only ever done with Tilly before now. He thought it was a great intrigue. Once, when her mother was out, Annie had taken Tommy up to her parents' room to show him the brooch. 'Cor!' he said, holding the sparkling jewels up to the light to make them sparkle more. He narrowed his eyes. 'Your mother must have done something very important for the person who gave her this as a thank you.'

Annie nodded. 'What could it possibly be? And why does my mother want to hide it away all the time?'

Tommy looked thoughtful. 'We have to work on this one,' he murmured.

Tommy had seen her. 'Hey, Annie,' he called. 'Want to come up here?' He leaned down to hoist her up next to him.

Annie sprang up and settled beside him.

Tommy gave her a gap-toothed grin. 'Want a gob-stopper?' He held out a crumbled white paper bag. 'They last a good long time and have some smashing colours.'

Sucking their gob-stoppers, the children watched the street party from their elevated position. It was now in full swing. The weather was swelteringly hot. Women wore thin summer frocks and hats to ward off the sun. Those men who did not care about appearing respectable at all times had sensibly taken off their shirts to reveal string vests beneath. Those who did, rolled up their sleeves as far as they could. Men downed pints and pints of beer, while everyone else drank glasses of barley water or lemonade to quench their thirst.

Later on Annie saw Sally Brown and waved to her

across the street. Sally was on the arm of a tall man dressed in an ill-fitting suit. He had a sharp, rat-like face. From the way Sally leaned heavily towards her companion and every now and then stumbled over her big feet, Annie could tell that she had probably also been enjoying a lot of the free beer. Annie was rather hurt when Sally walked right by without a flicker of recognition or acknowledgement. It was as if they had never had that private conversation on Sally's doorstep. Their talk had made a lasting impression on Annie and she had assumed that Sally felt the same way. In fact, ever since, she had felt a special bond with Sally, even though they hardly ever crossed paths. Now Sally was acting as though they had never met.

Next, they saw Maudie Sprackling wandering along the road. Her sad, downcast face stood out in the happy crowd. She had several sandwiches in her hands. She ate these methodically, lifting them up to her mouth and taking bites without pause. Her pasty moon face looked more bloated than usual, and Annie thought she looked even sadder, too. Perhaps happy people made her sad.

After a while Annie and Tommy jumped down from the wall and walked down to the far end of the street, near Annie's house. They passed Jack on the way. Annie could tell that he had been drinking beer with some of his mates. He was looking excited. He kept flicking his hair back off his face, which was flushed and hot. Most telling of all was his friendly greeting to his little sister: 'Hello there, Annie! Hello, Tommy!'

'Hmmm,' grunted Annie. 'Usually he ignores me.'

'Well a bit of beer always makes people friendly,' said Tommy.

'I don't know what my mother will say about Jack drinking beer,' Annie said with a self-important shake of the head.

It was time for the tug of war, always one of the most popular events of the day. It was Falkland Road versus the Cross-streeters, those from Leverton Street and Lady Margaret Road.

The men were lining up by the side of the road. The younger, stronger men showed off their bare chests and flexed their muscles in a display of strength. Those with weedy bodies just rolled up their shirt sleeves and waited, their arms hanging awkwardly by their sides. The two teams began to jeer at each other with mock rivalry.

Frank was in charge. He had marked out the area and drawn a line across the road with chalk. He had also tied his white handkerchief to the thick knotted rope. 'All right, boys,' he called, 'take your positions.'

Roger had taken up a position on the Cross-streeters' team. Annie felt a twinge of dismay as she saw her father talking to him in a friendly way. He too? It was bad enough that Clara was hanging around him.

Clara had stopped her jazz playing and had come to watch the tug of war. Watching Clara closely, Annie began to suspect that in all the cheering and shouting that was going on, Clara was actually rooting for Roger.

On the Falkland Road team, Jack had stripped down to the waist. His body had filled out and broadened in the past year. He looked more like a mature man than a fifteen-year-old. His muscles were sharply defined over his chest and back and along his arms. Annie was proud of her handsome brother, and pleased to see him narrow his eyes at Roger on the other side of the road. At least Jack had not chosen to forget what Roger had done. Annie was grateful for that.

It was an exciting contest, with the white handkerchief hovering over the line and moving slightly over to one side and then back again as the combined strengths of the two teams battled against each other.

Then suddenly it was over. The Falkland Road team faltered as one man lost his footing, with the others caught off guard. The handkerchief shot over the winning line, and the Cross-streeters fell backwards on top of each other as the tension on the rope was suddenly lifted. A great yell of victory went up. People blew whistles and cheered. 'Well done, Cross-streeters! Well done!'

It was a good-humoured contest. The losing side had to buy the victors a round of drinks in the Falkland Arms afterwards. There was not meant to be any bad feeling about it but Annie could see Jack looking quite disgruntled, especially as Clara had run over to Roger and was congratulating him. He was smiling at her and joking as he wiped the dripping sweat off his brow with the back of his forearm.

'Your sister seems to like Roger,' Tommy commented as they moved away.

'Mmm,' muttered Annie.

Much of the party was over, though many people looked set to celebrate until late into the night. Dolly had brewed the last of the tea. 'There's just beer and lemonade from now on,' she said. Annie was helping her clear up her table.

Suddenly she became aware of a loud bell ringing, and all around people were pointing and laughing. Then she saw why. Coming down the road swinging a large bell in his hand was Mr Spratt. His eyes were wide open and wild-looking, focusing on nothing as he approached. Annie stared aghast. From the top of his bald head to the tips of his gnarled toes, Mr Spratt was completely naked. He was yelling at the top of his voice: 'Bring out your dead! Bring out your dead!'

Women clapped their hands over their mouths and shrieked with laughter. Men looked away in embarrassment. Nobody did anything except gawp and laugh, until Dolly, who was not laughing, swept up her skirts and pushed her way through the crowds. 'Come on, now, Mr Spratt,' she said briskly, handing him her apron. 'Cover yerself up and let's take you home.'

'Bring out your dead!' Mr Spratt called. 'Bring out your dead!' He was oblivious to everything around him.

Dolly turned him around by the arm and gently led him back towards his house.

'He's been upset ever since his chickens died,' someone said behind Annie. 'A whole lot of them died for no good reason a few months ago. They just dropped dead. That young Clara Turner – bless her heart – bought him some new chicks to replace the ones he'd lost, but the poor old fellow's gone ever so queer.'

Annie turned her head to see that Clara had been listening to this conversation, too. Clara quickly looked way to avoid her sister's accusing eye.

Late that night when Annie was asleep in bed, exhausted by the events of the day, Jack and Clara were in Jack's room talking. They were in their nightclothes. Jack had been drinking more beer. Unused to alcohol, he felt

drowsy. They had been dancing until quite late when their
mother had finally told them to go to bed.

Clara fell back on the bed with a loud happy sigh.
'What a day! The best of my life!'

'It was pretty good,' he said.

'I just love to dance. It makes me feel so alive.' Clara
stretched her arms above her head.

Jack was feeling peculiar. He felt oddly excited but he
did not know why.

Clara lent backwards against Jack's legs, pushing her
toes under the soft eiderdown. 'I feel so safe and snug,' she
said dreamily.

Jack was aware of his sister's body beneath her white
cotton nightdress and the soapy fragrance of her skin. He
lay back against the bedstead and stared out of the window. The sky was blue-black. A midsummer evening. It
was now late but still not pitch-dark outside.
Unconsciously he ran his hand up and down Clara's arm.
He could feel the soft hairs on her skin. It was a comforting rhythm. Up and down. He was only vaguely aware of
his sister's hand on his thigh. She too seemed to be in a
trance as her arm moved along his skin. Up and down, up
and down.

Then they were aware and not aware. The pleasure of
the sensations they were creating was strong, so strong
that it overwhelmed any sense that what they were doing
was wrong.

Clara turned to Jack and reached up. As their lips
touched, powerful forces surged through their bodies.
Turning to each other, they pressed themselves close.

Jack knew that Clara felt the same. They should stop
but they could not. They wanted to go beyond the line,

they wanted to find out. And nobody would ever know.

Skin on skin. Flesh on flesh. Clara winced and shifted slightly as Jack pressed against her. She did not cry out. She did not tell him to stop. Their breathing quickened, their limbs tensed. Flesh in flesh, warm and enclosed. Once Jack opened his eyes to look. Clara's eyes were firmly closed, a sleepy sweet smile on her pink open lips.

In the middle of the night, Jack woke up with pins and needles in his arm. Clara was still in his bed and lying on his arm. She lay on her back, her mouth open, and her arm flung back above her head on the pillow. Jack pulled his arm away and shook his sister. Muttering in her half-sleep, but aware of the need to move, Clara stumbled next door to her own room and climbed between the cool sheets of her bed.

Annie slept soundly through it all. The sound of the bedroom door opening and Clara tiptoeing to bed were simply incorporated into her dreams.

The next morning as Annie went downstairs, she noticed something strange out of the landing window. There was something odd about Mr Spratt's chickens, and the way they were circling around in their run and making much more of a racket than usual. She ran downstairs and out into the garden to take a look. The fowl were looking quite extraordinary. Every one, including Marmaduke, had long dangling earrings clipped to its coxcomb. The unhappy birds clucked plaintively and shook their heads in a vain attempt to throw off the clinging jewellery – the late Mrs Spratt's best costume pieces in bright red, green, blue and silver – glittering as brightly as the chickens' frightened eyes.

And there was more. Annie caught sight of the chickens'

claws. Mr Spratt must have been up working all through night. Every one of his hens' talons was bright scarlet, beautifully painted with shiny red nail varnish.

Annie shook her head. Clara was going to have to say a lot of prayers in church that day to make up for what she had done to poor Mr Spratt.

CHAPTER 7

Jessie

THE KETTLE HAD BOILED. Taking it off the hob, Maudie Sprackling poured the boiled water onto the tea leaves, gave it a stir and popped the lid on. Covering the teapot with a red knitted tea-cosy, she placed it on a tray next to the jug of milk and bowl of sugar. She put two butter biscuits on a plate and then carried the tray next door to the front room, stepping around the heavy black pram in the hall as she did so.

She lowered the tray onto the small side table and then she sat back heavily into the armchair with a contented sigh.

She smiled gently as she looked around the room. There was the baby's rattle on the sofa, a discarded muslin nappy used only for the possets, the empty bottle on the side. She would have to boil that bottle soon, to sterilize it, she thought, and she must not forget to boil up the pile of nappies lying in the tin bucket in the scullery. If she washed the nappies before lunch, then she could hang them out to dry in the garden. There was a good wind outside so the chances were she could have them clean and dry by the evening.

Maudie stared at the bits and pieces lying around the room and thought how pleasant it was not to feel the usual urge to tidy up. No, if anything, she wanted to preserve the room as it was, to give her the chance to relish every bit of evidence of that young life sleeping so soundly upstairs.

What a lot of work it was looking after a baby! There was hardly time for anything. Just as she finished one thing, something else needed to be done. It was just as well that the baby slept so much. At least she could get most of her chores done while he was asleep – the chores at home, anyway. Going out shopping with the pram and all the business of getting the baby ready beforehand was still too daunting for her to attempt very often.

She poured herself a cup of tea and sat back in her chair. Sipping the milky drink, she reflected on how dramatically her life had changed over the last few weeks. Why, it had been less than three weeks since she had met Jessie, yet it seemed like an age.

She did not know why she had gone to Regent's Park on that Saturday morning. She did not know then and she was none the wiser now. Perhaps it was because she had been there once in happier days with Fred, when they had walked hand in hand and talked of their future life together, when she thought she knew what happiness was.

She had gone down there to listen to the brass band on the high bandstand and to wander around the ponds and watch the people in the rowing boats – happy people, laughing and splashing with their oars in the water. Happy people, unlike her, with her plodding legs and lumpy body. Life was a misery for poor Maudie. Everything was grey; she felt she had no feelings about anything any more. Even when the sun was shining and the sky blue, it all felt grey. She didn't care if she lived or died, and she only went on existing because she could not be bothered to think of anything else to do.

She worked a little, cleaning for Dr and Mrs Foster up in Highgate for three days a week, but she did not earn much because up until now she had not needed to. First, Fred had been earning enough working on the trams to pay for most things, and then after he left, she had just paid for the rent on the house with the money her father had left her when he died. It had not been much, but it had been a nest egg of a sort, and after Fred had run off with Connie Smith, it had come in handy. The trouble was it had almost run out and now she was becoming worried about what to do. Part of her could not be bothered to do anything. Life was so bad. But deep down she did care enough not to want to be thrown out of her home for not paying the rent. It was the house in which she had grown up. And her love for it had turned into a compulsive urge to clean it all the time she was there. She hated herself for doing it, but she could not stop herself. It made her feel safe, to keep busy that way, down on her knees and scrubbing.

She knew people laughed at her and thought she was going soft, but she still could not help herself. She did not care what any of them thought, not even those people who had been friends of her mum and dad. Maudie did not have friends any more.

As she had left the park she noticed a young woman pushing a large black pram along the pavement. The woman seemed to be struggling. She had two heavy string bags full of shopping so her hands were full already, and

pushing the pram was difficult. She had manoeuvred it to
the kerb where she was obviously planning to cross the
road. But the front wheels suddenly slipped over the edge
of the pavement, tipping the back end of the pram right up
into the air.

Maudie did not hesitate. She ran up to the pram and
pulled it upright. She held her hand out just in time to
prevent the tiny infant inside slipping out onto the road
with all its bedding on top of it. She pulled the pram back
to the safety of the pavement just as a motor car roared
past.

'Oh, thank you, thank you,' gasped the woman. 'You
probably saved my baby's life.'

Her accent was quite posh, posher than the woman's
appearance suggested. Her clothes were old and tatty, and
her shoes scuffed and unpolished.

Maudie smiled and shrugged her shoulders. 'That's all
right. I could see you were having trouble.'

The two women went into the park and walked along
together. The woman, whose name was Jessie, told Maudie
her astonishing life story without prompting.

She told her that although she came from a good family
and had grown up in a big house in south London, she
was now destitute. This sad state of affairs had come about
in little over a year. A year before she had been engaged to
marry a handsome young man called Larry. He was a
lawyer with a bright future ahead of him. Her parents liked
him and were pleased with the match. Because they were
getting married, they had been more intimate with each
other than perhaps they should have been, but tragically,
three weeks before the wedding, Larry was knocked down
and killed by a motor car. Jessie's grief was complicated by

the fact that a few weeks later she realized she was going to have a baby.

While she was pleased to have a child of Larry's, even in such terrible circumstances, her parents were horrified. They told Jessie that she would have to go away immediately before anyone they knew guessed about her condition, and that she could only return home after giving up the child for adoption.

Jessie had left the family home and given birth in a home for young ladies in trouble. 'My baby was born in the early hours of Christmas Day,' she said. 'At two o'clock in the afternoon, just at the time my family always sat down for Christmas dinner, I telephoned them from the hospital to tell them that they had become grandparents. But they would not speak to me. My mother put the telephone back on the hook. She put the telephone down on her own daughter.'

The two women were sitting on a bench in the park. They could hear the sound of the elephants in the zoo nearby bellowing for their tea, the chattering and shrieks of the monkeys and the shrill squawks from the bird house. Maudie listened to Jessie's story in fascination and when Jessie told her that she needed to find a place to live as she was not allowed to stay in the home for unmarried mothers for much longer, she did not hesitate to offer her a room in her house.

That had been a month ago and the arrangement had worked out even better than anyone could have expected. Jessie and her baby William moved in and the two women found that they liked each other. Despite the great differences in their backgrounds, they felt they had a lot in common. Soon they had arranged their lives to suit each

other. Jessie was very keen to get a job and earn some
money. She felt obliged to pay Maudie rent for the room
but she also wanted the independence her own earnings
could bring. However, she could not work unless she had
someone to look after the baby. She explained that
although she loved William, she did not enjoy looking
after him for every minute of the day. On hearing that,
Maudie did not hesitate to offer her services. And so Jessie
found a clerical job in a department store in the West End,
and earned enough to pay Maudie handsomely for the
rent and for looking after her baby. Maudie could give up
her cleaning job and now had a little baby to look after.
Even if she had to share him with Jessie, Maudie was
happy. William was a sweet-natured little boy and took to
being looked after by Maudie without any objections.
Four months old, with fair hair and huge blue eyes, he
laughed and chuckled at everything.

As Maudie was taking her elevenses back to the kitchen,
she heard William's high-pitched cry from upstairs. He
had woken up very hungry by the sound on it.

She removed the bottle of watered-down milk from the
saucepan of hot water on the cooker. Shaking it up, she
shook a drop of milk onto her wrist to test it. The temperature was just right.

By the time Maudie reached William in Jessie's bedroom upstairs, the baby was screaming. But the moment
he was picked up and gathered into Maudie's fleshy arms,
he stopped. Maudie held him gently against her shoulder
and rubbed his back. William smacked his lips together
hungrily and began rooting into her chest.

'Wait, my pet,' Maudie cooed, sitting down on the bed.
She held William in front of her and kissed him gently on

the cheek. Placing him on her lap, she began to unbutton her blouse. William's hunger was growing and he began to wail impatiently.

The bottle was on the side table but Maudie continued to undo her top clothes. She had wanted to do this for several days. Jessie was still nursing William in the mornings before she left for work and in the evenings when she came home. Maudie watched her intently every time, almost feeling the tug of the baby's demanding lips on her own large brown nipple.

Her heavy soft breast fell out of the brassière. William was whimpering and rooting hard against her white skin. Maudie grasped her nipple in the way she had watched Jessie do it, and guided it towards William's open mouth. William's gums sank with greedy relief onto Maudie's flesh. She jumped at the sensation, surprised by the strength of his mouth. For a few seconds, she gazed down at the baby on her breast, imagining the sight of her and William to be like the Madonna and Child. He was a Christmas baby, after all. She smiled, her eyes glistening with tears.

Suddenly William pulled away from the nipple with an angry cry. He plunged back onto it but pulled away again, his face red with frustration.

'Sorry, my darling,' whispered Maudie, reaching for the bottle and quickly pushing the teat into the baby's mouth. William sank into her arms with a sigh of relief, and gulped down the milk so fast that he nearly choked. 'There's nothing there for you,' cooed Maudie, pushing her breast back inside her blouse. 'I just had to know. I just had to know what it was like.' She smiled serenely. 'It was lovely,' she whispered. 'Thank you, love.'

*

The Easter bank holiday was always popular with the Turner family because of the traditional fair on Hampstead Heath. The children had been looking forward to it for weeks. Annie was particularly keen to win a goldfish this year. It was a popular fair with a carousel and rides for grown-ups and children alike, but it also had great side-shows with the Biggest Rat in the World, the Hairy Lady and (Jack's favourite) the Siamese Lambs, a freakish creature with eight legs and two heads. Frank had explained that although it was dead and stuffed, it was real. 'It wouldn't have been able to live for long,' he explained. Annie liked the two-headed duck, which was also stuffed, while Clara liked the twelve stuffed kittens all dressed up in pretty costumes and playing croquet on a pretend lawn. The kittens looked normal and Annie was afraid that there had been nothing wrong with them to make them die, which meant that probably someone had drowned them when they were a few weeks old. Her father probably knew the answer, but Annie did not dare ask.

Annie's mother had not been well that week – her joints had flared up again – so she said that she would stay at home and look after Bobby, who was too young to enjoy the fair properly anyway. So after lunch, Frank took the three older children on the Underground to Hampstead Heath.

The fair was in full swing when they arrived. Annie said she wanted to stay with her father, while Jack and Clara were keen to go off on their own. They had been fooling around a lot that morning, tickling each other and bantering loudly. When they acted like that, Annie always felt excluded, so she did not want to be with them anyway.

'We'll all meet up here by the candy-floss stall,' said Frank. 'At four o'clock sharp.'

Annie stayed with her father. Although excited to be at the fair, she was quite frightened by the jostling crowd of people who pushed and shoved her as though she did not exist.

The ground was getting muddy underfoot and her leather boots kept slipping. Only by holding her father's hand could she keep her balance.

What fun they had! Frank had his turn at the rifle range and hit three bulls'-eyes in a row. He won a rag doll which he handed to Annie. 'Look after my prize, my dear. It's for your mother. I've never once come away from here without some booty for Grace.'

Annie tried her hand with the table-tennis balls and the goldfish bowls but failed to get anything. She had never had an eye for the ball. They visited the Biggest Rat in the World and the Hairy Lady who was immensely fat and had hair sprouting out of her chin and down her cheeks. Oddly enough, she did not have much hair on her head.

Frank bought Annie a toffee apple which she ate with some difficulty but relished every bit of the crunchy crackly caramel sticking to her teeth. Every now and then they spotted Clara or Jack who were wandering around on their own. Annie watched her father hit three coconuts at the coconut shy.

'No more, sir!' called the man in charge. 'Give someone else a chance now.'

'There's one each for you three children,' said Frank.

'What about Bobby?' Annie always liked to be fair.

'Bobby won't know, and you can give him a bit of yours,' laughed Frank. 'How about a ride on the carousel?'

Annie smiled. She was touched that he had asked. She thought that perhaps at eleven, she was a bit old to want a go on the carousel but she still loved to ride on those garishly painted wooden horses, riding up and down, holding on tight to the reins as the music started up.

Seeing the look of eagerness on his daughter's face, Frank pulled out a coin and handed it to the operator. 'Next time you're on, Annie,' he called.

Annie rode on the most handsome horse she could find, holding her head high and pretending to herself that she was a prince galloping on a real horse across the fields in the countryside. The horse tossed his head in the air and snorted through flared nostrils. The earth thundered past under his hoofs. The music filled her ears. Annie was soon so entranced that she forgot to wave to her father as she went past him.

After the carousel, they went on to the Bowling for the Pig stand. Twelve large heavy skittles were placed at one end. Competitors had to roll the bowls to knock them all down. Ladies were allowed to start halfway up the stand.

'Roll up! Roll up!' The man in charge was heavily built with a crushed-looking face. He had a broken nose and scarred skin.

'This is your last chance to win the pig!' he bellowed through his cupped hands, turning from one side to the other. 'The play-off is in five minutes. This is your last chance to qualify!'

Annie peered into the banana crate next to the man. Lying on yellow straw, fast asleep, was a small pink piglet. Its tail was curled right round in a circle and its small snout twitched as he slept. Annie looked in wonder at the sparse white hairs growing out of its back. It was clean.

She knew pigs were really clean animals, that they liked to be clean if they had the opportunity. Her heart swelled with feeling for this baby animal, and her mind began to work out how she could look after it in the back garden. She had read a book once about a girl who had a pig for a pet. She squeezed Frank's hand.

'Oh Daddy, you have a go! You'll knock them all down.'

Frank laughed. He did pride himself on his strength and his accurate eye. 'I don't know what we'll do with a pig, Annie,' he said, 'but let's worry about that later.' He handed the man a penny and took the three bowls.

As Annie expected, Frank knocked down all the skittles with the three bowls. She jumped up and down with excitement. He had won! She had got the pig!

But she was wrong. Frank gently pointed out that three other men had managed to knock all the skittles down (albeit after several tries) and now there had to be a play-off.

A crowd gathered round to see the final of the bowling contest. Annie stayed close to the banana crate. The piglet had woken up now. He did not shift his position but his little eyes blinked sleepily.

Frank was the third to go. The first man was a young fellow with a patch over one eye. His first bowl was a disaster. It wobbled up the grass and missed the skittles completely. The other two bowls knocked down four skittles between them.

The next man managed to knock down six skittles after some bad luck when one bowl scooted between the targets without touching any of them. Then it was Frank's go. The atmosphere was getting tense. Everyone was quiet. Annie crossed her fingers and held her breath as her father bent down to pick up the bowls. With deft graceful movements, he sent the bowls down in speedy straight lines. The skittles went flying in all directions. 'Well done!' a cry went out. But there was one solitary skittle left standing.

'It's been put in a trench!' one wag called out.

The fourth man took up his position. Annie glared at him, willing him to fail, to let her have the pig as her friend. She leant down and stroked the pig's back. It flinched as she touched its thick, hairy skin.

The man bowled slowly and precisely. The first one knocked down six skittles, the other two the rest. A huge cheer went up. Frank laughed and shrugged his shoulders. Then he shook hands and congratulated the winner, completely unaware of the tears welling up in his daughter's eyes.

Annie stared at the pig sadly. It was too late now, there was no chance. He would belong to someone else.

The winner came over to inspect his prize. 'It's not a bad weight,' he said.

'Would have been better in the summer,' someone commented. 'The pigs are always bigger at the August fairs.'

Annie looked at the man who had won. He looked like a rough sort, not the type to love an animal.

'Too bad, Annie,' said Frank, cheerfully picking up his jacket which he had taken off for better freedom of movement. 'Can't win every time. Have to let others have a chance.'

'But, Daddy,' Annie said anxiously, 'what if that man doesn't have a garden? Where will he be able to keep the pig?'

The couple standing nearby heard Annie's remark and nudged each other. 'Oh, I don't think he's going to be keeping the pig in a garden . . .' the lady said with a laugh.

'No, more like an ice box!' They laughed again. Annie blushed. She felt angry and embarrassed. There was only one way a pig could fit into the ice box. It had never occurred to her that anyone would want to kill this sweet creature. She felt angry with her father for not winning the pig and saving it from such a fate. Surely he could have tried harder . . .

'Come on, Annie, it's nearly four o'clock. We've got to go to the candy-floss stand.' Frank picked up his coconuts and started off in the direction of the rendezvous. Annie lagged behind, feeling both sulky and sad. She had no pets, no rabbit, no pig, not even a goldfish.

The place was still crowded and soon Annie realized that she could not see her father who had been striding way ahead of her. She did not even know where the candy-floss stand was. She stopped and looked around, fighting the rising panic inside her. She realized now that she had lost her sense of direction completely. She was too short to be able to see over people's heads and she had no idea of where to go. She turned round and round in one spot. The ground was mushy beneath her feet. A couple of boys ran by chasing each other, knocking her sideways as they went. Annie lost her footing on the slippery grass and fell down heavily on her bottom.

She sat on the ground dazed. Suddenly a strong arm slipped under hers and pulled her to her feet.

'Up you get. Why, it's Clara Turner's kid sister, ain't it?'

Annie peered up at the person who had saved her. She shrank back. It was Roger Knight, looming over her now with a smile on his face. In his other hand he carried two jam jars with a goldfish in each.

'Thank you.' Annie brushed herself off and smiled stiffly. 'I've got to get to the candy-floss stand,' she said with a worried frown. 'I'm meeting my family there at four o'clock. I lost my father in the crowd.'

Roger took her hand. 'I'll take you there myself. Come on, then.'

Annie allowed Roger to lead her through the crowd. Her heart was pounding. She could not believe that she was holding Roger Knight's hand! Roger Knight, who killed Rabbit! She stared ahead, not daring to look at him. Where was he taking her? Could she trust him to help her find her father, as he said he would?

The glass jars hanging from his fingers clinked together. Roger lifted them up and peered at them. 'Here, would you like a goldfish?' he asked.

Annie stared at him as if she did not understand.

'I won them for my kid brother,' continued Roger, 'but he won't mind if he only gets one. He's got about six already.'

Annie's eyes widened. 'Really?' She breathed excitedly, staring at the goldfish darting about in the small jam jar. 'I'd love it,' she whispered.

'It's all yours!' Roger placed the jar in the palm of her hand and grinned. He looked steadily at her for a moment or two. 'Can't say I'd guess you was Clara's sister if I didn't know already. You don't look like her at all.'

Annie stared at her goldfish and pretended not to hear this hurtful remark. 'Thank you,' she whispered. 'It's very kind of you to give it to me.'

Roger waved off her thanks. 'It's nothing. Now, come on, let's go and find that family of yours.' He took her by the hand again and pulled her through the crowd.

As Annie ran along behind, trying to keep up with Roger's long stride, she felt all muddled. She did not know what she thought about Roger Knight any more. He had given her a goldfish. He had given her a pet. He had been kind to her, when he was supposed to be a bad person.

Everyone was by the candy-floss stand when they got there. Frank was surprised to see his younger daughter arriving holding Roger's hand but when he learned what had happened and how Roger had helped Annie when she was lost, he was openly grateful. 'When I realized we'd lost each other I thought it best for me to get to the meeting place and wait rather than try to find her in the crowd.'

Clara smiled coyly at Roger, while Jack eyed him suspiciously.

'It's time to get home now with all our booty,' said Frank. 'Let's walk back.'

'I'll join you, if you don't mind,' said Roger. 'I've had enough for the day.'

They walked back across the Heath. It was a bright afternoon still, and the light on the grass and trees was soft and warm. As they emerged out of one wood, they saw an enchanting sight. A young girl, of no more than fifteen, was sitting under a large beech tree and playing the accordion to a semicircle of people who had gathered around to listen. The Turners went to join them. The girl was a fine player and ran through all the popular songs. Annie watched and listened. Her heart felt uplifted by the sound. It had been a fun day even if she had not got the pig. She hugged the jam jar to her chest. After all these years, she had got her pet. And what a surprise that it came from Roger, of all people.

She glanced over at Roger. He and Clara were standing extremely close together, almost pressing against each other as they swayed to the music. Frank was watching the young musician and he did not seem to have noticed, but Jack had. He kept glancing at the two of them, his fists clenched tightly by his sides.

CHAPTER 8

❧

Danny Horder

GRACE TURNER WAS OUT in the garden carefully picking over her flowers and shrubs. In rare moments of peace and solitude when domestic affairs were under control, she would step outside to survey her fifty-foot patch of garden behind the house. And if her arthritis was not causing her trouble at that moment, she would begin to pull out weeds, prune a branch here, deadhead there.

Today, her joints were calm, the inflammation lying low. Her garden looked wonderful. The roses were showing off their white, red and pink flowers and the hollyhocks and dahlias were in full bloom. Grace loved this time of year when there was a dazzling display of colour amidst the green. The plants were all looking healthy, apart from the hostas. They were a sorry sight. Gazing in sad frustration at their leaves, now reduced to thin lacy skeletons, Grace had to admit that she had lost her battle with the snails. On Marion's advice, she had sprinkled gravel around the bottom of the plants. 'They hate getting anything on their bellies,' Marion had assured her. But the molluscs had still managed to reach the leaves and devastate them. Grace sighed. She could not think what the next step could be. Perhaps she should try growing them in pots. Or give up on hostas altogether.

At the back of the flower-bed was a large putrid jar full of dead snails. This lot had been lured into the trap by the inch of brown ale Grace had poured in. Perhaps she should put some more salt down. She did not approve of Jack's habit of pouring salt directly onto the snails to make them dissolve, but since the soil was dry, it wouldn't harm to sprinkle quite a bit around for the snails to crawl onto themselves. That way she wouldn't feel quite so responsible for their deaths.

The plight of her hostas made Grace profoundly sad. At her parents' cottage in Sussex where she had grown up, there had been magnificent hostas growing three feet high in large vigorous clumps, with leaves of various colours – powdery blue, pale green with creamy centres, grey-blue, dark green. And all producing the proudest racemes of violet or mauve flowers which crowned the foliage in mid-summer. Slugs and snails did not seem to like the sandy soil down there, for they had never been a particular problem, and the plants had always thrived.

As Grace's thoughts drifted to Sussex and the place where she had grown up, her face looked troubled. She picked up her thick canvas gardening gloves and stood up, straight-backed and rigid, a hand pressed against her ribs. Well, there wouldn't be any need to worry about any of her plants and flowers if war broke out. They would all have to go, poor things. The air-raid shelter would take up most of their patch of ground, and every inch of what was left would have to be given over to vegetables to feed the family. With images of cabbages, swedes, Brussels sprouts, onions and carrots, all thoughts of Sussex had faded to the back of her mind. 'Salt!' she said emphatically, picking up yet another snail from under the hostas and dropping it into the alcoholic pool of death. 'Salt it shall be!'

Annie was happy to run out and buy salt for her mother. Tilly had come round to see Annie that morning and they were glad to have an errand as an excuse to run around the neighbourhood, especially since Grace had told them they could keep the pennies left over and spend them in the sweet-shop afterwards.

Up the road, the two girls bumped into Tommy Smith. He was carrying a bag of books. He beamed at the girls when he saw them.

Now aged fourteen, Tommy had the beginnings of a beard on his chin. He had shot up in height recently and his voice had grown deeper. But he was still the same old grinning Tommy. He had never seemed embarrassed about the changes to his body, just taking them in his stride, as he took everything in life.

'Coming to the library, then?'

Annie shook her head. 'No, we've got to get some salt for Mother.' A musky smell emanated from him and curled around her nostrils. Annie liked it. It smelt foreign and grown-up.

'You're always going to that library,' remarked Tilly. 'You must be able to read very fast.'

'Yeah. I like reading.' Tommy grinned. 'I've decided to be a lawyer when I grow up.'

Annie nodded approvingly. 'That's good. You'll be the first in your family, I expect.'

Tommy threw back his head and laughed. 'That's true,'

he chuckled. 'But my family's had a lot of experience of the law, you know, so it's obviously in my blood!' The latest news from the Smith household was that the eldest boy, Keith, had been arrested for breaking and entering a shop in Holloway. He had stolen thirty tins of paint, and been sent to prison.

Tommy walked with them to Mr Nethercott's grocer's shop. As they passed the Horders' house, they heard a terrible sound, a sort of eerie wailing and howling.

'Have they got a dog?' The children stopped by the gate to listen.

'I think that's Danny,' said Annie. 'That's what Danny sounds like when he's upset. It's not usually as bad as that, but it does sound like him.'

Tommy went up to the door. It was locked. He peered in through the downstairs window, cupping his hands around the side of his face to get a clear look. 'I can see Danny,' he said. 'He's in there. He's crouching down on the floor.'

Annie and Tilly ran to the window to look. Sure enough, Danny was on his knees, rocking backwards and forwards, his huge hands covering his face. He howled in time to his rocking movement. There was no sign of Mrs Horder anywhere. Oddest of all, Danny seemed to be dressed in his stripy pyjamas, even though it was the middle of the afternoon.

Tommy tapped on the window. 'Hey, Danny! What's wrong?'

Nothing happened.

'Do it louder!' Annie's heart was pounding. Something was wrong.

Tommy banged hard on the glass with his fist.

Danny momentarily stopped his wailing and looked up.

Seeing Tommy standing by the window, he turned away and started up again, rocking backwards and forwards even more violently than before.

'Something must have happened to Mrs Horder,' whispered Annie.

'Perhaps she's just nipped out and left Danny at home for a few minutes,' suggested Tilly.

Annie shook her head. 'Mrs Horder would never do that. Danny can't do anything on his own. She takes him everywhere with her.'

'What about the people who live upstairs? Aren't they about?'

'The Spencers? No, they've only just gone away on holiday,' said Annie. 'They've gone to Blackpool for a week. Mrs Horder told me that only yesterday. I saw her and Danny coming home from the shops.'

The noise coming from Danny's throat was sounding more and more distressed. It was alarming. Annie banged on the window but Danny would not even look up any more. She felt confident that she could calm him but it was no good if he did not see her.

'I'm going to try to force the door,' said Tommy.

The girls looked on in wonder as Tommy pulled a penknife from his pocket. It was an old one he had had for years. He was always whittling pieces of wood with it or playing dangerous games of splits with other boys on patches of grass. He opened up the knife and pushed the blade between the door and the frame. He wiggled it up and down. Suddenly the door opened with a little click.

'How did you do that?' Annie was impressed.

'Well, since you ask,' Tommy grinned, 'it was me dad who showed me.'

The children stumbled into the dark hallway. Danny was in the front room where they had seen him. As they came in, he looked up at them.

Annie was shocked at the sight of him. His big round face was swollen from crying. His eyes were puffy and red. She noticed too that his cheeks were stubbly as though he had not shaved that day. She had never noticed that before. It had never occurred to her that the childlike Danny even shaved. Presumably Mrs Horder always did it for him.

'What's the matter, Danny?' Annie walked towards him, holding out her hand. 'Where's your mother?'

Danny's face was crumpled up with anguish. But he nodded when he saw Annie's familiar face. The other two children he was not so sure about, and he glanced at them sideways. He then got to his feet and reached out to take Annie's hand. She tried not to wince as he squeezed it tight. He squeezed it again and would not let go.

The house was quiet. It was as neat and tidy as ever. Nothing seemed different.

'Where's your mother, Danny?' Annie repeated the question in as clear a voice as possible.

Danny shook his head and frowned.

'Is she at home? Is she here somewhere?'

Danny stared at her with blank eyes. Then he frowned and looked away.

'I'm going to have a look upstairs,' said Tommy. He slipped out of the room. Seconds later he gave a shout. 'She's up here!' he called. 'She doesn't seem to be breathing. I think she's dead! She's all cold.'

Tilly's eyes widened. 'Oh, what shall we do?'

'You'd better run to Mr Nethercott's and ask him to telephone for the police and to call for a doctor.' Annie's voice was tremulous. Her hands were shaking too but she was only aware of Danny's tight grip on her upper arm now. He was leaning down on her heavily.

Tilly had gone. Annie sat down on the sofa. 'I think we'd better sit down here, Danny,' she said. 'We have to wait for some people to arrive now.'

Suddenly the house was full of people. The police arrived along with the doctor, and a crowd of people gathered outside in the street to see what was going on. People kept running up and down the stairs and nosing around the rooms. Then the police wanted to take statements from the children. They wanted to know exactly what had happened. Annie heard the doctor telling the police that it looked as though the old woman had had a heart attack in her sleep. 'It's the way to go,' he commented.

Annie was disturbed to see how rough the police were with Danny. They wanted to question him alone in the kitchen. But Danny would not let go of Annie's hand. Every time anyone came near him he started squealing like a frightened animal and huddled closer to Annie. 'Leave him alone,' she said. 'He's upset enough already.'

'It's all right, love,' said the policeman. 'We're not going to harm him. We just need to find out what happened.'

'What is there to find out?' Annie was getting cross with the way they frightened Danny. 'Mrs Horder just died in her sleep, didn't she? That's what the doctor said, I heard him. Besides,' she added, 'there's no point asking Danny questions. He can't talk. He's just like a two-year-old, just a baby, really, his mother used to say.'

The adults gathered around in groups and whispered. Tilly and Tommy were allowed to go home.

'Did Mrs Horder have any other relatives?' the police

sergeant asked Annie. 'Is there anyone else who can take charge of Danny now?'

Annie shook her head. 'Mrs Horder used to say there were only the two of them now.'

It was getting late. There was more whispering and talking. The light was failing outside. Annie was not surprised when her mother appeared. Tilly had informed her about what was going on. 'What's going to happen to Danny?' Annie asked. 'Who's going to look after him.'

Grace smiled and sat down beside Annie. Danny stared at her listlessly. He had dark circles under his eyes and he looked exhausted. 'Danny will have to go and stay in a special home where they will know how to look after him.'

'But he'll be frightened there,' Annie protested. 'He won't know anyone.'

'He'll get used to it,' Grace replied quietly.

'But he'll hate it. Surely he can stay. Someone can look after him here. Or perhaps he could come and stay with us. He is very gentle and kind, and he's very easy.'

Grace shook her head. 'Annie, love, we have to be realistic. Danny isn't like a dog we can take in off the street just like that. He's a full-grown man who can't look after himself. His mother devoted herself to him. Every minute of her day was spent looking after him. How do you think we could cope with him? He can't dress himself or', she lowered her voice, 'even wipe his own bottom.'

Annie's throat felt thick and congested. Tears welled up in her eyes as Danny's fate slowly became clear.

A van had drawn up outside. Some big men in white coats came into the house. There was more talking and whispering. One of the men came into the room and started talking to Danny.

'Would you let go of him, miss,' he said to Annie. 'It would be easier if you left the room now.'

Grace got up. 'I'll be waiting for you outside,' she said.

Annie tried to extricate herself from Danny's clasp but he clung on to her in desperation.

'Tell him to let go, if you would, miss,' said the man.

'Danny,' whispered Annie, 'you must let go of me now. These men have come to look after you.' She stroked Danny's arm soothingly.

Another two men had come into the room. They seemed to take up all the space. Danny slowly let go of Annie's arm. 'That's right, Danny,' she said. 'Good boy.'

'Now quietly leave the room, miss,' said the man. As Annie got up, Danny lunged towards her again. 'No, Danny,' she said quietly but firmly. 'You'll be all right.'

She quickly turned and walked out of the room. As she did so, the men pounced. Danny let out a great howl of outrage. Annie was led out of the house and into the street where she fell into her mother's arms.

'Let's go home now,' said Grace, trying to lead her daughter away from the crowd of people gawping on the pavement. The whole neighbourhood seemed to be there – including Maudie and her friend Jessie out pushing Jessie's baby William in the pram, and the Challen twins, and the Fenton sisters were standing on tiptoe trying to see over the heads of people in front. Even Dolly Pritchett had appeared, her large frame quivering with indignation as she glared at the men from the authorities.

There were loud screams coming from the house and the sound of breaking furniture. Men were shouting at each other over the unnatural screams of Danny himself.

'I'm not going home yet, Mother,' said Annie, pulling

away. 'I have to see. I have to see what they're doing to him.'

The noise had stopped. Five minutes later, Danny was led out of the house. Over his pyjamas he was wearing a strange white canvas garment which wrapped his arms around his body. Someone had pulled his boots on but not tied them up. The laces flapped at the sides as he walked. All he could do was waddle. Annie hardly dared look at him as they led him into the waiting van. She was relieved that Danny kept his head dropped down between his shoulders. She did not want him to look her in the eye and tell her that she had betrayed him. But Danny did not look up once. The doors closed behind him and the van drove off.

Danny Horder was never seen again. And it was a long time before Annie was able to walk past the Horders' home without feeling sharp stabs of guilt at the thought of her treacherous behaviour.

Annie's desire to become an artist was as strong as ever. The urge to paint and draw was with her constantly. She had recently become interested in perspective and how she could draw solid objects on a flat surface to make them appear as they actually do when viewed from a particular point. She was rarely seen without a green pencil in one hand and her sketchbooks in another. If she was sitting in the kitchen talking to her mother while Grace prepared the supper, Annie would be drawing everything before her, from the fruit in the bowl on the table, the plates on the dresser, the roast of meat waiting to be placed in the oven, blood oozing out of it, to the pile of knives and forks waiting to be laid. She drew her father at the piano, Jack bent over his school books, Clara combing and plaiting her long hair, her mother kneading dough. She even managed to draw Bobby, but only when he was asleep, for awake he never stayed still long enough for her to capture him on paper. She painted the Admiral butterfly she found dead on her window sill and the woodlice creeping about under the big rock in the garden. She painted the sky at night over Hampstead Heath, she painted the sky in the morning. Nothing escaped her attention, and her sketchbooks mounted up in the cupboard beside her bed. They were visual diaries of her life.

But as her passion for drawing and painting grew, so did her curiosity about her mother's brooch. It would not go away. She often found herself drawing it from memory over and over again, detailing all the diamonds and sapphires and the pretty gold setting. At night she would lie in the dark with her hands behind her head thinking about the mysterious jewel. She wondered why her mother never wore it but instead hid it away in the back of the wardrobe. Why did her mother refuse to talk about it, even with Frank, and why would she not even consider using it when it could help them, like when they were short of money and worried about treatment for her rheumatoid arthritis? Annie did not understand.

Annie had quizzed both Jack and Clara about the brooch, but neither of them seemed interested at all. Gradually it became Annie's obsession. She often crept into her parents' bedroom to look at it when her father was out and her mother busy with her chores downstairs. She would tiptoe across the room, reach up to the high shelf and pull out the box with the christening robe. She would unfold the tissue paper and hold the glistening jewel in her hand. It covered the whole of her palm. She would tilt her head one way and then the other to see the different patterns the light made as it hit the facets on the stones. Annie would pull down the sleeve of her cardigan and rub the diamonds. The brooch was beautiful, and highlighted by what looked like an aura all around it. Annie imagined that it was magic. Perhaps, if she rubbed it the right way, she might be transported away to some enchanted place.

Whenever she heard anyone coming up the stairs, Annie quickly wrapped up the brooch and slipped it back into the box with the silk christening gown. If found in the room, she pretended that she was looking for her sketch-book which she had left in there.

'Who gave Mother that brooch?' Annie looked up at her father hopefully.

'I've told you before,' replied Frank with a tolerant sigh, 'Mrs Pearson, the lady your grandparents worked for in Sussex.'

'But why did Mrs Pearson give Mother the brooch?'

Frank sighed again and put his arm around Annie's shoulder. 'As I have told you every time you ask me that question, I don't know. Your mother helped Mrs Pearson with something so Mrs Pearson gave her the brooch out of gratitude. If you want to know more about that transaction, you'll have to ask your mother. Perhaps you'll have more luck than I do.'

Annie shrugged and frowned. She could not ask her mother again. She did not dare. It would be too cruel. Whenever the subject of the brooch was brought up, however vaguely, Grace always looked distressed and unhappy.

Annie and Frank were walking down the road on their way to visit the National Gallery. Keen to encourage his younger daughter's artistic ambitions, Frank had promised for some time to take her on a trip to look at the nation's pictures. With all the talk of war in the air, he thought it wise to get Annie to see the country's art treasures before they were whisked away to some secret hiding place, as had been suggested in the newspaper the other day. Clara was supposed to have come too, but she was staying behind as a punishment, having been in trouble all week.

First, she was sent home from school after she had been discovered letting bees out in the classroom deliberately to disrupt lessons. Annie had noticed Clara's sudden enthusiasm for capturing bees in jam jars as they buzzed about the buddleia bushes, but she had not thought any more about it. It turned out that Clara had been letting out one every lesson for a fortnight. The school secretary had been searching everywhere in the playground for evidence of the source of these creatures. It had been serious. Two girls had been stung – one seriously, for it turned out that she was allergic to bee stings. She was rushed to hospital and was lucky to be out at the end of the week. Then Clara was found with a jar of bees in her pocket, and was sent home for two weeks. Then, she was supposed to have been studying for her exams at home but she kept slipping out to meet Roger on Hampstead Heath. This had enraged her parents, who only knew about it because Dolly Pritchett

had remarked on seeing Clara walking arm in arm with
Roger by the ponds one afternoon.

So Clara was in big trouble. No pocket money and no
going out until further notice. And certainly no treats. 'I
don't care,' Clara had shrugged. 'I like staying in my room.'

So Annie had the rare pleasure of going out on a trip
alone with her father. Halfway up the road they met Dolly
Pritchett. She was carrying two large string bags full of
groceries and was puffing as her heavy frame swung from
side to side. Frank greeted her in his usual friendly manner,
and then, as Annie shifted her weight from one foot to the
other and tried not to look bored because it was rude to do
so, there followed the usual exchange about what Mr
Hitler was up to in Europe and what the Prime Minister
was going to do about it all.

All anyone ever talked about nowadays was war, she
thought. She did not understand it much and it seemed
rather exciting, with talk of trenches being dug in the parks
and air-raid shelters in the gardens and gas masks to be
carried at all times. It also seemed far away from Kentish
Town, especially as no one seemed frightened. But her parents listened to the BBC news on the wireless every evening
and no one was allowed to make a sound, not even a
squeak, until it was finished. So perhaps they were more
worried than they let on.

Finally Dolly said her goodbyes and Annie and Frank
set off once more for the Underground station. They
turned down Leverton Street. Annie chattered gaily to her
father, passing on stories about her playmates as they
passed. They waved to the Challen twins and said good
day to the Fenton sisters who were just setting off on a
shopping trip to Queen's Crescent market. Annie waved to

Mrs Whelan, who was busy leaning out of the top-floor window and scrubbing the wall just below it. 'She'll fall out if she isn't careful,' she giggled.

But her father did not laugh. He was not even looking at Mrs Whelan. The laughter had gone from his face and he was looking rather stern.

'What's wrong?'

As Annie spoke, she noticed a woman sitting on the doorstep of the Smiths' house. She was about twenty-five. Although rather blowzy, she was attractive, with a neat compact figure. She had dark brown wavy hair, velvety brown eyes and clear white skin. She was looking up at Frank and smiling. 'Well, good morning,' she called in a cocky sort of way. Her voice was unusually husky.

Frank seemed to hesitate and draw back momentarily. For a second Annie thought that her father was going to bolt in the other direction. But a moment later he had collected himself. 'Good morning,' he said politely. Grasping Annie by the arm, he hurried her on. 'Come on. We mustn't dawdle any more.'

'But who's that?' she whispered, looking back at the woman sitting on the doorstep. The woman was watching them go, a smile on her full red lips. 'I've never seen her before.'

'That's Connie Smith.' Frank was striding ahead. 'Tommy's older sister.' He was matter-of-fact and brusque.

Annie had to run to keep up with him. 'Tommy's older sister,' she repeated. 'You mean, the one who ran away with Maudie Sprackling's husband?'

Frank nodded. 'That's right.' He didn't slacken his pace.

Annie was impressed. 'Well,' she mused, 'I wonder what Maudie thinks . . .'

'Not much, I should think,' said Frank. 'Now, come on, Annie, let's hurry . . .'

They spent the whole afternoon in the National Gallery. Annie felt in heaven. Never had she seen such paintings before. Some of them she had seen in books but she had never seen the brushwork on the oil paintings, or the textures or the colours. She was both awed and inspired by seeing the work of some of the greatest artists in history. Her head was spinning with their names – Michelangelo, Rembrandt, Leonardo da Vinci, Gainsborough, Reynolds, Goya – all painting so many different pictures.

'That should give you something to work towards,' said Frank as they had tea and scones in the Lyons tearoom in the Strand. 'Perhaps one day a painting by you will hang on those walls.'

Annie smiled and, with her finger, scooped up a blob of strawberry jam which had dropped down her front. 'If I work hard,' she said, popping her finger into her mouth and withdrawing it slowly as the sweet gooey jam spread out across her tongue. 'I'd like that.'

The early evening crowds were out as they walked back to Leicester Square Underground station. People were coming out from work and making their way home or arriving for an evening out at the cinema or the theatre or just a good meal in Soho. Annie suddenly noticed a face she recognized in the crowd. Across the road, she saw Jessie. 'That's Maudie Sprackling's friend, isn't it?'

Annie pointed and then quickly dropped her arm. She knew it was rude to point.

Frank looked up across the road. 'I'm not sure,' he said

hurriedly, and quickly guided Annie down the steep steps into the Underground station.

Later, as they emerged at Kentish Town station, they bumped into Maudie Sprackling pushing Jessie's baby, William, in the pram. Maudie had a gloomy expression on her face. She looked the way she used to before Jessie and William came into her life. Her face was red and blotchy as though she had been crying.

'Good evening, Maudie. Are you all right?' Frank could never let anyone go by without seeing if he could help.

'Yes, yes,' replied Maudie, looking away as if embarrassed by the giveaway signs on her face. 'It's nothing really.'

'We saw Jessie,' piped up Annie. 'We went to the National Gallery to look at the pictures. We saw her in town.'

Maudie nodded. 'Yes, she works late on Thursdays,' she said. 'The shop stays open until eight o' clock so she's serving customers and doesn't get back until late. It's my night for putting William to bed.' She smiled fondly at the sleeping baby in the pram.

'Well, we must be off,' said Frank. 'We must get home for our tea now.'

As he and Annie set off up Leighton Road, neither one of them said anything about Jessie. They had seen Jessie at five-thirty, when she was supposedly working. And she had looked different from normal. They had both seen her with rouge on her cheeks and bright lipstick on her lips, laughing in the company of a man who had his arm around her in a familiar way. Frank had a good idea of what was going on. For her part, Annie did not. But she sensed that what Maudie had told them about Jessie was not the real truth, though Maudie herself did not know that. Annie also knew that what she had seen down there on the street between Jessie and her gentleman friend was something to do with being a grown-up, and with what her parents sometimes did on Sunday mornings. It was not for discussion or comment.

CHAPTER 9

Connie

IT HAD BEEN A great summer holiday which culminated in the opening of the Lido at Parliament Hill. This was the huge new swimming pool complete with diving boards, chutes and clear blue water built for the pleasure of the local people. Everyone in the neighbourhood was up there to sample the delights of the water, whether they could swim or not. There was a grand opening and the sound of people shouting and splashing could be heard as far as Westminster.

Annie had gone up there several times with Tilly, and on a couple of occasions with Clara, too, when she was not trying to slip off to see Roger. Much to her parents' relief, Clara had claimed to have lost interest in Roger and announced that she was intending to concentrate on her schoolwork. But Annie and Jack knew better. They knew full well that Clara pretended to be going over to Marie's house but in fact was meeting up with Roger at the cinema or some place on the Heath.

Annie thought Clara was wrong to deceive their parents in this way but she never understood why Jack became

quite as angry as he did about what Clara got up to. If
Clara was out when Annie and Jack were playing gin
rummy or racing demon, Jack would keep looking at his
watch and murmuring under his breath about Clara's
behaviour. Once Annie asked him why he was so cross,
and he refused to answer. His face just went white and he
turned away.

If Annie did not understand her brother's feelings about
Clara, neither did Jack himself. As a boy, and the eldest, he
had always felt it his duty to look after his younger siblings. He had enjoyed their need for his protection. Now
Clara was breaking away from him and not wanting him
to look after her at all. He felt hurt and redundant. The
fact that she was attracted to Roger Knight, whom Jack
loathed, complicated matters further. He could not disentangle one lot of feelings from another. And neither could
Clara. She made it plain that she thought Jack simply
hated her seeing anyone.

Clara liked the idea of Jack being jealous. She assumed
that that night after the street party had been important to
Jack. In fact, it had been no more important to him than it
had been to her. What Clara refused to accept was that
Jack simply disliked Roger.

Annie was still too young to understand such matters.
She watched the goings-on with a cool indifference.
Generally, she was enjoying life. She liked school, and her
mother's rheumatoid arthritis was not too bad at the
moment, so she did not have to worry about that, either.
Her friend Tilly was also cheerful nowadays. Her father
had finally found himself a job in a small business in
Islington. It did not pay much but enough for the family to
be able to rent a larger place two blocks away in Countess

Road and afford a few luxuries. They even managed to get away for a short holiday in Wales. Both Annie and Tilly had passed the scholarship exam last term and were set to go on to the grammar school in Parliament Hill.

But once the summer was over, people started to talk more and more about the possibility of war. There was a lot of talk about air-raid precautions and an autumn drive for volunteers to man the services. Volunteers were needed for each road. After the Munich Crisis in September, gas masks were issued to everyone by hundreds of volunteers. It became illegal to go out without one.

People accepted the masks, for the fear of gas attacks was real, but they hated them all the same. They loathed the claustrophobic feel of the clammy rubber and the suf-focating condensation that built up on the celluloid eyeshields.

'Ugh!' said Clara, picking her mask with an expression of distaste. 'I'd rather be gassed than wear this.'

She stared at Annie who was peering out at her through the eyeshields. 'I don't want to look like a giant ant.'

Her mother laughed. 'When it comes to it, my guess is that you won't mind what you look like.'

The spectre of war loomed more and more by the week. It had been hanging in the air for so long, its presence was almost unbearably oppressive.

One morning Tommy turned up at Annie's house with some good news. His mouse had had babies and, as arranged, in a few weeks' time, Annie was going to be allowed to have one of them as a pet. Grace and Frank had finally given in to the pressure from their youngest daughter to have another animal.

'She's had six,' Tommy informed Annie. 'Last night.'

He held out his arm. Balancing precariously along Tommy's wrist and forearm, its tail flipping from side to side, was a black-and-white mouse. 'The proud dad.'

Annie jumped up and down with excitement. Ever since Tommy had suggested that she have one of his mouse's babies and her parents had agreed, she had been waiting for this moment. She had chosen the shoe box she would keep the mouse in. She would fill the box with scraps of coloured wool from her mother's knitting, and keep it under her bed. She would clean it out every other day so that it didn't smell and feed it with cabbage and nuts and perhaps some corn borrowed from Mr Spratt.

It had all been a surprise anyway: when Tommy went to the pet shop in Fortess Road and brought back two mice in a shoe box, he had told his mum that they were both male. A few weeks later, however, he realized that the white one with red eyes was getting fatter and fatter.

It was Annie's mother who had suggested that the mouse was about to have babies and was not just eating too much. Overhearing the conversation between Annie and Tommy about the fat mouse made her chuckle.

'I think you're about to have more mice to look after, Tommy,' she said the week before when Tommy had brought his two mice round to the Turners' house. The mice were tame and seemed quite happy to be handled. Grace held the albino mouse up to her face. She liked the way its whiskers never stopped twitching.

'I suppose they make easy pets,' she said thoughtfully.

'Oh, yes,' said Tommy, giving Annie a nudge.

So her parents had agreed. Now the moment had come.

'I couldn't bring the mother mouse along to show you because me mum said she should stay put. And she said to keep this one away from the babies. Mum said he might disturb them, or something. I have to keep him in a separate box for a while.'

'But when can I see them?' Annie asked anxiously. 'When can I see my new pet?' Suddenly she felt like a different person. Now she was someone who was about to be the owner of a mouse. Her ownership of the goldfish Roger gave her at the Easter fair had been short-lived. The fish was found floating on the top of the water after just a few days. Annie had not cried, though. The goldfish had proved to be a boring pet to have.

'Well, you can see it now, if you like. You can come to my house.'

Annie was surprised. Tommy had never suggested that she go to his house before. He had always been so eager to get away from it.

As they set off for Tommy's house, Tommy began to tell Annie about his sister who had returned after being away for a few years. 'She's great,' he said. 'She's always laughing and having fun.'

'But isn't she the one who ran away with Maudie Sprackling's husband?'

'Well, yes, but it looks like they're going to be good friends now.'

Annie glanced at him with surprise. 'But how's that possible after she stole Maudie's husband from her?'

Tommy shrugged. 'Yeah, it seems like that's all water under the bridge now. For the first few days when Connie was back, Maudie looked quite put out but Connie took her some flowers one day and they had it out. I don't know what was said, but now it looks like they're the best of friends.'

Annie was surprised by the state of the Smiths' house inside.

She had only ever been in it once before, when Tommy was ill and she had taken him some biscuits her mother had made for him. The squalor then had shocked her. The air was heavy with the sour odours of old cooking, cigarettes and unwashed bodies. Tommy's dad, as usual, had no work and he was sitting in the front room in his vest and trousers. A cigarette hung from his bottom lip all the time as though stuck to it. Annie had a quick glimpse of the kitchen and just saw piles of dirty plates and pots all over the place, on every surface but also stacked up on the floor. It seemed no wonder that Tommy was always commenting on how nice the Turners' house was.

But this time it was different. It was still cluttered and crowded but it seemed quite clean. There were no piles of dirty clothes or crockery lying around. The windows were open so fresh air circulated freely and there was even a small jam jar with a few marigolds on the table in the front room.

'Since she's been home, Connie's been doing the house cleaning,' Tommy explained. 'When our mum's out at work all day, she don't have much time for it. Now Connie does it instead.'

As he spoke, Connie appeared down the stairs. 'Hello, there, Tommy,' she said. 'Who's this, then?' She peered at Annie in a friendly sort of way.

Annie smiled shyly at her.

'This is Annie Turner,' said Tommy. 'She's come to see the mice.'

Connie nodded. 'So you're Frank Turner's girl, are you?

I remember, now, I saw you in the street with him the other day.'

'Yes,' whispered Annie.

'Nice man, your father,' said Connie. 'Always ready to help people, he is.'

Tommy led Annie out to the garden through the kitchen. At the table Tommy's two middle brothers were playing cards, beer bottles and cigarettes to hand. They did not even look up as the children went by. Annie recognized Eric from his broken nose. He was rather frightening to look at and she knew from Tommy that he had recently come out of prison where he had been for a few months for burglary.

Connie's influence stopped at the kitchen door. The garden really was a mess, filled with old bed springs and rusty cookers. They picked their way to the far corner where a space had been cleared for a large wooden crate. It had an old bike placed on top. 'I have to put this on to stop the cats knocking over the crate and getting at the mice,' he explained. 'Now, sssh . . .'

They crept over and pulled off the bicycle. Tommy slipped off the lid of the crate and peered over the side. 'You can see them all quite clearly now,' he whispered.

Annie looked into the crate. Her eyes opened wide at the sight of the white mouse lying down with six hairless pink creatures next to her. Their eyes were closed over and they moved about helplessly.

Annie was revolted by the sight but she hid her disappointment. She had imagined that they would be tiny replicas of their parents.

'When will they grow fur?'

'In a few days, I think,' replied Tommy. 'Yeah, they're not much to look at now.'

As he spoke, Connie called to him from the house. 'Want some biscuits, Tommy? There's enough here for you and Annie, if you're feeling a bit peckish.'

'Thanks, Connie,' Tommy called back. 'Just a sec . . .'

Annie peered back into the box. For a few seconds she stared at the animals in the box, trying to understand what she was witnessing. Suddenly she clasped her hand over her mouth as she felt the gorge rising in her throat. 'Aaagh! What's she doing? What's she doing?' She pointed into the crate for Tommy to see. 'Stop her!'

Like Annie, Tommy stared in open-mouthed horror at the sight before him. Frightened by the disturbance, the white mouse had started to eat her offspring, holding them in her front paws and chewing the pink and black skin as fast as she could, rushing from one to the next until the crate was littered with the pink and bloodied carcasses of her babies.

'It's too late,' Tommy said quietly. 'We've frightened her too much.'

Jack looked impatiently at his watch and frowned. Clara was late. It was typical. If only she could be on time, just for once.

The queue to the cinema was quite long now. The new film was clearly popular. Well, if Clara didn't come soon, she would miss it . . .

Jack nodded politely at Maudie Sprackling who was standing in the queue a good ten yards back. She seemed to be with Tommy Smith's big sister, Connie. How peculiar. The two women looked like the best of friends, laughing and joking together. Yet he had always grown up with the knowledge that Connie Smith had run away with Maudie's husband. In fact, he could just about remember the commotion when it happened. He could still see the look of excitement on Dolly Pritchett's face and hear the relish in her voice as she told Jack's mother about how Maudie's husband, Fred, had walked out after a row and never come back. And then it turned out that Connie Smith had disappeared that day too. Soon everyone knew that the two had run off and moved in together, without being married. It was quite a scandal at the time.

The queue had started to move. Where was Clara? She had said she just had to pop down to Daniel's, the department store, to buy some material to sew her sports badges on to. She would meet Jack at the cinema, she said, ten minutes before the film was due to start.

Time was passing fast. Jack felt crosser and crosser. He was not sure whether to go on waiting for his sister or just to file in with the crowd and buy one ticket and go in by himself.

But he didn't want to miss the film. He waited until Maudie, Connie and the rest of the queue had filed past and disappeared into the cinema. He looked down the road one more time. There was still no sign of Clara's blonde head bobbing up and down as she dashed in her characteristic way, late to whatever destination.

With a sigh of annoyance and disappointment – it was never as much fun going to the cinema alone – he bought one ticket and went in. Clara will just have to miss the beginning of the film and sit apart from me, he thought. That will serve her right.

Clara did not make it to the film at all. When Jack came out, he hung around to see if he could see her in the

Saturday afternoon crowd but there was no sign of her. She was definitely not there.

Now Jack began to worry that something had happened. Clara was famous for being late, but she always got there in the end. She had never not turned up before. Jack had always been protective of his sisters and now he began to be afraid that some harm had come to Clara and made her unable to meet him at the cinema as planned. After all, they had made the arrangement only thirty minutes before the film was due to start.

Jack hurried home. He feared the worst, though he did not know what that was. In his head he was working out how to tell his mother that Clara had gone missing. He had to do it without making her too worried in the process. He dreaded that look of panic which came over his mother's face whenever she thought one of her children was in danger. He had seen it quite a lot recently, too, particularly since his mother seemed to fret so much over Bobby. Even Jack's father had told Grace to stop worrying so much about the boy. 'Bobby's four years old,' he would say. 'He's quite old enough to climb down the stairs on his own without you holding him. He's got to become independent some day.'

This, of course, was different. Where could Clara be? Jack began to feel quite frantic as he approached the house.

All Jack's fears proved to be unfounded. And it was unnecessary to convey any alarming news to his mother after all. When he walked in through the front door, there was Clara playing the piano in the hall.

Jack was furious. 'Where were you? I waited for you until the last minute.'

Clara looked up, flashed a smile at him and then turned

back to the piano. Her fingers danced over the keys and the lively music filled the house. 'Oh, I decided not to come after all,' she said casually.

Jack stared at her. 'Why not?' He clenched his fists as his rage built up inside him.

'I met someone and we got talking.' Clara talked in a matter-of-fact voice. 'Then it was too late for the film.'

'Who was it? Who did you meet?'

His sister turned to look at him again. Her eyes stared at him defiantly. 'I don't think that's any of your business,' she said airily.

'Yes it is my business,' snapped Jack. He stepped towards the piano. It is my business if you say you're going to meet me somewhere and then leave me hanging around in a queue and nearly make me miss the film.'

'But you didn't miss the film.'

Jack lowered his voice. ' It was Roger you met, wasn't it?'

Clara began to play some brisk music very loudly, banging hard on the keyboard. She did not reply.

'It was Roger, wasn't it?' Jack repeated. 'You met Roger.'

Clara went on playing and ignoring him. Finally, as his throat tightened with fury, Jack reached out and flipped the piano lid shut. 'Didn't you?'

Clara looked up slowly. 'So what if I did?'

'He's no good. He's a bad influence . . .' The words spilled out from Jack's lips from nowhere.

His sister stood up and laughed. 'You sound just like Father.' She tossed back her hair. 'Leave me alone. I can be friends with whoever I want. And I don't need your permission to see my friends. I don't comment on the people you choose to have for friends, do I?' She stared defiantly

at him. Then she glanced sideways and raised her eyebrows
teasingly. 'I think you're a little jealous,' she said quietly.
'You're jealous of Roger because he's bigger than you and
he's got a job, when you're just a little schoolboy doing
your School Certificate.'

'Ha, don't be so ridiculous.' Jack sneered. 'Why should
I be jealous of a creep like Roger? Unlike Roger, I want to
get educated. I want to get proper qualifications to get a
good job and not spend my time just being a labourer,
which is all Roger's good for.' He squared his shoulders
and stuck his hands deep in his pockets. 'I just think you
should stay away from him. He's trouble.'

Jack started to climb the stairs to his room. Clara lifted
the piano lid and started to play again. 'Thanks for the
advice, bro,' she called gaily. 'I'll bear it in mind for the
future. I appreciate the concern, if nothing else.'

Jack went upstairs and shut the door to his room. He sat
on the edge of his bed and stared out of the window. He
could see his mother pottering about in the garden down
below while Bobby stayed in the sandpit. Annie was sitting
on the grass, sketchbook and charcoal in hand. Suddenly
Jack picked up the pillow next to him and punched it hard.
He rolled over, punching it again and again. The rage
roared through him. He was not jealous, he was angry,
but why and at whom he had no idea. It felt as though he
were filled with a crackling fireball of energy which was
desperately pushing him inside, seeking a release along the
path of least resistance.

Breathing hard, he rolled over onto his back. Staring up
at the ceiling, he was aware of how tightly his jaw was
clenched. His hand moved over his hip. Unbuttoning his
flies, he slipped his fingers under his shirt tails.

He could hear his mother calling to Bobby outside, and Bobby's shouts of joy. He thought of his mother, of the nape of her neck as she bent over her sewing. He thought of his sister Clara, laughing, throwing back her hair with a coquettish smile. But in spite of what happened between them, he did not want her now. He thought of Marie Whelan, but did not dwell for long on her long straight limbs and skinny frame. He thought now of a big tall woman with long red hair. Her small white teeth flashed as she smiled at him invitingly, beckoning him, holding her strong arms out to him as he came towards her. He could smell her, feel her. Jack's body arched in response. He let out a quiet groan of ecstasy as he sank into her soft warm flesh.

CHAPTER 10

A Murder

IN MARCH 1939, HITLER'S army invaded Czechoslovakia. As the Führer's attention focused on Poland, the British public was generally agreed that he had to be resisted. Everyone talked about the war and everyone had an opinion about what should be done, but few people had any real idea of how war might affect their lives. Everybody, except those who were either too young or too old to know what was going on, lived in a permanent state of anxious uncertainty.

The combination of the war threat and Grace's health had made the atmosphere in the Turners' house even more tense. Grace's rheumatoid arthritis was unpredictable and would come and go at different times. When the pains were under control she was remarkably cheerful, but when they were strong she withdrew into herself, leaving the family without a focus.

Annie found her mother's volatile state of health disturbing. With all this talk of war, she needed her mother to be certain and consistent. She wanted her to be a solid rock, at the centre of the family at all times, reassuring her children that everything would be all right. Annie craved it. Even though she understood that her mother was not to blame for being ill, she still expected her to be strong. Her mother was failing her. Sometimes Annie felt more like a carer than the one cared for.

Perhaps her older brother was feeling this, too; for much of the current problem at home stemmed from a change in Jack.

Having always been a compliant and easy boy, Jack, now sixteen, had suddenly become bolshy and difficult. He was sulky at mealtimes and he stayed out late at night without giving any explanation.

One morning, after Jack had once again stayed out until after midnight, Frank confronted his elder son. 'If you don't pull your socks up and spend your evenings studying instead of gallivanting around outside, you won't pass your exams.'

With what could be interpreted as insolent nonchalance, Jack slowly spread marmalade on his toast. He said nothing.

'You used to be so good about your studying,' chimed in Grace.

Suddenly Jack pushed the plate of toast across the table and leaped to his feet. 'Leave me alone!' he yelled at his astonished parents from the doorway. 'It's my life to do what I want!'

Grace rose from the table. 'Jack, dear, don't lose your temper . . .'

'Oh leave him be,' snapped Frank, pouring himself some more tea. 'He's got to learn to control that temper of his on his own.'

Jack had collected up his schoolbooks and left, slamming the door so hard that the whole house shuddered.

Upstairs Annie lay in bed listening to the shouting down below. She wanted to slap her hands over her ears to shut out the noise but at the same time she wanted to hear, not to miss anything that was said.

She was so tired of the arguments at the moment. If it wasn't Clara, it was Jack, and it didn't help that they were probably just going through a 'phase' as Dolly Pritchett had cheerfully suggested to Annie's mother that morning. 'They'll grow out of it and turn into lovely people,' she added. 'You'll see.'

In fact, Clara was much better behaved than she used to be. She seemed to have settled down a bit. She had even lost interest in Roger again and had been having fun flirting with other local boys, and not just to make Roger jealous.

No, it was Jack, who had never argued with his parents before, who was being sulky, distant and even rude. In fact, he seemed angry a lot of the time. Annie hardly dared speak to him at all at the moment for fear of being snapped at like everyone else. She just stayed out of his way.

Early one morning Grace and Annie set off down Kentish Town Road. They did their errands one by one. They bought pigs' trotters and a pig's head from the butcher, for Grace was planning to make a whole lot of brawn later that day if her hands weren't too painful, a big cottage loaf and Chelsea buns from the baker, carrots and greens for supper, and some beautiful material at Daniel's, the department store. Grace had promised to make Annie a new dress for the summer and she said that Annie could choose whatever pattern she wanted, and also the material, so long as it wasn't too expensive.

They looked through the pattern books, and Annie chose a pattern for a simple dress with a swing skirt. Next they went to the haberdashery department where they pored over the rolls of coloured cotton. Annie's head began to spin. The more she looked, the harder it was to choose. Finally, she pulled out a roll of blue cotton with a white polka-dot print. 'That's what I want,' she declared with satisfaction.

As the shop assistant measured and cut the material, she chatted to Grace. 'They say there's been something going on up the road,' she said. 'One lady said the police were running all over the place like a lot of chickens with their heads cut off.'

With the precious material in a brown paper bag under her arm, Annie walked with her mother and Bobby to their next port of call. As they moved from shop to shop, they heard more and more gossip about what had happened in Kentish Town that morning.

'I hear someone's been badly hurt,' one lady told the fishmonger.

'Someone's dead,' they heard at the haberdasher's. 'Been dead some time.'

'A young woman,' someone said in the street as they waited to cross the road.

'A woman, a loose woman,' said another.

'Got her come-uppance,' said someone with cruel relish.

'Up Fortess Road.'

'Somewhere in Leverton Street.'

'A terrible shock for the poor fellow what found her.'

Annie listened to the grown-ups passing bits of information backwards and forwards to each other and tried to piece together all the words to create some picture of what was going on. Although no one seemed to know the exact facts, it was clear that something serious had happened.

They walked back up the high street and turned for home. Annie realized that people were running past them towards Leverton Street, and a large crowd of people had gathered at the junction of Leverton Street and Falkland Road.

'Let's go on up Leighton Road.' Grace wanted to avoid the crowd. But Annie was having none of it.

'Oh, no, Mother, we have to find out what's going on. We must find out what's happening.'

When they got to the place where the two streets crossed, they could hardly move. The police had cordoned off Leverton Street between the junction and the oil store on the next corner. People were milling around and trying to see over the heads of the people in front of them, craning their necks and pushing.

They saw Dolly Pritchett standing next to Mrs Garcia. 'Whatever's happened?' asked Grace. Dolly glanced at Annie and lowered her voice. 'It's Sally Brown,' she whispered. 'Someone's done Sally Brown in.'

Annie's eyes widened in horror. 'Sally Brown?' Her words came out as a whisper. 'But we know her.'

Dolly went on to inform them that Sally had been found strangled that morning. The fact that her cat had been left out all night had alerted the neighbours because Sally always let it in at night. The animal had been scratching frantically at Sally's door, so they thought something must be wrong. Sally's door turned out not be locked anyway, and then they found her dead in bed.

'It's definitely foul play. She was a healthy young woman,' she muttered.

'One of her customers, no doubt,' added Mrs Garcia.

Dolly glanced sideways at Annie and frowned.

'What customers?' asked Annie. 'Why should Sally have customers?'

Grace put her arm around Annie's shoulders. 'Come on, Annie, let's get home.'

Annie walked along pushing the pram in a daze. Sally dead! Another person she knew was dead. First it was Mrs Horder, now Sally. But Mrs Horder died of old age, someone had killed Sally – had put a stocking around her neck and strangled her. Someone had choked her until she had stopped breathing. Someone had ended her life before it was supposed to end.

Sally was dead! It did not seem possible. She and Sally had sometimes sat on Sally's doorstep and told each other their secret dreams and hopes. Annie knew how much she wanted to have a fine husband, someone who would love her and look after her as a good husband should. Even though Sally used to ignore her when she had a friend with her – and come to think of it, they were always men – she was always friendly if Annie was walking past her house and Sally was sitting on her doorstep.

But now Sally was dead. Now she would have none of those things she had longed for, no kind husband, no home, no children. Annie's eyes glistened with tears as she thought about Sally's tall strong body stretched out on the bed, her beautiful long red hair spread out on the pillow like a halo. 'I liked Sally,' she murmured, rummaging up her sleeve for a handkerchief to blow her running nose, 'I thought she was nice.'

'Come on, Annie.' Grace urged her daughter on in a quiet voice. 'Let's get home.'

Mother and daughter went on as Mrs Garcia started to
relate to anyone who would listen the terrible thing that
had been done to her husband's horse the night before.
'It's sick,' she muttered. 'The person what did it was sick in
the head. Fancy attacking a dumb animal like that, in its
private parts. And in such a disgusting way, too, cutting it
up with a knife!'

The others nodded, their eyes open wide in horror at the
description of the attack on poor Juniper the horse.

They came for Jack early that same evening. The family
had just finished supper. The dishes had been washed,
dried and put away in the cupboards, the plates replaced
on the dresser. Bobby was asleep in his cot and Jack was
upstairs in his bedroom doing his homework. Moody
throughout supper, he had barely spoken a word. But since
he had been like this a lot recently, everyone else had
learned to ignore it.

Now the rest of the family were in the sitting room.
Clara and Annie perched on the sofa playing rummy while
Grace knelt on the floor with Annie's dress pattern and
polka dot material spread out before her. With her large,
heavy pinking-shears, she carefully cut around the markings on the thin tissue paper. In the corner, Frank sat in his
armchair smoking a pipe and reading the evening paper.

Suddenly there was a loud banging on the front door. It
was a rude violent noise, which made them all start and
look around at each other.

'Whoever can that be?' Grace frowned and glanced at
Frank who had folded his paper and got to his feet.

'I'll see,' he said.

They all waited to hear him going down the stairs, walk along the hall and open the front door. Annie held her breath as she heard the exchange down below.

'Good evening, officer.' Frank's voice was surprised and quiet. There followed a conversation Annie couldn't follow, but she heard the words 'your son Jack Turner', quite clearly. So did Grace.

'Jack?' Grace pulled herself up, wincing at the pain in her knees. 'Someone wants Jack?'

A minute later, they heard Frank coming slowly up the stairs. He stood in the doorway to the sitting room, his face grey and leaden. 'It's the police,' he stated. 'They're waiting downstairs. They want to take Jack down to the station for questioning.'

'Questioning? What sort of questioning?' Grace's voice rose in pitch as she flew at her husband. 'What are you talking about?' Clara and Annie glanced at each other in puzzlement and fear. Annie edged up to her elder sister for comfort.

'I don't know.' Frank's voice cracked. 'But it's obviously serious.' He turned and went on up the stairs to call Jack down from his room.

Moments later Jack appeared, followed by his father. Grace stood staring at him as he walked past them and down to the ground floor. Annie and Clara watched him from behind their mother's skirts. Jack looked straight ahead of him, not glancing at them once.

As the men reached the hall, Grace gasped as she heard one of the policemen say: 'Jack Turner, I am arresting you on suspicion of the murder of Miss Sally Brown of Leverton Street . . .'

The girls heard no more, for they rushed to their

mother's aid as she sank to the floor in a half-faint.

Once they had helped Grace into a chair, Annie moved to the window. Hiding behind the curtain, she looked down at the scene outside. Jack was being led out by two men. A policeman stood by a black car outside. A crowd of people had gathered around the car and were looking to see what was going on. Annie stepped back a bit. Down below she could see Dolly Pritchett, standing right at the front, arms akimbo, peering at Jack as he climbed into the car. There was Mr Spratt, Mrs Whelan, the Fenton sisters and everybody else from the block and beyond, it seemed. Everyone looked angry, shaking her heads and scowling. What did it all mean?

Suddenly Frank ran upstairs and into the room. 'I'm going down to the police station to sort this out,' he said hurriedly to Grace. He walked over to his wife and gave her a quick hug.

Grace clung to him, sobbing.

'Don't worry, sweetheart,' he said. 'It's obviously all some dreadful mistake. It'll be sorted out in no time.' He kissed her head. 'Look after your mother, girls,' he said, glancing quickly at Clara and Annie. With that, he left.

Annie watched out of the window at her father's figure disappearing down the road.

By eleven o'clock, Jack and Frank were still not back. Annie kept falling asleep on the sofa until her mother quietly told her to go to bed. 'I'll be all right,' she said quietly. 'I'm making myself believe that everything will be all right.'

Clara shrugged. 'I hope so,' she said gloomily. 'I just don't believe this is happening.'

Annie fell asleep the moment her head touched the pillow.

But she was woken a few hours later by the sound of excited voices. It was her mother welcoming Jack back home. Annie crept to the doorway of her room. She could hear the relief in her mother's voice, her father explaining that it was all a mistake. She heard Clara telling them that she had known they would be back in no time, and Jack quietly saying that he was exhausted and needed to go to bed.

Annie tiptoed back into her own bed. She could feel the sleep catching up with her as she pulled the sheets back over her. Everything was all right, she thought, snuggling down with a sigh. She would find out what happened in the morning.

But the next morning the atmosphere was not a happy one. When Annie came down for breakfast she found everyone sitting eating their porridge in stony-faced silence. They ate quietly. The only noise came from their spoons scraping the inside of the bowls. It was only afterwards, quizzing Clara, that Annie found out any of the story.

It seemed that Jack had been arrested because someone had reported seeing him coming out of Sally Brown's door on the night that she was murdered. Not only that, but his schoolbooks had been found in her rooms. An overzealous policeman had acted prematurely and pulled Jack in ready to charge him. But it only took a few hours to sort out the fact that although Jack had indeed been at Sally Brown's, he had left her home at 8.45, and been home at 8.50, a fact verified by Frank Turner. Not only that, Sally had been seen by at least two other people after 9.30 – by the tobacconist at the end of the road, who reported that she had popped in to buy a packet of Woodbines, and the ticket clerk at the Underground station who said he had seen her hanging around in Kentish Town Road at ten o'clock when he was coming off duty.

The police had let Jack go with apologies to Frank for their hasty actions, and advice to Jack not to associate with ladies of loose morals in the future.

Annie hung around in the hall trying to catch her parents' conversation while they sat in the dining room. The door was closed but Annie pressed her ear up against the door and could hear their words quite clearly.

'I still don't understand what Jack was doing visiting that woman.' Grace's voice was low and plaintive.

'What do you think, Grace?' Frank sounded tired and impatient. 'Why should any healthy young boy want to visit a woman known to have plenty of men friends?'

'I'm just so unhappy that my son should do such a thing, that he should need to do it. He's much too young.'

'He's nearly seventeen, Grace, he's a man. He was probably curious.'

Grace shook her head. 'He said he's visited her more than once.'

'I think you're focusing on the wrong thing here, Grace. Does it really matter if Jack's sowing a few oats? And better for him to do it with an experienced woman than a local girl he can get into trouble.'

'It's all my fault. If I were healthier I could have made sure this had never happened.'

Frank frowned. 'You can't blame yourself, Grace, it's certainly not your fault. Please don't say that.'

'It doesn't help that we live in Kentish Town,' Grace sighed. 'It's a difficult place for any child to grow up honest if he's in daily contact with prostitutes and criminals.'

'Come, now, Grace, you're exaggerating.'

'I'm not sure that I am. You know I've never much liked Kentish Town. It's a harsh place to live in and I've had to live here all my married life. To tell you the truth, I'm tired of it. But I know you love it and that's why I've put up with it.'

Frank pulled her to him and held her close. 'I'm sorry you still feel so strongly about it. I'm so sorry. When this war finally starts, nowhere is going to be an ideal place to be. But after the war, if we're still here, I promise we can move, if it means so much to you . . .'

Grace smiled up at her husband. 'Yes, Frank,' she whispered, 'I would like that very much.'

As Annie stood in the hall eavesdropping, the postman pushed a letter through the letter-box. It fell on the hall floor with a plop. Annie picked it up.

It was addressed to Mrs Grace Turner, and the hand-writing was unfamiliar. Annie screwed up her eyes to read the postmark: Petworth, Sussex. It must be from the lady who gave her mother the brooch. Why on earth should she be writing now?

Just as Annie placed the letter on the kitchen table so that her mother could not miss it, Tilly turned up at the front door. Under her arm she had a towel rolled up in a tube. She was hoping that Annie would go swimming with her.

As the two girls walked down to the public baths, Annie told Tilly about the terrible events of the night before. She told her how Jack had been taken off to the police station because he had visited Sally Brown on the night of her murder so the police had thought it was Jack who had killed her. 'So silly,' she laughed lightly. 'How could they think such a thing about Jack?' she said.

'But what was Jack doing at Sally Brown's house anyway?' Tilly turned to her quizzically. 'Why should he have been there?'

Annie frowned. 'I don't know,' she said crossly. 'How should I know?'

Annie went quiet. She was cross because she did not know the answer to Tilly's question but she was even crosser to think that Jack had been friends with Sally Brown without Annie knowing it. What right did he have to be friends with Sally? Sally had been Annie's friend, not his. Jack had even been in Sally's house and Sally had never in all their friendship invited Annie in. Her feelings were hurt. But then she felt guilty for being cross about someone who had just died.

Although Jack was in the clear, his reputation in Kentish Town had been tarnished. Having always been a popular, helpful boy, he was now shunned.

'Fancy a boy from a good family like that visiting a woman like that Sally Brown,' Mrs Rose tut-tutted in the grocer's shop as Grace went past. 'It ain't right.'

'I reckon there's more to it than meets the eye,' added Mrs Barnes.

'That's what I say,' chimed in Mrs Clark. 'There's no smoke without fire, and it's not as if they've caught the person what done it.'

While the local women did not make such remarks to Grace's face, she was aware, as she set about her errands, that they were stiff towards her, even cold. Even Dolly, who had been working for the Turner family for years, who had known the children since they were tiny, suddenly became unfriendly. She no longer relayed all the local gossip to Grace while mopping the kitchen floor or dusting the ornaments on the mantelpiece. She simply came in and got on with her job, receiving her money at the end of each stint with a quick nod.

Annie was not aware of these changes. All she cared about was the fact that that letter from Petworth, Sussex had disappeared and her mother had never said a word about it. She had also come to the realization that her father had stopped walking down Leverton Street. In fact, he went out of his way to avoid that particular street. Perhaps it was because of the murder, she thought, but thinking back, she realized that he had been avoiding Leverton Street for a long time now, certainly long before Sally Brown was murdered.

Annie waited for her mother to comment on the letter she had had that morning. In the drama of the day it arrived, it was forgotten. Nothing was said at supper that night, nor at breakfast the next day. Or the next. A few days later, as Annie cleared the breakfast things, she plucked up courage to ask her mother. 'Did you get that letter which came for you the other day? I left it on the kitchen table for you.' She tried to make her voice sound bright and innocent. Now she stared at her mother expectantly.

Grace did not pause as she began stacking the dirty plates by the sink. 'Yes,' she replied breezily. 'I got it.'

Frank looked up from his newspaper. 'A letter? Who wrote you a letter?'

Grace shook her head quickly. 'Nobody,' she replied. 'It was nothing.'

Encouraged by her father's look of interest, Annie's courage grew. 'The postmark was from Sussex,' she said. 'Wasn't that where you grew up?'

Her mother did not turn around. A plate slipped from her hand and fell with a crash into the porcelain sink. 'It was nothing. It was nothing interesting.' She began picking up the broken pieces of china plate but kept dropping them as though she were flustered.

Annie sensed she should stop there. She caught her father's critical eye and fell silent. Frank had decided to support his wife.

'It's rude to talk about other people's letters,' Frank said. 'You should know that, Annie, at your age.'

Feeling hurt and confused, Annie finished clearing the table and went upstairs to her room. What with Sally Brown's death, and all that business with Jack, and her parents being so secretive and excluding her, everything suddenly seemed to overwhelm her. She had a strong urge to creep into bed and stay there.

As she passed her parents' bedroom, she had an idea. She tiptoed over to the wardrobe and pulled a chair over. Standing on that, she reached up to the top shelf. To her disappointment, there was nothing new up there – just the box with the christening gown and the brooch. She jumped down and put the chair back in its place.

As she left the room, she noticed a lot of tiny pieces of paper in the wastepaper basket by the door. There it was, the letter, torn into tiny creamy fragments! Reaching down, Annie scooped up the scraps of paper and ran upstairs with the remains of the letter clutched between her hands.

Grace had torn up the letter into such tiny pieces that it

was impossible to put it back together again. For a good hour, Annie worked on it, trying to approach it like a jigsaw puzzle, matching the shape of the edges to each other. At the end of an hour she had tears of frustration in her eyes, and she had not got far. All she had was an address with S-U-S-S-E- and a few words, such as D-e-a-r, y-o-u, c-h-i-l-d-r-e-n, w-a-r.

Her frustration rose like gorge in her throat as she fought back the tears. What was wrong with her mother? Why wouldn't she tell Annie anything? Why wouldn't she answer Annie's questions about the brooch, about Sussex, about her past, indeed, about anything? What was her secret, or secrets? If her children were so important to her, as she said, then why could she not share everything with them?

Part Two

CHAPTER 11

Wartime

THE DECLARATION OF WAR in early September, 1939, brought with it an intense feeling of relief throughout the land. The build-up to war had been going on for so long that many people now felt a perverse desire for something, anything, to happen.

The news itself, though expected, still came as a shock.

On that Sunday morning of 3 September, the Turners had gone to church. As they sat in the pew and waited for the service to begin, the church was in silence. Everyone knew it was about to happen. Hitler had invaded Poland; the world was about to change. The vicar began the service, but ten minutes into it the verger hurried down the nave with a small piece of paper.

Annie felt all her courage draining out of her body as she watched the vicar look at the paper and climb the steps of the pulpit. She leaned against her mother. To her relief, Grace immediately placed an arm around her and hugged her tight.

'We'll be saved, my darling,' whispered Grace. 'We're going to win, I know we are.'

Her mother felt warm and solid. Annie was instantly less afraid.

The vicar cleared his throat. 'We are now at war with Germany,' he said in a quiet voice. 'We will go to our homes.'

Her mother's reassuring words and gesture remained with Annie for a long time. She clung on to them, even in times when her mother had withdrawn again. They carried her through the anticlimax of the phoney war, that strange period after war had been declared and nothing happened. They carried her through the long hot summer of 1940, with its warm sunshine and cloudless blue skies. But by the time the Blitz began, Annie was feeling very frightened again.

It was in early September of 1940 that the German Luftwaffe launched its savage attack on London. The East End and the docks were the main targets. On the first day, three hundred tons of high explosives and thousands of incendiary bombs were dropped onto the cluttered slums of Cockney London.

After the all-clear in the evening, Annie and Clara climbed out of their bedroom window onto the parapet outside. From here they could see the whole sky to the east was blazing red. The barrage balloons beyond were tinged pink from the reflection of the fires.

Clara shook her head in wonder. 'Half of London must be burning,' she whispered in awe.

Annie suddenly started to cry. She felt terrified.

Clara turned to look at her. Normally she would snap at Annie and tell her to stop blubbing, but this time she did not. This time she put her arms around her little sister and hugged her tight. 'Don't cry, Annie,' Clara whispered, 'you'll be all right. You mustn't be afraid. I'll always look after you.'

Clara's gesture made Annie cry even louder. Her eyes were flooded with tears of love and gratitude. Clara was the strong one. If she could rely on Clara's protection, she would always be all right.

For the next fifty-six nights, London was bombed from dusk to dawn. Vast areas of the city were destroyed. In spite of the devastation, the damage, the injuries and the loss of life, Londoners quickly learned to settle down to their regular routines. The German activities simply became the background to everyday life. Even at the peak of the bombing, in October, when it came very close to home and many bombs were dropped in Kentish Town and Hampstead, and Camden Town Underground station was hit and several people killed, the effect was to strengthen rather than weaken the collective resolve to win. 'We'll beat those buggers!' people would declare.

Extraordinary events can take so little time to appear normal. The sight of enormous bomb craters with fountains of water cascading from the broken mains, the smell of gas, and the burning after the bombing was not unusual anymore. After two and a half years of war, little seemed unusual. Everything was taken for granted. The absence of young men, the blackout, the rationing, the sand-bagged buildings and the shop windows smothered with tape and cigarette paper were all as ordinary as the sight of women in trousers, steel-helmeted police and ARP wardens patrolling the streets. Even the Blitz, which had been so terrifying at the time, seemed, with the protection of hindsight, like something they had all taken in their stride.

Annie lay in her narrow bunk one morning thinking back on those terrifying days of the Blitz. It seemed astonishing now that so many people had survived it at all. She stared up at the ceiling above her head. She had stuck lots of her drawings and paintings all over the shelter to cheer it up. She liked to examine them dreamily in the half-light of the morning while her thoughts floated in and out of half-sleep and she conjured up new paintings in her head.

She could hear her father's heavy breathing while he slept just a few feet away. Every now and then the even sound erupted into a snort. She could also hear Bobby's snuffling as he tried to breathe through his summer cold. Looking down, Annie could just make out her mother's face on her pillow on the lower bunk on the other side of the shelter. She looked serene and calm, and out of pain. At least sleep did bring Grace relief from the otherwise constant agony in her joints.

By the door of the shelter Annie could just make out the thermos flask of cocoa, the dried figs, and the thick slab of chocolate her mother always brought in to the shelter every night. By morning what was left of the cocoa was tepid, if not cold, but Annie still enjoyed sharing it with Bobby, pouring the sticky brown liquid into a tin mug and afterwards wiping off the dark moustache from her upper lip.

Looking across at the other top bunk, Annie could see that it was empty. She still could not believe that Clara was refusing to sleep in the shelter. Her sister had not slept there for days now. She had announced two weeks before that she would rather be bombed than go on sleeping in the smelly old shelter, and her father had agreed that now she was sixteen he could not force her to do much, even if he did not approve. So Clara had returned to sleeping in the house, though she had taken the precaution of creeping into a cot bed on the ground floor rather than her bed upstairs. She had made up the cot bed in the dining room, with the windows well taped and heavy dark curtains to prevent any flying glass falling into the room.

Annie was now wide awake. She put her hands behind her head and chewed her lip. Now fourteen, she had suddenly shot up in height and developed 'a bit of a figure', as her father would say, causing Annie to blush coyly. Although she did have curves of a sort, they did not amount to much. Besides, she felt clumsy and gawky most of the time, and she did not remember Clara ever appearing awkward.

Clara was right about this war; it was more than a nuisance. Ordinary the conditions might have seemed, but the war was still an endless bad dream, edging on a nightmare, spoiling their lives when they were supposed to be having fun. How could they possibly have fun with rations and shortages, sudden air-raid warnings and blackouts and bossy air-raid wardens ordering them around all the time? Most of their friends had disappeared from Kentish Town, with the eighteen-year-olds, like Jack and his friends, signing up in 1941 when the call-up age was lowered. And Roger Knight and all the older Smith boys were also conscripted and packed off for active service along with every other young able-bodied man in the country. Even Tommy had signed up and gone off to training camp. At sixteen, he was too young to join up but he lied about his age, and was believed. The powers that be never doubted that this big, fit, enthusiastic youth was a day under the age of eighteen.

So everyone who mattered had gone. Even the little ones at the beginning of the war had been evacuated to the country. It did not take long for huge numbers of them to come back, like William and his mother Jessie. They had left London on a crowded train full of crying children and mothers on Evacuation Day. Maudie had insisted that Jessie go, to get the child to a safer area. Jessie had been gone a week before she returned, disgusted by the way she was treated by the family who took her and William in. She was expected to sleep on a mattress on the floor in a box room and look after the woman's four children for her during the day. 'I'm not a maid,' she sniffed indignantly on her return. 'And even if I were, I still shouldn't be treated in such a way.'

So Jessie and William were back with Maudie in Leverton Street. Although Maudie worried openly about the child's safety, it was clear to all that she was really rather happy to have her family back with her. Maudie herself was always cheerful nowadays. She worked as a telephonist for the London Fire Service. Recently she had become much slimmer and her sweet round face always had a healthy bloom to it.

Annie and Bobby were, along with Tilly, now being educated at the emergency school set up in a big house in Leighton Road. Now that so many evacuees had returned to London, the schools were opening again, though not in their own premises, many of which had been taken over for civil defence purposes. For a short while, after a bizarre incident over the second letter from Mrs Pearson, the children had been educated by their mothers, Grace and Marion.

It must have been in August, 1939, two and a half years

ago and a few weeks before war was declared, that that other thick creamy envelope had plopped onto the hall mat. This time it was addressed to Mr and Mrs Francis Turner. Grace was still upstairs getting Bobby dressed, while Frank and Annie got the breakfast. Frank brought the letter into the kitchen and opened it. It was from Camilla Pearson, inviting Grace and the children to spend the necessary time at her home in Sussex 'while the danger is greatest in London'.

'What does this mean?' Annie was excited.

When Grace came down to find Frank sitting with the letter in his hand, her face went white as she realized what it was. She sat down suddenly as though her legs had given way under her.

Frank looked at her. 'It was addressed to both of us, Grace. Camilla Pearson mentions that you didn't respond to the letter she wrote earlier this year but hopes that this one will get to you now that the situation has become so critical.'

There was no escaping the situation for Grace. She could only sit down and allow the conversation to continue.

'We're invited to be evacuated to Sussex?' repeated Clara when she came down for breakfast five minutes later. 'Well, I'm not going.'

'The schools are all being evacuated anyway,' said Annie. 'Our school's going to Norfolk.'

Frank re-read the letter. 'This is a great opportunity, Grace,' he said. 'It can keep you and the children safe and together in the part of the world you know so well. Your own home, if you please! What could be better?'

Grace stared ahead of her at the butter dish on the table. 'We're not going,' she said quietly. 'Nobody's going.'

'But think of the children,' Frank protested. 'They'll be much safer in the country. The bombs will be coming for the cities and the children will be far from where they might fall.'

Grace shook her head. 'I don't care. You can't leave, Frank, you have to work, and I'm not leaving you. And I'm not leaving the children, either. I'll not be parted from them.'

Frank frowned. 'Shouldn't we put the children's safety first? They'll be safer out of London.'

Grace hesitated. 'Clara and Annie can go if they want . . .' Then she changed her mind again. 'No, they can be evacuated with their schools when it comes to it. We are just not going to Sussex.'

Annie stepped forward. 'But, Mother, I'd like to go and stay in the country. And I'd like to see where you grew up.'

Grace stared at her. There was a look of anguished uncertainty in her eyes.

'Well, I'm not going anywhere,' Clara announced. 'I'm staying put in London . . .'

'But it could become dangerous with the bombs,' Frank replied.

'I don't care,' said Clara. 'I'm a Londoner and I'm staying here. Besides, I can leave school soon and get a job doing something useful . . .'

Frank folded his newspaper and placed it carefully on the table. 'You're not leaving school, Clara,' he said. 'You've got a lot more studying to do before you start working.' Having enjoyed the fruits of his own hard work at night school, Frank was a firm believer in education as the path to progress and betterment. He was anxious that all his children get good qualifications. 'You know how I feel about this. And you'll thank me later in life when you know you can stand on your own two feet, and you've done even better than your mother and I. You can't always expect to be supported by someone else.'

Clara rolled her eyes. 'Studying is boring, Dad. And you can't make me stay at school.'

Frank looked wearily at his elder daughter. 'No, I can't make you stay at school,' he said. 'All I can do is give you some advice, and warn you.'

Clara sniffed. 'Well, thanks for the advice, Dad. I don't need it.' She hesitated and then smiled sweetly at her father. 'Maybe when the war's over, Dad, maybe then I'll go to college.'

Frank gave her a resigned smile. 'All right, Clara, you know what I think.'

And so no one left London in the end. Grace and Marion talked it over and decided to risk it. For Marion, too, felt reluctant to leave her husband, or be separated from her only child, Tilly. Together they could teach the children – meaning Annie, Bobby and Tilly – if there were no schools for them to go to. Both women felt that they did not want to be separated from their husbands who, in their early forties, were fortunately too old to be called up to fight, though were certainly useful for war work in London.

Annie had been bitterly disappointed not to go to Sussex, but the idea of going on her own to a strange home while the rest of her family stayed in London was daunting. It would have been different if her big sister had wanted to go.

And so Grace had replied to Mrs Pearson, thanking her politely for her kind offer but turning it down all the same. Grace then placed Mrs Pearson's letter in her wardrobe next to the brooch.

Frank was puzzled by Grace's decision. 'I'm surprised at you,' he said. 'It seemed such an easy way of making sure the children are safe.'

'As you said, no place is going to be safe, and since that's the case, I'd rather we all stayed together as a family. We'll manage all right in London, even in Kentish Town,' she added with a wry smile.

The bad feeling that had arisen over Jack's involvement with Sally Brown soon died down. After being rather cold for a while, Dolly had warmed up again in gratitude towards Grace for encouraging her to become an air-raid warden.

At first everyone had been astounded. Dolly had always been renowned for her hostility towards anything to do with the 'authorities'. 'No one has a right to tell me what to do,' she would always say. 'Never let anyone from the authorities into your home,' she warned people. 'They'll take over your life in a flash.'

At the beginning of the war Dolly had found herself in big trouble with the authorities in the form of the air-raid wardens. Before the Blitz, these volunteers did not have enough to do and tended to exercise their authority with a heavy-handedness that made them extremely unpopular. Dolly proved to be careless about her blackout curtains and was always being fined for leaving a light showing from her flat window. In no time, the local warden would be knocking on her door and shouting at her to black out the window immediately.

'It's not my fault,' Dolly would grumble to Grace. 'I just keep forgetting.'

'Accidentally on purpose,' Grace would whisper to Marion, rolling her eyes knowingly.

It was Grace who came up with the solution to Dolly's problems. 'I think you'd make a good air-raid warden yourself,' Grace said after Dolly had been complaining about another nosey parker who had ticked her off the night before.

Dolly's stared at her. 'Who, me? You must be joking!' She threw back her wide shoulders and roared with laughter.

'I'm not joking, Dolly,' replied Grace. 'You're very good at organizing things yourself – look at the way you do the street party – and everyone likes you around here. I think you'd be good at it because you know how to talk to people.'

Dolly laughed again. 'I've never heard anything so ridiculous.' But then she paused and thought about it. She shook her head. 'What a daft idea.'

'Why don't you volunteer? You know they need as many volunteers as they can get.'

Dolly was frowning. 'Well, even if I did, they wouldn't let me . . .'

'Why ever not? Of course they'd want you. You just have a bit of training, and that's that.' Grace peered at her. She sensed that something else was bothering Dolly.

Dolly shrugged. 'Na, there's no point . . .' She hesitated.

'What do you mean, there's no point?'

Dolly ran her hand over her hair and adjusted the bun on the back of her head. 'Well, just look at the size of me,' she said. 'They wouldn't have a uniform to fit me, would they!'

Grace had never seen Dolly embarrassed before.

Looking at Dolly's wide frame with her rolls of fat and ham-like forearms, she could see that Dolly was probably right. 'I could make you one,' she said quietly. 'It would be easy to measure you up and do it on the Singer.'

Dolly's face lit up. 'Really?'

'Yes, really,' nodded Grace.

And so Dolly became an air-raid warden and looked splendid in her custom-made blue uniform carefully sewn together by Grace.

That was the last garment Grace made. After that, she found it too difficult to thread the needle and manipulate the sewing machine. She handed over all her sewing things to Clara and Annie.

A large part of the garden was taken up with the Anderson shelter, but the rest of it was dug up and laid out for growing vegetables. Like the rest of the population, the Turners were digging for victory. Every inch of garden was used for growing food. Hampstead Heath and Parliament Field were covered with allotments, as was the moat around the Tower of London. Those people without any land of their own were given permission to use the gardens of empty houses. Next door to the Turners, Mr Spratt had extended his chicken run and reared even more chickens than before. Now that eggs were rationed to one per person per week, his eggs were even more precious and in demand. Many people kept chickens now. The clucking of hens was heard throughout the streets of London.

But Grace seemed to have lost interest in gardening, just as she had lost interest in so much of life. She claimed that now that she could only grow vegetables, she no longer felt joy in seeing plants grow. 'There's nothing unpredictable,' she said wistfully, 'nothing uncertain.' And when she said it Annie felt she was talking about more than simply her garden.

Grace had become sadder and more remote at times. Annie thought it was probably her arthritis but she also thought it might be something else. For although it was true that Grace's condition had worsened, there did seem to be more to her sadness than that. Something else seemed to trouble her as she sat so frequently staring into the distance, her thoughts miles away, in another place, another land, another life. Who knew? All Annie knew was that sometimes she felt that she did not have a mother any more.

Grace was also becoming increasingly religious. She had always been a believer, sending her children to Sunday school, and attending the service every Sunday. Her involvement in the church had seemed normal, no more or less than what other people did.

But recently she had taken to going every day, and sometimes Annie would go out to the church and find her down on her knees in a pew, praying half aloud and staring up at the stained-glass window above. Even at home, when Grace was sitting in a chair, her lips moved quietly as if in prayer. Nobody said anything about it in the family, but Annie could tell that her father was not happy with his wife's growing religious fervour.

As for Frank, although he had never been religious, he had been happy about the children being sent to Sunday school because for years it had meant that there was some peace and quiet for him to have sexual relations with his wife. But now he was growing more concerned about Grace's love of the church. Like everyone else, he felt increasingly excluded from Grace's thoughts and life. He had certainly been excluded from her embrace for a long time. Her body, which had once been so yielding, soft and receptive, was now brittle and rejecting. Now it seemed that the only person whose presence brought Grace to life was Bobby.

Bobby was the apple of his mother's eye; he could do no wrong. An attractive boy with his father's curly brown hair and high forehead, he had twinkling blue eyes under dark eyelashes. His puckish smile and quick tongue made him a popular fellow wherever he went. Sturdy and well co-ordinated, he was athletic as well as clever. But there was a strange naiveté about him. Unlike the other children of his age, Bobby had no common sense, no sense of self-preservation against the world. Frank was sure that Grace was to blame for this; she had overprotected Bobby so much that the child had no idea of how to look after himself.

One Saturday in the autumn, Frank took his daughters to the ARP dance at the St Pancras Town Hall. It was quite an affair. They had been sold tickets by Dolly, who was helping to organize the event, and originally Grace had said she would get Mrs Whelan to look after Bobby so that they could all go. On the day itself, Grace had bowed out. 'My aches are too bad today,' she said. But Annie knew that she had never intended coming, since her mother had never mentioned the occasion to Mrs Whelan in the first place. But she did not care. She would rather go with her father and Clara, who both loved dancing, than her mother who might not want to join in at all.

It was a grand affair. Everyone from the neighbourhood

was there. There were few young men between the ages of seventeen and thirty-five, but it did not seem to matter. Everyone was dolled up in their best clothes determined to have a good time. The music was wonderful. Jimmy Rope crooned to the Alf Rogers band. The large hall was decked out with coloured lights hanging from the four corners of the room, directed at a large revolving glass ball, high up beneath the main chandelier, and a never-ending stream of multi-coloured lights flooded the walls, ceilings and floors. The waltzes in the dark were particularly popular, with the old codgers pressing their prickly cheeks against the soft skin of shy fourteen-year-old maidens, and fresh-faced young boys dancing with their mothers.

Annie was having a wonderful time. She was dressed in a skirt and top Clara had lent her for the evening. Although she did not fill it out well, the soft lawn cotton of the blouse and the full skirt swirling around her legs made her feel alive and full of energy. Many times she danced the Lambeth Walk with her father, clinging on to his strong arms, kicking her legs proudly as she marked out the steps, feeling the heat of his body. At one moment she buried her face in her father's chest and felt a strange pull inside her. It seemed like a deep primitive feeling, a longing for something she did not know. It was as if in that fleeting moment she had crossed the threshold to womanhood and she understood that she was longing for love. Then the feeling was gone.

She waved to Dolly, who was dressed in her uniform and going round trying to persuade more people to volunteer for the ARP. She waved to Marion and her husband, who were dancing close like two love-birds. She waved to Maudie Sprackling who was there with a man

Annie had never seen before. Maudie looked great. She was a normal size now and really quite pretty. Annie was pleased to see that Maudie's companion had a kind smiling face. She felt a quick rush of happiness for poor old Maudie.

Clara was in an exuberant mood, too. She looked lovely, with her straw-coloured hair pulled back into long tresses down her back, her lips red and her cheeks flushed with excitement and the beers she was surreptitiously drinking in the corner. She hardly stopped for a moment, throwing her head back, stamping her feet, gliding over the floor with effortless grace. Her vibrancy was clearly appreciated by many; often when she stopped dancing there were murmurs of appreciation from the onlookers standing around the edge of the hall.

Across the room, Annie saw Connie Smith. She was wearing a dress that was a little too tight for her. It accentuated her curves in a slightly disturbing way. Annie kept glancing at her, but looked away in embarrassment whenever Connie noticed her and waved.

At the end of the evening Frank walked home with his two daughters. They held each other's arms and guided themselves by the light of the moon and the white painted markings on the pavements. Annie felt happy, as did Clara. It was not so late. People were still up, putting the cat out or listening to the wireless. A dog barked in the distance.

'If the bombers come now and we die tonight,' Clara stated, throwing back her head, 'it won't matter. Nothing matters. I have lived my life to the full.'

Frank laughed and put his arms around his daughters' shoulders. 'Well, I hope you'll have a little bit more life ahead of you,' he said. 'Let's hope Hitler grants you that . . .'

The house was dark when they got home.

'Your mother must have gone to bed already.' Frank yawned. 'Well, I'm knackered, too.' He shook his head sadly. He used to be able to dance until the early hours.

He heated up some cocoa for all of them and went off to bed in the shelter, leaving the two girls sipping their hot drinks in the kitchen.

Annie loved to sit up late talking to her big sister. Recently she had been enjoying Clara's company a lot. True to her word, Clara had ignored her father's wishes, and left school to get herself a job. She had found work in a factory in Leyton making parts for aeroplanes.

Annie could never hear enough about Clara's working day and all her new workmates. They sounded so grown-up and fun, these fast-talking young women who wore their hair tied up with scarves, or used pipe cleaners as hair pins, and shared their lipsticks and any other cosmetics they could get their hands on in wartime. She also liked to hear what Clara said about the soldiers and sailors she and her workmates often met at dances. They were all boys on leave wanting to meet some nice girls in the short time they had before being sent off to fight in some part of the world they had never heard of.

Clara seemed so grown-up and sophisticated as she sat at the table, dragging on a cigarette and then blowing out the smoke slowly through her pursed lips, her eyes half closed.

Watching her sister, Annie felt a great surge of pride rush through her, pride at her sister's beauty, her talent, her charm and, above all, her courage. She seemed not to be afraid of anything. Clara was so uninhibited; Clara was a free spirit.

They talked on into the night. Clara told Annie that she had received a letter from Roger. 'Just a note. It was from somewhere in Africa. It didn't say much but he sounded a bit fed up. He doesn't like being a soldier. I suppose he doesn't like being told what to do.'

Annie was intrigued. 'I thought you weren't friends any more.'

Clara shrugged and laughed. 'I suppose he wanted to write to a girl and he knew my address.'

The girls talked on until Annie's eyelids began to droop. She wanted to stay up forever but her fatigue was taking over. 'I think I might stay in the house tonight,' she said. 'I could sleep on the sofa.' Yes, she could be brave, too.

Clara leaped up. 'Great! I'll get you some sheets and blankets.'

Wrapped up snugly on the sofa, like a chrysalis, Annie listened to Clara's chatter with a delicious exhaustion taking her over. Then just as she was drifting off, the silence of the night was shattered by the loud wail of the air-raid siren starting up.

Annie leaped off the sofa, the bedding dropping to the floor. 'Oh help!' she shrieked. 'We're going to die!'

Clara sniffed. 'There's no need to worry,' she said cheerfully. 'Just stuff some cotton wool into your ears. You'll get used to it.'

But Annie was already collecting up her clothes and putting on her slippers. Picking up her clothes, she bolted out of the room. She was not going to take any chances. It was going to be a long time before she was brave enough to stay indoors.

Annie crept outside and into the Anderson shelter where her parents and Bobby were all sleeping soundly. With a sigh of relief, she climbed into her bunk and snuggled down to sleep.

Within moments, she was asleep and dreaming of her little brother Bobby. He was standing high on a hill and holding his arms out to her and calling out her name into the wind.

CHAPTER 12

Sussex

EVERY NOW AND THEN Annie had an overwhelming urge to touch and look at the mysterious brooch in her mother's wardrobe. It had been several months since she last looked at it, and suddenly, again, the urge was irresistible.

The house was quiet. Her mother was out with Bobby, queuing at the shops in the hope of getting a pig's head from Mr Worth. He had been expecting a supply for some time, and Grace planned to make plenty of brawn as well as serving up the tongue and the ears in some delicious form. It was fortunate that her family loved offal as much as it did, since it was one of the few foods that were not rationed.

Annie crept upstairs to her parents' bedroom and reached up to the shelf in the wardrobe. She had grown taller so she no longer needed to stand on a chair to reach it.

The brooch was looking quite a bit duller. The sheen had gone from the gold and the jewels did not seem so dazzling in the light. It all needed a good polish. Annie rubbed it against her sleeve, then turned it over slowly in her hands.

'Tell me what you mean,' she said. 'What is your secret?'

She stood there motionless, as if she were half-expecting a little whisper in her ear which would explain everything. But there was just silence.

As she put the brooch back, she noticed an envelope on the shelf of the wardrobe, pushed right back into the corner. It was the letter Mrs Pearson had written to her parents at the beginning of the war, the one offering to take the children.

Seeing the letter suddenly gave her an idea. She scribbled down the address, shoved the envelope back in its place, and disappeared up to her room. Later that day she went to the post office, bought a stamp and posted a letter into the letter-box in Fortess Road.

Mrs Pearson's reply came three days later. She was delighted that Annie had written and invited her down to the house near Pulborough on the following Saturday. She included details of the train times, and suggested Annie catch the late morning train which arrived at Pulborough just before lunchtime. 'Please let me know if you are not going to be on that train,' she wrote.

For the next week, Annie could barely sleep. She lay awake in her bunk in the Anderson shelter imagining her meeting with this mysterious woman, and going over and over in her head the conversation she was going to have with her. She could barely contain her excitement. She was certain that this meeting was going to change her life dramatically for ever. At last she was going to find out about the brooch. At last the mystery would be solved.

Annie did not tell anyone about her plans. With foresight she was proud of, she prepared the ground by saying in advance that she and Tilly were planning a picnic with friends that weekend, and were going off together for the day.

Annie felt uncomfortable about deceiving her mother. She tried to avoid spending too much time in her company for fear that she might guess what she was up to. She was convinced that her intentions were written all over her face.

Saturday was a clear, sunny day, with a fresh breeze and just a few wispy clouds floating in the sky. Dressed neatly in a blue cotton skirt and white blouse, Annie scurried along the road to the Tube station with her head down, hoping that no one would notice her. She was wrong.

'Hey there, Annie!'

Annie gasped and spun round, her face hot with a guilty blush. It was Tommy.

The sight of him filled her with a mixture of relief and confusion. She barely took in his words as he explained that he was home on a forty-eight-hour leave from his army training. Seeing him kitted out in his smart uniform, Annie blushed more deeply. She was sure that he would know that she had dreamed about him several times over the past few weeks, and they had not been the innocent dreams of the past. They had been quite embarrassing in their content, with Tommy removing his uniform, and embracing her in his strong arms. These dreams had surprised and shocked Annie for the adult longings they revealed deep within her.

Fortunately, Tommy did not act as though he knew about her dreams. He was his usual friendly self. He had always been a confident boy and now he seemed even more sure of himself than ever. He had always known about Annie's mother's brooch, so she hurriedly told him where she was off to that day.

'Well, I'm coming with you,' he said. 'At last we'll learn what the mystery is all about. I was hoping to see you today, anyway,' he added, 'so it doesn't matter if it's on a train or on Hampstead Heath.'

Annie was touched that he felt like that. She was also pleased to have a companion for her trip, for she was nervous about going down to Sussex on her own. Quite apart from meeting this formidable Mrs Pearson, she was worried about navigating her way there. She was not experienced at travelling on her own and she was terrified of getting on the wrong train.

Tommy had grown up and filled out a lot since she had last seen him. His hair was short, his shoulders broad and solid. His khaki serge uniform made him look big and strong.

He grinned. 'I'll just tell Connie to tell Mum we're off for the day. They're all at work in the day so they won't miss me.'

Annie waited outside the Smiths' house while Tommy ran indoors to tell his sister he would be back that evening to see them all. As she stood there, Annie could see Mrs Whelan peering at her from behind the lace curtains next door.

Tommy reappeared a few minutes later. 'That's all right, then,' he said. 'Connie didn't seem too pleased that I was going off. I suppose she thinks I should be stopping home all day.'

The couple took the Underground to Victoria station, changing at Charing Cross. Once there, Tommy bought some cigarettes at a kiosk.

The train was packed with soldiers. Corridors were full, with men hanging out of the windows, talking and smoking.

One man gave up his seat for Annie. She settled down on the soft bench seat while Tommy stood beside her, holding on to the wooden luggage rack above her head.

Watching Tommy's strong body and legs from her position, Annie suddenly felt self-conscious. A part of her was pleased to see Tommy again, and she realized how much she had missed his company over the past year, but another part of her was aware that they had both changed. Before they had just been pals, children who caught sticklebacks together in Highgate Woods. Now they were boy and girl, man and woman. She found herself being conscious of how she looked – her hair, her clothes, her skin.

For his part, Tommy did not seem to be aware of any difference. He grinned his gap-toothed smile as he joked about his family and the neighbours. As the train pulled out of the station and set off creakily across the Thames, he told her stories about his training and about some of his mates at the training camp. He enjoyed the army. 'But I can't wait to get out there to kill a few Germans,' he said. 'We'll show that Hitler.'

Annie did not really follow or understand much about what was happening in the war. All she knew was how it affected everyday living for her and her family, the restrictions and the shortages, the making-do and the bravery. It was a completely different kind of war from the war that Tommy knew.

Soon they fell silent as the train chugged through south London and out into the Surrey countryside. Annie stared out of the window at the backs of the houses, the little gardens and then the fields passing by. Soon they were in the country. It all looked so tranquil. Who would know what horrors were going on abroad? She suddenly had a mental image of those lush green meadows overrun with Germans. She shivered and looked up at Tommy. She was immediately embarrassed to see that he was looking down at her with a thoughtful expression on his face. He had clearly been looking at her for some time. She smiled shyly and quickly looked away.

One hour later, they arrived at Pulborough Station. Annie and Tommy alighted from the train and walked towards the platform exit. Annie let the other passengers pass her. As the doorway cleared, she could see standing next to the ticket collector a tall, elegant woman dressed in a tailored dark-blue suit and a blue hat. She was peering at all the female passengers as they went past.

'That must be her!' Tommy dropped his voice to a whisper.

'Mrs Pearson?' Annie straightened her back and approached the woman with a nervous smile.

'Yes.' The response was hesitant, almost cold.

But then she responded, leaning forward to grasp Annie's hand. 'Anne, my dear . . .' She paused and looked at Tommy. 'Oh,' she said, 'you have a companion.' She smiled at Tommy who was standing back a few feet away from Annie.

Annie suddenly felt confusion swamp her. As she opened her mouth to explain, Tommy stepped smartly forward and held out his hand. 'Thomas Smith, ma'am,' he said with cool confidence. 'I'm a family friend and I accompanied Anne because her parents were concerned about her travelling on the train alone. I'll just wait here for her now and accompany her back to London when you've all finished your business. I have a book to read.' He patted his pocket.

Mrs Pearson frowned momentarily but then smiled again. 'I won't hear of it, my boy,' she said with the insistence of one who was used to having her own way. 'You must join us for luncheon. It will be most pleasant to entertain a young man for a change.' She flashed another radiant smile at Tommy, who nodded.

'Well, if you're sure, ma'am, I'd like that. It's kind of you to invite me.'

Annie was relieved that Tommy had given in and was coming, too. Confronted with Mrs Pearson, she was suddenly feeling out of her depth. She could not imagine how or why she had initiated this meeting.

'That's settled, then,' said Mrs Pearson with satisfaction. 'Now, come over here. I've brought the pony trap. I tend to use it whenever possible now, what with this tedious petrol rationing.' Mrs Pearson pointed to the station forecourt where a small grey pony stood patiently between the long wooden shafts of a dark green trap.

Perched high up on the seat next to Mrs Pearson, with Tommy squashed into the space at the back, Annie enjoyed the fresh breeze on her face as the pony trotted smartly along the narrow lanes. The hedgerows were thick and high, so it was only when there was a gate or stile that she could get glimpses of the wide green meadows and yellow cornfields beyond.

Above the soft thud-thud of the pony's unshod hoofs on the road, Mrs Pearson conversed. 'I'm living in the mill cottage at the moment. The army has taken over my house for their operations. I couldn't really stop them, though I thought it a bit outrageous. But my husband died several years ago and I live here alone with only a few staff now. I can't say I'm delighted by the arrangement. The house has been in my family for generations and I feel that I'm the caretaker for my descendants, so I'm always worrying about the place.'

'I'm sure the army will recompense you for any damage done,' Tommy said cheerfully.

Mrs Pearson nodded. 'Yes, I'm sure they will, of course. I just don't want them to do any damage in the first place,' she said wistfully.

'No, of course not,' Tommy agreed tactfully.

Annie was hardly listening to their exchange. She had noticed Mrs Pearson's hands. How elegant they were! They had long tapering fingers and long nails. In fact, with her neat hair and smooth white skin, Mrs Pearson was an elegant woman in every respect.

'Did you say you're living in Mill Cottage?' she asked.

'Yes,' replied Mrs Pearson. 'It'll be interesting for you to see the house your mother grew up in. Of course, it looks different inside. I've brought quite a few bits of furniture with me from the house, and various objects I couldn't live without.'

After about ten minutes, they turned into a wide drive with tall plane trees on both sides. They had arrived. An old man dressed in a dark suit immediately emerged from the front porch to help Mrs Pearson and Annie down from the trap. Then he led the pony and trap away while Mrs Pearson took her guests in through the open door of the cottage.

Annie was feeling increasingly nervous. The unexpected venue had made her feel even more anxious about bringing up the subject of the brooch. She found herself wondering why she had ever had the mad idea for making this trip in the first place.

They sat in the small sitting room. The warm sunlight shone through the open window. Mrs Pearson showed them photographs of her son Julian who was away at school.

Annie looked carefully at the photograph. Julian was a tall good-looking youth with floppy wavy hair falling over one eye and a cool gaze as he stood holding a shotgun, a black labrador at his knee.

'He's a very good shot,' commented Mrs Pearson. 'He says he can't wait to go off to fight, which worries me dreadfully. He's only sixteen, after all.'

'Oh, the same age as me,' said Annie.

Mrs Pearson glanced up at her. She hesitated momentarily. 'Yes, indeed, of course you are exactly the same age,' she said with a smile. But it was a strange smile, a secret sort of smile about something she was not going to share.

'I can understand how your son feels,' said Tommy. 'I feel the same.'

The smile had gone. Mrs Pearson sighed heavily. 'I think it's dreadful that you young men idealize war. War is a ghastly business . . .'

She fell silent and stared down at the photograph in her hands. 'I just don't know what I would do if anything happened to Julian.' She seemed to be talking more to herself than anyone else, and neither Annie nor Tommy felt it wise to comment.

They ate a light lunch of cold ham and potato salad. Mrs Pearson was gracious. She showed a genuine interest in Annie's family, and asked about Tommy's with interest. She expressed her condolences when Annie told her that her mother's health was not good.

'I remember your mother so well as a child,' said Mrs

Pearson, offering slices of freshly baked bread. 'Remarkably shy,' she said. 'At least with us, she was . . .

'There was a time when we played together quite a bit – I think after my brothers had gone off to boarding school and I needed a companion to play with. I liked her parents, too – your grandfather managed the farm. My father always thought he was the best employee he'd ever had. But I liked your grandfather because he always let me see the calves being born, which my mother didn't approve of at all. He'd beckon me from behind the stables and lead me into the barn to see them. He'd let me feed the orphans and the rejected ones with a bottle. Yes, he was a nice man. He understood children. He knew what interested them.

'And your grandmother, of course, taught me my first French words. I remember her standing in front of me – I can't have been more than about three – and making me repeat *un*, *deux*, *trois* . . .'

She paused and shut her eyes for a moment. 'Goodness, what a long time ago all that was!' she said, opening her eyes again and shaking her head. 'And so much has happened since. My dear brothers were both killed in the Great War. That's how I came to inherit the house.' She stared out of the window. The light coming in caught the tears glistening in her eyes.

For a moment Annie thought she was going to cry. She did not know what she was going to do if she did. 'I'm sorry,' she murmured.

'Yes, yes.' Mrs Pearson blinked several times. Now there were no tears. 'People die,' she said with a sudden sharpness. 'It's a fact of life. A sad one, but a fact of life nevertheless.'

Tommy placed his buttered bread on his plate. 'And

sometimes,' he added, 'people have to die if it's for a good cause . . .'

Mrs Pearson turned and stared at him. 'Well, I'm not sure that either of my brothers died for a good cause. Theirs were stupid, unnecessary deaths which nearly destroyed my parents. I don't believe my mother ever recovered. My father was upset that neither of his sons would inherit the house, which has been passed down from father to son since 1640. But although I wasn't the right sex, at least I could ensure that the house stayed in the family.'

Her voice drifted off again as her thoughts went back to a past age. 'And now Julian will take it on after my death,' she added quietly.

Annie thought it best to change the subject. 'Do you live here all alone?'

'Yes,' replied Mrs Pearson. 'There's just Dobson and his wife now. All the young staff went off when the war started. So it is probably just as well that I'm not in the big house at the moment.'

After lunch, Camilla Pearson offered to show Annie and Tommy around the garden. 'You might like to see the motor cars, Thomas,' she said, waving an arm in the direction of the stables. 'My husband had quite a collection and I've never had the heart to get rid of them. We use just the Riley nowadays but Dobson keeps all the other ones tuned and in good condition. I think it's become his hobby.' She laughed. Annie was pleased to see Mrs Pearson relaxing again. She seemed like a nice woman, even if she was fierce.

Tommy was delighted to be able to examine the old Bentleys and Rolls-Royces in the coach house while Annie

walked with Mrs Pearson around the garden. Before
Annie went off, Tommy caught her eye and winked. She
knew it was meant to give her courage to ask the question.

It's now or never, thought Annie, bracing herself. She
took a deep breath. 'The reason I wanted to see you and
talk to you,' she said, staring down at her shoes, 'is that I
thought you might be able to solve a puzzle for me . . .'

'Oh yes?' Mrs Pearson turned and fixed her gaze on her.
Her brilliant blue eyes seemed to pin Annie to the spot.

'My mother has a brooch,' said Annie, 'a valuable
brooch, which she told me you gave her.' She paused. Mrs
Pearson gave no indication of knowing what she was
talking about.

'I wondered if you would be able to throw some light on
the brooch – on why you gave it to my mother in the first
place. It would help me to know these things, you see . . .'

Her voice tailed off as she felt those blue eyes burning
into her. 'I mean . . .' she had started to stammer, '. . . my
father would . . .' She swallowed hard as her voice dried up.

Mrs Pearson stopped and turned to face her. 'And has
your mother told you about the brooch?'

'Only that you gave it to her.'

Mrs Pearson turned away and walked on. 'Well, it's up
to your mother to tell you, child. It's not for me to say.'

Annie ran to catch up. 'I know, but she won't tell me. I
just hoped that you would be able to . . .'

'I'm sorry.' Mrs Pearson's voice was suddenly hard and
cold. 'It's not for me to tell you anything. If your mother
hasn't told you, she has her own reasons for that. Does she
know you've come down here?'

'No.' Annie looked down at the ground. 'No, she
doesn't.'

'Well, then, it's a bit naughty of you to come here behind her back, don't you think?'

Mrs Pearson's tone of voice changed as she deftly changed the subject. 'Come, now, let's see what I can give you from the kitchen garden. We grow most things here so we don't go without.'

She led Annie through a gateway into a walled garden laid out in neat rows of vegetables – lettuces, runner beans, carrots and sweet green peas.

Mrs Pearson bent down and pulled up a lettuce, shaking the dark crumbly soil off the roots. 'And have some salsify, too.' She pulled up a long black root. 'Oyster plant, some people call it, because it tastes like oysters. A wonderful delicate flavour – divine!'

For a few minutes Camilla Pearson bent and stooped as she pulled and picked a generous armful of vegetables. Handing Annie a wicker basket filled with the freshly harvested vegetables, Camilla Pearson peered at her again. 'You've got a pretty complexion,' she commented, 'and pretty eyes. You've got some potential there. And you've certainly got some brains in your head . . .' She paused. 'Now what about this young man?'

'You mean Tommy?' Annie stared at her. All afternoon she had had the impression that Mrs Pearson had taken to Tommy.

'Yes, Thomas.' Mrs Pearson paused. 'Of course, you're far too young to be thinking of these things but sometimes it's good to be aware . . .'

Annie did not know what she was talking about. 'I'm sorry?' She stared at the older woman in puzzlement. 'Be aware of what?'

Mrs Pearson hesitated but then spoke again. 'Difference,'

she said flatly. 'He's a nice enough young man. In fact, he's a nice young man. But he's not, in my opinion, good enough for you. I'm sure your mother would agree. Why, I find it quite hard to understand what he is saying.' She reached over and touched Annie's arm. 'When the time comes,' she said in a confiding tone, 'you can do better . . .'

Annie drew her arm away. 'But he's my friend,' she said quietly. She was shocked. Until that moment, Mrs Pearson had given the impression that she genuinely liked Tommy.

'Yes, yes, I understand,' said Mrs Pearson, collecting her trowel and secateurs, 'and that's perfectly all right, just so long as it stays that way. Just regard it as advice from an old woman.' With that, she strode out of the garden, leaving Annie staring after her in astonishment.

On the train home, Annie felt gloomy and disappointed. The high expectations with which she had started out were dashed. 'What a wasted journey,' she murmured. The train was not quite as crowded as the earlier one and there were a few empty seats so they were not as cramped.

Tommy laughed. 'In some ways it has been, yes,' he said, 'but in another way it's been very interesting. If Mrs Pearson doesn't want to tell you about the brooch, then she and your mother must have done something too terrible to tell anyone.'

'But that's awful,' said Annie. She was now afraid that what her mother had done was illegal, and she could not bear it if she went to prison. It made her frightened of stirring things up.

'Maybe,' said Tommy, 'but it's all the more intriguing. And I've certainly enjoyed myself. I've always wanted to look at a Riley at close range. What beauties those cars are!' He looked at Annie and smiled. 'But the best thing about the day has been being with you.'

At Horsham two passengers got out, leaving Annie and Tommy the only people in the compartment. Tommy moved over and sat closer to Annie, placing his arm behind her shoulders as he did so. 'I rather liked your Mrs Pearson,' he said. 'She seems a nice enough person, even if she didn't solve the mystery for you.'

Annie felt her throat tighten. How could she tell him about Mrs Pearson's unkind comments? How could she tell Tommy that he had been taken in by Mrs Pearson's hypocrisy? She couldn't hurt his feelings or his pride. And now his hand was on her arm and her skin felt as if it were burning where he touched it.

She blushed. 'Oh, Tommy.' She looked away in embarrassment, turning to stare out of the window, not daring to turn back to look at him.

Tommy reached over with his other hand and turned her face towards him. With a soft sigh, Annie allowed him to pull her over and kiss her gently on the lips. His chin felt hard and prickly, his lips dry and firm. 'Oh Tommy!' Annie buried her head in the rough uniform on his chest as Tommy folded his arms around her and held her close.

The train chugged along towards London. Annie's head rolled gently against Tommy's shoulder as she stared out of the window. Sometimes they kissed again, and she marvelled each time at the sweet hard-softness of his lips. Her head spun, full of confusion from the events of the day. It was all too much to take in, in too many ways. She did not want anything to spoil this delicious feeling of closeness. She wanted it to go on forever. She wanted to hang on to this feeling rather than think about the bitter disappointment she also felt at failing to learn anything at all from Mrs Pearson about the brooch. No, Mrs Pearson had proved to be as reluctant to talk about it as Annie's own mother had been. She had had such high hopes, such high hopes that were now dashed. Never had Annie felt so helpless and dispirited.

CHAPTER 13

❧

The Visitor

WHEN CLARA FIRST CONFIDED in Annie that she was pregnant by a GI she had met at a dance, Clara's attitude was casual. 'It's all a mistake anyway,' she told her younger sister breezily. 'You're not supposed to get caught if you do it standing up. So I can't really be blamed for it, can I?'

Annie had not seen many of these American soldiers since their arrival in Britain after the Japanese bombed Pearl Harbor, for they did not have much reason to come to north London. But she knew that Clara and her friends spent a lot of time with them when they were not working, enjoying the gifts of Lucky Strike cigarettes, chewing-gum, Hershey bars and nylon stockings. Now it seemed that one of these generous men had given Clara something more.

It was late. The sky was dark outside and the girls' parents had taken themselves off to bed in the shelter some time before. Annie was taken aback by the news, and Clara's offhand attitude did nothing to reduce the effect of her comment on her sister. 'You're going to have a baby?' She stared at Clara with her mouth open.

Clara rolled her eyes. 'No, silly, I'm not going to have a baby.'

'But you just said you were pregnant, that you haven't had the curse for three months.'

'That's right, I did,' replied Clara, staring back at her steadily.

Annie frowned. 'I don't understand,' she said. Clara's contradictory statements were making her feel stupid.

Clara cocked her head to one side. 'Listen, I am pregnant, that's for sure, but people don't have to have babies if they don't want them. There's a way of getting rid of them.'

'There is?' Annie looked at her in puzzlement. 'So what happens to the baby?'

'Oh, nothing, it's just got rid of, that's all.' She frowned back at Annie as if to warn her off asking any more questions.

'The point is, Annie, that I know about someone who can help me. One of the girls at work has given me the name of a man who helps people in trouble. I'll have to go sooner rather than later because it gets more difficult as time goes on. Also, Annie, I don't want Mum and Dad to ever know about this, so I have to trust you to keep this as a secret.'

Annie nodded. 'Of course, Clara, I won't tell anyone. I'll help you in any way I can.'

The next day Annie had accompanied Clara on the bus to a dispensary in a row of shops in a leafy street in Hampstead.

Clara had been cheerful on the bus. She had been laughing and joking and acting as if she did not have a care in the world. Perhaps it really was not something to make a fuss about. Everyone made a big fuss when you had a baby. Perhaps the opposite was true when you did not have one. They got off and walked half a mile up the road until they reached the dispensary.

The shop was closed but Clara rang the bell and the chemist arrived to let them in. He was a tall, middle-aged man with a bald head and a small brown moustache. Annie thought that his clothes were rather shabby. He led the girls through the dark shop to a room at the back. Annie was told to wait there while he led Clara into another room beyond.

As Annie sat on the chair outside, she wondered what the man was doing to Clara on the other side of the door. She stared at the dreary posters on the wall opposite and tried hard not to think about how she might have been an auntie. No, that was really selfish of her. She thought about how Clara could not possibly have a baby when she wasn't even married. But killing a baby! That had to be wrong. Annie's head felt completely blocked with confusion. She could not think clearly at all. What she did know was that if Clara had a baby when she was not married then their mother would be very upset indeed. And their father would not be pleased, either. At least if Clara did something so that there was no baby after all, their parents would never know, and they would never need to know. Annie felt relieved to know that something made sense even if it did not feel right.

The clock on the mantelpiece was ticking loudly. The ticking noise seemed to get louder and louder until it felt as if it were actually striking her each time. What was happening? How much longer was she to wait?

Now she could hear noises next door. There was a clink of metal falling on the floor, a groan and then a sharp cry. Then there was another groan. Annie could hear the man's voice, muffled and incomprehensible.

She watched the door anxiously. Her hands were clutched together tightly in her lap.

It felt like an hour but the clock on the wall informed Annie that the procedure had taken twenty minutes. The door opened at last. The chemist came out first, drying his hands on a blue towel. He was followed by Clara.

Clara looked like a different person from the blasé young woman who had marched into that room twenty minutes before. She hung her head low. Her movements were slow and cautious and her lips, which were usually such a healthy red, looked yellow and waxen.

The moment she saw Annie, Clara's face crumpled up. She reached out towards her. 'Annie . . .'

Annie jumped to her feet and cried out, just as the chemist spun round in time to catch Clara as she collapsed into his arms.

Annie's fears that her sister was dead were soon dispelled. The chemist told Annie that Clara had just fainted. Soon he had Clara on a chair with her head down between her knees. He poured some sharp-smelling liquid onto a cloth and held it briefly under her nose. Clara jerked her head back. For a few moments, her eyes opened and flickered. Then, although her eyeballs seemed to be rolled back, her lips regained their colour.

'You're perfectly all right,' the chemist said gently. 'This sometimes happens. It's nothing to worry about. You're just a bit shocked, that's all.'

Once Clara had recovered enough to go home, the

chemist repeated what he had told her before. 'Go home and take it easy. It will happen within twelve hours or so.'

He squeezed Annie's shoulder in a friendly way. 'You'll look after her, will you? She should have someone with her.'

Annie nodded. He seemed like a kind man. He was clearly concerned about Clara and was trying to help. But Annie did not really understand what was happening. She did not know what had happened behind the closed door and she could not imagine what was going to happen within the next twelve hours. She also did not want to ask.

The chemist took them back through the shop and unlocked the door. 'Good luck,' he said as the girls left. 'And remember, we've never met . . .'

'Yes,' said Clara meekly. Her voice cracked. 'Thank you.'

Going back on the bus, Clara was quiet

'Has it gone?' Annie asked quietly.

'What?' Clara barked at her.

'Well, the baby . . .'

'Of course not, yet!' Clara snarled at her. 'What do you think that man was talking about when he said it would take twelve hours, you idiot?'

After that, Annie did not dare say anything. She kept wondering what the baby would look like, and whether she would get to see it. She also wondered whether she would cry when she saw it.

Back home, Clara told her mother that she wasn't feeling well because of her monthly, and took herself off to her bedroom. As soon as she could after supper, Annie followed

Clara upstairs to look after her, as she had promised the chemist she would.

The pains started at about nine o'clock that evening. At first they felt like the usual cramps but then gradually they grew more powerful. Clara had been pacing around the room. Annie looked in horror as Clara suddenly let out a deep groan and bent over double. A minute later, Annie noticed a crooked line of dark red blood trickling slowly down Clara's bare leg.

Feeling the wetness, Clara looked down. 'Get some towels, Annie!' She sounded quite desperate. 'Oh, goodness, I think there's going to be a bit of a mess . . .'

By the time Annie had returned, Clara was lying on her bed curled up into a ball and hugging her knees. Every now and then she pulled her legs in closer and winced as her face became screwed up with pain. Her hair, damp with sweat, stuck to her forehead in frizzy yellow curls.

'Is it getting any better?'

Annie sat at the end of the bed, one hand resting reassuringly on Clara's leg. This had been going on for over half an hour now. Surely it had to be over sometime soon?

The problem was that Annie did not have a clue about what was to happen. But surely the situation could not get any worse than this? Surely Clara had suffered enough already?

There was a terrible mess. By the time Clara's baby had been expelled from her body, five thick towels had been soaked with dark blood.

Clara endured the ordeal with hardly a sound. When a cramp came, her face went red and then white. She bit her lip and tears welled up in her eyes as sweat beads rose on her forehead. But not once did she cry or scream.

Annie held her hand throughout.

And then it was over. Annie gathered everything up, the blood-soaked towels, the massive clots of blood, and the tiny baby itself. But she did not look at it. She tried not to look at anything so that she would not retch. Everything that needed to be destroyed, she put in a bucket ready to put into the fire of the kitchen boiler later that night.

Once it was over, Clara was calm again. She was exhausted, and lay on the bed, staring at the ceiling. 'Thank you, Annie,' she whispered.

Much later, when the night was still and Annie was certain that her parents had taken themselves and Bobby off to the shelter in the garden, she started to take everything downstairs.

'Thank you,' repeated Clara.

'That's all right,' returned Annie. She closed Clara's bedroom door and carried the bucket and towels downstairs.

She burned the contents of the bucket in the boiler and dumped the bloody towels in the bath. As she scrubbed and rubbed, she thought about Clara's terrible experience that day. It was all a disaster, a terrible, terrible thing. No, that was never going to happen to her. Not in a million years.

It was Saturday morning and the butcher's shop was crowded with people. That morning Mr Worth had in a batch of chickens for the first time in months. Chicken was not rationed but it was an almost forgotten luxury so word about Mr Worth's delivery had spread quickly around Kentish Town.

Annie was quite high up in the queue so she had a good

chance of being one of the lucky ones. As she waited her turn, she thought about how they could make the chicken go as far as possible. If she cut it up into pieces and rolled them in batter, perhaps they could get two meals out of a few ounces.

At the thought of the delicate meat, her mouth began to water. The hundreds of dreary meals of spam or pilchards she had eaten over the past few years had deadened her taste buds, but suddenly she was excited at the thought of food.

The Fenton sisters were standing in front of her in the queue. Annie said good morning to them with a smile. The old women paused for a moment in their conversation to say hello back and then resumed what seemed to be an argument over how many people had been injured by the bomb that had fallen on Peckwater Street two nights back.

As they argued, Mrs Whelan joined the queue behind her. 'Hello there, Annie,' she said. 'And how's your mother?'

'Not too bad today,' replied Annie, 'but her arthritis has been playing up recently.'

Two places up in the queue, Mrs Rose turned and eyed Annie. 'Is your mother taking herself off to church more often or am I imagining it?'

Annie nodded. 'Yes, she has been going up there a bit more than usual. She likes to go there to think.'

The Fenton sisters nodded in unison. 'They say that often happens to people. They get more religious as they get older,' said Ada.

'Mrs Turner's not that old,' replied Emily.

Ada frowned at her sister. 'Maybe not, dear,' she said with a touch of sarcasm, 'but she's older than she was.'

Emily rolled her eyes. 'Well, there's no denying that,' she said. 'But you could say that about all of us.'

The conversation then turned to the latest air raids and the damage caused by the bomb that had fallen on Peckwater Street. It had landed in the middle of a terrace and killed two people.

'It's a wonder no one else was killed,' said Mrs Whelan. As she talked it became clear that she knew most of the details, having spent quite some time standing by the bomb site watching the rescue teams bringing out the dead and wounded. 'One old chap was sitting in his front room. Dead drunk, he was. He didn't know what had hit him. He staggered out but it was the drink what made him stagger, not the shock.'

'Well, that's one way to deal with it,' muttered Mrs Rose.

At that moment, Mrs Whelan stepped towards the window and peered out over the sausages and pork pies. 'Well, will you look at that! There's that Maudie Sprackling, indeed!'

Along with everyone else in the queue, Annie turned her head to look. Walking past was Maudie Sprackling leaning on the arm of a handsome young man. She looked radiant. Now slimmed down, she had a strong shapely figure, and under her blue-and-white hat her face revealed clearly defined features – a well-shaped nose and high cheekbones.

'That's her fiancé,' said Bob Worth, wiping his hands on his apron.

'Why isn't he away fighting, then?' demanded Mrs Whelan. 'He looks fit enough to me.'

'He's got asthma, apparently,' returned Mrs Rose. 'Nice bloke, though. And since you mentioned it, I think it was quite a blow for him not to be able to fight. And they're getting married next month,' she added.

'Well he can't want any children, then,' sniffed Mrs Whelan, who never liked to be filled in on the details of anything, especially when it concerned one of her own neighbours. 'Everyone knows that Maudie is as barren as the Sahara desert.'

'You can't be too sure of that.' The husky voice called across the shop from the doorway. Everyone turned to look. There was Connie Smith standing at the back of the queue with her shopping basket over her forearm. 'It takes two to tango, you know,' she continued, 'and it's not always the woman who's at fault.' She smiled and tossed her head defiantly.

Mrs Whelan drew herself up and pursed her lips. She sniffed sharply through her thin nose. She had never tried to hide her disapproval of Connie Smith for stealing Maudie Sprackling's husband, Fred. 'Well, I suppose you would know more about that than the rest of us,' she said primly, turning her back on Connie, 'but I'm not quite sure how, since you didn't have any children either.' This last remark was uttered in a softer voice but loud enough for everyone to hear.

Connie smiled confidently. 'All I said was that you shouldn't assume it's the woman's fault. No more, no less.' She stepped back. 'I'll return later, Mr Worth,' she called. 'When the shop isn't so crowded.' She stared pointedly at Mrs Whelan, and left.

For a few minutes silence reigned in the shop. All that could be heard was the heavy thump-thump of Mr Worth's cleaver on the wooden chopping table. But then the women started to chat again, the earlier exchanges forgotten.

In spite of being weighed down by the heavy wicker baskets on her arms, Annie decided to go up to Peckwater Street on her way home to have a quick look at the bomb damage.

It was quite a shock to see it. The bomb had devastated the Victorian terrace, blasting the fronts and backs of the houses so that the rooms were pitifully exposed to view like dolls' houses. There were drooping roofs and sagging floors; doors were wrenched off; furniture had been tossed all about, and wallpaper was blasted and tattered. Yet in some houses pictures were still hanging on the walls – slightly askew but otherwise intact. The sight offered poignant snapshots of life seconds before the bomb exploded. Mugs were still on kitchen tables, children's toys were scattered about the floors, clothes were laid out carefully over the back of a chair. And all around these cameos was chaos – shattered wood and bricks and rubble, and dust everywhere. Even houses that were not seriously damaged had had all their windows shattered by the force of the explosion, and were now boarded up with planks of wood.

Long wooden barriers had been placed across the road to keep people away from the rubble and the mess. Wardens were picking through the piles, while the police kept potential looters at bay.

Annie stood by the barriers for some time. This scene was always shocking, no matter how often she had seen it before. People had died and other people's lives were ruined for ever. It made her think about what her house would look like if a bomb were ever to fall on it, too. She imagined a young girl like herself looking in at Annie's house, with Annie's paints and pencils scattered across the floor of the dining room, her paintings lying buried in the dust and bricks.

As she stood wondering and imagining, she heard a small noise behind her. A young ginger cat, no more than a kitten really, came out of the rubble and rubbed its body against her bare leg.

'Hello, cat.' Annie bent down and scratched the cat behind the ears. The kitten pushed itself against her even harder. Then it climbed into Annie's wicker basket which she had put on the ground by her feet.

Annie pushed the animal out and set off for home with the basket on the crook of her arm. Halfway home, she realized that the kitten was following her. 'Go home! You can't come with me!' She waved her arms at the cat who stared at her and opened its mouth in a silent wail.

Annie set off again with the kitten in tow.

When she came to Falkland Road, Annie saw a large, sleek, black car parked outside her house. A chauffeur sat in the front. Small children were circling the vehicle, peering in through the back window and running their sticky fingers over the bodywork. No one in the street owned a car so this was a cause for much excitement and curiosity.

Annie was puzzled at first but then she recognized the face of the driver – the old retainer from Sussex. The car was Mrs Pearson's Riley. Mrs Pearson had come to visit!

With her heart thumping, Annie quickened her pace and ran indoors, unaware of the ginger kitten following close on her heels.

Her father was sitting at the kitchen table reading the paper. Bobby was also sitting at the table trying to push a skewer through a conker. He was concentrating hard, his head tipped over to one side. Holding the shiny brown nut in one hand, he twisted the metal skewer into the flesh. Tiny, damp, pale yellow flakes fell on to the wooden table.

'Your mother has a visitor,' said Frank, looking at Annie over the top of his newspaper.

'It's Mrs Pearson, isn't it?' said Annie. 'Why is she here?' She had never told her parents about her visit to Sussex.

Frank shrugged and looked back down at his paper. 'How would I know why she's here? It's your mother she's come to see.'

Annie unpacked her shopping and put the food and provisions away in the larder. She filled the kettle and put it on the stove to make a pot of tea.

'Who's this, then?' Frank pointed to the ginger cat which was poking its head round the door. 'It seems we've got an open house today.'

Bobby jumped off his chair and crouched down at the cat as Annie scooped it up in her arms.

'Hey, want to hear a good joke, Annie?' Bobby hovered around her excitedly. He smiled at her; the gaps where his milk teeth had been falling out seemed to be growing. Several teeth had all come out in the same month. He had collected quite a few pennies from the tooth fairy recently.

'All right, go on then.' Annie was a resigned and sympathetic listener to Bobby's jokes. She could remember when she was that age and was trying out most of these same jokes on her long-suffering parents.

'Here we go: why did the chicken cross the road?'

Annie rolled her eyes tolerantly. 'Well, I've heard that one before, Bobby, you asked me that only yesterday, and the day before that.'

Bobby chuckled gaily. He was a happy little boy. 'Yes, yes, don't spoil it. There's another part, a new bit . . .'

Annie nodded patiently. 'The answer is, because it wanted to get to the other side.'

Bobby wriggled with pleasure. 'That's right. Now,' he said, 'why did the chewing gum cross the road?'

Frank raised his eyes over the paper. 'I hope Clara hasn't been giving you more gum, Bobby. Your mother won't be pleased, you know.'

Bobby frowned. 'Oh, don't spoil it, Dad.'

Annie laughed. 'I don't know, Bobby, you've got me with that one. Why did the chewing gum cross the road?'

Bobby jumped to his feet and shouted triumphantly: 'Because it was stuck to the chicken's foot!'

Annie and Frank both laughed.

'That's not a bad joke, Bobby,' said Frank, 'not bad at all.'

'Clara taught me that,' the boy said with a satisfied look.

Annie was no longer listening. Her thoughts were now upstairs, in the sitting room where her mother sat with the visitor. If her father had not been there, she would have crept upstairs by now to press her ear against the closed door to hear the voices on the other side.

Inside the sitting room, Grace was on the sofa against the far wall. She had a nervous and pinched expression on her face as she watched the other woman pace across the worn blue carpet. At times, she even looked afraid.

'I must emphasize the importance of keeping everything secret,' Mrs Pearson was saying. 'I was alarmed when Anne came down to see me, but it was evident that she did not know anything. As I said, I am here to make sure that you continue to keep everything under wraps. If anything ever got out about what we did, there could be serious consequences for everyone. I don't have to remind you that what we both did was against the law . . .'

Grace raised her head and a rare flash of emotion showed in her grey eyes. 'Of course it's a secret. It always has been and always will be. Anne is a girl with a lot of curiosity and I'm not surprised that she came to see you like that. Obviously, I'm glad you didn't tell her anything, either.'

Mrs Pearson looked at her fiercely for a moment. 'You should have got rid of the brooch,' she said accusingly. 'Or at least made sure that no one ever had reason to wonder about it.'

'Well, then you shouldn't have given it to me in the first place,' returned Grace. 'I never asked you for it.' She looked away.

'I want to say one more thing before I leave.' Mrs Pearson stood over Grace's form on the sofa. 'There is no point in thinking about the morality of our actions. It all happened a long time ago now, and there must be no regrets. The best thing is to put it out of your mind completely. I think you'll find it never bothers you if you do.'

Ten minutes later, Annie watched from the kitchen doorway as Mrs Pearson swept down the stairs and let herself out of the front door. She could not see clearly but Annie was sure that the expression on Mrs Pearson's face was one of great satisfaction.

Annie was surprised and even a little hurt that Mrs Pearson had left without seeking her out to say hello.

The black limousine drove off, scattering the urchins hanging around it. A few minutes later, Annie heard her mother's slow footsteps on the stairs. 'I'm going out for a while,' Grace called. Her voice was soft.

'Is everything all right?' Frank called back from the kitchen.

'Yes, thank you,' replied Grace. 'I won't be long.'

Annie knew that her mother was taking herself up to the church.

That evening, Grace called Annie in to the sitting room.

'Close the door, Annie and come and sit down here. I have something to tell you. I've thought about this long and hard and feel that I owe you an explanation.'

Annie was amazed. She walked slowly into the room and sat down in the chair facing her mother.

Grace looked down at her hands. Annie noticed that she was unconsciously running the fingertips of one hand up and down the back of the other. 'Annie, dear, I know you saw Mrs Pearson today, and I understand that you went down to visit her a few weeks ago to ask her about the brooch. I won't chastise you for going to Sussex without telling me. Let's just say that I was a little bit hurt. I'll leave it at that. If I'd known that you were so desperate to know about the brooch that you would take yourself off to Sussex like that, I would have told you myself. I certainly think you're old enough to understand now.'

Annie bit her lip. 'Sorry,' she muttered sheepishly.

'But I will tell you about the brooch,' continued her mother. Grace turned her head and stared out of the window as she began to speak.

Annie looked up in surprise. Her mother's words were so unexpected.

'A long time ago,' Grace began, 'when I was still living at home with my parents and before I had met your father, I helped Mrs Pearson. That is why she gave me the brooch. I helped her do a terrible thing.' She turned back towards Annie, her eyes filled with tears.

Annie shifted uncomfortably in her chair. Was she really going to learn the truth she had longed to know for so long? Her heart was racing. Her mother had helped do a terrible thing? She waited for more.

'Camilla was not then married – she was called Camilla Heathcote in those days. She had a liaison with a young man . . .' Grace paused and added, 'I know you're old enough to hear what I have to say . . . In any event, she found herself in trouble, which is a terrible thing for any young woman, but especially in a grand family such as hers. She was panic-stricken and, having no one else to turn to, she confided in me. She did not dare tell anyone else. As it happened, before any decision could be made about anything, she lost the baby. It was a godsend, in a way. Or so it seemed at the time, and I hope God will forgive me for saying that. Camilla was about five months gone and the baby was a fair size.' Grace's voice was getting fainter and fainter. 'She asked me to get rid of the baby for her.' Now her voice sounded choked up. 'I took it out in the night and buried the body in the grounds.' She paused before continuing. 'We never spoke of it again but a few days later Camilla gave me the brooch. It was, she said, a symbol of her gratitude, for being there when there was no one else she could turn to.'

Grace stopped and smiled wanly. There was a terrible sadness in her eyes. 'I'm sorry that it's taken you so long to learn this. I'm sorry that you had to learn of it at all. What we did was a sin. The child was conceived in sin and then buried in unconsecrated ground. I trust you to keep this secret to yourself. I should be grateful if you spoke about it to no one, not Clara, not your father, not Jack, nor Bobby. It's between you and me. I know you will respect that request.'

Annie nodded meekly. She walked over to her mother and kissed her on the forehead. 'I understand,' she murmured. She left the room thinking about how she had tipped Clara's baby into the boiler to burn, as if the poor little thing had been pitched into hell's fires. No consecrated ground for that baby, either. As she climbed downstairs, her face burned with shame.

Later that night, Annie lay in her bunk bed in the shelter. Her mind was racing as she stared up into the darkness. Over and over again she replayed her mother's words in her head. She felt uneasy as she turned them over in her mind, trying to imagine the scenes between the two young women – Camilla in trouble, her mother creeping out in the middle of the night with the dead baby, the unwanted dead baby. They were poignant images which she could picture easily in her mind.

But there was something wrong with it all. Something made her feel uneasy. A cramp was seizing her leg so she shifted position. Something about her mother's account did not ring true. There was a problem. And that problem was that she did not believe that her mother had been telling her the truth. Her sweet, God-fearing and gentle mother had been telling her a bundle of lies.

CHAPTER 14

Annie in Love

IT HAD NOT TAKEN long for Annie to realize that she was falling in love with Tommy. She did not know it at first. It started with her observation that her feelings for Tommy were changing. She noticed that she liked to think about him, to conjure him up in her mind's eye or recall his voice in her ear. She had warm feelings at the thought of him and sometimes even a slight lurch in her belly. She could amuse herself for hours just thinking about him and when she did a smile appeared on her lips and her dreamy eyes would sparkle. Slowly it dawned on her that what she was feeling was love. She was falling in love.

At first she was frightened of the change in their relationship, shifting from a simple friendship to something far more serious, something mysterious and alluring. And these feelings were stronger than any crush she had ever had at school, stronger than anything she had ever felt before. It marked her development from child to woman, as did the physical changes that were still happening to her body.

As an artist, Annie had become very interested in the

human body. At every opportunity, she would draw a hand, a foot, the profile of her mother's head as she read her *Good Housekeeping* magazine, or Bobby's back as he leaned over his Meccano set. Her sketchbooks were filled with anatomical studies. Soon she became fascinated, too, by the way light casts shadows on human flesh, changing the image significantly. Her mother's face could look worn and tired in one kind of light, yet another kind of softer, gentler light could recapture the pretty bloom of youth.

Annie also began to think about her own body and how different it was from Clara's or her mother's. Whereas they both had strong, lean bodies with rounded curves, Annie's frame was slight and angular. Her slender wrists and ankles looked positively fragile against Clara's robust bones, and generally, Annie felt she lacked a womanly shape.

These differences bothered her considerably. Not only did they revive her old fears about being different from the rest of the family but they also made her think that Tommy could not possibly find her attractive.

One day, when Tommy was home on a brief leave, they went for a walk in Highgate Woods. There had been heavy storms the night before and the rain was still dripping off the leaves of the trees and falling on to the brown leaf-mould below. There were few people about – just the occasional woman walking her dog, and apart from the low rumbling of the trains coming into Highgate station, the woods were quiet and still.

Annie and Tommy walked hand in hand. Both were silent and thoughtful that morning.

'I sometimes find it hard to believe you genuinely like me,' Annie ventured.

Tommy gave her a puzzled look. 'Of course I do. What are you talking about?' He squeezed her hand and pulled her to him.

Annie smiled but pulled away. 'I'm being serious,' she said. 'I can't believe that you don't find Clara more attractive than me.'

'Clara?' Tommy looked surprised. He thought for a moment. 'Clara is attractive, of course,' he said, 'but you're the one I like best. And I find you very attractive.'

'But Clara's got curves. All men go after curves. I'm just straight and thin, like a stick insect.'

Tommy laughed. 'Attraction is not just about curves, you know. And besides, do you think I'd court a stick insect? You insult me!'

Annie looked away with embarrassment and he squeezed her tight. 'Annie, love, don't you know, you're very beautiful. You have a gracefulness and elegance that Clara will never have. She is very womanly, yes, but you have something special. I don't know what it is, exactly, but I know I like it. You're like a swan.'

Annie grunted. 'You mean an ugly duckling.'

Tommy placed his hand over her mouth to hush her. 'No, a swan.'

They had come to a clearing. Taking his hand away, Tommy placed his lips on Annie's half-open mouth. He pulled her to him, causing her to stand on tiptoe, and squeezed her tight. One hand ran down her back. Then he pulled up her skirt at the back to allow his hand to continue up her inner thigh.

The feeling of Tommy's rough hand on her sensitive skin sent a tingling between her legs and up to the pit of her belly. Annie felt excited in a way she had never been before.

She leaned towards him, rubbing her own hands up and down his back. She was trembling with new sensations, twinges and deep longing. This poor despised body of hers had suddenly sprung to life.

Tommy kissed her neck. 'You're my swan, Annie,' he whispered, running his lips down her neck. 'Do you believe me now? Just look at this exquisite neck!'

Annie smiled and nodded weakly. 'My father says I take after my great-grandmother,' she whispered.

'Then I'm grateful to your great-grandmother,' Tommy replied.

After that, Annie had no doubts about Tommy's interest in her, and she looked forward to his short furloughs with longing. They spent every minute of his leave together, walking hand in hand across Hampstead Heath and on to Highgate Woods. They rowed on the boating ponds at Alexandra Palace, or swam in the icy cold water of Highgate Pond. They lunched in the British Restaurant in Highgate and went several times to the cinema. They saw a Gracie Fields film at the Hampstead Picture Playhouse, and *Mrs Miniver* at the Court cinema in Malden Road. And at the Kentish Town Forum, they saw Clark Gable and Spencer Tracy in *San Francisco*, which they had first seen years ago, before the war had started.

Sitting next to Tommy in the cinema stalls, Annie often felt she was living a dream. Her head was floating but she remained acutely conscious of Tommy's leg against hers, his fingers interlaced with her own and the musky male smell of his body as he leaned against her.

So many times in the past, Annie had snatched a look at

the courting couples sitting in the back rows of the cinema oblivious to the world as they kissed, or just sitting with blissful expressions on their faces as they enjoyed the simple pleasure of being completely caught up with another person. What heaven it was!

At last Annie had joined the grown-ups, or at least the big girls, with a kind, handsome boy of her own, a decent fellow who treated her with respect and dignity.

On one occasion when Tommy came home it was clearly going to be his last leave for some time.

'I can't talk about it, Annie, you know that, but something big is going to be happening soon,' he said. 'I don't know when myself. No one knows, except the big shots.'

They had gone back to Tommy's home after a walk on Hampstead Heath. At first Annie had not wanted to go to the house in Leverton Street, for she was aware that Connie had had some change of feeling towards her. Tommy's big sister had always been so friendly towards her in the past, but over the last few months she had appeared cold and distant.

However, Tommy assured Annie that no one was at home. It was the middle of the afternoon and his parents and Connie would still be at work.

The house looked neat and tidy. Connie was still keeping it well. Tommy made a pot of tea and they sat in the front room together on the broken-down sofa. It was propped up underneath with some bricks. They talked about their plans for the future, how Annie wanted to apply for art school and Tommy to study law. They talked about the return of Roger to the neighbourhood, after being invalided out of the army. 'He smashed up his leg in a motor-bike accident,' explained Annie. 'He spent a long time in an army hospital but he was sent home a few months ago. His leg was in plaster for ages, and Clara visited him a lot at home.' She sighed. 'I suppose that will all start up again now,' she added wearily. 'He's got a job working for a builder now.'

'There's plenty of that work to be done, that's for sure,' said Tommy.

Then, after a while, Tommy placed his hand on Annie's and they began to kiss, as they had done at every meeting since that first time. Now Annie had got used to the hard prickles of Tommy's chin which had made her own skin sore and red at times. And she no longer felt repelled by the feel of his tongue on hers. Sometimes, she even felt bold enough to move her own tongue against his.

This time, there was an urgency in Tommy's breathing. His hands, rubbing up and down her back and shoulders, seemed stronger, bolder.

'Annie, Annie,' he whispered, taking her hand and placing it against his trousers.

Annie moved her hand away and sat upright. 'No, Tommy,' she said. She straightened her skirt primly.

Tommy placed his hands around her face and stared into her eyes. 'This might be the last time I see you, my darling,' he whispered. 'Let's show our love for each other in the way we are meant to . . .'

Annie swallowed hard. She was feeling excited herself. In fact, she was feeling an almost unendurable urge to let Tommy sweep her up in his arms, pull off her clothes and consummate their love. She longed to be taken over, to give up all control, just like in the films, with all that rich, stirring music in the background. But she did not yield. Because however strong that impulse to surrender herself

to Tommy, there was no escaping the image in her mind of
Clara squatting over the chamber pot and the bloody
remains of that tiny dead baby in the bucket.

She buried her face in Tommy's chest. 'Tommy, Tommy,
I love you,' she whispered. 'But I can't do it yet. Let's just
kiss.'

Tommy shuddered and immediately pulled away. He
looked disappointed and for a few moments was quite
subdued. But he respected Annie and did not want to
push her if she wasn't keen. He knew, too, that he was
partly responsible for feeling so let down. He had fool-
ishly allowed himself to believe his mates back at the
army base when they advised him on how to succeed with
his girl.

'Never mind, then,' he said, adjusting his trousers and
trying to sound cheerful. 'Let's have some more tea.'

As Annie poured out the tea, they heard the front door
open. Then Connie appeared in the doorway. The sight of
Tommy and Annie sitting close together on the sofa did
not seem to please her at all. Annie saw that she was
frowning.

'Oh, it's you, Tommy,' said Connie.

'Well, who did you think it could be?' asked Tommy.
'The seven dwarves?' He laughed.

'Hello, Connie,' Annie said shyly. Connie used to be so
friendly towards her. What could have happened?

Connie left the room and disappeared into the kitchen
to cook some tea. Could it have anything to do with
Tommy and her getting so close? The thought suddenly
seemed to make sense. But why on earth should Connie
mind? Annie was hurt and confused. What was wrong?

Nothing more was said, and Tommy certainly seemed

unaware of any problem. Perhaps it was just in Annie's own head. She tried to persuade herself that it was.

Annie could not have known that Connie's strange reaction stemmed from fear, not disapproval. Connie had just woken up to the fact that Tommy and Annie were extremely serious about each other. They were so serious that Connie could no longer ignore their friendship. Worse than that, she knew that she would have to do something about it.

When Annie left to go home, Tommy kissed her hard, giving her a long, lingering kiss on the mouth. Annie walked backwards up the street waving goodbye to him. Tommy was off early the next morning and she would not be seeing him again before then. Perhaps it would be the last she would ever see of him, but she did not think so. It suddenly struck her that, deep down, she was not afraid for his life. She just knew that he would survive the war, and that they would be together afterwards.

When she reached her own front door, she was surprised to hear someone playing some lively music on the piano. Her spirits rose even higher than before.

Clara was sitting at the piano. She flashed a smile at her sister as Annie came into the hall. Annie had not heard Clara play the piano for a long time and certainly she had not played any music as gay as this for many years.

'Hello, sis!' Clara beamed at her.

Annie nodded. 'You seem happy,' she commented.

Clara's eyes were sparkling. She nodded back, her blonde hair bobbing up and down. Then she stopped playing and held up her left hand with the fingers spread out like a fan. 'Look at this,' she said. 'Roger's asked me to marry him.' She laughed gaily. 'It's an engagement ring. I'm engaged.'

Annie stared at her sister's finger and the ring with its small modest stone. 'Engaged?' She repeated the word slowly. 'To Roger?' She could not hide her disbelief.

Clara leaped to her feet and grabbed Annie's hands. 'Yes, yes, I'm going to get married!' She laughed again, spinning Annie round in a circle. 'I'm about to become a respectable woman!'

Annie's parents seemed resigned to the match.

'He's a nice enough boy,' remarked Grace. 'He's grown up a lot and he's got himself a regular job since he came out of the army.'

'The army was probably good for him,' said Frank. 'Gave him a sense of discipline he never got at home. He said as much to me only the other day.'

'What counts is Clara's happiness,' said Grace. 'She certainly looks happy enough now. And,' she added with a soft smile, 'if they get married in the autumn, we could be grandparents within the year!'

Annie frowned. 'If Clara gets married then she probably won't go to college, will she?'

Frank sighed. 'I've lost that argument, yes. And if marriage is what Clara really wants, then there's no stopping her,' he said. 'Clara's always been one to get what she wants.'

Annie listened to these conversations with interest. She felt her father's disappointment that Clara would not go to college and get some qualifications. And she sensed that beneath her mother's excitement at the idea of a wedding and what it meant, there was a touch of regret that Clara had not done better for herself in her choice of husband. Apart from his charm and good looks, Roger had never given any reason to be considered a catch in any way.

Sometimes, too, Annie felt quite uneasy about Roger. There was an unpredictable side to him that scared her. He could be quite moody, one minute full of laughter and big ideas for having fun, and the next silent and brooding. Annie also noticed that he sometimes spoke sharply to Clara, which never used to happen, and that Clara, to Annie's surprise, tended to take notice without argument. This unpredictable behaviour was disturbing. But generally, she quite liked Roger. She could see through his rough-tough exterior to a softer fellow beneath. He was always kind to her and teased in an affectionate sort of way. Annie liked the way Roger seemed to look up to her father, in the way that Tommy did sometimes, too, as a fatherless boy does. It made her proud of her family, and the way it welcomed outsiders into the fold.

By the time Tommy had returned to camp saying that something big was about to happen, the bulk of Europe, from the Ukraine to the Pyrenees, was an undisputed German fiefdom. D-Day, 6 June 1944, was to change all that.

Ten thousand aircraft took part, each one painted with stripes the night before for recognition. The planes towing gliders and carrying paratroops formed a nose-to-tail stream more than one hundred miles long that morning.

Seven thousand vessels, from midget submarines to the mightiest of battleships, were to head for the Normandy beaches. And so crowded were the British ports that some ships had to sail from as far north as Scotland.

Over a hundred and fifty thousand Allied men set foot on French soil that day, as well as fifteen hundred vehicles.

All were landed on open sandy beaches fortified and protected by wire, mines and steel traps. And all done in atrocious weather.

Everything had been planned with utmost secrecy. The whole of south-west England was an army camp, and a huge armada had gathered.

Annie's first inkling of the importance of that day came as she was hanging out the washing. High above her, the sky was almost dark, full of planes, wing to wing, streaming towards the coast.

Like everyone else in the land, the Turner family gathered round the wireless that evening, listening to the BBC's accounts of the landings and thinking about Jack, Tommy and every other boy they knew who was out there that day.

After D-Day, most people thought that surely the war was over, but soon afterwards a new kind of German aircraft started terrorizing London: Hitler's revenge bombs. Unmanned and extremely noisy, they flew at just the height to avoid both the light and the heavy guns. The engine would suddenly cut out and then a huge explosion would follow within seconds. The doodlebugs, as they came to be known, were then followed in September by an even more frightening weapon: the flying rockets. These could be launched from over two hundred miles away and gave no warning at all. Both weapons represented a sinister development at this stage in the war when the Allied troops were supposed to be taking control of Europe. But still Londoners kept going, making jokes about those cowardly men fighting at the front while those back home were suffering the worst of it.

*

If marriage had put paid to Clara's plans to go to college, Annie was still determined to make her way to art school. Now seventeen, she was able to apply but she decided to wait until the next year to do so. In spite of the doodlebugs and the rockets, the war had to be in its last stages. There were already signs of peace. In September the blackout gave way to a dim-out, and on Christmas Day, churches could light their stained glass windows for the first time since war had begun. Two days later, car headlights' masks were abolished. It would all be over by next year, and Annie wanted to wait until it was. She wanted the certainty. Until then, she wanted to get out and contribute properly to the war effort like everyone else.

Tilly felt the same way, so the two girls got themselves jobs in a small home factory in Camden. It had been started by a group of women who had got together to set up shop at home, testing screws for aircraft engines. It was monotonous, boring work but the camaraderie and friendly atmosphere in the room where they all worked made up for that. Annie listened to the conversation of the older women with great interest. She listened to the stories of their husbands and fiancés. She heard confessions of infidelity and raucous laughter at the foibles of men. Annie tried not to look too shocked when the women talked bluntly about their men's inadequacies in bed but she liked the way that the women showed a genuine affection for their husbands, even if they did regard them as naughty children. Sometimes the conversation became quite explicit, and Annie would look down and pretend not to listen, or sneak a glance at Tilly, who was always equally embarrassed. But she loved the fact that the women treated her as one of them and did not feel it necessary to clean up their language to protect innocent young ears.

One day, coming home from work on the bus with Tilly, Annie saw a strange sight. Outside the pub on the corner of Islip Street and Kentish Town Road she saw her father deep in conversation with Connie Smith. The bus had been held up by a lorry backing out into the road from a side street, so Annie could watch the scene from her position on the top of the bus. Her father was frowning and shaking his head, while Connie, who looked serious and concerned, was nodding her head vigorously and making the same gestures over and over again.

Annie watched with them with fascination. She could not think what they were talking about but she had a feeling that it was serious. It was most odd. As far as she was aware, they hardly knew each other.

The bus moved on but even as Annie alighted and set off up Falkland Road with Tilly, the image of those two adults in animated conversation lingered in her mind.

Later at supper that evening, Annie thought her father was acting rather strangely. He was uncharacteristically detached and quiet as Clara and Grace discussed the wedding plans. It was decided that the wedding would be in the autumn.

'If the war's properly over by then, perhaps Jack will be home,' said Grace hopefully.

Annie pushed a forkful of mashed potato into her mouth and said nothing. Thinking of how much her brother disliked Roger, she knew he was not going to be pleased at the news of Clara's marriage. She knew how possessive Jack could be about Clara. She did not know why he was, but she had always been aware of it. And she knew that the idea of having Roger in the family would make Jack angry.

Throughout the discussion, Frank was quiet. He stared down at the table and said little. Even when Bobby tried to tell him his latest joke, Frank was hardly able to raise a smile in response.

Annie was to find out why immediately afterwards.

After the washing-up had been done and the plates dried and returned to their positions on the dresser, Frank picked up his hat and announced that he was going out for a stroll. 'Would you like to come, Annie?' he asked.

Given her father's silent mood, Annie was surprised to be asked. But she always enjoyed going for a walk with her father, which she often did. They would walk and talk and discuss whatever was on their minds.

But this time Frank continued to be rather quiet. He rolled a Woodbine cigarette between his fingers and then lit it. 'Have you heard from Tommy lately?' he asked casually.

Annie smiled but shook her head. 'Not since after D-Day,' she said. 'I got that postcard saying he was well – just like the one we got from Jack. I'm sure he's well. Deep down, I know he's safe.' At the thought of Tommy, a warm feeling crept through her.

Frank was quiet again. The he took a deep breath. 'I have to talk to you about Tommy,' he said.

Annie looked quizzically at her father. 'What do you mean?'

'I want to talk to you about Tommy and your friendship with him.' Frank looked ill at ease and uncomfortable.

'We haven't done anything, if that's what you mean.' Annie blurted out the words defensively.

Frank shook his head. 'No, that's not what I mean, not really. Though, of course, I'm glad to hear you say that, too. No, it's more than that . . .'

'What do you mean, it's more?'

Frank turned and faced his daughter, looking her directly in the eyes. 'Annie, Tommy's a nice boy, you know we all like him. You know that. But I don't want your friendship with him to go any further.'

Annie stared at her father, unable to respond.

'You have to go to art school and do great things with your life . . .'

Annie narrowed her eyes suspiciously. 'So . . ?'

'Well, I want to see you do all those things. I don't want you to give up your ambitions for the sake of a boy. I'm sad that Clara has done that herself.'

He paused and shuffled from one foot to another. Then he came out with it. 'I don't think Tommy is good enough for you. That Smith family is trouble and I would hate to see you a part of it.'

Annie stepped backwards, letting out a light gasp. Her face quickly flushed red with indignant rage. 'How dare you suggest that Tommy is trouble! How dare you suggest that he's not good enough for me. I've heard that said before, and it's not fair. Tommy's the best person in the world. He's worked hard and done well in spite of his family. He plans to go on studying when the war's over and he'll get a good job and earn good money. And I still plan to go to art school. You know that. I've never said I wouldn't. I don't understand why you don't like Tommy. It's so unfair when you don't seem to worry about Clara marrying Roger. And you can hardly say that Roger is the most reliable person in the world. He certainly hasn't got a spotless reputation.'

Frank winced. Taking off his hat, he ran a hand over his forehead and rubbed his eyes. He looked tired and drawn. 'You're right, Annie. You're too clever to be fooled.'

As he started to talk, Annie knew that something extraordinary was about to be said to her and she knew that it had something to do with the scene in Kentish Town Road that she had witnessed that evening.

'I have to tell you the truth. I can't order you to keep it a secret or to keep it from your mother but I can hope that you will. I personally think that it would kill her to hear what I am about to tell you.'

'What, Daddy?' Annie gripped Frank's arm in panic. 'What are you talking about?'

'What I'm talking about is Tommy,' said Frank, 'Tommy and you. You cannot have a friendship. You must not take it any further.' The next words felt like a physical blow. 'The fact is, Annie . . .' Frank was sweating. His hand had dropped to one side and the expression on his face was one of extreme anguish. 'The fact is that Tommy is your half-brother.'

Seeing the incomprehension on Annie's face, Frank grabbed her by the shoulders and pulled her round to face him. 'You see, Tommy is my son.' His voice cracked as he pulled her against his chest. Burying his head on her shoulders, he let out a series of loud, choking sobs.

CHAPTER 15

❧

Frank's Secret

ANNIE AND FRANK sat on the wooden bench in the churchyard. It was a summer evening and the air was still. Two sparrows squabbled over a crust of bread someone had thrown over the brick wall. The sun was disappearing rapidly over Parliament Hill, the sky was streaked with crimson and grey. The light was rapidly fading as Frank Turner began to tell his story.

'I never thought I'd have to tell anyone about this,' he said. 'I thought of it as a mistake twenty years ago and I still do. It never occurred to me that there would be any consequences. You just don't when you're young. I can still hardly believe it myself, though deep down I know that it's true, that Tommy Smith is Connie Smith's son. He is also my son.'

Annie looked vexed, a small frown between her eyes. 'I don't understand,' she said. What do you mean he's Connie Smith's son? He told me that he was Connie's cousin. He was just brought up by his Aunt Jan as her son.'

'That's what Tommy believes because that's what he's

always been told. Tommy doesn't know, Annie. It's what everyone's always been told. And it does add up, doesn't it?' replied Frank. 'It all adds up.

'Soon after your mother had Clara, it happened. It just happened once. I can't explain exactly why, Annie, but you must know that what goes on between a man and his wife is an important part of a marriage.' He looked away but Annie could see his face in the descending darkness.

'Once your mother started having children, she became less interested in – how can I say this? – the physical side of marriage. Once we started having a family, she lost interest, except when she wanted another baby. It was hard for me, you understand.'

Frank was looking uncomfortable. His handsome face was contorted into an ugly grimace of pain as he confronted his past sins.

'It's not right for a father to talk to his own daughter about these things but the circumstances mean that I have to.' He paused and cleared his throat with a dry, cautious cough.

'I don't drink much nowadays and I have never been much of a drinking man. But there was a time, before you were born, when I would go for the occasional pint at the Pineapple. I used to meet up with friends or just go in for a gossip and catch up on the news.'

Grace placed the sleeping infant in the cot and stood over her for a few seconds. Frank watched her standing there, her clean profile outlined against the wall in the dim light. As his wife slipped silently into bed and dropped the covers over her body, Frank reached over and placed his hand on her hip. He felt the soft flesh stiffen.

'Not now Frank, please,' said Grace. 'I must sleep while I can.'

The baby let out a small cry but then settled back to sleep. Frank pulled his hand back and rolled over on his side, his back to his wife. How much longer was she going to be like this? She had never taken much pleasure in sexual union but she had not objected to his needs. Why, in the early years of their marriage, he had sought comfort in her warm flesh every night. What joy that had been! Every evening as he bicycled home after work, he would look forward to sinking into her arms and abandoning himself to that exquisite pleasure. It had not lasted, of course. His needs were the same but Grace began to resist them more frequently. If he had been a violent man he might have insisted on his rights with a firmness which showed he meant business. He often imagined taking Grace by force but such actions remained in his thoughts only. Frank was essentially a gentle man.

'I'm sure your mother has talked to you about what goes on between a man and a woman.' Frank scratched his ear.

Annie was silent. She could feel a blush creeping up her neck.

'I'm not excusing myself,' he continued. 'What I did was wrong. But sometimes the need is so great . . .'

The pub was quiet that evening. Frank sat and talked to old Jim Horder for a while and shared a joke or two with Mr Garcia. After they had drunk a couple of pints, Mr Garcia fell silent and Jim Horder became maudlin about the tragedy of his idiot son Danny. Frank knew it was time to go. He downed the rest of his pint and pulled on his coat. He felt quite light-headed. He rarely drank so the two pints of bitter had set his body tingling. 'Night all,' he muttered as he left the pub.

Outside, the night air was cool on his face. He set off down the road with his hands in his pockets. The period after Jack's birth had been difficult. He had felt left out, redundant then. But Grace had still allowed him his pleasure. This time round, long before Clara had even been born, Grace had shut him out. She seemed to be completely wrapped up with the baby and her needs. Clara was a colicky baby who cried a lot and often. Frank often spent evenings with hardly any communication between him and Grace that did not concern young Jack or Clara. Frank had not even been able to play the piano as Grace was afraid it would set Clara off again.

Deep down, Frank was sure it would be all right in the end. It was just a period they had to go through. In the meantime, it was tough.

On the corner of the street, he saw young Connie Smith. Connie was a buxom girl of about seventeen. She had a deep husky voice and thick brown hair coiled around her head, and the most compact, neat body he had ever seen. Her tight clothes accentuated her figure. She was always laughing and joking. She was the one member of the Smith family whom Frank liked. He had been to school with her brothers. All three had been ne'er-do-wells then – not incapable of picking the pockets of their teachers – brash and cocky. He had never trusted them, either.

But Connie was different. She had a warm heart. Perhaps being the only girl and the baby of the family had made her different. Everyone knew how helpful she was to her mum and she was frequently helping out the neighbours – always willing to baby-sit or run an errand.

'Hello, Frank,' she called.

Frank nodded and smiled. He pulled out his packet of cigarettes.

'Have you got one for me?' Connie asked, sidling up to him coyly.

'Here.' Frank held out the packet for her. She reached out to take a cigarette with the tips of her fingers. He could smell her freshly washed hair and the cheap perfume she had dabbed onto her wrists and neck.

She pressed her hand gently on his forearm. 'Got a light then?' she asked. She stood closer to him, holding the cigarette in her pouting lips.

Frank's heart was beating fast. All he had to do was touch her, and he knew it. His willpower had disappeared. The descending darkness made him feel safe from prying eyes.

'I was wrong,' he said to Annie. 'But I couldn't help myself. I took advantage of her for my own purposes.'

Down a back alley off Falkland Road, Frank pushed Connie against the wall. Hanging on with her arms around his neck she had wrapped her legs around his waist, and was kissing him hard. Her enthusiasm excited him as he had never been excited before.

Frank could not tell his daughter how much he had enjoyed those moments with Connie. Once, fast, against the wall like that, and then again, ten minutes later on the grass. The second time, it had been more gentle and loving, closer to what he longed for from his own wife. Connie had run her fingers through his hair and called him 'love'. And she had groaned in quiet ecstasy when she climaxed. Frank had never known that women could climax like a man, and it thrilled him. But he could never tell anyone how wonderful those moments had been. Many times since then he had gone over the occasion in his head as he lay frustrated beside Grace's sleeping form.

'The moment it was over, I regretted it,' he told Annie. 'I

resolved never to have contact with Connie again. I was disgusted with myself. For the sake of a moment of pleasure, I had failed Grace and the children, my children. After that night, I stayed away from Connie's house and crossed the road whenever I saw her. And I almost stopped drinking altogether as a direct result. I've never gone to the Pineapple on my own since that day.

'Then I heard that Connie had suddenly left the neighbourhood, but she came back again after a few months. A little while later we learned that her mother, Mrs Smith, had adopted her baby nephew. Although Tommy was a cousin, he was brought up as another brother in the family. Some time later, we all heard rumours about Connie carrying on with Maudie Sprackling's husband, and that turned into a scandal when they ran away together.

'Anyway, Annie, Connie has just told me that Tommy is not her aunt's child at all. He is not her cousin. Tommy is her own child, born nine months after that evening with me. She says Tommy is my child. And I believe her.

'When she discovered that Connie was having a baby, Mrs Smith sent her away. No one – not even Connie's mother – knew who the father was. Her mother was disapproving but did not want the baby to be adopted by anyone so she agreed to take him in and pretend that he had been born to another relative. Connie has never breathed a word about Tommy's father to a single soul. She never intended to tell anyone. There was never any reason to. But when she saw that you and Tommy were getting so close, she became concerned. She has told me because she wants me to put a stop to it. She has never told Tommy the truth about his father. And she doesn't plan to, either.'

Annie turned to stare at him.

'How can you be sure that you really are the father? Connie Smith ran away with Maudie Sprackling's husband. How can you trust a woman who is capable of stealing another woman's man?'

Frank shrugged.

'I can't be sure,' he said. 'And you're right to question it. But I do think she's telling the truth. I don't see why she should lie. She's not trying to get anything out of me. She just wants the best for everyone.' He paused for a moment, then said: 'And I do believe that Connie has a good heart.'

Annie sniffed. 'Tell that to Maudie.'

'Oh Annie! That was a long time ago. And Maudie seems set on a happy path now.'

Annie fell silent. Staring at the tombstones in the dark, she felt cut off from everything around her. It was true. All that had been said was true. Tommy was Frank's son, she knew it. She had always known it, in a way. She recalled Connie's words in the butcher's shop about how it's not always the woman who's infertile. Connie had said that because she knew she wasn't infertile. And she knew that because she had given birth to Tommy. But most of all, Annie knew it was true because one of the things she liked most about Tommy was that he reminded her so much of her own father.

A strange noise erupted from her belly and rose to her throat. With a great howl, Annie flung herself against her father's shoulder. Father and daughter clung together in the dark.

After a while, Annie finally spoke. 'Mother mustn't be told,' she said quietly. 'It'd break her heart if she knew.'

Frank nodded. 'Yes. Connie's not prepared to tell Tommy,

either. She doesn't want to upset the apple cart. If Tommy knows the truth, it would cause a lot of trouble in both families . . .' He squeezed her arm.

'I'm sorry, Annie . . .'

Annie stared at the church steeple silhouetted against the night sky. It was up to her. No one wanted to tell Tommy the truth, and she could barely take in the truth herself. They were related. They were half-brother and sister. They could not get engaged and be married. Those would be sins against nature. They could not make love and have children and do all the things they had been planning and hoping to do.

It was Annie who would have to act. She had to break off with Tommy. It had been left for her to deal with, yet she wouldn't be able to tell him why.

Annie bit her lip and fought back the tears. She felt trapped, wanting to escape in every direction, to run away from it all. There was too much to take in – her mother's unhappiness, her father's betrayal, Tommy's ignorance of the truth. There was not room in her head even to think about any one of them. What could she do?

In a way she had no choice about what to do. Too many people stood to lose, to be hurt if the truth came out. But it was the two innocent ones she cared about most – Tommy and her mother. Her responsibility towards both of them made it clear what course of action she had to take.

With her head bowed, she rose to her feet and set off down the road towards home, leaving her father sitting alone on the bench in the dark church graveyard.

CHAPTER 16

❧

Bobby

FOR AS LONG AS he could remember, Bobby Turner had wished that his mother went out to work so that he could have a bit of freedom in the hours after school, like so many of his friends. But she did not, so his mother was always there, every minute of his time at home. And it drove him mad.

Grace Turner fussed over her younger son as if he were still a baby, and every day Bobby hated it more and more. His only consolation in this humiliating situation was that at least he wasn't the only one to think that his mother fussed too much. Recently his dad had been telling his mum to stop pampering him, too.

'Ease up on the boy,' Frank had said only the night before. 'He's got to learn a bit of independence, Grace. There's no danger outside now. The war's practically over, there's no chance of bombs. Bobby's got to learn to look after himself. You're turning him into a sissy.'

Grace frowned slightly, as though put out by the remarks, but she had taken in her husband's words. The Germans had been all but defeated. What with Hitler's suicide in April, she knew it was only a matter of time before Germany surrendered. She had to agree that she no longer had the excuse she had been using for so long. 'Perhaps you're right,' she said, after some thought. She was, in fact, well aware of how much she worried about Bobby. Only she knew the reason why. 'Perhaps I do mollycoddle him too much,' she admitted.

Frank was pleased that his words had had such an immediate effect. 'Let the boy have a friend round and let them go out together after tea. That Davey seems a sensible boy. He'll keep Bobby out of trouble.'

Davey was Bobby's best friend from school. He lived with his mother in Ascham Street, just a few blocks away. His father was away fighting and his mother had a job in a shell factory in Acton from which she did not arrive home until late in the evening. Davey was therefore free to do whatever he wanted after school every day. And Frank was right about him; he was a bright boy who did not look for trouble more than the average eight-year-old boy.

For several weeks now Davey had been telling Bobby about the bomb-sites he had been exploring, and badgering him to come too. Now at last Bobby had been given permission to go out with him. It was great!

Bobby was overjoyed by this sudden chance to be independent. He could hardly believe that it was true. For the whole of that day at school, he and Davey plotted what they were going to do once they were free of adult control. They came home from school together, having agreed to keep their plans top secret.

They ate their Marmite sandwiches and slabs of chocolate, whispering together excitedly. Grace served their food and poured their milk, trying to fight off the tension in her chest. Bobby was so excited that he nearly choked as he bolted down his food.

'Now make sure you're back home by six,' said Grace. 'I don't want you going to bed late, what with school tomorrow.'

'Promise, Mum,' called Bobby, running down the street after Davey. 'Bye!'

The boys ambled along side by side. Bobby shoved his hands into his shorts pockets and kicked stones across the road, scuffing the toes of his leather boots. Davey looked well built and stocky beside Bobby's slight frame. With his skinny limbs and pale skin, Bobby looked like a small plant that lacked enough sun to make it thrive.

Weedy or not, Bobby felt on top of the world. He was feeling exhilarated, but he did not dare tell Davey quite how exciting it all was because he did not want Davey to know that this was his first time out on his own without his mother trailing along a short distance behind him.

'Let's go over to Hilldrop Crescent,' called Davey. 'There's a smashing bomb-site over there, where Crippen's house was – you know, the man what murdered his wife. We might find all sorts of things there.'

'Yeah!' Bobby ran after Davey as fast as he could.

The bomb-site was vast, with huge piles of rubble, bricks, wood and glass in high mounds. Several house walls were still standing but some looked dangerous, leaning outwards, close to collapse. Awaiting proper demolition, they were roped off, with large signs which read: DANGER, KEEP OFF.

The boys ignored the warnings and scrambled up over the bricks and rubble, lifting planks and stones as they went. And they found all sorts of things – a pipe, a leather shoe, a drawer full of knives and forks and serving spoons. Bobby even found a rusty penknife which he stuffed into his pocket. He'd have to remember to take it out and hide it before he got home, or his mother would question him about it if she found it.

Bobby approached one of the standing walls. The stairs ran all the way up one of them, and he started to climb.

'Hey! Look at me!' he called cockily to his friend, stamping his feet hard as he ran up the echoing wooden stairs.

Suddenly a few bricks fell down from above his head, dropping heavily to the ground below.

'Watch out!' Davey called.

Bobby stood still, flattened against the wall. He stayed that way for a few minutes then, feeling quite safe, he started to climb again. He had never felt so free. Next he chased up onto the ledge of a shattered window which he could just reach, pulling himself up with a quick, agile movement.

'Look at me!' he called again, standing up so that he filled the window frame.

Davey was laughing. 'That's great, Bobby!' he called. 'I bet you can't climb along to that window over there . . .' He pointed to the next window. 'I bet you can't . . .'

Bobby looked over to where Davey was pointing. He looked down at the fifteen-foot drop below him.

'Yes I can,' he called to his friend. 'Watch this.'

Bobby edged along the brickwork, scraping his knees as he went. His heart pounded with fear and excitement.

Just as he reached up an arm to grab the side of the other window, a great shout went up. 'Hey! You! Get down from there, you stupid kid!'

Startled, Bobby turned his head to see Dolly Pritchett waving a fat arm at him. She startled him. He looked desperately at Davey and then at Dolly. At that same moment, he lost his footing. In a few split seconds, he scrabbled to get his hold again but the skin and flesh on his fingers were scraped to the bone as he dropped straight down to the ground below.

He never had a chance. His head smashed against a large block of concrete. Bobby Turner died almost instantly.

When news was first brought to the Turners' house of the terrible accident that had taken place on the bomb-site, Grace screamed and ran out into the road. She was hysterical with grief. 'It's all of you!' Her screams carried a long way down the street so that even Mrs Garcia a block away could hear her. She had been tying up herbs for drying, but she put them carefully on the floor in order to go out and see what the fuss was about. 'You've killed my baby!' screamed Grace. 'You've all killed my baby!'

It was Frank who grabbed her and dragged her indoors to make her lie down on the sofa. 'It's your fault,' she started to scream. 'You made me let Bobby go. I knew he shouldn't go, and you made me.'

Frank frowned. Hardly able to take in the news of his child's death, he was shocked to be attacked now. He remained silent. It was not the time to argue.

As her hysteria subsided, Grace sank into a quivering, sobbing heap. She knew that her outburst at her husband and Kentish Town was unjust. She knew only too well that her anger was not at anyone other than herself. It was her weakness and foolishness that had destroyed every bit of happiness she might have had. She had been born with the chance of a good life and it was she, only she, long ago, who had thrown away that chance when she was already grasping it by the hand. It was she who was at fault. And there were no chances left. What she had done had affected many people. She threw herself on her bed and wept. She wept aloud for all her babies, wherever they were. But most of all she wept for her second daughter, the one she had treated worst of all.

After Grace's dramatic display of emotion, she gave up on life altogether. For a few days just before Bobby's funeral she seemed surprisingly strong, though not engaged with the world around her. On the day itself, dressed dramatically in long black clothes and veil, she stood and stared at the small wooden coffin being carried off in the hearse. No emotion showed on her face.

Annie watched it all, unaware that her mother's anguish was for more than the loss of a child. Most of the neighbours were at the funeral but the atmosphere was strange and strained. Annie herself had been shocked by the size of Bobby's coffin. She knew that Bobby had been just a little fellow, but the many funeral cortèges she had seen – during which the strong black horses pulled the heavy black hearse up Lady Margaret Road to the church – had been for old people, adults who had reached the end of their natural lives. She realized that she thought all coffins were the same size. The sight of Bobby's little box, almost completely lost among the flowers and wreaths, caused the salty tears to flood more heavily to her eyes than they had done already.

Afterwards, Clara and Annie sat in their room unable to speak. Annie felt as though she were in a fog, disconnected from the world around her. She would never see Bobby again. It was impossible to imagine that he would never again pester her with his silly jokes, or to play snap or racing demon together. He would never again tease the cat and then complain that she had scratched him. Never again would she see his cheeky gap-toothed grin, so like Tommy's at that age, she could now see. And no one to talk to about it, either. Everyone was alone in their shock and bereavement. She dreamed about Bobby every night and woke up with her cheeks wet with tears.

In the face of such tragedy, how could she even begin to think about her own problem? It seemed so minor compared with her little brother's death.

Grace's accusation at the neighbourhood did not go down well with the local people. Although Frank was well liked, his wife had always been regarded as an outsider who had been determined not to fit in. Years of resentment at Grace's aloofness rose to the surface. The less generous of her neighbours accused her of putting on airs and graces, but others tried to be kinder.

In the Pineapple pub and the Falkland Arms, people talked about the situation over their pints of beer.

'Well, we paid our respects for Frank's sake but she's got a cheek saying it was anything to do with us.'

'Bloody nerve, if you ask me,' said Mrs Rose. 'How dare she say it was little Davey's fault.'

'I'd say she's more to blame herself, for mollycoddling that child. She always did, right from the start.'

Dolly Pritchett placed a bowl of pork scratchings on the table. 'I don't think it's right to go that far,' she said, settling her bottom onto the wooden bench. 'No one's to blame for that child's death. It was a tragic accident. We can't blame Mrs Turner any more than she can blame us folks in Kentish Town. The poor woman's in distress, you have to make allowances.'

The others muttered into their drinks and shrugged.

The day after the funeral, Grace Turner took to her bed. The atmosphere in the house in Falkland Road became heavy and claustrophobic. No one played the piano. No one laughed. Everyone lived their own lives in their own way.

Annie cooked the supper, which they ate in silence with their father. Grace's food was taken up to her on a tray and brought back down half and hour later, barely touched.

Grace started to write in a notebook incessantly, writing with a slow, painful hand, her lips moving as she did so.

Sometimes Annie sat in her mother's room trying to keep her company. Sitting in the chair in the corner she would sometimes suddenly see her mother as others now must see her – as a grey-haired woman with a hunched body and a face pinched with pain.

Grace was cut off from her. She would answer questions if asked but otherwise just stared out of the window, her beautiful grey eyes dull and blank with grief.

Grace's condition threw gloom over the good news from the outside world, too. But even though Grace stayed at home, the other Turners could not fail to join the rest of the country and the whole population of Europe in celebrating the end of the war.

That Tuesday night, thousands of north Londoners made their way to the hills of Hampstead Heath, Parliament Hill and Alexandra Palace. Although it was dark, there seemed to be a special aura around the outlines of the night.

Enormous bonfires had been lit. Fireworks exploded in
the sky, competing with the thousands of flickering silvery
beams from the searchlights down below. All around,
public buildings, flooded with light, loomed eerily.

Gaily coloured bunting and flags hung everywhere – the
Union Jack and flags from the Allied nations flew from the
flagpoles on Hampstead Town Hall. No building anywhere
was without some form of decoration and the British flag
hung proudly across every shopping parade in the land.

Women and girls twisted coloured ribbons in their hair.
Men and boys stuck red roses in their buttonholes. And
while the beer lasted, public houses did a roaring trade.

Frank and his children had joined the gathering crowd
on Parliament Hill. What had been a small bonfire had
grown into a raging inferno as more wood was added over
and over again. The moment was right. As the fire began
to burn fiercely and leaped up towards the stars, a lumpy
stuffed effigy of Hitler was thrown on top. In the red glow
of the flames, crowds set off more fire crackers, waved
sparklers in the air and sang and danced to all their
favourite tunes. The night throbbed with the sound of
'When the Lights Go On Again All Over the World' and
'When They Sound the All-Clear'.

Down in the streets of Kentish Town fires burned, as
they did in almost every street in Britain. Gramophones
and pianos had been brought out into the streets, and all
around them danced jubilant citizens, free at last from the
dreariness of war. In the windows of their houses coloured
lights flicked on and off. And while thousands were rejoicing with noisy abandon, many others were quietly praying
to God in the churches.

Lying in bed at home, Grace barely noticed it. It all

made so little difference to her now. She did not notice the streets being filled with young men again after so long. She not notice the happy, relaxed faces, the look of hope on people's faces as they looked forward to the new world that the politicians spoke of and newspapers wrote about with such enthusiasm.

Grace had so lost interest in life that she even missed Clara's wedding. Instead of being the festive occasion that had been planned, the ceremony ended up being a quiet affair in the registry office in St Pancras town hall with Frank and Annie as witnesses. No one from Roger's family came. His father had died of cirrhosis of the liver a couple of years before, and his brothers were still away in the forces. Annie felt rather sorry for Roger. It was sad not to have any family at all at your wedding, she thought. But Roger did not seem to care. Or if he did, he did not show it. He looked happy to have acquired a father as well as a wife.

Annie guessed from the slight swelling of Clara's belly under her smart blue suit that their first baby was already on the way. Afterwards, Frank took them out for a meal in an Italian restaurant in Charlotte Street where they celebrated over plates of spaghetti bolognese and a bottle of Chianti in a wicker basket.

Watching her big sister so happy with her new husband, leaning up against him and touching him at every opportunity, made Annie happy for her but very sad for herself. Every tender gesture between the newly-weds reminded her of the task that still lay ahead for her. Tommy had not come home but he had sent a letter telling her to expect him any day now.

The happiness of the young married couple did not last for long. Clara and Roger had set up house together in two rooms in Camden. Roger had regular work as a labourer, for there was much work to be done rebuilding London. For a while Clara seemed happy and settled in her new role as homemaker and wife. She would proudly show Annie some new curtains she had made on the old Singer which her mother had given her, or press on her a slice of cherry cake she had just baked that morning. But every now and then Annie would sense that under the show of domestic bliss there lurked something not so good. Sometimes she sensed that Clara was holding back some information about her new life as an adult, as if there was something too painful to talk about. Sometimes when Annie saw Clara and Roger together, she felt something unspoken and fierce hovering between them. At other times Annie simply did not like the sharpness with which Roger spoke to his new wife.

Back home, every evening, with Grace upstairs in bed, Annie and Frank ate their suppers in near-silence. There was nothing to be said.

Marion Banham was proving to be a good friend to Grace. She came almost every day to sit with her and talk to her. At first it was a monologue, but over the weeks there were sounds of a conversation taking place between the two women. It soon became clear that Marion was the only person Grace really talked to, but what the two women talked about, nobody knew. What did it matter? Annie agreed with her father that it was simply a good thing that Grace was talking to anyone.

With the war over at last, the men were returning home – the local boys Annie had been at school with were now coming back as men, hardened and brutalized by the grimness of warfare. Not a game, not fun, but a place where people died or were hurt and maimed. Brother Jack came home, too, a decorated hero. Apparently he had shown particular bravery and saved the lives of several of his fellow soldiers.

Jack had grown a lot since they had last seen him, now broad and strong, with lines on his face and a hard expression which Annie had never seen before, and it frightened her.

For his part, Jack was shocked to find his mother in such a state. He had been informed by letter of Bobby's death but having lost so many friends in the fighting, he had not really absorbed the tragedy of the news at the time. He was upset about his mother's condition but was equally upset to learn of Clara's marriage to Roger. 'She might have waited until I was home,' he grumbled. And when Annie suggested that there had been a certain urgency at the time (Clara was indeed to have a baby soon), Jack's gaunt face twitched. He said nothing.

The day after Jack's return, Clara came round to the house. Now heavily pregnant, she looked tired and drawn. She kissed her brother warmly on the mouth.

'Congratulations, Clara.' Jack was stiff but not cold with her.

Clara laughed, her lovely, deep, throaty laugh. 'Well, you know I only married Roger to annoy you,' she teased. And Jack had to smile. Then he hugged her tight.

'You'll come to like him, Jack,' said Clara. 'He's a lovely man, you'll see. He's got a lot of troubles, that's all, and it's not surprising after the way he was brought up in that family.' Then she smiled sweetly at her brother. Rather too sweetly, and for a second too long, thought Annie, as though Clara was having trouble convincing herself that her husband was a lovely man.

With the family gathered round Grace's bed, Jack unpacked his heavy backpack, pulling out all sorts of gifts from all over the world. He had beautiful silk jackets from Singapore which he had swapped with a mate in the navy for a German pistol he had captured. He held out a brilliant turquoise jacket for Clara. 'This was made for you,' he said.

Clara laughed and snatched the jacket from her brother's hands. 'It's hardly going to fit me while I'm in this condition but I'll try it on to see if the back fits!'

She pulled off her woolly cardigan and tried on the jacket. As Clara pulled on the silk sleeves, Annie noticed black and brown bruises all along Clara's upper arm. She was tempted to say something immediately but she did not. If anyone else noticed, they chose not to comment either.

Later that evening Annie sat on a stool in the sitting room, balancing a sketchbook on her knee as she did quick portraits of Jack as he sat talking to his father about his life over the past four years. Jack's descriptions of his experiences barely entered her consciousness as Annie sketched and shaded with rapid speed. Her thoughts were not on Jack or the war at all. They were on Clara and those bruises on her arms. It puzzled her that Clara did not comment on them, did not mention them at all. It puzzled her that Clara never complained about Roger hurting her. In fact, she seemed to go out of her way to boast about how kind Roger was to her, bringing her flowers and little presents when he came home from work. Perhaps she was wrong about how those bruises got there. Perhaps Clara had just had an accident, banged herself against the door, for instance. Annie reassured herself that nothing was wrong after all.

While Jack Turner thought about what he was going to do now that he had been demobbed, he hung around at home doing very little. There was plenty of female interest in him. Jack had always been popular with the girls. Even Tilly Banham confided to Annie one day that she found her brother 'irresistible'. 'He's so brave,' she rhapsodized, 'and so attractively aloof!'

Annie rolled her eyes at such comments. She felt uncomfortable about Tilly's interest in her brother. It seemed to change their friendship. Seeing Tilly's look of puzzlement, Annie smiled, but she felt a little sad. Whenever anyone alluded to love in any way, it just reminded her of the terrible task ahead of her when Tommy returned.

It was another six months and spring before Tommy did eventually return. He had been in North Africa and then stayed on in the army to fight in Palestine where his part in capturing some terrorists had won him a medal. All this meant that it would take much longer for him to return home. Tommy had written to say he was definitely on his way. 'I can't wait to look at your sunny face,' he wrote. Annie had felt pained by the innocent excitement in his letter.

Annie was out in the garden pruning the summer clematis which her father had planted for her three years before. It was a healthy, vigorous plant which produced a profusion of pale blue flowers each summer. Each spring, Annie cut back the plant right down to the roots, just as her mother had taught her in the days before Grace had lost all interest in gardening and given it up, along with everything else.

Annie was bending down over the flower-bed when she heard a shout. Turning round, she saw Tommy standing by the back door. Dressed in his khaki uniform, he had a broad smile on his tanned face.

'Annie,' he said. 'Here I am. Home at last!'

Annie jumped. She had been expecting and dreading this moment for so long. She thought she was prepared for it, having rehearsed it in her head many times over the past year. She was supposed to stand still and say nothing. The look in her eyes would be enough to tell Tommy that it was over between them. He would hesitate and then bow his head and leave in silence. The scene would be enacted without a word, like a silent film.

The reality, of course, was different. Tommy bounded across the garden with his arms stretched out towards her. 'Annie, my darling Annie!'

She could not help herself. Instead of standing firm, she gave in to her instincts. Letting out a little cry, she ran towards him and flung her arms around his neck. Their lips met in a long lingering kiss.

'Annie, Annie,' murmured Tommy. 'I've dreamed of this moment a thousand times.'

Annie shivered and buried her face in Tommy's chest. What a fool she was. A reprimanding voice started to order her around. She had to act now to save them both. She longed to prolong the kissing and the feel and smell of Tommy's strong body against her own. How easy it would be to have it that way, for just one more time. The voice began to order her to act and act soon. This was not supposed to have happened. Now she had messed up everything and made it all more difficult for both of them.

Her body longed to continue to lean against Tommy but her head suddenly cleared. She pushed herself away and smoothed down her hair.

'Oh, Tommy,' she said quickly, 'I do love you, I really do.'

Tommy laughed and tried to grab her wrists again. But Annie twisted her body round, away from his reach.

Now Tommy looked startled by her unexpected movement. Annie took another step back and looked him straight in the eye. The anguish in her face could not be missed.

'I do love you, Tommy,' she repeated, 'and this has nothing to do with you or anything you've done . . .' She twisted her hands together like a worried child. 'But it's finished between us, it has to be over.' Her voice cracked as she spoke these last words.

She stared at Tommy. He had to believe her. He had to know she was being serious.

At first Tommy laughed again, but the smile on his lips faded when she did not smile back. A muscle in his cheek twitched as his quick mind assessed the situation. Then he knew. 'It's over, isn't it.'

Annie dropped her head and nodded shamefully.

'But why? Tell me why.' Tommy suddenly looked angry. He shifted his weight from one foot to the other and placed his hands on his hips. 'Is there someone else?' he demanded. 'You'd better tell me about it now, if there is.'

Annie stared at him, still unable to respond. Now her head was racing with thoughts, with possible lies she could tell him to soften the blow. It would be easier for him if there were another person. She opened her mouth to speak but no words came out. She turned away.

For a few loaded seconds, Tommy stood facing her, his face twisted with confusion and disappointment. Then his expression suddenly changed, and he looked calm.

'Well, I'll go,' he said quietly. 'I'll go. This has happened to plenty of men before me.' He turned on his heels and began to walk back to the house.

As Annie lifted her head to watch him go, tears began to stream down her cheeks. Part of her wanted to shout to him, to tell him to come back and sweep her up into his arms. But that bullying voice in her head prevented her from doing it. She watched Tommy's back as he went, walking out of her life forever.

She picked up the garden fork and smashed it hard into the roots of the clematis, striking it again and again. The green shoots splintered and fell onto the earth.

'Damn you, Father!' she hissed, attacking the earth around the plant's roots and hacking at it relentlessly with the heavy garden fork. 'Damn you, damn you, damn you!'

CHAPTER 17

❦

Jack's Revenge

TO ANNIE'S RELIEF, TOMMY did not make any attempt to get her to change her mind. This did not surprise her for she knew how proud he was. In any case, too many of his army mates had been betrayed by their girls back home and he did not think he was any different. Obligingly, he stayed away from Annie and her family. Annie never even saw him in the street, though she purposefully avoided Leverton Street for several weeks.

Annie settled into a quiet way of life, going out to work and looking after the home for her parents. Grace needed a lot of caring now and was unable to do much in the house. Annie's spare time was taken up with housework and laundry. Occasionally she managed to get out to the cinema with Tilly, if there was a new film on at the local. She rarely had time for her painting now, though the truth was that she had lost much of her enthusiasm for it. That in itself made her feel deadened inside.

At some point Dolly informed Annie that Tommy had gone off to study law at university.

'Always was a clever boy, that Tommy,' Dolly remarked.

She peered at Annie. 'You used to quite fancy him, didn't you? You don't seem to be interested in him any more.'

Annie turned away. 'No, we've gone our separate ways,' she said, swallowing a hard lump in her throat.

Annie tried her best not to think about Tommy at all. She felt she had no right to be concerned about her own sorrow anyway. Clara was giving her far too much cause for worry now. In fact, over the months, Annie had become extremely concerned about Clara.

Clara had given birth to a baby boy earlier in the year. When the little fellow was born, Annie felt strange. Sitting next to her sister's bed in the hospital ward and holding the tiny baby in her arms, she was swept right back to the day of Bobby's birth when she had clutched Rabbit in her arms like this. Poor little Bobby, who had had such a short life.

Within two months Clara had declared that there was another baby on the way. It was difficult nowadays for Annie to get a chance to talk to Clara on her own and it was hard to know what was going on between her sister and Roger. Annie had the distinct feeling that Roger did not want Clara to spend much time with her family. He wanted her all to himself, away from the Turners. He even seemed to have lost his admiration and respect for Frank as a surrogate father. Indeed, Clara and Roger rarely came round to the house at Falkland Road and never invited people back to their flat in Camden, so Annie did not see them often. But when she did, she noticed that Clara frequently had bruises on her arms now, and once she even had one on her cheek.

This time Annie asked about it. 'I fell against the door,' Clara replied hastily.

One day Annie decided spontaneously to drop in on Clara on her way home from work. There she found her sister in a desperate state. It was only a few weeks before the next baby was due and Clara was enormous. Her clothes barely stretched across her huge belly. Ten-month-old Anthony had just gone down for a nap in his cot so the place was quiet.

It was also in a terrible mess. Clothes and toys were strewn all over the floor and dirty plates and dishes were piled up in the deep porcelain sink and on the sideboard. It looked as if Clara had neither the energy nor the inclination to do anything about her squalid surroundings. Annie was shocked.

Clara looked exhausted. Her face was puffy and her features seemed heavy and coarse.

'What's happened?' Annie looked around the room. 'Is everything all right?' she asked warily. Even as she spoke, Clara's face suddenly crumpled.

'Oh, Annie, I'm so unhappy.' Clara slumped into a chair and covered her tearful face with her hands.

Annie moved across the room to her and gently put her arms around Clara's shoulders. 'Why? Tell me, what's the matter?' she asked quietly.

It was several minutes before Clara was able to control her crying enough to speak. 'It's Roger,' she finally said into the palms of her hands. Her words were muffled. 'I just don't think I can take any more . . .'

For the first time, Clara began to talk about Roger. She told Annie that she thought she had made a mistake in marrying him. She revealed that Roger could never control his temper. He hit her whenever he was angry about anything, and humiliated her whenever he chose. He made her do things to him that she hated, and did things to her that made her feel degraded. She feared for the safety of this new baby inside her.

Annie listened in horror and growing rage at her brother-in-law. She did not know for sure what Clara was talking about at times, for she was not explicit, but she knew that they were intimate matters she need not enquire too closely about. It enraged her all the more. How dare Roger treat her sister in this way, and turn her from that brave laughing creature into this frightened person who did not know what to do! Her wonderful big sister, who had once wanted to grow up to be a mermaid. The exuberant Clara, who once pushed drawing pins into the soles of her shoes and tap-danced all the way down Kentish Town Road. All that spirit gone! Clara had always known what to do! What monstrous things had Roger done to her to make her so cowed?

Clara sat with her head in her hands. 'The worst of it, Annie, is that I still love him, even after all this. There is a soft side to him, a soft, almost frightened side to him, which no one knows about. I love him when he's like that, he's almost like a child. But it's been a long time now . . . he hasn't been like that for a long time.' Her voice tailed off. 'It's just as if sometimes something seems to snap inside him . . . It feels disloyal talking about him like this, but I have to tell somebody. And I know I can trust you not to tell anyone else about it.' Clara looked at her with a pleading expression.

Annie waited, dreading some new revelation even more shocking than the last.

Clara continued in a faltering voice. 'There are particular times when he's bad . . .' She coughed. Her words were drying up. Clara took a deep breath and started again. 'There are particular times – just sometimes – when Roger can't do it – you know – in bed.' Clara was blushing more than Annie as she blurted out the words as quickly as she could. She looked down at her knees; her fists were clenched tight. 'He is very demanding about it but he often can't do it. That's when he gets angry, so angry that . . . that's when he hits me . . .' Her voice was suddenly drowned by sobbing as she finally broke down. 'I know it's not really me he's angry at . . .'

Annie hugged Clara tighter as she sobbed into her hands. The two sisters clung to each other in silence for some minutes.

Then Clara began to speak again. 'Do you remember years ago when Mr Garcia's horse was hurt?'

Annie nodded. She remembered the combination of thrill and horror when they heard that someone had cut Juniper's private parts with a knife.

'Roger did that,' Clara said quietly. 'He told me just the other day that he did it.' She started to tremble, her voice breaking again. 'And he said he'd do the same to me too if I wasn't careful.'

Annie left Clara's house feeling shocked and churned up inside. Clara had sworn her to secrecy over what she had just told her. 'You mustn't tell anyone else. You see, I still love him, and I think he loves me too,' she added pathetically.

Clara did understand her husband but she overestimated her ability to help him. She knew that no one had loved him as a child and she had tried to make up for that loss. But Roger was too damaged to be helped. He had never seen how a loved one might be treated. In a home where the only physical contact was a belt around the head, he learned that any frustration was dealt with by violence. It was only when he was in the very best of moods that he could ever meet love with love.

The promise to keep Clara's words a secret left Annie feeling hopeless. She longed to help her sister, to make her life better, but she did not have the faintest idea of where to begin. Everything seemed so grim. Here was her sister so unhappy and trapped in a marriage with a cruel and dangerous husband. Annie's own unhappiness about Tommy seemed minor by comparison. Besides, that was all in the past now. Tommy had long ago gone off to law school, his fees met by the army in payment for his contribution to the war effort. He had climbed onto a train and gone out of her life forever. There was no other young man in Annie's busy life but at night in her dreams she was back in Tommy's arms, loving and kissing, laughing and cuddling. Many mornings she awoke with her cheeks wet with tears at the bitter-sweet memories she had shored up inside her.

Although he was by all accounts a cruel man, Roger did love Clara as much as she believed he did. He loved her as much as she loved him. But sometimes she made him angry, and when she made him angry he could not help hurting her, hurting somebody, or something. He could not stop himself lunging out at her, wanting to strike, to stamp her out, to show her that he was the boss. He did not like to sense that she was defying him, or that she was stronger than he. It was a rage that took him over, causing his jaw to lock and his eyes to become blurred. Ignoring Clara's cries that he would hurt the baby, he would go on, wanting to penetrate and overpower her. But then often, too often, his flesh would fail him. He could sense the sudden softness rising up through his otherwise rigid body. The rage burned even hotter inside him. He had to keep it burning.

When this happened, he pulled Clara roughly by the shoulders and rolled her over onto her belly. Knowing that it was pointless to struggle, Clara let her body go limp as he manoeuvred her into the position he wanted. Her eyes squeezed back tears as she bit into her fist, fighting the urge to scream.

Roger pushed into her. Now she could not stop herself crying out. He was in. There was no softness now; the weakness had vanished. This was the only way, the only way to release the rage that burned in his gut.

Then he was a boy again, lying on his stomach, his head pushed up at an angle against the wall. He was Clara, she was he. It was his whimpering he could hear in his ears as a heavy dark shape pushed into him from behind. Deep inside. He could feel the fumbling hands on his skin and smell the sour odour of beer as it crept around his neck.

His brothers slept in the next room. His father, the brother of the man who took over Roger's body, lay in a drunken stupor on the kitchen floor. His father did not stop what was happening. He could not, he did not. He did not care. And no one heard Roger's stiff cry for his mother – the only person in the world who might have protected him. For she lay buried in the grassy graveyard up the hill.

Roger did not want to hurt Clara and he could not bear to hear her cry. He was always sorry after it was over. But he could not help it. He had been the chosen one, picked out by his uncle as special. He was special. It was his fault. It was Clara's fault.

After her conversation with her big sister, Annie felt very anxious and upset. She felt she ought to be doing something to help Clara, to protect her just as Clara used to protect her when they were little. But what could she do? And since Clara had sworn her to secrecy she could not ask anyone's advice about what to do, either. She felt powerless.

One day she decided to make a batch of mince pies for Christmas. Spending the morning in the kitchen in the comfortable company of Tilly lifted her mood. By midday, they were ready to go out and distribute the pies around the neighbourhood. This was something Grace Turner had done for years until her arthritis and the war had made it too difficult to continue. It had been Annie's idea to start doing it again, and this was the first Christmas they had done it since the war had ended.

The mince pies were still warm as Annie and Tilly gently packed them up, nestled six at a time into brown paper bags. The girls enjoyed making them, measuring out the flour and fat, mixing the greasy crumbs between their fingers and into the bowl, kneading the dough and then cutting out the pastry in small precise circles to fit into the pie dish. They did not talk much as they worked, both preoccupied with their own thoughts. Tilly indulged herself with fantasies about Jack, while Annie worried about her sister.

Wrapped up against the cold, Annie and Tilly set off from home to visit the old people, handing them a branch of holly and a bag full of warm mince pies.

One of the recipients was old Mrs Anderson who lived in Leverton Street opposite the house where Sally Brown had once lived. As they passed Sally's house, Annie had a quick wistful memory of her talks with Sally on the doorstep so many years ago. How simple life had seemed to her then!

Mrs Anderson had been widow for many years. A short barrel of a woman, she was well into her eighties and now toothless and fairly deaf.

'Come on in, my dears,' she said, shuffling ahead of them into her front room. The air was heavy and airless. A musty smell curled around the nostrils. A small coal fire burned in the grate.

'I don't get many visitors nowadays so I hope you'll have a cup of tea and keep an old lady company for a short while.'

The old lady was dressed in a green woollen dress under a floral pinafore. She wore thick brown stockings and slippers which revealed the outline of her misshapen feet. Dark food stains ran down her lumpy front. Long grey hairs grew out of her chin and her fingers were swollen and crooked from arthritis. Annie noticed them straight away. They were worse than her mother's.

Mrs Anderson let herself down in an armchair with a deep sigh. 'Oh, my rheumatism is playing me up right terrible today. Don't get old, darlings, it's no fun.'

Annie and Tilly politely sat on the sofa, sipping tea from greasy cups and nibbling seed cake. Delighted to have willing ears, Mrs Anderson talked to them. In a rasping voice she talked and talked about the old days.

Each time Annie or Tilly said something, she would peer at her through her spectacles. 'Eh, what's that?' She

screwed up her wrinkled face and cupped a hand over her
ear. 'You'll have to speak up,' she said. 'My hearing's not
what it used to be.'

Tilly explained that they had made a batch of mince
pies for her, for Christmas. 'We've made them for several
people around here,' she added.

They stayed for a while talking to the old lady. Her
memory was quite good but occasionally she lapsed into
confusion and was not as lucid as she first appeared. At
one time she started talking about her friend Amy Horder.
'Had a cup of tea with her the day before she died, I did,'
she said. 'Terrible shock, that was.' She leaned forward
conspiratorially. 'Her son Danny's not quite right in the
head, you know, but you mustn't tell Amy. She won't have
any of it. Thinks he's perfect, she does.'

Annie and Tilly exchanged glances.

'What did you say your names were?' Mrs Anderson
slurped her tea and nibbled her biscuit, dropping crumbs
down her bulky breasts.

'Anne Turner and Matilda Banham,' replied Tilly.

'Turner, eh? Are you related to that Ada Turner what
used to live in Falkland Road . . .'

Annie was about to say that Ada Turner was her
grandmother when Mrs Anderson interrupted again.

'She really was a one, that Ada,' continued Mrs
Anderson, her thoughts drifting. 'She stole my young man
from me, she did, and I never forgave her for that . . .'

She was warming to her theme. 'Well, she was a right
one, that Ada. No shame, that's what I said at the time and
what I say now.'

She sucked her toothless gums. Her watery eyes
sparkled with the memory. She looked animated. 'Well, of

course, it came back to her. You can't behave like that and get away with it . . . I got my own back, I did.' She chuckled quietly. Then she paused and narrowed her eyes. 'Well, you're too young to remember any of this, you must have been little kids when it happened . . . I've seen a lot in my time, all the comings and goings in this street. I always knew what was going on.' She tapped the side of her head. 'Nothing misses me, I can tell you. Like there was a young woman over there, see.' She indicated a house across the road. 'A low-class sort of girl, if you know what I mean . . .' She leaned forward and whispered, 'A prostitute, she was.' She spat out the words primly.

It slowly dawned on Annie that she was talking about Sally Brown.

'Well, the young lads in the neighbourhood used to visit her, creeping in at all times of the day or night. She used to entertain them all, she did. Disgusting, it was.

'Well, that young woman got her come-uppance, too. Murdered, she was. Strangled one night.'

Annie sat on the edge of her chair waiting for the old lady to say more. Then she prompted her. 'What boys? Do you remember what boys?'

Mrs Anderson was well into her stride. 'Well, I told the police about seeing Ada Turner's grandson there – I can't remember his name. But he used to go in there a lot. He got into big trouble.' She smiled in quiet satisfaction to herself.

'Were there other boys that night, too, then?' Annie was trembling with excitement and afraid that her interest would be obvious.

'Well, yes, come to think of it, there were . . .'

Mrs Anderson hesitated. 'Well, I suppose it can't do any harm now, it was all so long ago. Just water under the bridge now. Yes, me own great-nephew was there that night.' She paused and then added, 'But I didn't tell the police about him. You wouldn't, you see, because blood is thicker than water. Not that he would have done what they said was done to that girl. He was a naughty boy but not bad. No, he was kind, always kind to his old aunt, he was. He used to take me to the street parties what they used to have round here each year.

'Now, I know that you two nice girls wouldn't say anything to cause me any trouble, would you? Not that it matters. I know Roger would never hurt anyone. He used to be a good boy to me, not that I've seen him for a long time, not since before the war started. I heard he was back and got married, but I don't keep in touch with his family, you know – troublesome lot, they are, a bunch of no-goods, they are.'

Finishing their tea, Annie and Tilly escaped into the street. After the hot clingy atmosphere in the old lady's room, the air outside felt deliciously fresh as it hit their faces.

Annie gripped Tilly's arm. 'Did you hear what she said?'

Tilly shook her head. 'It doesn't mean anything,' she said. 'The old lady is so senile, she's probably got her memories all mixed up.'

'No, she definitely said she chose not to tell the police about her great-nephew. She wasn't mistaken.'

Annie felt both excited and frightened. It was terrifying to be plunged back into that nightmarish time just after Sally was murdered when everyone was convinced that Jack had done it.

The girls delivered the last batch of mince pies to Maudie Sprackling.

Maudie opened the door. She looked radiant. Her eyes

sparkled and there was a fresh bloom to her face. Maudie had been married three months now. The married state clearly agreed with her.

She thanked the girls for the pies and hesitated in the doorway. 'I have to tell you something . . .' She glanced left and right. 'I just have to let you know, because you've always been good to me, that Arthur and I, well, we're going to hear the patter of tiny feet . . .' She smiled at them coyly, waiting for a response.

Annie threw her arms around Maudie and hugged her. 'Oh, Maudie, how wonderful!'

Maudie hugged her back. 'I've got more news, too, about Jessie. Jessie's found herself a nice young man and she too is to be married. She's made up with her family, too. Her mum approves of Ken and thinks he'll make a good son-in-law.'

'So Jessie and William will be moving out?'

Maudie nodded. 'Yes, they're going to rent a nice little house in Islington. There'll be plenty of room for William, and any other little ones that happen to come along . . .'

Afterwards, they set off for home. 'I always thought Maudie couldn't have children,' said Tilly.

Annie shook her head. 'That's what everyone used to say. Now it seems that it must have been Mr Sprackling who couldn't have the babies.'

Tilly nodded. 'You know, Connie Smith was always hinting that it could be him who was to blame. I could never work out how she knew that. After all, she didn't have any children with him, either. How would she know it wasn't her?'

Annie was silent. Loyalty to her father prevented her from telling Tilly, her best friend, the truth about Tommy.

She had lied to Tilly about her reasons for breaking off with him. 'I've just gone off him,' she had said; she did not feel it right to reveal the family secrets to anyone.

Her mood fell and she found herself thinking of Jessie and the day she and her father had seen Jessie in town on the arm of a disreputable-looking man. She had guessed for some time that Jessie had been on the game, before she got her job at Daniel's and became more respectable.

But now Jessie was going to get what she wanted – a nice husband to take care of her and William. Annie thought sadly of her conversation with Sally Brown all those years ago. Poor Sally, who longed for a home and a husband and ended up strangled. How different life might have been for her if she had met a nice young man at the right time. Both Maudie and Jessie were getting what they wanted in the end. Yet she, Annie, could never have what she wanted. Connie's conversation with her father had seen to that.

Tilly sensed her friend's gloom. She had no idea that it could be connected to Connie in any way. 'Well, the big question now is are you going to tell Jack what you learned today from Mrs Anderson?'

Annie shrugged, a look of despair on her face. 'Am I going to stir things up? Things that are better left undisturbed? I don't know if my family can take any more.'

'Yes, but just think, if Jack's name can be cleared once and for all – and some people around here still like to believe that he was guilty . . .' Tilly sounded urgent. Her passion for Jack was evident.

'Yes,' said Annie, 'but you have to remember that Roger is part of the family now. He's married to my sister. He's the father of her children. It's not simple at all . . .'

*

Jack was not at all pleased to hear the news.

'I wish you'd never even told me,' he said to Annie. He had been brooding on the information all morning ever since his sister had quietly told him what the old woman had said. They were out in the garden dismantling the Anderson shelter with their father. Frank had gone off to buy a rake for the new lawn he was proposing to sow. As usual, Grace was sitting in a sad state in her bedroom upstairs.

'I've put all that behind me,' said Jack. 'It was a mistake. The police saw that straight away. There was no harm done and I don't want to think about it any more.'

Annie stared fiercely at him. 'How can you say there was no harm done? Sally Brown was murdered. You call that no harm done? She was killed and the person who did it was never caught. Now it looks as if your own sister could be married to the murderer. Don't you care?'

Jack shook his head. 'Of course I care, Annie. But you don't know if what Mrs Anderson said is true. And even if it is true, there's no evidence that Roger killed Sally Brown. Roger could simply have been leaving the house, just as I was.'

'Yes, but the police still ought to know, don't you think?'

Jack shrugged. 'I don't know,' he said wearily. 'I don't know if I want any of that business stirred up again. It was bad enough at the time – there was a lot of bad feeling which still exists, I think. I often think that people think of me as someone who got away with it, from remarks and looks I get sometimes.'

'That's not true!' exclaimed Annie. 'Nobody thinks that. They know you were innocent.'

'Maybe,' said Jack flatly.

'But if Roger is the one who killed Sally Brown, then we should care that he's married to Clara. He might hurt her . . .' She hesitated as she remembered her last conversation with Clara. She was tempted to tell Jack about how badly Roger did in fact hurt their sister. But she had been sworn to secrecy.

'Of course I care about Clara,' Jack said sharply. 'But it's precisely because they're married that I'm reluctant to do anything. Do you want Clara to be a grass widow? Do you want her children to be without a father?'

Annie felt as if all her energy was draining out of her. 'I see,' she said quietly, hanging her head.

Jack could see that he had disappointed Annie. 'I'll sleep on it,' he said. 'Let me have a think about it. It's hard to know what to do, especially since the only thing that's actually happened is that a senile old lady has said something about an event that took place years ago. It's hard to act on hearsay.'

Jack did sleep on the information and he did not do anything. In fact, he did not mention it at all until the day Clara came round to Falkland Road with Anthony, a swollen face and a black eye. In a choking voice, and with tears flooding her blue eyes, she blurted out to both Jack and Frank that she could not take it any more. She was afraid for her and Anthony's safety and had had to run away.

As Annie and Frank comforted Clara and tried to clean up her face, Jack took himself down to Clara's home in Camden. He found Roger asleep on the sofa, in a drunken stupor after a visit to the pub.

Jack lunged at Roger's sleeping body and yanked him to his feet. He pulled his arm round in a half-nelson and charged him towards the wall where he banged his head again and again. 'I'll teach you to hit my sister!'

Momentarily stunned and confused, Roger staggered and stumbled. But then he woke up, suddenly alert as he realized what was happening. All his instincts as a street fighter, sometime leader of the Torriano gang, were unleashed. He let out a great roar and spun round, locking himself into a tight hold around Jack's body.

The men tussled and fought for several minutes, falling about the flat, smashing furniture. Roger was bigger and heavier than Jack and at first seemed to have the advantage. But Jack was nimbler and more agile, and concentrated on trying to get a firm grip to pin Roger down.

As they fought, the people who lived in the other flats in the building slowly emerged from their doors to see what the noise was about. Someone ran for the police. Others gathered in the doorway to watch the spectacle of the two men fighting.

Jack and Roger were unaware of the spectators who were crowding around the door. Over and over they rolled, punching and kicking when they could. Finally Jack got the upper hand. He managed to manoeuvre himself into a position sitting on Roger's back with his arms in a full nelson. Roger's head was wedged against the wall and every now and then Jack pushed him up against it hard, squashing his face with brutal strength.

'Leave my sister alone,' Jack hissed into Roger's ear. 'You touch her again and I'll kill you.'

'That silly bitch deserved what she got.' Roger was defiant.

Jack rammed Roger's face up against the wall. Roger cried out in pain. 'I don't want to hear you say that!'

'She should watch her tongue,' Roger blurted out. 'It was her own fault. She asked for it. She's just like the rest of them, all bitches, all castrating bitches.'

'You mean like Sally Brown?' Jack threw it in.

'Yeah, just like Sally Brown, the stupid bitch. Well, she really got what she deserved. I got her.'

As he spoke, they could hear the sound of heavy boots on the stairs. Two constables appeared, pushing their way through the small group of onlookers at the door.

They pulled the men apart and took them both down to the police station to sort them out. When Jack told the police sergeant that he had new evidence that could solve the Sally Brown case, the sergeant sniffed. But when one of the men who had witnessed the fight from the door confirmed that Roger had indicated that he had hurt someone, or worse, the policeman took more notice. They decided to take up Jack's suggestion to question old Mrs Anderson again after all these years.

CHAPTER 18

Grace

THE AMBITIOUS YOUNG DETECTIVE at Kentish Town Police Station was excited by this unexpected new lead in the Sally Brown murder case. Although it had happened over eight years before, the case had never been closed. And while his more cynical colleagues warned him that it was more than likely to be a groundless accusation motivated by a family feud, as was usually the case in Kentish Town, he felt that Jack's suggestion was worth taking up.

Although old Mrs Anderson did indeed have a failing memory, the detective suspected that she was pretending to be more senile than she was. After some clever friendly questioning, the young man – who had considerable charm when he needed it – got her to admit that she had indeed seen someone else leave Sally Brown's house on the night of her murder, and that that person was in fact her great-nephew Roger.

This information was enough for the detective to arrest Roger and pull him in to the police station again for questioning. He had grave doubts about whether the case would hold since he had good reason to believe that the old lady's memory would conveniently fail once she realized what trouble her great-nephew was in. But he need not have worried. To his astonishment, after a night in the cell and half a day of heavy grilling, Roger broke down and confessed to Sally Brown's murder. He told them that he had done it because she had laughed at him and humiliated him when he found himself unable to make love to her. He remained without remorse for what he had done. No man would put up with a woman laughing at his sexual prowess. 'Would you?' he asked of the young detective, confident that he would win himself some sympathy. He was wrong.

Roger continued to confess his guilt. He was a broken man. He had no fight left in him. Every night while awaiting trial he cried for his mother.

Six months later he was sent to prison for twenty years for the murder of Sally Brown. Each night the pubs of Kentish Town were packed with people discussing the merits of the case and the morality of Jack's actions. A surprising number thought that he had done wrong.

'He could have let sleeping dogs lie, that's what I say. She was only a prostitute, after all.'

'Well he's gone and made a grass widow of his own sister and made those kids fatherless. I wonder if he thought of those consequences beforehand.'

'Yes, it's not really done, not round here, it's not. Roger's own family is right done in. There weren't no need for it, really, not after all this time.'

'And it sounds as if the woman did deserve it, if she really did what he said she did.'

'What I can't believe is that young Jack ratting on his own family.'

'Yeah, you'd think he could have just kept quiet about it.'

'Well, you know that family always have been a bit hoity-toity, always thought they were a cut above the rest of us.'

'Yeah, just because they had a bit more money than most.'

'To be fair, you have to admit that Frank is a good man . . .' Someone felt he had to put in a good word.

'Well, it was that wife of his. She always did think she was better than the rest of us.'

At Falkland Road, the atmosphere in the house was even heavier than usual. Grace had found strength with which to castigate herself.

'It's all my fault that this has happened,' she sighed from her bed. 'Perhaps if we had moved away to a better neighbourhood, our children would never have got themselves mixed up with ne'er-do-wells like this. Bobby wouldn't have died and Clara wouldn't have a husband in jail, our grandchildren wouldn't be fatherless. It's all my fault. I should have insisted that we move away.'

'Don't say that,' said Frank. 'It's too easy to blame Kentish Town. Nobody could have helped any of them. Nobody could have stopped Bobby dying and we certainly couldn't have stopped Clara marrying Roger. You know the girl's got a mind of her own. And you certainly mustn't blame yourself. You have enough of a burden to carry on your shoulders without adding to it. Please don't castigate yourself.' He grasped her by the shoulders. 'I'll tell you what,' he said urgently, 'I'm going to start looking for another house for us to move to, like I said we would. We can get away from Kentish Town, up the hill, to Highgate or Muswell Hill, if you like. What do you think of that? That'll make you happy, won't it, my darling?'

Frank had tears in his eyes as he tried to sound bright and enthusiastic. But he knew his offer was too late.

Grace shut her eyes and sank back with a sigh. 'It doesn't matter any more, Frank. I just don't care any longer.'

In spite of her husband's reassurances, Grace chose to add to her burden of sorrows. The weight quickly proved too much for her. She really did seem to give up on life. She stayed in her bed and for much of the day lay motionless, facing the wall. She would spend perhaps an hour a day writing in her journal, and Marion Banham would come in to visit her in the evenings. Her strength seemed to be seeping from her. She ate little and was listless. She grew thinner and thinner. Everyone understood why: she had nothing left to live for.

Annie was desperately worried about her mother's health and hurt that she could do nothing to cheer her up. Nothing she said or did could bring even a flicker of a smile to her face. It was as if she did not matter to her mother at all. Annie would lie in her bed and cry herself to sleep like a little child. She felt so lonely, meaning nothing to her mother and cut off from Tommy, the one person she loved without reservation.

Jack had had enough. One day he announced that he was heading off for Australia, to make a new life there. His parents were shocked and saddened and Frank pleaded with him to change his mind. 'It'll break your mother's heart,' he said.

But Jack was adamant. 'Mother's heart is broken already,' he replied. He had bought his ticket and was sailing in a fortnight.

The night before he left, Jack knocked on Annie's bedroom door. She was in bed reading.

'I hope you understand why I have to go away,' he said. Even in the soft flattering light cast by the bedside lamp, his face looked tired and drawn.

Annie put down her book and smiled. 'I think I do,' she said. 'Things are difficult here.'

Jack sat down on the bed and took her hand. 'I don't want you to think I'm abandoning you all.'

Annie shrugged. 'But you are . . .' Her voice tailed off. She fiddled with the edge of her eiderdown where some threads had become loose. She could feel tears trying to spill into her eyes but she concentrated hard on the fraying material and pushed the tears back.

Leaning forward, Jack lifted her chin with his forefinger. 'I want you to understand that I have to leave this place. If I'm to make a proper life for myself I have to go somewhere completely new, somewhere I'm not known, somewhere I can't be reached.'

'But Australia's so far away.'

Jack nodded. 'Yes, but there are more opportunities out there, as well as lots of space.'

Annie lifted her head and looked straight at him. 'Don't you care about us, Jack? Is that why you're going?'

Her brother looked away. His voice cracked as he spoke. 'Of course I care, Annie. I care about you all very much. I worry about Mother. I feel guilty as hell about Roger, and I can hardly bear to see Clara in the state she's in. I keep thinking it's all my fault. And it is. I just have to get right away for a while. It may only be for a couple of years, it may be more. I feel I have to get away to sort out exactly what I do feel about myself and the family. Once I know, I'll be able to come back and not feel swamped by it all, as I do now.'

Annie could not hold her tears back any longer. 'Just keep in touch, please,' she sniffed.

'I promise,' replied Jack. 'And perhaps you'll come and visit one day.'

When Annie kissed her big brother goodbye the next day, she had a feeling that she would not be seeing him again for a long time, if ever. She did not cry. She was beginning to feel a hard, bitter core inside her that had no room for tears of any sort.

Tilly Banham cried for a whole day for her unrequited love. But then a few weeks later she met an amorous GI who in no time had helped her forget about Jack Turner.

Hank Jackson was a handsome, stocky fellow with a crew-cut and a loud laugh. He met Tilly at a tea dance in Bloomsbury where she and Annie had gone one Saturday afternoon. The dance hall had been packed with GIs returning home from the war and Annie had hated every minute of it. She had not wanted to go anyway and she had a headache brought on by the hot smoky atmosphere. But Tilly was having the time of her life, and was being unusually exuberant. It was almost as if something had been released in her to allow her to be suddenly vivacious and outgoing. Whatever it was, she caught Hank's eye and won his heart. He quickly set out to win hers.

After that tea dance, Annie hardly saw Tilly at all, for they had both stopped working and Tilly now chose to spend her free time with Hank rather than Annie. Annie was happy for Tilly but it seemed that she was losing everyone who had ever been close to her. She began to feel sorry for herself.

Living is always a kind of battle in which there are only so many blows a person can take before they lose the will to fight on. Then the body takes over, dropping all the defences that have protected it until then. Perhaps Jack's leaving was the final blow for Grace Turner. A few months after her eldest child had gone, Grace developed bad pains in her belly. But she ignored them and endured them without a word until they were too excruciating to bear any longer. Frank took her to the doctor who informed him flatly that his wife had an advanced cancer and that there was little that could be done. 'It probably wouldn't have made any difference if you had brought your wife in earlier,' he said. Then he added that Grace probably had a few weeks left. In fact, Grace was dead within the week.

Annie did not cry. It was for the best. Grace had had no life to speak of for years. And now she would be out of her suffering. It could only be a good thing.

Her father was distraught at the loss of his wife. He shut himself up in his study for three days, drinking himself silly with a large supply of whisky.

The funeral was held at St Benet's Church up the road. There was not a huge turnout. The bad feeling that had been created by Roger's arrest and imprisonment was stronger than any goodwill felt towards Frank. Grace had never been one of them, and no one was grieving for her apart from her family and her good friend, Marion

Banham. Jack was not there either. Frank had sent him a telegram at the address he had given in Sydney. But they never heard from him so they did not know if he got the message or not. But most of the closest neighbours did come, even if they did not make a big show of it. Annie saw Mrs Garcia and Mrs Whelan standing at the back of the church. But they did look as if they were there out of obligation more than feeling. There were not many tears.

Afterwards, Clara and Annie had prepared the house for sherry and sandwiches. More people dropped in then, more, it seemed, for Frank's sake than to pay their respects to Grace. No one said anything but Annie could sense the coolness these people felt towards her mother. She felt it in the way they looked around the house, peering in the rooms and scrutinizing the furniture and decorations. Well, Grace had rarely invited people in, so they were in their rights to have a good look now. It was not surprising. Grace had made little effort with them and she had hurt their feelings.

Dolly Pritchett popped in for a brief time. She looked tense and uneasy as she settled her bulky frame on the edge of a chair and knocked back a glass of sherry without pausing. 'You all right, then, Frank?' was all she said.

Mr Spratt came in from next door, too. He looked much the same as he always had, perhaps a little thinner. However, he was almost completely senile now. He wandered around the rooms talking to himself. 'My wife's come home, you know,' he repeated over and over again. 'She's just gone up the road to visit some friends. I can't think why she ever left me.' He shook his head plaintively.

'Don't know why she left. I cooked her some dinner and she never came home to eat it. My wife's come home, you know . . .'

Marion Banham was there, warm and smiling as she helped pass food around. 'You're lucky to have such lovely daughters, Frank,' she said. Clara was there with Anthony and Lizzie, now aged two. And Tilly was there, too, now full of excited talk of Hank Jackson who wanted her to cross the ocean and marry him in the United States of America. She did not know what to do, and Annie certainly couldn't advise her.

It was a heavy, tense day. After the last visitor had finally gone, and Clara and Annie had cleared up the front room, Frank began to drink hard. Tumbler after tumbler he filled with whisky which he then gulped down with scarcely a moment's hesitation. Then he became maudlin and talked at length about the old days when he and Grace had been a courting couple.

The night wore on. Clara's babies had been put to bed hours before, and now Clara decided to turn in. She had moved into the house the week before, just after Grace had died. 'To keep you all company,' she said, but it was clear that she did not want to go back to her dismal flat in Camden which still smelled of Roger in every corner. Clara put her children to bed and retired upstairs herself.

Frank sat slumped in the armchair staring into his lap. He was motionless.

Clearing up the glasses and plates, Annie glanced at him. 'Are you all right, Dad?' Her voice was soft. She walked over to him and knelt down. Then she placed her arms around his neck just as she used to when she was a little girl.

Frank burst into tears. He tried to cover his face with his hands as he sobbed uncontrollably.

Annie did not move. She stayed still and quiet, her arms around her father while he wept.

'Annie, my darling, I'm so sorry,' he cried.

'Shh . . .' Annie whispered.

'I'm so sorry for all this mess, and all these terrible things . . .'

'Don't say that, Daddy,' Annie reassured him. 'It's not your fault that anything has happened.'

'Yes, it is, you just don't know . . .' Frank's words were drowned by his crying.

Annie was horrified to see her big, strong father in tears. It frightened her to see him showing such emotion. She had to get him to stop. She ran her fingers over his face and hugged him. 'Please don't,' she whispered, 'I can't bear it . . .'

As she spoke, she began to cry herself. She couldn't help herself. Everything had welled up inside her at once.

Frank was hugging her back. 'Don't you start,' he said, smiling at her through his watery eyes. He kissed her temple and Annie buried her head in his shoulder.

Suddenly she was aware of her father's hands on her arms, then on her chest, running over her breasts. He was holding her firmly.

She pulled away, astonishment on her face. 'Dad!'

As she spoke, Frank pulled her face down towards his and kissed her hard on the mouth. Then he rubbed his rough face against her cheeks.

Annie recoiled. 'Daddy, stop! What are you doing?' She pulled herself away and jumped to her feet. 'What are you doing?'

From her greater height she looked down at the pathetic broken face of her father looking up at her, his tearful blue eyes now full of shame.

'How can you do this to your own daughter?'

Frank could barely speak. He mumbled something and more tears flooded his bleary eyes. 'Oh, I'm sorry, Annie. I'm sorry, so sorry. I didn't mean it. Jesus Christ, you must hate me!' He covered his face in his hands and started to sob again, loud racking sobs which made his whole body shudder.

Annie stared at him. 'What is the matter with you? What are you doing?'

Frank lifted his head once more. He swallowed hard and composed himself as much as the alcohol in his body would allow. 'I'm sorry, I shouldn't have done that in any circumstances.' He said nothing more for a moment or two and then he said it: 'But I have to tell you something more. I have to tell you that you are not my daughter . . .'

Annie frowned at him. 'What are you talking about?'

'I'm not your father,' repeated Frank. 'Your mother left a note for me to open after her death. She says I'm not your father. No more, no less.'

'I don't believe you.' Annie stared at him, waiting for him to tell her it was a joke.

But he did not. 'It's true, Annie. I wouldn't make up such a thing. In other circumstances I might not have said anything about it at all. It wouldn't really have mattered, not at this stage in anyone's life. I've brought you up as my daughter, and you are in my eyes my daughter and always will be. But I have already done you an injustice by destroying your friendship with Tommy.'

Annie turned away. 'Why are you bringing up Tommy?

He's got nothing to do with anything,' she said bitterly.

'Well, he does, Annie.' Frank spoke softly, grabbing her wrist. 'Because if you're not my daughter, then you are free to marry Tommy. If that's what you'd like to do.'

Annie was silent. 'It's all a bit late for that,' she said angrily. 'You destroyed whatever chance I had for that a long time ago.'

Frank winced. 'It's not my fault, Annie,' he said quietly, 'but I am sorry.'

'So who is my father then, if you're not?' Annie glared at him angrily.

Frank shook his head. 'I don't know,' he said. 'Your mother wrote the briefest note just stating that fact. It didn't say anything more.'

Annie thought about her mother sitting in bed or reclining on the sofa writing in a journal. 'Mother's journal!' she exclaimed. 'Where's her journal? She was always writing in it. There must be a clue in there . . .'

'I don't know where she kept it,' replied Frank. 'I only ever saw it when she was writing in it.'

Annie opened the door. 'I think I know.' She closed the door and quickly ran upstairs.

Moments later she was reaching up into the wardrobe and the top shelf. As she did so, it brought back flashes of the past, of the many times she had snooped in this room over the years. But since her mother had become an invalid and remained in her room, she had not had the opportunity to have a look.

There was nothing there. Annie had been so convinced that the journal would be there next to the other secret thing in her mother's life that she was shocked when it was not. And disappointed.

But it was worse. Not only was there no sign of the journal but the brooch was not there either. Annie tore off the tissue paper wrapped around the christening gown, and rummaged all around the box and the rest of the shelf. But the shelf was empty. Both journal and brooch had vanished.

CHAPTER 19

❧

The Confession

IT WAS MARION BANHAM who produced both the brown diary and the brooch the next day.

She arrived on the doorstep at Falkland Road and handed Annie a bag. 'Your mother gave these to me when she knew she had no time left. She told me to give them to you in person, the day after her burial. She wanted me to make sure you got them.'

Marion's expression was grave and sympathetic. 'Your mother loved you very much, you know. She wanted you to know that.' She reached over and touched Annie's arm with her hand. Giving a quick smile, she turned and left.

Annie was shaking as she carried the bag upstairs to her room. She shut the door and sat on the bed. For a few minutes she did not move. Then she opened up the bag. Inside was a small red box and the large brown notebook.

Annie quickly looked inside the red box. There, settled on the nest of tissue paper, were the familiar diamonds and sapphires of the brooch. She felt a strange rush of old feelings go through her.

With trembling hands, Annie opened the notebook.

It was three quarters used, filled with writing in her mother's hand – thin and delicate but sometimes suddenly uncontrolled in patches when the writing went spindly and untidy. Grace had struggled to write in the diary even on days when her arthritis had been bad and made writing painful.

Annie riffled through the pages, forwards and backwards. Her heart was racing and her mouth was dry. She hesitated. Could she take any more secrets now? Her father's revelation the night before had caused her to have a wakeful night, turning over confused and muddled thoughts in her head at an exhausting speed. Her sensibilities had been knocked so many times recently that she felt almost too numb to care about anything. Nothing could surprise her now. She was powerless to do anything about the truth anyway. What had happened, had happened and nothing she could do would change the facts. What more could she possibly learn that would make any difference?

She swallowed. There was more to learn, of course, and it might make a difference. If Frank's outburst the night before was based on a truth, then perhaps this journal would reveal who her real father was.

Whatever misgivings she had, Annie knew that she had to read the journal. Swallowing back a deep feeling of dread, she curled up on the soft eiderdown, opened the notebook, and began to read:

My darling Annie,
I want you to know from the start, before you begin to read this journal, that I love you very much and always have. What you are about to read will no doubt change

your view of me forever but I hope it won't make you
hate me. I hope that by the time you have finished reading, you will understand what happened and why it
happened. And I hope that having that understanding
will enable you to forgive me.

I know that I am going to die soon. I don't know if I
am doing the right thing in telling you the truth but I
hope you will be strong enough to allow me to release
my conscience before I die.

This is the truth, Annie. I am ashamed to say that I
have lied to you in the past – perhaps you guessed that
at the time. But whenever you have questioned me about
why I am in possession of a valuable brooch that I never
wear or use for my own purposes, I have been too
stricken with panic to be truthful. I was afraid of saying
the wrong thing which would be wrongly interpreted
before I could explain. This way, at least, I can get it all
down. You can read this account or explanation as
many times as you want, and then you can think about
it in your own time.

In my worst moments (and I have many of them), I
think that you have every reason to hate me and to curse
me for the rest of your days. But when I'm feeling
strong, I believe that our lives together and my love for
you will have made an impression on you enough to
withstand the blow I am about to inflict on you. I know
you are a sensitive girl with the ability to imagine what
I was like twenty-two years ago and not so much older
than you are now.

You have always been interested in the diamond and
sapphire brooch ever since that day it fell out of the
wardrobe when you were reaching for Bobby's christening

gown. I still remember that moment with the same horror I felt then! I evaded your questions about it then, and more recently I did worse. In the hope of satisfying your curiosity and stopping your questions, I lied to you about why Camilla Pearson had given me the brooch. I don't know if you believed me then but I know I didn't feel convincing at the time. You haven't mentioned it since or asked me anything else but I don't know what that means.

Now I am going to tell you the truth, dear Annie. I can't face telling you in person. I shall be gone when you read this and I'm sorry if there are any more questions left unanswered. I shall try to cover everything – I owe you that, at least.

As you know, my parents were employed by Camilla's parents, Colonel and Mrs Heathcote. The Heathcotes were kind people who took seriously their responsibilities towards the community they lived in. They paid for new labourers' cottages in the village, for instance, to house young married couples who could not otherwise afford accommodation of their own. They also donated land for a sports field and paid for the building of the pavilion on it. And they were always exceptionally kind to the people they employed.

My parents lived in a tied cottage on the Heathcote estate. My father managed the farm for them while my mother, who was a quite well-educated woman and half-French, taught French to the three Heathcote children when they were small. There were twin boys, Piers and Hugh, and one girl two years younger, Camilla. She was my age.

As small children, we often played together in the

grounds, but when Piers and Hugh were sent off to boarding school at the age of eight, Camilla was particularly glad to have me as a playmate and we spent quite a lot of time together. As I said, I always liked the Heathcote parents. They were unfailingly friendly and generous. But their children were different. They knew they were privileged and they thought they were better people because of it. Now I'm afraid that it was a failing in the parents that must have made their children think this way, though I did not see it at the time. In spite of their superior attitudes, I quite liked Piers and Hugh. There was a good side to them. By contrast, I always found Camilla bossy and sometimes unkind. But since I was an only child, I was also happy to have someone to play with, so I went along with what she wanted. She could be overbearing and mean, even as a little girl. Once she made me eat a worm we had found under a stone. She ordered me to eat it, saying that my parents would be thrown out of the cottage if I did not do everything she said. It was pathetic, but I believed her. I can still taste that worm in my mouth to this day.

As we grew older, we saw less of each other. Camilla soon developed a crowd of riding friends and then she, too, went off to boarding school when she was twelve. After a time, we had nothing in common at all. Tragically, both the boys were killed in the Great War. I remember the terrible heavy air of tragic loss hanging in the house for months on end. Camilla was the only one left.

After going to finishing school, Camilla married a lawyer several years older than herself. She had a huge reception in the grounds of the house with three hundred guests. Soon afterwards, I married your father, whom I had met through a family friend. We had a more modest party. How lucky I felt to be with Frank!

I was very much in love with Frank but I was sad to leave Sussex and move to London. I have never got used to the dirty air in London and it was also so far away from my parents. My father was not at all well with a bad heart, and not so long afterwards he died – just before Jack was born. The Heathcotes were exceptionally kind to my mother. They paid for my father's funeral and assured her that she could stay in the cottage for as long as she wanted. They had sold off the farm soon after the war and the cottage wasn't needed by them or their staff at the time.

After Jack, Clara came along quite quickly. Camilla had not produced any children, which was a worry for her parents, who were elderly by then. My mother often sat and read to Mrs Heathcote in the afternoons, and it was the old lady who said that Camilla's husband, Robert Pearson, was desperate for a son and heir. 'A lot of nonsense,' she had said to my mother. 'He should be ready to be parent to any child, whatever the sex, but at this rate it looks as though he won't have that privilege.'

On the occasions when I visited her, my mother would fill me in on all the latest talk from the big house. I remember her telling me that Camilla had been consulting the Queen's gynaecologist and that there was a great concern that she might not be able to have babies.

Once I met Camilla in the grounds when we were both visiting for the weekend. I was walking with Jack and Clara and introduced them. I never forgot the pained look on her face – it was almost a grimace – as she looked down at the babies I was showing off so proudly. I did feel sad for her then.

A year later, everything changed suddenly. First Colonel Heathcote died and his wife followed soon after. Camilla inherited the house and estate. Soon afterwards, I learned that I was going to have another baby, and my mother informed me that Camilla had recently announced that she was expecting. It has always struck me as sad that her poor dear parents did not live to hear the news or to see the birth of a grand-child. And if they had, how differently things might have turned out!

Sadly, my own dear mother died when I was eight months into my pregnancy. I arranged the funeral in the village church. There was a good turn-out, for my mother had been popular in the village. Even Camilla came, which I appreciated at the time, but I think it was only because she wanted to talk to me afterwards. She was looking blooming as she awaited the birth of her child.

After the funeral, when most of the mourners had left, Camilla asked if I would clear my mother's belong-ings out of the cottage as soon as possible because she had recently appointed a married couple as staff, and she preferred to have them living in the cottage rather than in the big house.

I was rather shocked and distressed by the speed at which she asked me to do this. I had hoped that she would wait until after I had had the baby. But I was in no fit state to protest, and it's not in my nature anyway, so I agreed. I said I would go down and sort it all out the following week.

As it turned out, it was an extremely difficult time for us back home. Your father had just started a new job at the piano factory and he was unable to take time off work. Fortunately Dolly kindly agreed to look after Jack and Clara while I went back down to Sussex to sort out my mother's affairs.

The journey down was exhausting to me in my condition, though I was fortunate to be healthy throughout the time that I was expecting. That helped me get through the ordeal. I was more than a little annoyed to find that by the time I got there, the cottage had already been cleared out and all my mother's belongings had been pushed into the carriage house. I was upset not to be able to pick through the things myself and hurt by Camilla's insensitivity at such a time, but I reminded myself of how kind Camilla's parents had always been to me over the years, and decided that was what counted most. Life had changed. One era had passed and another one had begun.

Camilla was apologetic and charming about what she had done and she invited me to be her guest in the big house. Everything was in turmoil: her husband was away in London and the new housekeeper had suddenly become ill with influenza. It seemed that most of the neighbourhood was down with it and I was worried about catching it myself. Camilla said she had hired a temporary maid from an employment agency to help in the house. She kept complaining about the expense and I remember thinking that her mother would never have complained in such a way.

I sensed that Camilla was glad to have my company, just in the way she had when we were children. I was better than nothing. Her confinement was closer than mine; in fact her baby was due the following week. We were both easily tired, but I have to confess that just a short time away from the demands of my little ones seemed to restore quite a bit of energy in a short time, even after a day of going through my mother's things.

We ate supper together both nights. I remember being struck by the way Camilla talked about her baby, referring to it constantly as 'he'. I thought at the time it was sad that her desire for a son was so blatant. Although her husband had been anxious for her to have the baby in a maternity clinic in London, Camilla had insisted on having it at home in Sussex with the family doctor in attendance. 'Dr Potter's father delivered me and my brothers,' she said, 'and I want Dr Potter to deliver my baby.'

In the middle of the second night, I awoke suddenly knowing that my baby was coming. I managed to ring the bell for the maid, who came and told me that Mrs Pearson had also gone into labour soon after going to bed. The district midwife was on her way. They had telephoned for Dr Potter but learned that he was in bed with influenza and unable to attend.

My labour was extremely short. By the time the midwife had arrived, the baby, a boy, had already been born. Although he was nearly three weeks early, he was well-formed and a good weight. He gave no cause for concern at all. The midwife checked that the baby and I were all right and then got the agency maid to clean us up while she concentrated on assisting Camilla, whose labour was longer and more difficult.

The third time round, it seemed so easy. I felt calm

and relaxed. I settled back in bed with my new baby and drifted in and out of sleep.

When I awoke in the morning, I learned that Camilla had given birth and that all was well. She had had a little girl.

The midwife checked over the babies and mothers for a second time and declared everyone fit and well. She said that she would probably be back the next day to check on us, and to fill in the registration papers. But with any luck, she said, the doctor would be well enough to come himself. I remember that she seemed a bit confused about who was who. She was new to the area and quite a young thing. I think it was her first job, and the idea of two babies being born on the same night in a private house was overwhelming to her.

Later that day I was in my room worrying about how I was going to get in touch with Frank to tell him the surprising news, when Camilla appeared carrying her baby in a shawl. After my initial elation, I had begun to feel a bit fuzzy-headed. The birth of the baby, coming so soon after my mother's death, suddenly took its toll. I certainly could not think straight, and I felt completely helpless and incompetent. I could not imagine how I was ever going to be able to get back to London and my family. I was feeling close to not coping at all.

Holding her baby, Camilla sat down on the end of my bed. She was looking wild-eyed and nervy. Then she burst into tears and started to talk in a choked voice. She told me that she was desperately upset not to have a boy and that she was scared for her marriage. She kept rubbing her brow and frowning, and she kept telling me over and over again how lucky I was to have a boy. I was lucky to have a boy and a girl already, she told me, so the sex of this third baby had never mattered at all. 'Can you imagine what it's like,' she cried, 'to want something for so many years and then get exactly the opposite?'

I began to feel sorry for her. She was right, I was lucky to have a boy and a girl and not to care about the sex of the next. But I don't think I ever cared very much either way about whether my babies were boys or girls. All I cared about was that they be healthy. But Camilla's words began to eat into me until I began to feel guilty for having what she envied me for. It was a strange feeling which I had never had before. In the past, I was the one who envied Camilla.

She said that the doctor had telephoned earlier to say that he would be coming that evening to visit both mothers and babies. Camilla paused for a few seconds and then she told me what she wanted to do. The reason she had come into my room was to ask if I would consider swapping the babies.

The tears had gone when she spoke, looking me directly in the eye in the way she always did. 'We could exchange babies and no one would ever know,' she said.

I was horrified at such a suggestion and I told her so. It was a barbaric and ridiculous idea. But now Camilla had started to cry again, as if she could not cope with my refusal. I had hardly ever seen Camilla cry and I found it disturbing. Camilla went on and on about her fears and how miserable she was not to have a baby boy. She talked about her beloved brothers who had died and how her husband had wanted a son, how much she wanted a son. She went on and on until I wanted to clap my hands over my ears to shut out her voice. Then she began to remind me of all the kindness her family had shown to my own parents. On and on she talked until I could bear it no longer. I was worn down. She was right, they had always been so kind to my family. I owed it to them to be nice to theirs. I felt sorry for her. And I wanted to help. I was completely overwhelmed. I could not withstand the pressure she was putting on me. I had never been able to stand up to her when I was a girl playing games with her, and I couldn't stand up to her any better then.

To my shame, Annie, I gave in. I finally agreed. I thought I would go mad if she did not leave me alone. She wore me down. She made me feel guilty for having exactly what she wanted and didn't have. Dear Annie, I am crying as I write this because it is the hardest part of the letter. I am reminded of what I did not only to you but also to my baby son. But it was the only way to stop her tormenting me. So I did it. I gave in. I agreed to swap my baby for hers. I handed over my boy and took her baby girl, you.

The moment I agreed, I knew that there was no going back. Camilla looked delighted. The moment she held my baby in her arms she seemed to be revitalized. She assured me that as long as we did not breathe a word to any one about what we had done, no one else would ever know. She had worked it all out. It was just her good fortune that the housekeeper was ill and that the only staff in the house was the temporary maid who was due to go that day, with a replacement arriving later. No one would ever be aware of anything untoward having taken place.

There was no going back once I had agreed and there

was certainly no hope of going back once we had lied to the doctor about which baby belonged to whom and signed all the necessary papers. No, there was definitely no going back. The deed was done. This terrible sin bound us together forever.

Camilla was happy to send a telegram to Frank in London to inform him of the birth of his second daughter and that mother and baby were well. I remember thinking at the time that for someone who had just had a baby, she had a frightening amount of energy.

When Dr Potter came to the house, he only knew that two babies had been born in the night. You were duly registered as my child, and the boy presented as Camilla's son.

Soon after the doctor had gone, Camilla's husband arrived from London to take his son and heir into his arms and celebrate. While a delighted Robert Pearson held his son and talked about his plans for the future, Camilla took me aside and kissed me on the cheek. Then she slipped a diamond and sapphire brooch into my hand. 'I'll be grateful to you forever,' she whispered into my ear. 'It's worth a lot, that brooch.'

Camilla was glowing with happiness. Everything had worked out perfectly for her. Extraordinary chance and a fair bit of natural guile had enabled her to get exactly what she wanted.

I returned to London with you in my arms. Frank borrowed a car and motored down to Sussex to collect me. By the time he arrived, I had already convinced myself that I had given birth to a girl, that you were mine. It was the only way, you see. I knew that if I were to live with this lie, I had to convince myself from the start that it was true. It is remarkable what you can make yourself believe if you have to.

And I did, I think. I did fairly well. I always, always thought of you as my child, my daughter. Away from Sussex, it seemed possible, especially now that my mother was dead. I had no reason to go down there.

For the first few years it was easy. I simply forgot about the circumstances of your birth. But then, inexplicably, I lost two babies in succession. Those deaths seemed too terrible not to have some meaning. Slowly the deed began to gnaw at my insides. At first it was just the occasional twinge but gradually over time it grew and grew to monstrous proportions. I fought against the notion that those dead babies were punishments for what I had done, but it was hard. When I started to get the symptoms of my rheumatoid arthritis I began to feel that I had poisoned myself with my deeds.

And, of course, however hard I tried to throw off such thoughts, there was always a reminder, a link with Sussex and my terrible misdeed in the form of the brooch, my payment. I stuffed it into the top of my wardrobe as I could never bring myself to touch it. I could neither wear it nor sell it. It seemed wrong to benefit from it in any way.

Then Bobby was born and everything seemed wonderful again for a while until my health got worse and then, of course, Bobby was taken away from me, my precious replacement boy. There is nothing I can say to describe the pain I feel about Bobby's death. And I know that I am largely responsible.

My conscience has burned for the past few years. My greatest regret is that I cannot go back in life and do things differently. I have felt tormented. I have felt so cut off and remote from you children. I was living a lie which grew to an unmanageable size.

The Reverend Richardson was helpful to me over the years. It was originally his suggestion that I reveal the truth to you; to lift the burden off me. He told me he thought it was your birthright to know.

I don't know if he was right, dear Annie, and I'm sorry that he passed away and is not here to talk to you about it. He was a wise man. Marion is also wise, and she will always be willing to talk to you if you need someone to talk to. She has been a good friend to me and a strong person. Watching her cope with the problems they've had in that family makes me feel that Marion would never have given in to Camilla as I did. That realization makes me feel worse, because for many years I had convinced myself that I had no choice, that anyone would have done what I did. Now I know that if I were a different character I might not have been so weak.

Apart from Marion and the priest, no one else knows. Frank does not know the truth. It is up to you, Annie, to tell him or not. But remember that if you tell him, he may want to search for a son he never had. It is a terrible burden and I'm sorry to place it on you. It was my weakness a long time ago that is responsible for all this now.

I shall be leaving you the brooch to do with what you like. I have never known what to do with it. I could never abide the sight of it but I could not get rid of it, either. I am leaving it to you because it will mean something to you, though that meaning will be different.

Perhaps after all you will be able to benefit from it in some way. It is worth a lot of money and should give you a start in life.

I know that I am not well. Over and above my arthritis, I feel there is something wrong with me and that it is serious. I feel such sadness looking at the state of the family as I shall be leaving it, with Jack now thousands of miles away in Australia, Clara married to a murderer and alone with her babies, however adorable they are, little Bobby in his grave . . . Poor Frank, abandoned by his happy wife many years ago. And now you, dear Annie.

I want you to know that I have always thought of you as my daughter, whatever my private agonies, and that my love for you is as strong as a mother's love can be. Although I regret what I did, of course, if I had not done it, then I would not have had the pleasure of having you as a daughter. And I would regret that.

I hope you will forgive me and that you find happiness in whatever it is you choose to do.

PS: At the end of this notebook you will find some photographs. They are of happier days to show that I was different once. I was happy with myself. Please remember, though, that I have always been happy with you. M.

That was the end of the writing. About a quarter of the pages remained clean and untouched. Annie turned to the back of the notebook. On the inside cover there was a small pouch with three photographs inserted into it. She pulled them out and laid them before her.

There was a grainy picture of her parents she had never

seen before. They both looked so young, standing close together with their arms around each other and smiling directly at the camera. Frank's curls were thick and dark, while Grace's fair hair was tied back in a French plait. Her lips were dark with lipstick. Annie could see now how much Clara looked like her, with her rangy limbs and strong, well-balanced features – widely spaced eyes, broad cheeks, full lips and small chin. It could almost be Clara standing there. There was also a photograph of a baby, a standard studio shot. On the back was written: 'Anne Turner aged six months'. Finally, there was one of Annie aged about eight. She had a page-boy haircut, and was wearing a dark tartan skirt, white blouse and a Fair Isle cardigan. On her feet were the Clarks sandals which she remembered so well. She was holding Rabbit and beaming into the camera.

'Oh, Rabbit,' Annie sighed, as she gathered up the photographs and slipped them back into the pouch at the back of the notebook. 'Oh, Rabbit, I wish we could go back and start again.'

Annie closed the notebook and stared at her long fingers spread out over the brown cover. She could hardly take in her mother's words. Her thoughts swirled around her head like leaves in the wind. She was not her mother's daughter. She was not her mother's daughter. She was not her father's daughter. She was nobody's daughter.

Annie felt battered by wave after wave of shock. She had barely absorbed the information her father had given her the night before. Mother was not her mother. Yet she was her mother, she was the only mother she had known. She had not grown inside her body as Jack and Clara had done. She had been born to a woman who had promptly rejected her just because she had been the wrong sex. It was not personal. It should not matter, but it did. Deep inside her a terrible wound had been inflicted on her for nothing. But this at last was the truth, and the whole truth. Now it all made sense – the brooch, the parentage.

Annie opened the journal again and gazed at the open page. She let her eyes slip out of focus, allowing her mother's writing to swim before her in a blurry haze. Her whole life seemed to pass in front of her eyes, with everything slipping into place as if by some pre-ordained pattern.

Now she understood all the mysteries of her childhood. She knew now why there had been that hint of sadness in her mother's dark brown eyes all the time. She winced at the thought that it was her very presence that was the cause of that sadness. Annie was a constant reminder of what Grace had done.

Now she also understood why she had been so different from the others, why she had a small, angular and delicate body instead of the strong athletic frames of Jack and Clara. Now she knew why she was tone-deaf when everyone else had a sharp musical ear. Now she understood why Mrs Pearson had made that puzzling remark about Tommy not being good enough for her when she and Tommy had gone down to visit in the middle of the war. Everything about her past was suddenly clear.

It was also very confusing. She just did not know who she was any more. A few years ago she had been Annie Turner, third child of Frank and Grace Turner, and for a while, the girlfriend of Tommy Smith, the boy who lived down the road. Then everything changed. First she was no longer Tommy's girlfriend; she was his half-sister. Just as she tried to get used to that idea, she learned than this was not, in fact, true after all. She was not Tommy's half-sister, as she had been told. Now she had learned that she was not the sister of Jack and Clara, either. Or that she was not the daughter of either Frank or Grace but of a man she had never met and a woman she had met only once in her life.

She could go back to being Tommy's girlfriend (if it was even possible) but only at the cost of her very identity. For who is anyone if not in relation to other people?

Annie certainly did not know what to do now. More responsibility had been heaped on her. Should she tell her father? Should she show him the diary? Deep down, she did feel that Frank remained her father, even though her real father was a dead lawyer she had never even met.

She did want to talk to someone, to ease the pain and the pressure. But she was also scared to. If she started talking, she might start something she could not stop. How could she talk to anyone? No one had ever told her anything until it was too late. Wasn't that a lesson to her now? It was impossible to make any decision about what to do except to decide not to act at all. That way, the information she had just learned could at least be kept under control, for a while.

CHAPTER 20

Beginning Again

IT TOOK SIX MONTHS for Annie to decide anything. When Frank cautiously asked if she had finished reading her mother's diary, Annie had simply said yes and ignored the questioning look in his eye, the look that begged her to tell him what had been in Grace's diary. 'I have finished, and it's private,' she had replied, unnecessarily sharply, she thought afterwards.

Since the night of her mother's funeral, relations between Annie and Frank had been strained. Frank was still ashamed of his behaviour and waited for Annie to forgive him. But she remained stiff and cold with him. They ate their dinners in silence and conversed about little. Annie did the housework and went out to work. Although she functioned enough to apply to art schools and get herself to interviews, she felt that she might as well be paralysed, so incapable was she of deciding what to do. Certainly she had ceased all sketching and painting. She had not picked up a drawing pad for weeks. When she was offered places at two art schools, she was unable to decide even then what to do. She did not want to reply to either, and then finally, after requests from the institutions themselves for an answer, she wrote to say that she was turning down their offers. No, she decided, perhaps she ought to forget about studying art and just stay at home and look after Frank and the house.

She also felt sad on the day of Tilly's departure for America, off to the New World to marry Hank Jackson, who was waiting for her on the other side of the ocean. Marion was quiet that evening, sad that her only child had chosen to live so far away, but she was philosophical about it. 'I believe people should do what they feel is right for them,' she said.

And even though Marion knew the truth and perhaps was waiting, hoping, for Annie to turn to her for advice, to become a surrogate daughter to her, Annie felt unable to do that. Perhaps one day, but not for a while yet.

Then Camilla Pearson's letter arrived. Soon after Grace's death, Frank had sent a death notice to Camilla Pearson, who had replied with a polite note of condolence, which Frank had not even bothered to show to Annie. Six months later, Camilla Pearson wrote a letter to Annie herself.

Annie's hands were trembling as she tore open the envelope, staring at the bold, confident handwriting. It was eerie to think that this was the handwriting of the woman she had been born to.

The letter was brief but intriguing. Camilla was inviting Annie down to Sussex again. 'Now that the war is over, certain developments mean that we have some matters of mutual interest to discuss.'

It was too tantalizing an opportunity to miss. Annie telephoned Mrs Pearson and arranged to catch a midday train the following Saturday.

It was a hot, steamy day with little breeze. The train was slowing down as it approached Pulborough Station. Annie had combed her hair and given her nose a quick powder. Peering at herself in the mirror of her compact, she hoped she looked more composed than she felt. It was an extraordinary journey. Here she was on her way to meet the mother who was not her mother, the woman who gave her up at birth simply because she was not a boy.

How different this all was! How different she felt this time! Last time, travelling down with Tommy, Annie had been excited by the prospect of learning the truth about the brooch. Now, six years later, she knew the truth about the brooch, and much more. There were no more secrets to be had, at least she thought there were no more. Perhaps in fact there were. Perhaps the final knots in the tangled thread were ready to be untied at last. What could the matters be that Camilla Pearson wanted to discuss? Annie's curiosity had, of course, made her respond to Camilla Pearson's request. She was also nervous about seeing Camilla again and seeing her in a new light. Knowing what she did now, she was not sure how she would behave towards her.

All her thoughts and feelings were topsy-turvy. She did not want to go but she also had a deep urge inside her compelling her to go. Go on, find out! A voice whispered constantly in her head. At last it will be over. Go, go!

She was met at the station by the chauffeur who led her into the big black Riley parked outside in the station forecourt. Annie sat on the beige leather seat at the back of the car staring out at the lush green foliage of the hedgerows and fields rushing by. The sun was hot. Hazy heat rose from the tarmac of the narrow roads. Annie's mind felt both full and blank. She did not know what to expect yet she dreaded what lay waiting for her.

The car swept into the driveway and took the side road down to the cottage where Annie's grandparents had lived for most of their lives. Camilla Pearson was standing by the front door. She was wearing a blue and white paisley dress and brown shoes.

'Hello, there,' she called. Two black labradors ambled over to Annie, pink tongues hanging out, as she stepped out of the car.

Camilla strode over and grasped her hand. 'Welcome,' she said. 'Have you had a good journey? How good to see you again.'

Camilla led the way into the sitting room of the cottage where she offered Annie a chair.

Camilla Pearson had changed considerably in the years since Annie had last seen her. She looked much older and thinner. Her hair was now grey and the eyes had sunk into their sockets. With her slightly drooping mouth, Camilla's once handsome demeanour had given way to a forlorn and sad expression.

'I was sorry to learn that your mother had passed away,' Camilla said, offering Annie some tea.

'It was mercifully quick,' replied Annie, repeating the words she had heard so many times from other people's lips over the last few months.

Camilla talked about the house. 'The army has left at last,' she said, 'but I have to say that they have left the house and grounds in a disgraceful state. I shall get some compensation, I hope, but it's going to be quite a struggle to restore it to the way it was.' She paused and stared out of the window. 'It needs so much doing to it.' Her words were hardly audible. 'I don't know if I have it in me now . . .'

Her eyes were suddenly glistening with tears. She turned to Annie, her lips pressed together in an unnaturally tight line. 'You know that my son Julian died . . .'

Annie shook her head. 'No, I'm so sorry, I didn't know.'

Camilla raised her hand. 'It's been over two years now. He was killed in his first week of training for the RAF. It was an accident, a stupid freak accident. The pilot who was training him had a heart attack while they were in the air. He had been perfectly fit up until then. Julian, unfortunately, was not experienced to control the plane in such an emergency . . .'

She sighed softly and turned back to look out of the window, into the gardens beyond the cottage. 'He was only eighteen. He was going to inherit the place, to bring it back to its former glory. We would have had parties on the terrace again, dances in the ballroom.' She smoothed her hair with the palm of her hand. 'It was going to be the way it used to be . . .'

Annie shook her head. 'I'm sorry,' she repeated.

Camilla turned to her now, her blue eyes staring intently at her. 'Anne, my dear, I have something to tell you which I know will be a terrible shock to you . . .'

Annie waited. She had decided earlier that she would not let on that she knew anything until she had to. She wanted to hear what Camilla had to say.

'The fact is, my dear, you are my daughter. I am your mother.'

Annie stared at her silently.

'We swapped, you see, your mother and I. I so dearly wanted, needed, a son because my husband had been quite desperate to have someone carry on his family name.

There were no other men in his family, you see. Your mother didn't mind. She already had a boy and a girl and she wanted to help . . . She was the kindest creature, you know.'

Camilla was talking fast now, almost gabbling, as though disconcerted by Annie's blank expression.

'It was good of her, very good of her. Grace was a good person, she always was . . .'

Suddenly Camilla broke down. A deep sob erupted in her throat and she hid her face in her hands. More sobs followed, her shoulders shook uncontrollably. 'I've lost my son and you've lost your mother, or the person who brought you up . . .' she added quickly. She raised her head. 'But you are my daughter, my real daughter, and now you can come and be mistress of this estate. I want to welcome you as my daughter and have you come and live with me here. I can promise that life here will be much more comfortable that what you're used to.'

She paused, waiting to see Annie's response.

Annie's nervousness had vanished. Now all she felt was a hard core of anger rising up inside her. 'I am not your daughter,' she said.

'But what I have just told you is true . . .' Camilla interjected.

'Oh, I know it's true to some extent,' replied Annie. 'In fact, I know it's true because my mother had already informed me . . .'

'She did?' Camilla looked surprised.

'She did, yes, because she loved me. She told me everything, all about how you bullied her into swapping babies.'

'That's nonsense!' Camilla sat back in her chair and frowned. 'That's unfair. Your mother agreed quite readily.

And she never changed her mind about it. She could have . . .'

Annie shook her head to silence her. 'You may have given birth to me but you're not my mother. My mother brought me up and loved me for being me. She was tormented by what you did, by what you made her do. You are only interested in me now because Julian has died and you want someone to take over your responsibilities. You said so yourself. Well, I'm not interested. I'm not your daughter.'

Camilla stared at her for a moment and then rose to her feet. She came over and placed a hand on Annie's shoulder. 'Dear child, please forgive me . . .' Her eyes were brimming with tears again. 'I'm so unhappy, so lonely.'

For a moment, Annie nearly gave way, nearly relented. But then she visualized her mother's journal, and the agonized expression of her mother's torment. 'My mother was unhappy, too,' she said quietly. 'For many years she was unhappy, and all because of you. I find it hard to say this because it goes against the way my mother brought me up, but you deserve to be unhappy. I don't want to have anything to do with you. Now, I'd like to go. There is nothing more to discuss. I'd like a lift to the station. I'll wait there for the next train back to London.'

The train home took a long time. Some children had dropped a boulder on the line from a bridge so there was a long delay at Horsham. Annie did not mind. While the other passengers sighed and rolled their eyes impatiently, Annie sat in the corner of the compartment lost in her own thoughts which raced about her head.

It was early evening by the time Annie had arrived back

at Victoria. By then she had decided what to do. She caught the Tube home and, with her jaw set in an expression of sheer determination, she marched round to the Smiths' house in Leverton Street.

First she knocked on the door, then she banged on it. No one was in. She knocked again.

Mrs Whelan opened her door and stepped into the street. 'There's no one home. The older folk have gone to the bingo in Camden, and Connie went out about half an hour ago.'

Annie nodded and thanked her, only slightly irritated by Mrs Whelan's busybody ways. But with her earlier intentions foiled, she felt deflated. She walked home dragging her feet. She felt almost overwhelmed by a sense of gloom and despair. She felt she would seize up if fate dealt her another blow.

As she walked in through the front door, she was surprised to hear the unfamiliar sound of laughter coming from the kitchen. She could hear her father's deep voice, animated and excited, and a woman's, a familiar woman's voice. It was Connie Smith.

Frank and Connie Smith were sitting at the table having a cup of tea. The remains of a seed cake lay on a plate before them.

'Why, it's Annie, my dear.' Frank leaped to his feet and hugged Annie tight.

Annie stiffened. She was unable to respond naturally to anything. She nodded hello to Connie.

'Connie made me a delicious cake.' Frank lifted the plate towards Annie. 'There's plenty left. Help yourself.'

'No, thank you.' Annie poured herself a glass of water from the tap.

'We've been talking about the old days, haven't we, Connie?' Frank laughed at Connie. 'We go back a long way, don't we?'

Connie laughed. 'We do indeed. I can't remember when I didn't know your father. How's your day been, then?'

Connie smiled at Annie in a kind way. She was the way she had been on that day when Annie had come over to see the mice with Tommy, warm and friendly. She was not at all cold in the way she had been since she didn't want Annie seeing Tommy. With her sparkling eyes and red cheeks, Connie was looking pretty.

'It was all right,' grunted Annie. 'But I'm tired. I'm going upstairs.'

As she climbed the stairs to her room, she felt a mixture of rage and relief. How could her father be laughing and joking like that so soon after her mother's death? How could he sit in Grace's kitchen and banter with Connie as though he did not have a care in the world. How dare he?

But as she walked into her room and shut the door, a voice inside her challenged her. Why shouldn't he? Why shouldn't he have some fun after all these months of misery? Months? Why, it had been years of misery for him. Everything had been so grim for such a long time, she should be glad that there was a change in the air.

The sound of the piano rose up the stairwell. Nobody had played the piano for years.

First there was music, her father playing so deftly, his fingers running lightly over the keys. Then she could hear Connie singing along in a lovely clear, pure voice that reached up to the top of the house. Then her father joined in, singing with Connie, his deep, rich voice circling and joining Connie's in the duet.

It was a lovely sound which took Annie straight back to her childhood. She lay on her bed listening. She suddenly felt a great weight lifting from her. Her father had a right to be happy. He also had the capacity to be happy. And if being with Connie made him happy, then she, Annie, would accept that. She realized then how much she loved him and how little all the recent revelations had really changed things.

She sat up suddenly. That was right. Nothing had really changed. Even if Grace and Frank were not actually her parents, her feelings for them remained the same. She loved them very much. She also loved Tommy very much, as much as she always had. And she, too, had a right to be happy.

Leaping to her feet, she went to the window and stared out at the view across London. The music from the hall was loud and constant, uplifting and exuberant at the same time. The view across to the Kent hills was for once clear. Annie's thoughts were suddenly very focused. Everything had fallen into place. She knew exactly what she had to do.

She went downstairs to ask Connie for the information she had wanted before.

The next morning Annie caught the bus down to Camden Town.

Clara was at home in her flat, to which she had returned some months before. She looked tired, and the children were running noisily around her feet.

'I can't stay,' said Annie. 'Here, this is for you.' She thrust a small package into Clara's hands. 'It's worth a lot of money. Sell it and get yourself a nice place to live. You need it more than I do.'

Clara was speechless as she opened up the paper to

reveal the diamond and sapphire brooch twinkling in the palm of her hand.

Annie reached over and gave her a great hug. 'I've got to dash,' she said. 'We'll talk about it when I get back . . .'

Hurrying away, Annie slapped her hands over her eyes. 'Please, God,' she prayed, 'please bring my big sister back.'

An hour later, Annie was sitting on a train again, this time heading for an address in Bristol which Connie had given her that morning. Tommy was going to be surprised to see her, she was sure, but she was also sure that he would be glad.

The train rolled along with a comforting clackety-clack, clackety-clack. Once again Annie thought of her mother's diary and what the revelations in it really meant to her. Her mother's voice in that diary had been strong and direct. Her mother had still existed right up until the end, even though for years she had faded away to almost nothing. She was still a person with thoughts and feelings, and love and hope.

Annie thought of her family and the happier times of her childhood. She pictured her mother smiling gently, bent over her sewing, while Clara and Frank sat at the piano playing their duets. She pictured the many family meals around the kitchen table, sometimes fraught, sometimes full of laughter, but always safe and containing.

She thought of Tommy, whose origins were, as it now turned out, so similar to hers. Was that why they had been drawn to each other in the first place?

Of course, Tommy did not know about his origins. Connie did not want him to know. Frank did not know about Annie's either. She had not yet been able to tell her father the truth. Telling him the truth would mean telling him that he had had a child, a son, he had never known.

Clackety-clack, clackety-clack. The train thundered on towards the west. Annie stared out at the green fields racing past, the hedgerows and trees, the hills in the distance, the cows and sheep standing mournfully in the meadows. If she wanted to stop with any one scene in front of her, she could not. The train was beyond her control. She would not say anything to Tommy, and she would not say anything to her father, either. It was not for her to pass on anything. But Annie knew that she could not control these things. Secrets work their way up to the surface, however long ago or however deeply they were originally buried. These secrets were no different, and would no doubt work their way out at some time in the future too.

But in the meantime, she was not going to let secrets spoil her life. She would push them to the back of her mind and only look forwards from now on. She was going to write back to the art schools and see if they still had a place for her. If not, she would reapply next year. Frank did not need looking after, and even if he did, it wouldn't be for her to do it, not now.

She sat back and breathed a soft sigh, letting her body roll gently to the rhythm of the train. There was Annie Turner, a pretty young woman going to meet up with the man she loved, a light smile on her lips, an excited sparkle in her eyes. For that moment, at least, she was ready for anything.

The Cry of the Children

For my siblings,
Simon, Mark, Jane, John and Adam

Do ye hear the children weeping, O my brothers,
  Ere the sorrow comes with years?
They are leaning their young heads against their mothers,
  And *that* cannot stop their tears.

from 'The Cry of the Children' by Elizabeth Barrett Browning

PROLOGUE

London's Kentish Town in the late 1960s. A place of change and social upheaval. One hundred years before, the Midland Railway cut a heartless gash through he area, across the playground of St Luke's School in Islip Street, dividing one part of Kentish Town from another and cutting off the whole of Kentish Town from the green, open spaces of Parliament Hill and Hampstead Heath.

For one hundred years, the railway industry smothered the streets with filthy sooty air, mucky debris from the steam trains and shunters' yards in Kentish Town and in Camden Town, just down the road. Large, drifting particles of soot blackened the bricks and windows of the Victorian terraced houses of this north London village which, before the trains, had been regarded as a healthy country retreat for city dwellers. The railway made the winter air a thick yellow, the summer air a choking grey.

During this period, people who could choose generally shunned Kentish Town, preferring instead the leafy sub-urbs or the fresher villages of Hampstead and Highgate further north.

Now it was changing. In the 1960s, a decade after the steam engines had been replaced by electric trains, and the clean air legislation prohibited the burning of coal fires in domestic grates, the air was clearer and cleaner. Young professionals who could not afford the areas their parents moved to in the Forties and Fifties, were turning their attention to Kentish Town, attracted by its Victorian family houses with decent-sized gardens, and by its proximity to the city centre.

The other new immigrants of the Sixties were also arriving from abroad – Cyprus, India and Pakistan – adding to the social mix and, with their corner shops, were offering exotic, unfamiliar foods and smells, and slowly changing the landscape and character of the smaller streets off Kentish Town Road.

In 1968, Kentish Town Road itself remained much the same as it had for years, with its Boots the Chemist, Sketchleys, West the butcher, Woolworths and the Post Office. Although the trams no longer trundled up the hill, the road was as congested as ever by traffic, the cars, taxis and red double-decker buses jostling for space on the main artery to the north.

A pedestrian walking up from the Northwestern Polytechnic at the junction of Prince of Wales Road would pass the Saxone Footwear shop and Jennings, the solicitor. The Scotch Wool Shop stood next to Broadmead Radio and TV, which rented out most of the televisions in the council flats on the Torriano or Peckwater Estates. Walking on up the road, the pedestrian passed the Wimpy Bar and the Council for Unmarried Mothers, the Nina Hunt School of Dancing and Dawson & Briant, the jewellers.

As this story begins, Sainsbury's is advertising in the local papers for staff to work in its new self-service store, which will compete with the Tesco at the top of Fortess Road. Tesco now has late-night shopping on Fridays and has just started to give away Green Shield Stamps. In

Highgate Road, the ABC cinema – once called the Forum – is showing a new film, *Camelot*, starring Richard Burton and Vanessa Redgrave.

Over the last few years, Camden Council has bought up at least half of the properties in the area and is currently locked in battles with numerous Residents' Groups and Housing Associations about whether the mid-Victorian terraces should be renovated or flattened to make way for vast housing estates of high-rise blocks. As the new house-owners do up their homes (gentrification is beginning), squatters are moving into and occupying the council's many empty properties, to be sharp, nagging thorns in the councillors' sides.

There is squalor but there is also care. In the summer of 1968, as America fights a war in Vietnam and the whole world seems to seethe with rebellion and revolt, many back gardens in Kentish Town are quiet, well tended and verdant. Flowers bloom, trees grow. Blackbirds sing loudly and pull worms from the surprisingly fertile soil.

That pedestrian walking up Kentish Town Road might buy some milk and cheese at the Express Dairy, order some fresh cod fillets at W. Starling, the fishmonger, and purchase a couple of punnets of strawberries and a pound of ripe plums from Lipman's, before popping into the new premises of the public library to borrow the latest new novels.

Concentrating on the errands of the day, and shutting out the sounds of the busy street, that person, like everyone else walking outside at that moment, will not hear another sound in Kentish Town.

It is the sound of a child crying, sobbing quietly. A little girl locked in a small room in a big house. No one hears her. They never do.

When she is finally released from her prison, her eyes will be dry. Her eyelids will flicker. She is just a child and quite powerless. But she is clever, and ambitious. And she knows that she will not be powerless for ever.

CHAPTER 1

May, 1997

Distant Voices

Lunchtime in Shepherd's Bush, London. It is a sunny May day. A tall, lean-limbed woman walks down the street. Her flat leather sandals slap on the hot pavement. On her slender body she wears a simple white sleeveless blouse, and a dusty pink denim skirt swings around her long legs.

Two bare-chested builders sit on a flight of steps eating thick fried egg sandwiches. They simultaneously eye up the woman as she goes past. One of them, a chunky young man with curly blond hair, wipes the egg yolk off his rough chin and is tempted to whistle. He particularly fancies older women.

But something holds him back. Perhaps the look on this woman's face prevents him from doing what usually comes so spontaneously to him. Today, however, even he is sensitive enough to guess that perhaps a cocky message from him is not appropriate.

The woman has a pleasant face – still pretty, even though she must be in her late thirties, the young builder reckons. She has large chocolate-brown eyes, wide cheekbones, small chin – framed by a well-cut bob of brown hair.

As she walks by, the woman's dark brown eyes do not notice the presence of the admiring builders. Nor do they take in the smile from Mehmet, the gentle Asian grocer who is stacking his fruit and vegetables in artistically shaped piles on the wooden shelving outside his small, crowded corner shop. Mehmet is used to exchanging greetings with the woman, but he, too, knows that she is troubled today. He thinks she looks a little less worried than she did when she walked past an hour earlier but he can tell that all is not well with her.

In fact, Mehmet has been thinking for some time now that something was up with her. The sparkle in her eyes is less bright, her smile less ready than when she and her handsome husband first moved to the neighbourhood three years ago.

A devoted family man with four healthy children (three sturdy sons and a daughter), Mehmet is fairly sure of the reason for the woman's troubled expression, and when he discusses his theory with his placid fecund wife, she agrees with him.

The woman turns into Melrose Gardens. If she could read Mehmet's thoughts, she would tell him his theory is right. She is a woman in crisis. Until recently, she has always regarded herself as a perfectly normal person. Now she feels herself turning into a very abnormal person. At the moment she does not think that life can get much worse.

Unfortunately (or perhaps fortunately), she does not realise that it can indeed get worse, and that it will. She also does not know that the telephone she can hear ringing as she turns the key in the lock marks the beginning of the next stage of her life. And that this stage is going to be far harder than anything she has ever encountered before.

*　　　*　　　*

The telephone was ringing as Lucy came in through the door of her flat. By the time she reached it, the ringing had stopped. Never mind. If it was important the person would ring again. She retrieved the bag she had flung down in the hall and began to unpack her shopping in the small fitted kitchen.

She made herself a tomato sandwich and settled down at the kitchen table to read the newspaper with conscious satisfaction. Lunchtime was her favourite time of day. Her husband, Simon, who had worked in a newspaper office for over ten years, laughed at her for it. For in spite of being freelance and able to organise her days as she liked, Lucy liked to stick to office hours, starting work promptly at nine am and working through until twelve forty-five pm. She would look forward to catching up with the news during her lunch hour.

Simon thought she was absurd. 'The whole point of being your own boss is that you can work when you like,' he laughed. 'You can work at night and go to the cinema in the afternoon and avoid the crowds.'

Lucy disagreed. 'It still makes me feel as if I'm bunking off school,' she replied.

'You're just not a natural freelance. Perhaps you should work in an office again,' Simon said.

'I didn't become a freelance by choice,' she reminded him sharply.

This morning, of course, had been disrupted by the visit to the doctor, so she had not got much work done. She was copy-editing a dreary consumer guide to family law and had promised the publisher that she would finish it by the end of the week. She would probably have to work late into the night.

The telephone rang again just as she bit into her sandwich.

Damn! She hated to be disturbed while eating, and she had forgotten to put on the answering machine. She could not just let it ring, she was incapable of ignoring it.

To her relief, it was Rosie.

'Lucy Montague! I've been trying to get hold of you all morning.'

'I've been out. I had to see the doctor.'

'Everything okay?' Rosie was briefly, but genuinely, concerned. 'At least, nothing serious?'

'No, nothing serious. I just felt I had to do something about the fact that I can't get pregnant. I can't go on like this for much longer and I've asked to be referred to a specialist.'

'Ah. Oddly enough, that's what I was ringing about,' said Rosie.

Lucy sensed a suspicious cheerfulness in her voice. She waited.

'I wondered if you would mind doing a small interview on just that subject for me. Please say if you really don't want to, but we're desperate to get hold of someone. The person we lined up let us down at the last minute and it occurred to me that you might just agree to do it . . . Of course, I'll understand entirely if you don't want to do it,' she added disingenuously.

Lucy smiled. She was used to helping Rosie out at the last minute. Rosie was Associate Editor on a woman's magazine, in charge of features, and she shamelessly used her friends as interviewees whenever necessary. Over the past two years, Lucy had been interviewed about six or seven aspects of her deeply interesting life experience. How the children of doctors view their own health; being made redundant; freelancing; one was about having a homosexual brother (that was strictly anonymous, as was the one about oral sex). In fact, Lucy's life could be mapped out through the pages of *High Spirits*. As could the lives of most of Rosie's friends.

At least Rosie did talk to real people nowadays. She had found herself in big trouble with her editor last year when it was discovered that she had written a series of articles without interviewing a single real person. She had simply made them all up.

'Real people never say the right things,' Rosie defended herself. 'I can think up much more interesting and apt quotes than your average person. Sometimes you find people who've done something interesting but when it comes to talking about it, they might as well be pond life.'

'That's not the point,' snapped her editor. 'Do that again and you're out.'

Of course, the editor knew and Rosie knew that this was not true. Rosie was far too valuable to the magazine. She was full of ideas for every section, from features to fashion, she wrote like an angel about any subject, and she worked all hours. Rosie was headed for stardom, and everyone knew it. She was frequently approached by rival magazines and she was clearly just waiting for the right offer to come along. Indeed, when Rosie won a major media award for that same series of articles (submitted before the misdemeanour had been discovered), nothing was said about it. Proud to have an award-winning journalist on her team, the editor put up Rosie's salary, gave her a generous clothes allowance, and prayed that *Private Eye* never found out the truth.

'You can be interviewed anonymously, Lucy,' Rosie continued. 'I wouldn't expect you to put your name to it . . . we'll just describe you as Milly, a thirty-five-year-old lawyer.'

'That's what you called me in that article on blow jobs,'
laughed Lucy.

'No, I've never used the name Milly before.'

'I mean the thirty-five-year-old lawyer.'

'No, you were thirty-four last time.'

Lucy sighed wearily. 'Yeah, from blow jobs at thirty-four
to IVF at thirty-five. Except that I'm thirty-seven.'

'That's a small detail,' replied Rosie. 'Oh, go on, sweetheart, say you'll do it, please. I'm really desperate. This last
woman got cold feet at the last minute. I told her she'd
be anonymous but she's terrified her mother-in-law will
recognise her and make trouble for her and her husband.
Ridiculous! But you can't make someone talk if they don't
want to.'

'No, indeed.' Lucy did not feel sure about what she was
agreeing to.

It had been hard enough talking to her GP that morning
about what was going on. Her doctor had quite shaken her
up, talking about unconscious reasons for infertility, and she
had not yet had a chance to think about it properly.

But the visit to the doctor had shaken her up in some way
that made her feel slightly different about it, too. She was
surprised to hear herself agreeing to Rosie's request. 'All
right,' she said. 'I'll do it, as a favour to you, Rosie, but you
owe me one . . . Tell the journalist to ring me this evening
at about six thirty, before Simon gets home.'

'You're a true doll.' She could hear Rosie blow a kiss
down the phone. 'Thanks.'

Lucy went back to her sandwich and newspaper, trying
to concentrate on the daily news again. Instead, she found
herself replaying her visit to the doctor that morning.

Lucy had always liked Dr Kenny, who was not much
older than Lucy herself and had an endearingly friendly,

no-nonsense manner. She even liked her enough to forgive her for having young children. She had once seen the doctor shopping in Marks & Spencer with a toddler and an infant in a buggy; the toddler, she had noted with satisfaction, was howling its head off.

But here Dr Kenny was in a professional role. When Lucy sat down in the chair next to the doctor's desk and burst into tears, Dr Kenny had handed her a box of tissues and waited in silence for her to stop. When Lucy managed to blurt out that she had decided that perhaps it was time to be referred to the fertility clinic – or was it the infertility clinic? – Dr Kenny had nodded and smiled, and said, 'Of course.'

If Lucy had a complaint about Dr Kenny it was that she was sometimes just too correct in her behaviour. The health centre was very geared up for counselling and therapies of various kinds, so it was no surprise when her doctor stared at her and said, 'Perhaps you should think about talking to someone about what you're going through.'

Lucy sniffed through her tears and frowned. 'What do you mean?'

The doctor shuffled her papers. She was clearly treading carefully. 'I am going to refer you to the clinic at the hospital but it may take a while to get an appointment. It seems to me that you are possibly more upset about your difficulties in starting a family than you think.'

Lucy rolled her wet eyes.

'It sometimes helps to talk about your feelings,' Dr Kenny continued, 'get them out and not keep them bottled up.'

Lucy felt herself cringing. This intelligent woman was sounding like something out of Rosie's magazine. 'I don't need to talk to anyone I don't know,' she said. 'I talk to my friends.'

The doctor smiled. 'Fair enough. Sometimes friends are

all you need. But sometimes they're not. Just remember that if you do feel the need to see someone, we can arrange it. Just let me know.'

Biting the inside of her lip, Lucy smiled. She was grateful for the concern, if nothing else. She did not feel she got much real support from anyone around her but that was mainly her own fault; she did not like to talk to anyone about her problem.

The doctor continued. 'You know, there's been quite a bit of research done on why people don't conceive. Psychological factors can play a large part.'

'So what?' Lucy snapped, taken aback by her own rudeness.

Dr Kenny paused and smiled again. 'I'm just saying that sometimes there can be a psychological component.'

'You mean that I unconsciously don't want to be a mother? Unable? Unready? Unwilling? That sort of thing?' Lucy scratched her forehead and looked defiantly at her.

Dr Kenny shrugged. 'I don't mean anything specific. It's just that a lot of women can go for years with unexplained infertility – when there's no obvious reason – and suddenly find themselves pregnant. As far as I'm concerned, yours is unexplained. All the preliminary tests have shown that you're ovulating. You've never had a pelvic infection, so far as you know, Simon is producing perfectly good sperm, and plenty of them. Yet you're not getting pregnant. It can often be like this. There is no obvious reason and then suddenly it happens. We all know about couples who have been trying for years to adopt a baby and then suddenly the woman finds herself pregnant with no help at all.'

'Of course I've heard of that,' Lucy said impatiently. 'But I don't see what it's got to do with me. I'm sure there's something physically wrong and since those first investigations I've had over the last three years have not thrown anything up, I feel time is running out. I want to get to a clinic and be investigated properly. A year ago I still thought it was just a matter of time. Now I have less time to play with. I'm thirty-seven. I can't afford to wait much longer.'

Dr Kenny nodded. 'Fine. I'll write to the consultant today. They're very good at the Hammersmith.' She scribbled in her notes, looked up and smiled. Lucy's time was over.

Lucy picked up her bag and rose from the chair. 'Thank you for all your help. I'll let you know how I get on.'

The doctor nodded gently. She did not seem to have taken offence at Lucy's rejection of psychological help. 'Let me know if you haven't heard from the hospital within three weeks.' She caught Lucy's eye. 'And you may be right. Perhaps they'll pinpoint the problem at the clinic and fix it. Physiological problems are usually the easiest to fix . . . But I think you'll be all right. Most couples end up with the baby they want nowadays, whatever the original problem is.'

Biting into her tomato sandwich, Lucy thought that she was not about to tell anyone that her doctor thought it was all in the mind, but she was aware that something inside her had eased. As she ran water into the kettle for coffee, she realised that she could manage to talk about it to a stranger. Perhaps it was good to talk, just to articulate and clarify her thoughts about the whole business. And it might also help someone else in the same situation to learn that she's not alone, that she's not the only one.

The kettle boiled. As Lucy poured the water on to the instant coffee, she chuckled at how Rosie had persuaded her to be interviewed. Rosie was so clever, and so incorrigible! And she had always been like this. She had an inborn talent for getting her own way in the most charming manner imaginable.

At university, where they had first met and become friends, Rosie edited the student newspaper, took the leading roles in the productions of the drama club, and made all her own clothes from designs she had pinched from the swanky boutique in the high street. In her second year, she had been banned from several clothes shops in the town after being regularly spotted measuring up the seams of dresses and writing down the details in a red notebook. The shops naturally thought she was a spy for a rival in the garment industry but in fact she simply went back to her lodgings and cut out her own paper patterns to recreate the dresses on her old Singer sewing machine.

On top of all this activity, Rosie always had a string of boyfriends waiting for her favours. She treated all of them quite badly and Lucy was forever handing out comforting cups of tea to the latest reject. They trooped round regularly to their shared flat in the hope of a reconciliation, only to find that Rosie was out with somebody else.

The only time Lucy ever showed any disapproval was when Rosie slept with three men in one day, dashing from one set of digs to another across town and back, until she returned home, alone and exhausted.

But even then Rosie was immune to criticism. 'The trouble is,' she said artlessly, as she collapsed on the sofa, 'I like all these boys in their way, and I don't like to hurt anyone's feelings. I can't bear to reject any of them. You know, Tom's much better in bed than Bill but Bill always makes me laugh. And Martin's so spiritual – he's teaching me Tantric sex, though I don't think it's really for me. It probably suits B-type personalities more. And then James, well, poor old James. I haven't got the heart to disentangle myself, he's insecure enough as it is . . .'

Rosie's looks always attracted attention. She had thick glossy brown hair and the most unusual mouth with naturally dark-red lips which turned up at the corners to give her a permanently content and bemused expression. Ripe and buxom, with a small waist, she had always dressed well, from her home-made dresses at university to the Nicole Farhi suits she could afford now that her magazine salary was topped up with a dress allowance – all part of her 'package' from the magazine.

Lucy always loved Rosie's company. Rosie's mind was as vivacious and lively as her body, and made Lucy feel more alive in her presence. She was full of ideas and laughter, and she could rarely sit still for a moment. It was no wonder that men were always attracted to her. But Rosie always manipulated them as she wanted. Unlike most people, she did not seem to be longing to find a partner with whom she could settle down and reproduce. 'If I have a biological clock at all, it must be electronic – because I can't hear it ticking,' she would say with a laugh.

For Rosie, work took precedence over the boyfriends. She just wanted to do interesting and stimulating work and have a good time. And the fact that Rosie was not longing to settle down and have babies made her a safe friend for Lucy. Unlike many of Lucy's old friends, Rosie was not going to go off and betray her by getting pregnant!

Of course, all that running around at university had been in the late Seventies, before anyone had ever heard of AIDS. Fired up by the women's liberation movement and easy access to contraception, women were encouraged to flex their sexual muscles and enjoy them without the risk of disapproval or fatal disease. In those days, all you had to fear was pregnancy.

Lucy often reflected on the irony of that. All those years spent trying not to get pregnant. All those days following a rather too carefree night anxiously waiting for the stomach cramps and dark menstrual blood. How welcome they had been then! Now the telltale twinge in her belly and the blood flowing through her cervix each month sent her plunging into gloom.

With her thoughts back on her infertility, she wondered if she was really ready to be interviewed by a complete stranger about something so personal.

The journalist telephoned at exactly six thirty, by which time Lucy had begun to feel agitated. She did not know whether her nerve would abandon her and leave her to sob pathetically into the receiver and blurt out her misery. Talking to her doctor that morning had brought on tears; she had no idea whether this favour to Rosie was going to be better or worse. Was she going to find herself blubbing uncontrollably? Pushing back the nervousness, she reminded herself sharply that she had agreed to do this interview, so there was no going back now . . .

Lucy did not catch the woman's first name and she had forgotten to ask Rosie what she was called. It hardly mattered. In fact, the more anonymity on all sides, the better, especially if she was going to cry.

The woman was a sympathetic and sensitive interviewer with an attractive husky voice. At one point Lucy thought it sounded a little familiar. But Lucy was surprised to find how easy it was to talk like this over the telephone, to recount her experiences over the past four years. She told her the whole story, about how she used to be a book editor in a publishing company, how she got married to Simon, a journalist and the Deputy Editor of a local newspaper in south London. She used to have a wonderful job, she told her, but then everything changed. There were cutbacks and 'downsizing' and she found herself being laid off with a bit of redundancy money and a lot of rejections from other publishing houses that were also shedding staff.

It was at this point, she explained, that she had decided to look on the bright side, and to regard this event as no bad thing. She and Simon decided that now was probably the time to start a family, as they had always planned to do. If Lucy could build up enough contacts doing freelance editing, she would be able to work from home and be available for the children.

Such hopes! Lucy felt such sadness as she described the excitement of having her coil removed by the GP, and being tested for rubella in preparation for conception. Then there was the joy of having sex without contraception. In those early days, the knowledge that it might result in a baby added a thrilling edge to sex. Their sex life during those early months seemed electrified by the possibility of creating a new life, by their sense of omnipotence. 'We had sex at every opportunity,' Lucy laughed, 'in bed, on the kitchen floor, across Simon's desk, against the washing machine . . .'

She had not expected to get pregnant straight away (though she had secretly hoped to). For the first three months, when her periods came on the dot, on the twenty-seventh day of every cycle, she tried not to be disheartened. She knew it could take time. But gradually her feelings changed. The onset of each monthly period was marked in her diary with a large, disappointed 'P'. Friends who had started trying to get pregnant around the same time would suddenly announce their success, and then fall quiet. Most disappeared; Lucy could not bear to see them in their fecund happiness.

Month after month went by. Sex became a chore. The four days of the month during which she was supposed to be fertile became crucial, marked out in red in the calendar in her head. One night Simon had flu and simply did not have the energy to arouse himself in any way – he could barely lift his head off the pillow.

Lucy sat downstairs and wept into glasses of neat whisky, bitterly disappointed that that month's chance was lost.

Into the mouthpiece of the telephone, she described the isolation and anger of being infertile, of how she felt excluded from ordinary life. Although she deliberately avoided her friends as they settled into domestic family living, she still could not avoid the rest of the world. Everywhere she looked, there were pregnant women, and the streets were crowded with women holding toddlers and pushing buggies. Nappy advertisements filled the television screens night after night. Novels were full of descriptions of childbirth and mother love. Even the children's section in the local library seemed to accentuate her misery as she walked past the door.

Her despair was a repeating pattern, following her menstrual cycle relentlessly, month after month. It disappeared for the four days after ovulation, allowing Lucy's spirits to rise each month as the twenty-seventh day approached. Then they would crash at the first twinge of cramp in her belly, and the painful lumpiness in her breasts followed by the unkind presence of blood cleansing her womb, washing away that month's ovum and all chances of its fusion, implantation and survival.

Then there was the pressure she felt from her mother

to produce a grandchild. She did not describe in full her mother's tactlessness or insensitivity, but she did describe the sense she often felt of her parents' disappointment when she was with them now. Omitting the fact that her brother Andrew was unlikely to produce grandchildren, ever, Lucy did hint that if her parents were ever to have grandchildren, they would only be from her.

Lucy also realised, but did not say it, that there was a hope deep inside her that if she could produce a grandchild, then her parents might become a bit happier, that her mother would stop henpecking and her father would stop retreating from the world. A child might give them a new interest and bring them alive again.

Perhaps it was talking to a faceless stranger on the telephone but Lucy found it surprisingly easy to articulate thoughts and feelings she had never expressed before. She talked about the loneliness of infertility, how it set her apart from the rest of the world. 'I have become painfully sensitive,' she explained, 'to the most innocent enquiry from anyone who asks if I have children or am planning to have them. I blush bright pink and feel almost attacked and exposed. The worst of it,' she continued, 'is that I have actually become quite phobic about children. I avoid them if I can. I no longer see old friends who have children and I tend only to mix with couples without children. It's pathetic, isn't it?' Saying all this made her feel like a sad person.

But there were some things she did not divulge to this journalist, and never would divulge to anyone, such as the time the telephone had rung at six o'clock one morning when she and Simon were fast asleep. Simon answered the phone. The exclamations and joy in his voice said it all. His sister's firstborn was a boy. A twelve-hour labour. Mother and baby were doing well. As Simon went into the kitchen to put on the kettle, too excited to go back to sleep, Lucy turned her face to the wall and wept.

Nor did she mention how the romantic weekend in Rome (carefully scheduled to tie in with her fertile days of the month) was ruined for her by the presence of a bawling baby in the row behind them on the flight home.

For years Lucy could hardly bear to admit to anyone that there was something wrong. Seeking medical help would be an admission of need. Simon had persuaded her that they should at least do the basic tests to check that all was well, so she had gone along with that. Anything that did not mean going to hospital. As the daughter of a doctor, she had mixed feelings about hospitals and clinics. The thought of invasive medical tests made her panic. She could not bear the idea of having metal instruments inside her, fiddling with her reproductive organs. She even thought that if she ended up with a baby at the end of that, it might be a metal robot.

'But now the time has come for me to brave the next step,' she said, 'since just letting Nature run its course has not worked. That's a change in my thinking. I'm not sure what I'm going to do if they start talking about laparoscopies or hysterosalpingography, or other ways of fiddling around with your insides. But,' she said with a light laugh, 'I'll have to deal with that when it comes to it.'

She told the journalist how it had affected her relationship with Simon and how it had put pressure on him to have sex on certain days of the month and be kind and supportive when her period started. 'But Simon has always been wonderful,' she said. 'And continues to be so. Luckily he has never had a burning desire to reproduce himself, so he never makes me feel I'm letting him down as well as myself. He's a brick,' she added, 'and always has been.'

She had said far too much, she knew. All this woman had

wanted from her was a few quotes. 'I'm sorry to rabbit on,' she said. 'I don't know what came over me.'

'That's all right,' replied the woman on the other end of the phone, 'you've said some very interesting things and given me some strong lines.' She paused and said, 'Thank you so much, Lucy. I do wish you luck. I hope you get the children you want.'

Lucy's throat contracted at the genuine warmth of the remark. 'Thank you.' Her voice cracked. 'By the way,' she said, collecting herself, 'I didn't catch your name.' She had a sudden urge to connect with this woman.

'Vita. My name is Vita Cumming.'

'Vita.' Lucy repeated it. 'It's an unusual name. I knew a Vita once, a long time ago. There was a girl up the road from us called Vita.'

'What's your name? Is Montague your married name?'

'My maiden name is Butler.'

As she said it, a sharp shiver of excitement ran through her. She knew what the voice down the phone was going to say next.

'My maiden name is Valentine. I'm Vita Valentine. And you're Lucy Butler who used to live down the road. You're Dr Butler's daughter!'

'Yes,' Lucy whispered. An image appeared in her head, an image of a large rambling house with a vast garden in Kentish Town. There was shouting and laughter, and a crowd of chattering children jostling and playing together. There was a beautiful dark woman in a long exotically coloured kaftan, leaning on the arm of a tall, handsome blond man in the background. The adults were smiling, looking on, detached but proud.

Now she knew why the husky voice was familiar. She recognised it as the voice of her friend Vita, the friend she

had during that long hot summer before her parents moved
away to south London. She remembered her now, a pretty,
vital girl whom she admired with a passion. A wonderful
friend and, in some ways, it felt now as if she had been the
most important friend she had ever had.

'What about you?' Lucy's voice was almost a whisper.
'Do you have children?' She dreaded the answer.

'Yes.' The reply sounded almost apologetic. 'I have two
girls, eight and six.'

'And your husband, or partner? What does he do?' It was
always a risky question but Lucy wanted to know.

The pause was followed by an unexpected answer. 'He's
dead. He died three years ago. I'm a single mother.'

'I'm sorry,' said Lucy. 'How sad to be widowed so
young.'

'Yes,' replied Vita, but she did not sound sad. 'Life goes
on,' she said, 'especially when you have children. Oh shit,
I'm sorry. Just what you don't need to hear again.'

'That's all right,' murmured Lucy.

Vita sounded excited. 'Now, do you think we should meet
up? See what we both look like after all these years?'

'But, of course!' exclaimed Lucy, her heart pounding in
her throat. 'We have to. God, how amazing! I'd love to
see you again. Let's meet for a drink.' She was astonished
by her excitement; it was almost uncontrollable. 'It will be
wonderful to see you again after all this time.'

'Let's meet at the Groucho Club in town – do you go
there? We'll meet up without my children – it sounds as if
you've had enough torment over the past few years.'

That night at supper Lucy tried to tell Simon about the
extraordinary coincidence of being interviewed by Vita
Valentine. She tried hard to explain about the Valentine
family and why she was so excited about making contact

with Vita again. But Simon was keen to eat his pasta quickly and watch the highlights of the cricket on television. He did not express much interest in Lucy's news. Perhaps the Valentines did not sound interesting to him, or perhaps he felt uncomfortable because Lucy had gone public about their fertility problems. Simon was a taciturn man at the best of times, and he was also tired after a difficult day's work on the paper.

That night Lucy woke in the early hours thinking about Vita Valentine and her extraordinary family. She had thought about Vita frequently all her life, ever since her family had moved away from Kentish Town to Dulwich, in south London.

Simon's long, solid shape lay beside her. The night was quiet, apart from the occasional cat calling in the garden and the roar of cars speeding down Shepherd's Bush Road four hundred yards away.

Lucy moved over to cuddle up against Simon's back, fitting her body around his. She rubbed her nose against his skin and took in his heavy male smell. Her thoughts spun in her head.

Thinking it over in the warm bed, Lucy thought how odd it was that she and Vita had lost touch with each other so completely. Yet Lucy had thought about Vita and her family many times over the years, wondering what they were all up to. Certainly whenever she drove through Kentish Town, she thought about her friends from the past and all those things she used to do with them.

Once she had even plucked up the courage to ring them unexpectedly and see if she could pick up the threads of their friendship again, but when she looked them up in the telephone book there was no Valentine listed in Lady Margaret Road, NW5. They had moved away. The contact had gone.

Then the older she became, although the yearning to see them remained, Lucy also grew more fearful about actually meeting again. After all, Vita had never bothered to get in touch with her, either. Until today. And even that had been a surprise for both of them.

Lucy was nervous about it, there was no escaping that. What would Vita be like? What would she look like? What would she make of Lucy now? Would they have anything in common now that they were adults with lives of their own? Vita was a widow. She had married someone who had died. And she had children.

Lucy felt so inexperienced and childlike by comparison. Nothing had happened to her in her adult life to make her feel properly adult. She had hardly grown up and she felt that she would never grow up properly until she had produced a child, until she had become someone's mother.

'Life goes on,' Vita had said, 'especially if you have children.'

Vita had apologised for her tactless remark but it did raise an important question. But what if you do not have children? What if you want them and never get them? Does life still go on then?

Lucy scratched her leg and shifted position in the bed. She pushed the pillow under her neck and sighed deeply. As she lay there, her breathing gradually evened out and she slowly slipped back into sleep. Dreams filled her head. First she dreamed that she was surrounded by young children. They were all shouting at her and pulling her by the arms and clothes in different directions. Then she dreamed that she was in hospital where she had given birth to a baby with no backbone. She was crying but no one came to help her.

When the alarm clock went off at seven o'clock the next morning, Lucy was shaken awake by the bell, relieved that the start of the day had released her from the night terrors.

CHAPTER 2

July, 1968

The Family Up the Road

Lucy Butler was the nine-year-old daughter of a family doctor in Kentish Town. Her father, Gordon Butler, ran a small practice in Falkland Road. He was on his own but ran the practice with the help of his wife, Hilda, a former nurse. A quiet man, totally dedicated to his work and patients, he left the practical side of running the surgery, from the two ground-floor rooms of their three-storey terraced house, to Hilda and a part-time secretary.

Hilda Butler was a conscientious woman who enjoyed some pride in her own virtue. Thin and wiry, she was a woman in constant motion, tidying the sofa cushions, straightening the rugs, wiping the kitchen surfaces or patting her hair to check the state of its perm. Although she was no fool, she was prey to foolishness, of prejudice and irrational thought. In spite of her nursing training and marriage to a doctor, if pushed, she would opine that virtue could keep someone in the state of good health. And she was proud that she had not spent a day in bed for twenty years.

Hilda was well known in the neighbourhood for her

competence and efficiency. Her husband's patients tolerated her fussiness, which they put down to 'nerves' for they knew that Hilda was essentially kind at heart, and, when need be, got things done. And she was also always fair. If someone needed to see the doctor urgently, it was Hilda who decided who got through the door, and when. She never made mistakes and she made a conscious effort to be fair and decent to everyone, while remaining consistently firm with those who needed staunch handling.

Hilda's reward for such fairness was a high social standing. This meant a lot to her. As wife of the local family doctor, she was on a par with the vicar's wife – people came to her for advice and support – and she took her role and responsibilities seriously.

On Saturday afternoons, after the morning surgery and family lunch of roast chicken, peas and baked potatoes in their kitchen on the first floor, Lucy Butler loved to sit on the worn carpet that covered the floor of her father's surgery while he went through his notes and dictated letters for his secretary to type up on Monday morning.

The waiting room was on the ground floor in the front of the house, with the surgery at the back. The surgery was a comfortable, comforting room. On one side, against the wall, stood a high examining couch and a screen behind which patients could undress with some modesty. On the other side was a wall covered with bookshelves that were bowed from the weight of the medical textbooks and neat piles of issues of *The Lancet* and the *British Medical Journal* going back many years.

The third wall sported large photographs of her grandfather and great-grandfather, both doctors.

Against the fourth wall was a large wooden cabinet which was always kept locked. This was full of boxes of pills, powders, linctuses and capsules of all different shapes, sizes and colours.

Lucy always thought it odd that this cupboard was locked when her father was so careless about all the other drugs that came in, sent as samples by the drugs companies or handed in by patients who had given up on their treatment halfway through the course. She often watched him throw these samples carelessly into the bottom drawer of his desk, and wondered why he never bothered to lock them up with the rest of the medicines in the cabinet. When she asked him he would laugh and nod in agreement. 'You're right, I ought to lock them up or do something with them. I shouldn't leave them lying around. I'll get round to putting them away or throwing them away one day.'

But he never did.

During these quiet Saturday afternoons, Lucy liked to sit on the floor and leaf through the medical textbooks which revealed the shocking population of medical curiosities, the people doctors were really interested in. She was particularly fascinated by the grainy black-and-white photographs of Siamese twins, babies born physically joined. One of the pictures was of two live babies who were simply connected by skin. But the pictures that excited her most were of the ones that had two heads and bodies joined at the waist, with two arms each but only two legs between them. Those ones were dead. There was another picture she liked to pore over. This was of a living baby which looked normal in every way, except that it had one complete extra leg growing from its groin – the evidence of the second twin, the caption simply informed her.

She also liked to look at the children with Down's syndrome. She knew by heart the typical features of a Down's child – the eyes sloping upwards at the outer corners, the folds of skin covering the inner covers of the eye, the small facial features, the large protruding tongue, the short, broad hands with the inward curving little finger and the single transverse crease. Several people who looked like that – children and adults – came to her father's surgery once in a while. Her father explained to her that they had been born like that and they tended to be born to women who had babies late in life.

When Gordon Butler was in a light-hearted mood and not too busy, he would tell her what some of his patients had been up to the previous week, like the woman (he never revealed their names) who ate her prescription because she thought it was the treatment, and the man who was worried because every time he blew his nose his hair stood on end. (This was, in fact, true, Dr Butler recounted with a laugh. The fellow had an unusual sinus that ran up his forehead and under his scalp, causing the skin on his head to blow like a balloon when he blew his nose.) Dr Butler would chuckle in a gentle way about the patient he was particularly fond of – Henrietta, who was clearly a spastic, suffering from cerebral palsy. She could only have been born with it, he told Lucy, but he was too kind to contradict Henrietta's own version of her medical history – told to her by her mother – that she had been born perfect but then swallowed a nappy pin as a baby and this had worked its way through her body to ruin her backbone for ever.

Lucy knew many of the patients herself. She would see them coming into the house to sit patiently in the waiting room at the front of the house, and then she might see them another time in Kentish Town Road, at the fishmonger's or butcher, or browsing around the shelves in the library.

There was Elsie, the woman with popping eyes and hair falling out, who lived in a council flat in Bartholomew Road.

She would come with her ten-year-old son who had thick dark hair all over his face like a young werewolf. Then there was old Mr Potter, who lived in Ascham Street and suffered from patches of horrible red scaly skin all over his unhappy face. Lucy always felt sorry for him. Another regular visitor to the surgery was Miss Norris, a very thin lady whose enormous ankles swelled over the tops of her shoes as though someone had pumped water down inside the skin of her legs.

Otherwise Dr Butler attracted a lot of ordinary patients, with ordinary minor ailments and aches and pains. There were the young mothers with their chubby babies, the bent old ladies hobbling in with their corns and bunions, the elderly men with their rasping coughs and troublesome old war wounds. And some of them came to confirm that they were close to death.

It always saddened Lucy to hear that her father had just certified the death of someone she knew. Only last year old Mr Turner died, and she could hardly believe it. Frank Turner had lived in Falkland Road, just two doors down. He had always been so friendly towards her. He used to invite her in for tea and biscuits and tell her about his grandchildren, who lived in America and Australia. Then suddenly he was dead, a heart attack in his sleep. One day he was there, the next he was gone.

She had cried hard at that news. Her father had comforted her. 'Everyone has to die at some time,' he said. 'We're all mortal, even the Queen. And let me tell you that dying in your sleep isn't a bad way to go. That's the way I'd like to go myself.'

Lucy scowled. 'Oh, don't talk about you dying, Daddy,' she protested. 'I can't bear the thought.'

*   *   *

Dr Butler sat at his dark mahogany desk with his back to the cabinet. At thirty-five, he was a good-looking man with black hair showing streaks of grey. His gentle brown eyes and a quiet manner helped make him a popular doctor. He enjoyed his work and was a conscientious physician who had lived in Kentish Town for nearly ten years, since just before Lucy was born. With the help of his wife, he had built up a moderate-sized practice. Hilda had proved to be a great asset; she ran the practice as efficiently as she kept the home.

On the desk, below the photographs of his father and grandfather, was a large colour photograph of his children – nine-year-old Lucy, beaming at the camera, and seven-year-old Andrew, glancing shyly sideways, a smile perhaps about to appear on his lips.

There was another photograph of his wife in a tan leather frame. It was his favourite photograph of Hilda, taken soon after he had met her at University College Hospital, where he had trained as a doctor. She was a newly qualified nurse. In the photograph she was laughing, her curly brown hair thrown back off her face. She was looking so young and carefree then, long before their marriage and the arrival of the children. Well, they had indeed been more carefree then, in their early twenties, with their whole lives stretching out before them, before they had lived long enough to have experienced too many tragedies or dark moments. As a doctor, he saw such tragedies and dark moments all the time, but they were in other people's lives. The Butlers had, of course, had a few moments of sadness, but no more than the average.

It was quiet in the room. The clock ticked softly on the mantelpiece. Lucy felt peaceful and happy. The house was always blissfully quiet and still when her mother was out. She took the busy atmosphere away with her. That afternoon, Hilda Butler had taken Andrew over to Jones Brothers in the Holloway Road to get him fitted for new shoes.

The telephone rang at about three o'clock. Dr Butler answered it and listened before asking a few questions. 'I'll be along within fifteen minutes,' he said, and put down the phone.

'I have to make a home visit,' he told his daughter. 'It's just up the road. Do you want to come or stay here?'

'Can I stay here by myself?' Lucy was delighted that her father considered her old enough to stay.

As she said the words, she could see her father's face change, the expression suddenly uncertain. 'On second thoughts, I think you'd better come with me. Your mother might not be so pleased if she knew I'd left you on your own. You can come and wait for me while I see this young child. It's just up the hill. It won't take long . . .'

Lucy did not try to hide her disappointment. 'Oh, Daddy, I'm nine years old, and I'm perfectly old enough to be left alone. Please.'

Her father shook his head. 'I'm sorry, Lucy. You know if it were up to me, I'd let you stay. But your mother worries a lot and I think it would be better to ask her first rather than making a unilateral decision.'

Lucy did not know what unilateral meant. Normally she would have asked but she fell back into a sulky silence. She was tired of being treated like a baby. Her parents never let her do anything on her own or trusted her to be sensible.

Dr Butler picked up his heavy black leather bag. 'Come on, slowcoach, we'd better go and see this young patient. It's one of the Valentines, that family in the big house at the top of Lady Margaret Road. They've only recently registered with me, and I've hardly seen any of them. They seem like a healthy lot. There are a lot of children, about six or seven, I think, or maybe more.'

As father and daughter walked up the hill, Dr Butler thought how he was glad to have this opportunity to make contact with the family. His wife had told him they had registered, after their old family doctor in Tufnell Park had died and they did not like the new one who took over. Dr Butler remembered precisely when that was – in May. He remembered because it was around the time of the student riots in Paris. There was a lot of debate on the television and radio about students and student issues, and Anthony Valentine was often on as a guest, always very outspoken on behalf of the student cause. He was an academic of some sort.

Dr Butler noticed Anthony Valentine's name again in June when Danny the Red, one of the most famous students in Paris, came to Britain after a row about his visa. (Hilda had thought it wrong that he was granted a visa at all.) He came to take part in a BBC debate with students from other parts of the world. Anthony Valentine had taken part in that, too, totally on the side of the students, their sit-ins and complaints.

The Butlers learned from that debate that Anthony Valentine was a lecturer at the London School of Economics, where Danny the Red gave a talk to the students the day after.

Since then, the Butlers had occasionally seen Anthony on television discussing his views about the Student Question, or being quoted in the *Hampstead and Highgate Express* criticising Camden Council and the town planners for pulling down perfectly good houses and building characterless housing estates, all in the name of slum clearance and progress. He was very active in local politics and even seemed to support the squatters who had taken over many of the empty council houses scattered around the borough. Hilda did not approve of such things, but Dr Butler was undecided. As a doctor he had visited some pretty squalid homes and was aware of the disgusting conditions that many poor families were forced to live in. The council had a duty to build better homes for people to live in but Camden had been particularly bad about clearing houses and then doing nothing with them, allowing the empty houses to fall into even worse states of repair. If squatters moved in and did them up and looked after them, surely it was better than leaving them empty.

They had had squatters living two doors down from them for the past six months. Hilda had been most upset when they first pushed their way in and settled down there. The house had been lived in by an old patient of Dr Butler's, Frank Turner, a widower, who died in his sleep only last year. The house was already run down but it had fallen into an even worse state of repair·very rapidly until it looked as if it was about to fall down brick by brick. Even Hilda had to admit that the young squatters – gentle people who wore flowing clothes and long hair – had improved the house no end. They removed the buddleia bushes from the crumbling mortar, replaced the rotting woodwork, patched up the masonry, painted the windows and door, and even planted brightly coloured flowers in the front and back gardens. The house had not looked so good in years.

No, thought Dr Butler, the squatting issue was not a simple one at all.

The Valentines' residence was a rambling double-fronted Victorian house at the top of the hill, just before Brecknock

Road, where Lady Margaret Road ran down towards Tufnell Park. Lucy had noticed this house before because its unusually massive size made it stand out from the others around it. Built in 1860 by a prosperous Victorian merchant who had made his fortune in railways, it was surrounded by a large walled garden shaded by tall poplar trees. From the top-floor windows there were sweeping views of London in every direction, to the Kent hills in the south, Hampstead Heath to the west, and the hills of Crouch End and Muswell Hill, and Alexandra Palace to the north. It was really a vast suburban villa amongst city terraces.

Lucy had often heard children's voices drifting over the garden wall. There were always lots of them, which had led her to believe that there were often parties going on from which she felt excluded. It had never occurred to her that they might just be the voices of the children who lived there.

It was about 3.15 when Dr Butler and his daughter stood on the blue-and-white ceramic tiles of the front doorstep and rang the bell.

The door was opened by a short woman with brown, shoulder-length hair. Lucy immediately noticed her straight sharp nose and thick, shapeless lips. Behind her, a small pretty child with long curly black hair and deep blue eyes clung to her skirt.

'Mrs Valentine?' Dr Butler was momentarily confused.

The woman stepped back, opening the door to let them step into the house. 'No, I'm the housekeeper,' she said. 'Mr and Mrs Valentine are out at a concert this afternoon. They left me instructions to call you if the child worsened. He's upstairs in bed. He was listless this morning and stayed in bed. But an hour or so ago he started vomiting. I called you after he was sick for the third time.'

She spoke softly but clearly with a distinct Welsh accent.

Her pale face showed little expression. She was not casual but she did not give the impression of being particularly worried, either.

Lucy smiled at the attractive little girl who was still holding on to the housekeeper's skirts. The child stuck out the pink tip of her tongue and curled it round the corner of her lips, in the manner of all the world's babies in moments of shyness, and looked away.

The housekeeper pushed the girl to the side with a firm gesture. 'Stand out of the way, Celestria,' she said. 'Let the doctor pass.' Then she started to lead Dr Butler towards the stairs.

Dr Butler hesitated. 'Is there somewhere my daughter can sit while I go upstairs? I apologise for having to bring her but my wife is out. I think she should stay downstairs while I see the patient.'

The housekeeper nodded. She opened a white door off the hall to the left of the stairs. 'You can wait for your father in here,' she said to Lucy.

Lucy wandered into the room. A dog, a brown cocker spaniel, was lying on a rug in front of the fireplace. It jumped to its feet when it heard her. For a second it eyed her nervously, but then relaxed and wagged its tail gently before settling down again, licking its chops.

Lucy sat down on a dark blue three-seater sofa, sinking into the comfortable soft cushions. Above the mantelpiece there were two life-size portrait paintings in ornate gilt frames. One was of a young woman of great loveliness, with huge dark eyes and long flowing black hair which fell in soft curls around her graceful neck and bare shoulders. Her face seemed perfectly proportioned and, draped in a diaphanous white shawl, she stared out at the world with a dreamy intelligence.

The other portrait was of a young blond man. Dressed in a crisp white shirt, open at the neck, he looked out boldly and confidently, his dark blue eyes proving the only colour against his pale skin and yellow-white hair.

Lucy was staring up at these portraits, and so engrossed that she did not hear the children come in.

She was startled by a voice behind her.

'Those are our parents.'

Lucy jumped and turned to see three girls standing in a row before the door. The dog jumped out of its basket and walked over to the girls, its claws clicking on the floorboards, its docked tail wagging in greeting.

The littlest girl bent down to pat the dog's head. 'Hello, Dido, lovely dog.' She kissed its ear and the dog licked the child's hand appreciatively.

'Hello, I'm Vita,' said the tallest of the three. She looked about the same age as Lucy, but she was tall and slender with thick black hair and dark eyes. She held out her hand. Lucy shook it shyly.

'Hello.'

'I'm nine,' said Vita. 'This is Perdita. She's eight, and this is Lorelei. She's five.'

Perdita and Lorelei stepped forward to shake Lucy's hand. These two did not smile but scrutinised her with their big calm eyes. Perdita's were as pale as Vita's were dark.

All three girls wore blue jeans and rather grubby white T-shirts.

Lucy realised then that these children were not unfamiliar to her. She had seen them many times in the street – either on bicycles or on roller skates, careering along the pavements as bold and carefree as any child she had ever seen. She had never seen them in the company of an adult, and Lucy had often been aware of her own envy of such freedom to roam at will.

Now that she could study them close up, Lucy was struck by how Vita and Perdita were beautiful, graceful and dark like their mother, though Vita had dark olive skin and Perdita had creamy white skin and a mole on her cheek. Lorelei, with her handsome wide cheekbones, white-blonde hair and deep blue eyes, evidently took after her father.

'The portraits were painted when our parents were students at Oxford,' continued Vita. 'They were very clever and the most handsome couple in their generation. These paintings were done by a friend of theirs who is now a very famous artist.

'They're older than that now, of course,' she added. 'The paintings were done fifteen years ago.'

Lucy nodded and smiled. Thinking of her own parents with their ordinary looks and features and their normal clothes, she found it impossible to imagine what it must be like to have parents who were so famously good-looking and handsome that they had to be painted. 'They're big pictures,' she murmured. 'It must have taken a long time to paint them,' she added.

The girls did not seem to notice the lameness of her comment. They now crowded round the sofa, quizzing Lucy relentlessly about herself. Where do you live? Where do you go to school? How old are you?

Glancing from one inquisitive face to another, Lucy told the girls what they wanted to know. She informed them that she lived in Falkland Road, just off Lady Margaret Road and opposite the Methodist church that was hardly ever used nowadays. She was nine years old, she told them. She attended St Luke's Church School in Islip Street, and when she was eleven she was going to go to Camden School for Girls.

As Lucy answered their questions, she found herself looking around the room. The large French doors were open on to the verdant back garden. The heavy maroon velvet curtains moved gently in the breeze which blew in from the outside. Three walls were crowded with pictures – oil paintings, watercolours, prints of all sizes. The fourth wall was lined with bookshelves, from floor to ceiling, all of them jammed tight with books. The small tables against the wall had colourful Tiffany glass lamps and simple Chinese vases of subtle delicate colours. The floor, dark polished boards with red and blue Persian carpets, bore piles of newspapers, magazines and reviews. Everywhere she looked there was something to read – books, newspapers, magazines and journals – *New Statesman*, *The Spectator*, *The Economist*, *New Scientist*, *The Times Literary Supplement*, *Vogue* and *Queen*.

A few minutes later the door opened again. The children stopped their chattering and fell silent as Olwyn the housekeeper came in carrying a round wooden tray with a glass of milk and a small plate of home-made butter biscuits. 'Here are some refreshments for you,' she said, without looking at Lucy. She was a short, stolid woman wearing a short skirt which stopped two inches above her fleshy knees.

Lorelei was stroking Dido, the dog, which backed away quietly and slunk off to its basket.

'Thank you,' replied Lucy. She watched in puzzlement as Dido nervously eyed the housekeeper.

Olwyn placed the tray quietly on the side table next to Lucy and left the room. None of the other girls said a word. It was an odd silence that had descended upon the room. But the moment the door clicked quietly behind the housekeeper, the children became animated again, and Dido's ears pricked up cheerfully.

'Are those just for me?' Lucy asked, greedily eyeing the pile of biscuits.

'Drink your milk and you can come and see my room, if you want.' Vita smiled at her with friendly openness.

'Don't you want a biscuit?' Lucy was puzzled that there was no milk and biscuits for the others.

Vita shook her head quickly. 'We're not supposed to eat between meals,' she said, 'and tea's in an hour.'

'Oh, that's what Olwyn says, anyway,' said Perdita with a quick laugh. 'But she's not here. I'll certainly have half a biscuit if there's one going.' She took Lucy's offering and ate it swiftly, wiping away any telltale crumbs off her red lips.

After Lucy had finished her snack, Vita took her on a tour of the house upstairs, all the while talking rapidly about her family.

'There are eight of us children. Our parents aren't even Catholics, they just like having children. Our mother was a twin and she has had two sets of twins herself – you know it runs in families. I might easily have twins myself when I have children. There's Constantine and Achilles, they're identical twins and they're fourteen. Then there's Byron, who's twelve. They all go to boarding school, where they have lots of fun. They're all out playing tennis on Parliament Hill this afternoon. They're very good at it. Then there's me, then Perdita, then there are the other twins, Lorelei and Florian. Last is Celestria, who's three.'

'What unusual names you all have,' remarked Lucy.

Vita nodded. 'Mmm. Our mother likes names,' she said. 'She says that sometimes a person's name is more interesting than its owner.'

Everywhere they walked in the house – up the stairs, along the corridors, into rooms – the walls were covered with bookshelves crammed with books, and any gaps between shelves were filled with pictures and ceramic pots.

Finally, Vita led Lucy into a bedroom and said, 'This is my room.' The walls were painted a sky blue. Bunk beds had been pushed against the wall, and on the walls were posters of the Beatles and the Rolling Stones. There was a record player in one corner and a box full of LPs. One poster of Paul McCartney was inscribed: 'To Vita, with all my loving, from Paul'.

Lucy looked at it with surprise. 'Is that really Paul McCartney's signature?'

Vita nodded casually. 'Yup. We've met the Beatles. They're friends of our parents. They've even been here to supper.'

Lucy was impressed. She had never heard the Beatles singing but she knew from her friends at school who were allowed to watch *Top of the Pops* that they were the coolest thing. It seemed astonishing that the Beatles had actually been to Kentish Town and eaten supper just a few hundred yards from her own house. Why, no one would believe her if she told them! She scrutinised the books stacked on the shelves running across the whole of one wall. 'You've got some great books here,' she told Vita. Lucy loved reading and always had at least three books out from Kentish Town Library at any one time.

'You can borrow them whenever you like,' said Vita. 'So long as you return them.'

Lucy smiled gratefully at these words, for they suggested that she was going to see this interesting family again – and that Vita, at least, was happy to see more of her.

'Thank you,' she said.

Vita smiled back. 'Take one now, if you like, and bring it back when you've finished.'

Lucy knew exactly what she wanted. It was a beautiful old edition of *A Little Princess*. She had spotted it the moment she walked into the room. She had been planning to get it out of the library next time but this edition, with its gold lettering and old-fashioned pictures, was so interesting. And what a coincidence! She reached out and gently slid the book out of the shelf.

Vita nodded with approval. 'I love that book. It's one of my favourites. And that particular book used to belong to my grandmother. She gave it to me.'

Clutching *A Little Princess* under her arm, Lucy looked on with interest while Vita then showed off her collection of fossils.

'I found them in Sussex, near my grandmother's house,' she said. 'It's very chalky around there, and good for fossils.'

A voice was calling from downstairs: 'Vita! Come down now. Dr Butler is leaving.'

Vita pulled on Lucy's sleeve. 'You've got to go,' she told her. 'But you must come again soon.' Her smile was warm, her pink lips revealing small white teeth. She spoke with the confidence of an adult. 'Any time.'

'Thank you,' said Lucy. 'I'd like that.'

As they walked down the stairs Lucy could see her father by the front door, dressed in his brown corduroy trousers and green tweed jacket, giving instructions to the housekeeper.

A small, sturdy dark-haired boy of about eight suddenly appeared from a doorway, crept across the hall and disappeared down the basement steps.

'Is that one of your brothers?' asked Lucy.

Vita frowned. 'Who, him? No. That's just the Brat,' she said dismissively. She turned away and said no more.

There was no time to find out more. Lucy's father turned and reached out his arm for her. 'There you are, Lucy,' he said. 'Time to go home now. The patient is quite comfortable.'

Olwyn the housekeeper had opened the front door for them. As father and daughter walked out into the garden, and the heavy door was closing behind them, Lucy heard the sweetest words she could have hoped for.

'See you again soon,' Vita called. 'I hope you'll visit us again.'

At supper at the Butlers' house in Falkland Road that evening, Lucy listened as her parents discussed Dr Butler's visit to the Valentine family. Andrew, as always, was lost in his seven-year-old thoughts at the other end of the table. Hilda Butler was noticeably interested in the fact that her husband had been to their house that afternoon, and she quizzed him in detail about what it was like inside.

Dr Butler slit open his baked potato and spooned in a slab of yellow butter. He shook his head and frowned.

'I wasn't there to inspect the decor, Hilda. I had a sick child to attend to.'

'It is very big with lots of rooms,' Lucy offered. 'There are books everywhere you look – on the walls and the floors, too. It's crammed with things, beautiful things to look at.'

'Such as?' demanded her mother.

'Oh, beautiful bowls, rugs, vases and statues, and stained-glass table lamps, things like that.'

Hilda nodded in the ostentatiously knowing way she had. Lucy could guess that her mother was mentally tut-tutting at the amount of dusting such objects required. She did not give her the pleasure of knowing about the light film of London dust that lay on the bowls, vases and statues, or how untidy the place had been with piles of books stashed in corners on the floor and mountains of dirty clothes in the children's bedrooms.

'I met some of the children, too,' she went on. 'They were very friendly. One of them, Vita, said I should come again.'

'How many children are there?' asked her mother. 'I know there are a lot of them.'

'Eight.'

'Oh, they must be Catholics, having that many children.' Mrs Butler seemed pleased to have worked out something else. 'That explains why I never see them in church.'

'Perhaps they simply don't go to church,' said Dr Butler. 'That's possible.'

'No, they're not Catholics,' chimed in Lucy. 'Vita specifically told me they're not.'

Her mother did not seem to hear. 'They must be well off to be able to afford so many children.'

'I expect there's a bit of private money there,' replied Dr Butler. 'The house seems to be full of heirlooms.'

'What's an heirloom?' asked Andrew from the end of the table, where he had been struggling with his baked potato and listening quietly.

'Don't talk with your mouth full, Andrew,' his mother said tolerantly. 'Hold your knife and fork properly. And please, darling, sit up straight!'

Lucy caught Andrew's eye and smiled sympathetically as their parents continued to exchange what bits of information they had about the Valentine family. Lucy lapped it all up as she heard the snippets of information and gossip.

'He's very left-wing, the husband, isn't he?' Lucy could

tell from the sharpness in her mother's voice that this was not necessarily a good thing – whatever it meant to be 'left-wing'.

'He certainly doesn't seem to side with the Establishment, in anything he says or writes,' replied Dr Butler. His own political views were neutral except when it came to the National Health Service, which he loved dearly and defended passionately.

Mrs Butler's attention switched to Mrs Valentine. 'She is very good-looking, I have to say that. I see her sometimes in Kentish Town Road. She wafts about in long kaftans and the most unsuitable kinds of clothes. Her mind always strikes me as being somewhere else. I've stood behind her in the butcher's on more than one occasion when she's held up the queue while she scrabbles around for her shopping list, which she's usually lost somewhere among the folds of her garments.

'But I don't think she has much to do with the house, really. That housekeeper of hers is always doing the household shopping, as far as I can tell. I'm not sure how much she does with the children, either. Seraphina Valentine – isn't Seraphina her name? – extraordinary, isn't it . . . ?'

As her parents continued to discuss the Valentines, Lucy learned that Seraphina was a writer and artist who had had some success at both.

'She writes poetry, I think, and novels. I've seen her books in the bookshop,' said Hilda. 'Historical novels – not really my sort of thing.' Her own taste ran more to straightforward romantic fiction. 'And once when we went to the Camden Arts Centre there was an exhibition of her paintings. Not to my liking at all. Very modern.'

Now Lucy's mother struck her final blow.

'It makes you wonder, though, doesn't it? To go out to a

concert when one of your little ones is ill. Fancy leaving it to the housekeeper to arrange for the doctor to come.'

'That's a bit harsh, Hilda,' said Dr Butler. 'People are allowed to enjoy themselves, and the child was not that ill.'

'But they didn't know that, did they? Besides, I don't trust anyone who hands over her children to another woman to look after. What's she doing having so many children if she's not going to look after them herself?'

'Perhaps that's precisely why she does have so many children . . .' muttered Dr Butler drily, impressed by his own insight.

Ignoring him, Hilda went on cataloguing her disapproval. 'And I always see them running around the place, unsupervised, in a way that *I* would never tolerate. Shaking her head, she declared that the Valentines were 'bohemians'. The tone in her voice made it plain to Lucy that they were not quite as wonderful as she, Lucy, thought, that there was something other people did not like about them.

As a result, Lucy was fascinated by her mother's reaction to the Valentines. They seemed to bring out all sorts of opinions she probably knew her mother had, but she had never heard them expressed before.

But in spite of this disapproval, Lucy could tell that the Valentines fascinated her mother, just as they fascinated her.

After supper, Lucy went to bed and settled down to her evening reading of *The Lion, the Witch and the Wardrobe*. She had started it the week before and was enjoying it a lot but now she could not wait to finish it so that she could begin reading Vita's copy of *A Little Princess*, which now lay on her bedside table. Lucy had placed it there carefully so that she could see it even when she was lying down with her head on the pillow. Earlier, she had run her fingers over the soft brown binding and admired the delicate tissue paper covering the pretty coloured picture plates inside.

Immersed in the world of Narnia, Lucy did not hear Andrew come into her room.

'Hello,' he said.

Lucy turned to look at him. She smiled. He looked cute, dressed in his stripy blue pyjamas and sucking his thumb.

Climbing on to Lucy's bed, he snuggled down next to her, as he did every night.

Lucy smiled again and moved over to make room for him. She liked her little brother and was always pleased when he asked for things from her.

'Read a book to me, Lucy,' said Andrew. 'Read me some more of *The Lion, the Witch and the Wardrobe*. When you've finished, I'll read it myself but I like the way you say it out aloud.'

So Lucy read to Andrew for ten minutes until his eyelids closed and he fell into a deep sleep beside her.

Dr Butler came up to say goodnight and to move Andrew back to his own bed. 'Goodnight, Lucy,' he said, as he turned off the light, the sleeping boy in his arms. 'It sounds as if you've made some new friends today.'

Snuggling down in her warm bed, Lucy still felt exhilarated by the afternoon's visit. Her head was swimming with images from the Valentine house up the road. How happy she was that those girls had been friendly. It would be wonderful if her father were right – she would so much like to be friends with them!

Lucy turned over restlessly. The more she thought back on the day, the more she felt that she had been on some electrifying journey to a new and exotic land. She had not known that people could live like that, surrounded by hundreds of books and beautiful objects – the richness of the velvet curtains, the deep warm colours of the rugs on the floor, the bright modern prints and the thickly textured oil paintings in their gilt frames, even the freshness of the breeze from the garden – and have so little regard for untidiness or dust. These were the two things that her mother could not abide.

Her eyelids fluttered and she let out a drowsy sigh. Lucy fell asleep trying to imagine what she would have been like if chance had made her be born into the Valentine family instead of her own. She would have liked to be Vita's twin. How lucky she would have been then!

CHAPTER 3

May, 1997

Old Friends

The night before her planned meeting with the adult Vita Valentine, Lucy was tense and nervous. At home in bed, her jaw felt tight and rigid, her teeth clenched. Even a bit of warm bedtime sex did not help her relax much, but then sex rarely helped her relax nowadays, now that it had become associated with procreation and nothing more. Sleep finally came by midnight but Lucy was dismayed to find herself awake again three hours later after an unpleasant dream about blind babies encircling her and reaching out their chubby arms to her in despair. Why was she suddenly dreaming these awful baby dreams?

Simon lay in a deep sleep beside her, his curly hair just visible under the blue duvet. His breathing was deep and regular. Lucky sod, he never had trouble getting to sleep – or staying there, for that matter. Simon was such an uncomplicated man. Phlegmatic and calm at all times, nothing fazed him. Or at least it never appeared to.

Her thoughts spun around her head as she thought about the Valentines again. Vita she remembered as a striking beauty, with long black hair, white skin and flashing black eyes. Thinking about her, Lucy felt quite old and faded, particularly since she knew that Vita was also a mother, something Lucy herself had been unable to achieve at this great age of thirty-seven. Thirty-seven! With no children and no significant career to speak of! Here was Vita with two young children *and* a successful career as a journalist. Now she was aware of it, she had seen Vita's byline in numerous publications. Lucy felt as if she had done nothing by comparison.

But if thoughts of Vita made Lucy feel inadequate, then memories of the Valentine parents made her feel even worse. They couldn't have been much older than Lucy was now, yet at that time they were famous. And they had eight children! How could she fail to feel she had just wasted her life in the face of that?

The birds outside the window were starting up the first notes of the dawn chorus. Why could she not sleep? There was no hope; her thoughts churned on round and round her head.

Well, at least, she thought, she was still married and seemed to have been quite successful at that. Lucy consoled herself with the other fact that Vita had told her, that Vita was widowed. So not everything could be perfect for her. Terrible things had happened in her life. Lucy felt a pang of guilt about feeling glad that life was not perfect for Vita Valentine. She was not glad that Vita had been widowed but she was glad to know that she had not always had a charmed life.

Now she was more awake, Lucy realised how much she was clenching her jaw. Sleep had not entirely gone away, it hovered about her. Her thoughts were slipping in and out of consciousness as she recalled that first visit to the Valentine house with her father that Saturday afternoon. Was it a dream or memory when she saw in her head the group of

Valentine children crowding around her in a big room filled with beautiful objects? Were they dreams or flashes of broken memory, these feelings that she experienced now? There was the deep longing to be part of that household, her excitement at being in their presence, her great joy at being accepted as a friend of Vita and Perdita, her younger sister.

Dreaming and not dreaming, she visualised the wonderful paradise of the grandmother's house in the country, swimming in the river nearby, running through water meadows, the long grass tickling her bare legs as a crowd of children ran chasing each other and falling over in their excitement.

The dawn chorus grew louder. Lucy was awake but she realised that she had a smile on her lips. What great friends they had been that summer, those Valentine girls!

Lucy rolled over. Tucking the pillow under her neck, she tried to get more comfortable. So long ago. She had been nine. It was the year they went to Norfolk for their summer holiday for the third year running. It was the year *Yellow Submarine* came out, and when the Beatles opened their shop in Baker Street. The Valentines had known the Beatles, she remembered that, too.

She had a strange memory – or was it a dream? – of her father laughing and making jokes. Lucy could almost feel the happy atmosphere in the house. Was she imagining it or did she have a memory of her mother sitting at the table, smiling and relaxed? Hilda is looking across the table at her husband, the doctor, a proud look on her face as he talks and laughs in an animated way. Was there a time when her parents had enjoyed each other's company and relished family life?

Her thoughts were drifting out of control. Oh, it must be a dream. Lucy frowned in the grey dawn light as she worked through another strange thought. She had been nine when her parents moved away from Kentish Town. They moved soon after that amazing summer. What was so astonishing to her now was that Lucy had only known the Valentines for a very short time, for that one summer of 1968, yet it always felt as if it had been years. The Valentine family had impressed itself in her consciousness so deeply that she was always surprised to remind herself that their intense relationship had not lasted for years.

And yet, once her father got that other job in south London and they moved, it seemed that she had no more contact with the family. That was strange, but indeed, she had no recollection of seeing Vita – or any of them – after the move. She did not remember even keeping in touch by letter. How odd that so much of that summer had become a part of her and other bits were so dark. Memory was a strange thing. And the strangest thing was the feeling she had that life had somehow become completely different after her family moved away from Kentish Town. Maddeningly, she could not remember why. What was it that made one remember some things and not others?

Oh, she was tired. She lay awake for a while longer until finally sleep did overcome her. Her steady soft breathing began just as she had started to wonder again what Vita Valentine would look like.

They were to meet at the Groucho Club at seven. Vita lived in West Hampstead, Lucy in Shepherd's Bush, so it was easier for them both to travel into the centre of town and meet there. And Vita was a member.

Lucy had been to the Groucho Club a few times with Rosie, who had been a member from the early days, and she was not delighted by the choice. Those crowds of noisy, confident young people made her nervous, but she did not have an alternative venue to suggest.

Lucy arrived early and sat on the sofa in the foyer waiting for Vita to arrive. Sitting perched on the edge of the seat, she watched the cocky journalists and young advertising executives, dressed in their slick suits, walk in through the revolving doors, kissing each other on the cheeks, greeting each other with loud exclamations of joy and delight. The short skirts, well-toned bodies, high heels, and air of self-importance made Lucy want to shrink away and disappear into the upholstery, so unconfident and small she felt.

Vita was late and Lucy's discomfort grew, sitting there on the green sofa. She tried to look casual and offhand, and listened in to several banal conversations one advertising executive had on his mobile phone, talking loudly so that all could hear.

Just when Lucy was beginning to think she had got the date wrong, Vita walked in through the door. Lucy recognised her immediately, though it was twenty-eight years since their last meeting. Jumping to her feet, Lucy smiled with obvious relief.

'Hello, Vita.'

The thick hair was still black, pulled back off her face and tied in a loose plait down her back. Her skin still had that olive Mediterranean sheen inherited from her maternal grandmother, and her eyelids still looked heavy over her dark eyes. Her features were clean and strong. Lucy instantly recalled the portrait of Seraphina Valentine on the wall in the sitting room. Vita had grown up to look just like her mother. She held out her hand to Lucy and smiled, showing a flash of strong white teeth. As Lucy responded, she placed her other hand over Lucy's, pulling her to her, and kissed her on the cheek. 'Hello, there! You look just the same. And you look wonderful!'

Lucy blushed. She did not feel wonderful at all, and Vita's well-cut black suit made her feel even more dowdy in her neat little Marks & Spencer skirt and blouse, and her polished brown shoes from Next.

'What will you have to drink?' Vita asked, leading Lucy into the bar and waving casually to the waiter.

'What are you drinking?' Lucy asked.

'Large Scotch on the rocks.'

'I'll have a white wine spritzer,' replied Lucy.

They sat side by side on a lumpy blue sofa under the window, oblivious to the noisy crowd surrounding them in the bar. It was odd at first as they slowly filled each other in on their lives since the age of nine. In her husky voice, now made even huskier by the untipped Gauloises she consumed in great numbers, Vita told Lucy about her family's activities. The whole family moved, in 1969, to California, where Anthony Valentine was given a teaching post at Berkeley. The children all went to American schools but then came home to go to university at Oxford.

'We all went to Oxford. It was expected of us.' She said this breezily but without boasting. 'I read English and my sister Celestria read medicine. She's a consultant paediatrician in Yorkshire. Everyone else read law, including Perdita, whom I'm sure you remember. Perdita's a barrister here in London, but my older brothers – Achilles, Constantine and Byron – they're all lawyers in the States. They have a law firm together in Washington DC, and specialise in civil rights cases. And Florian and Lorelei, the other twins, are solicitors with their own firm down in Croydon. They concentrate mainly on legal aid and mental health cases.'

'So they're all left-wing, like your parents . . .'

Vita looked at her curiously for a moment. Then she laughed. 'I don't think any of them are particularly interested in politics, but I suppose there seems to be a family gene that wants to make things better in the world.' Pausing briefly, she added without looking directly at Lucy, 'Or perhaps there's a need to look after the underdog . . .'

'And are they all married?' Lucy wanted to know all the details. 'Do they have children?'

To her surprise, Vita shook her head. 'Some got married but they all seem to have split up. I'm the only one with children, and all the others seem a bit hopeless when it comes to relationships. I don't know if they're going to reproduce or not. I do know that Perdita certainly doesn't want children, and Celestria seems too busy looking after other people's children to have much time for a social life. The rest, I don't know . . .'

'That must be sad for your parents,' said Lucy, thinking of her own mother's longing for the next generation.

But Vita shrugged. 'Oh, I don't think they're bothered. They're not particularly interested in grandchildren. They hardly see my children. They still live in California and rarely come to Europe nowadays. We talk on the telephone.'

It was clear that she did not want to dwell on her parents, and she proceeded to tell Lucy more about her adult life. Soon after graduating, she married a fellow graduate from Oxford. He was a brilliant classicist, quite exceptional, who got a starred First and an academic post at Queen's College. But in his early thirties he became very peculiar, she said. He started to do odd things and was finally diagnosed as manic-depressive. By that time, they had two young children.

'Until I had children I was working as a journalist on the *Oxford Mail* but I stopped working the minute the children came along.' She paused. 'At the time it seemed very unfeminist to do such a thing, and I was criticised by several of my female colleagues on the paper. But I really wanted to look after them myself. It was important to me, for one reason or another,' she added softly.

'When the little one was just two,' she continued, 'Chris became out of control. He stopped taking his pills and ran up massive credit card bills, bought two new cars and a whole Smallbone kitchen one weekend. Then a week later he flew to Rio de Janeiro and back. He offered three people jobs on the plane.

'Immediately after that, the low started and he became more depressed than I'd ever seen him before. After a while he began to get better again and I thought he was all right. But then on Easter Sunday, he shot himself in the garden of a cottage we had rented for the holidays. I don't know where he got the gun from. It was a 12-bore shotgun. He put the muzzle in his mouth and lay on top of it so that the kickback wouldn't throw him off target. I found him when I came back from a walk with the children . . .' A deep line ran down her forehead as she toyed thoughtfully with her glass. 'I relive that scene every week of my life, and I still have a section of his skull, which I picked up afterwards.' Raising her head, she looked directly into Lucy's eyes. 'It's very smooth,' she said.

Lucy wanted to reach over and touch Vita, but she held back. 'I'm so sorry,' she said. 'It must have been terrible.'

Vita shrugged. 'Yes, it was. But the worst thing was that I was almost relieved when he killed himself. It was really the only way out of what had become a nightmare for him, for all of us.'

There was a brief, awkward silence as Lucy tried to imagine what Vita had gone through.

Then Vita sat up straighter and asked in a brighter voice, 'What about you, then?' It was clear that she was not hoping for pity.

'Well, there's not much more to tell you, really. I've had an unexciting sort of life,' apologised Lucy. 'I went to York University and then got a job in publishing. The worst thing that happened was that I got made redundant. I got married five years ago and I am still happily and boringly married. Simon is Deputy Editor of the *South London Examiner*, where he's been for years. He is not the ambitious type, he's happy on the paper, and I think just likes a relatively quiet life.'

It was Lucy's friend Rosie who had first introduced Lucy to Simon. She had met him at a dinner party and then invited him to a small drinks party of her own. Amazingly, Rosie had not slept with him. 'Grab him before I do,' Rosie had whispered soon after she had introduced him to Lucy on that occasion. Shoving the chilli dip under Lucy's nose, she hissed, 'Offer him some of this – it's nice and spicy.' Rosie placed her mouth against Lucy's ear. 'Go for it! You deserve him and I *think* he deserves you.'

The start of the relationship was simple and straight-forward. Simon and Lucy had taken to each other at that party. Simon invited Lucy out the next week and it grew from there. Simon was a great letter writer and proceeded to flood Lucy with long and passionate declarations of love.

Their relationship had grown slowly, thrived and flour-ished over the years. It had survived the few calamities, such as Lucy's redundancy, and they had weathered the unpredictable storms of infertility for a long time without breaking up, as many couples did.

Lucy looked sadly at Vita. 'The major event in my life is a non-event – I just haven't managed to conceive. And now I'm really beginning to feel that time is running out . . .'

'What about your parents?' asked Vita. 'Is your father still practising?'

'Yes. He's coming up to retirement soon but he's still working as a family doctor in Dulwich. He's been doing that since we moved away from Kentish Town.'

'And your mother,' asked Vita, 'she's still going?'

Yes, Lucy told her, her mother was still going. What she did not say was that her mother was more of the same – fussy and anxious, worrying about minor details and avoiding important issues. Lucy did not want to say too much about her mother's henpecking and constant nagging of her father. Age and experience had helped Lucy realise that her mother behaved in such a tight and rigid way because what was going on inside her head felt so messy and unbounded that she was terrified that it might become unleashed. Hilda needed to keep that internal chaos under control at all cost.

'My mother's not an easy woman to live with, but my father's worked out his own way of handling her. I suppose that's what couples do when they've been together a long time.'

Again, she did not describe in full her father opting out of conversation and family discussions in order to avoid arguments with his wife. It seemed that he always gave in to her. Lucy could tell that her father felt it was just not worth standing up to Hilda. It was just not worth getting into conflict with her, for whenever he did, Hilda would retreat to the bedroom in distress and tears, and Gordon would not have won any victory. As a result, Gordon Butler spent much of his spare time concentrating on his own interests

– listening to the opera on weekend afternoons, gardening, and reading detective novels.

'My parents have developed their own way of dealing with each other,' repeated Lucy sadly.

Vita raised her eyebrows and gave Lucy a cynical smile. 'My parents have never had that problem. They've always been more interested in each other and their work than in anyone else.'

There was another uncomfortable pause as Lucy could not think of how to respond. In the past, she had never once thought to criticise the Valentine parents in any way. They had seemed like dream parents to her at the time.

In her confusion, she found herself asking a question she would normally avoid. 'Tell me about your children . . .' But at the moment she had a singular feeling of closeness to Vita, as though they had been friends all their lives and had seen each other only last week rather than almost thirty years ago.

Vita looked pleased and opened her black leather hand-bag. Lifting out a photograph, she handed it to Lucy. Two black-haired girls with dark eyes and long eyelashes were standing with their arms around each other's shoulders and giggling into the camera.

'They're beautiful,' said Lucy. 'They look very lively.' A twinge of envy ran through her. 'They look just like you.'

Vita smiled. 'They're good girls. They've survived everything very well, so far.'

She went on to explain that she had a local woman – a mother herself – who looked after them after school and during the holidays, but as a freelance journalist she was working at home most of the day.

'I can keep a good eye on things,' she said, 'and make

sure everything's okay. She comes on a daily basis – I'd never have a live-in nanny.'

For a moment Lucy thought that a strange look came into Vita's face and, as she caught Vita's eye, a peculiar feeling spread over Lucy herself. She felt distinctly uneasy, but had no idea why.

'So, tell me about the rest of your family,' she said. The two women drank some more. The strange feelings receded and disappeared as the effects of the wine crept through her body. Lucy sank back on to the sofa. She was beginning to feel very relaxed and comfortable in Vita's company again. They drank some more and talked and laughed, still ignoring the crowds around them.

'Do you remember the time we ran that funny old go-cart down Lady Margaret Road at about five in the morning? And the time we left our footprints in the wet cement on the building site?'

Vita giggled and nodded. 'We had great fun,' she agreed. 'I remember a lot about that time, actually.'

Lucy felt a flicker of pleasure at the words.

'That holiday I had with you and your family up in Norfolk,' said Vita, 'that was lovely.'

'Did you enjoy that? I don't remember it being particularly memorable. I always worried that you were bored with my family. Yours always seemed so much more exciting.'

'Oh, I wasn't bored. I liked your parents a lot, especially your father. He was so great to talk to, and I learned a lot from him. He liked children, you could always tell that about him. He was interested in what children had to say. That's quite rare in an adult.'

Lucy looked thoughtful. 'It's interesting that you say that. Thinking about it, my father's been pretty good as a parent, to me. I've probably never properly appreciated how much he's supported me over the years. Mind you, I don't think he had particularly high expectations for me because I was a girl. It was different for my brother. When Andrew decided he didn't want to be a doctor, even after going through medical school and qualifying, my parents were disappointed. I think Dad's always felt that Andrew let him down because he did not become the fourth generation to go into medicine. He's still hoping, of course, but he won't get his wish. Andrew is far too happy not being a doctor – he runs his own computer graphics company, and loves it.'

As Lucy spoke she realised that Vita was looking distracted. Perhaps she was bored by Lucy's tale, or perhaps she was disappointed after meeting her old friend.

But Vita looked up at her again with an enigmatic smile on her red lips. 'It seemed to me that you were pretty lucky with your parents . . .' Her voice tailed off. Looking at her watch, she grimaced in dismay. 'Oh, I've got to get home, I'm afraid, before the children go to bed.'

She got to her feet. It was time to go.

As Lucy jumped to her feet also, she felt an impulsive rush of warmth towards Vita. 'You must come over for a drink and meet Simon,' Lucy said generously. 'Being journalists, you probably know all sorts of people in common.'

They parted on the mosaic ducks on the step of the Groucho Club, hugging each other tight. Vita smelled of expensive French scent.

'I'm glad we met up again,' Vita said in a forthright tone of voice as she stepped back. 'It's been great seeing you.'

'Oh yes,' said Lucy. 'Same here.' She felt quite dazed by the success of their meeting. It had been far better than anything she might have imagined.

Vita set off for Piccadilly and Lucy headed towards Tottenham Court Road tube. Lucy's spirits were soaring,

and she suddenly recalled this same elation from the old
days; Vita had always had this effect on her; it seemed as
if nothing had changed.

Feeling quite high, Lucy sat on the edge of her seat in
the tube train home. Her head buzzed with memories of that
summer of 1968. Most of the memories came into her head
vivid and unprompted, but there were others, too, vaguer
ones. But whenever she tried to concentrate on these, they
hovered in her mind and then veered off into the blackness
beyond her mental reach. A peculiar sense of frustration
came over her, as if some elusive thing were allowing her
to go so far and no farther.

The excitement of meeting with Vita Valentine was forgotten two days later when she received the telephone call from
Patrick Toller, her brother's live-in partner.

It was a call she had been awaiting for four years.

'Andrew's in the hospital,' Patrick said. His voice trembled. 'He's got PCP. They say they think he'll be all right,
they've got it in time.

'He's at the Middlesex if you want to visit him. I'll be
there this evening, too. Andrew wants you to call your
parents and tell them.'

Lucy put down the phone. Her lips trembled like a child's
as she fought back tears. It had started now. This was
it. Patrick's news heralded what would be a quickening
downward spiral of hospital admissions until death.

Until now, in spite of being HIV-positive, Andrew had
been perfectly healthy. After an attack of shingles four years
before, which was what prompted him to be tested for HIV,
his health had been fine. He was a tall, strapping young man
who played tennis and swam regularly. He always looked
so well.

But Lucy knew that the virus would eventually win. She had read enough to know that the HIV-positive status eventually led to 'full-blown AIDS', that, in spite of the efforts of modern medicine to combat the disease, the virus gradually destroyed the body's immune system until the significant illnesses started, creeping up relentlessly, slowly destroying strong resilient human tissue and finally reducing it to a feeble mass of skin and bone. She did not know exactly what lay in store for her little brother, but she knew his future was going to be wretched.

PCP. This was a new term to her. She looked it up in her book on AIDS, which she had surreptitiously bought at Waterstones a year ago, and found that the initials stood for '*Pneumocystis carinii* pneumonia'. *Pneumocystis carinii*, the book explained, was a parasite that commonly caused lung infection and pneumonia in people with HIV infection. 'It is not known to cause illness in people with healthy immune systems. In many cases, PCP is an AIDS-defining illness. The immune deficiency syndrome makes its presence known as diseases appear that are caused by microbes ordinarily living in perfectly healthy human beings whose normal body defences prevent disease.'

Patrick had said that Andrew wanted her to tell their parents. This was the hardest bit. At some level Lucy felt angry with Andrew for dumping that task on her; he could have told them himself.

Yet Andrew had hardly seen his parents in five years. They could barely control their anger and annoyance over Andrew's rejection of a career as a doctor after all that time at medical school, when they'd been so proud of him. He had qualified, got his medical degree, but then announced that he did not want to practise as a doctor. His parents were disbelieving at the time, certain that he would change his mind.

But then Andrew packed up his backpack and set off for a trip around the world 'to find himself'. After spending two years in Australia, he returned to London a happier-looking man and now certain that he did not want to be a doctor.

In Australia he had discovered a talent for art and design which he had also combined with computer skills. He intended to set up a design company and have nothing to do with medicine at all.

He looked fit and well, slimmer and well-toned. When he introduced Lucy to his partner Patrick, Lucy was shocked at first, but then when she thought about it, she was not so surprised. The signals had all been there for many years – the absence of obvious girlfriends, the men's perfume, the fastidious dressing, the increasingly exaggerated gestures and mannerisms.

Andrew's parents concentrated their annoyance on his refusal to be a doctor. His sexuality was never discussed. Both the Butler parents had found Andrew's rejection of medicine difficult to accept, though it was Gordon who generally found it easier to accept what his children actually were, even if he had to struggle with himself a little. Hilda Butler, by contrast, had a tendency to expect things of people and then be disappointed and unforgiving when they didn't turn out that way.

Lucy always felt that by not becoming a nurse and marrying a successful doctor as Hilda had done, she herself had failed her mother. And by not producing grandchildren, she had failed her even more.

But at least she continued to have a relationship with her parents, while Andrew did not. Whenever his name came up in her parents' presence, her father would busy himself with the newspaper while Hilda pursed her lips, and allowed her eyes to take on a glassy stare.

*   *   *

Now Lucy had to tell her parents of Andrew's condition, when they had never even acknowledged that he was homosexual. Her hands shook as she tapped out the phone number and held the receiver against her head.

As always, her mother answered the telephone. Without any other warning, Lucy just blurted it out: 'Andrew's in the hospital. He was admitted today.'

She heard her mother let out a little gasp at the other end. The unguarded gasp of a mother.

Lucy had decided in advance not to let her mother do any of the talking. She had a message to convey, and convey it she would.

'He's in the Middlesex. I'm going to see him this evening but he'd like to see you, too. He specially asked me to call you.'

There was hesitation at the other end. Then a quiet voice. 'But what's wrong with him? Is it something serious?'

'He has pneumonia, Mother. But they say he's going to be all right.' She did not add, 'this time'; but that was what she was thinking. 'He'll be in for a few days,' she added.

There was a silence on the other end, then her father got on the line. Hilda had handed the receiver to him.

'What's all this then, Lucy?' Lucy repeated what she had told her mother, aware from the grunts on the other end that her father was taking it all in. He had worked out what was going on.

'He's in the Calder Ward,' she said. 'You can go and visit at any time . . .' She hesitated before saying more. But she decided to anyway. 'It's the AIDS ward, Daddy.' Her words spilled out as she broke down at the words.

Dr Butler's voice was calm and gentle. 'Yes,' he said, 'I thought it might be. Don't worry,' he added with an uncharacteristic firmness in his voice. 'We'll be there. Tell Andrew, when you see him, that we'll both be in to see him tomorrow.'

As she put down the phone, Lucy heard Simon, home from work, coming in through the front door. She stumbled across the room and threw herself into his arms.

That night she dreamed that she gave birth to a baby with two heads. One head was laughing and jeering at her; the other was crying pitifully. She woke up sweating, greatly relieved that she had been spared the task of killing the monster and both its heads.

CHAPTER 4

July, 1968

Paradise Found

Vita Valentine rang Lucy the next day, just as the Butlers were beginning to get ready for church.

'I wondered if you would like to come over to play this morning,' she said.

A thrill ran through Lucy as she heard these words. Vita wanted her company. She wanted to be her friend. Vita's voice was strong and confident. 'You can stay for lunch as well, if you like.'

To Lucy's surprise, her mother seemed pleased to hear about the invitation. In fact, for a momentary flash, she thought she looked excited.

'Tell Vita you can go up after church. I'll drop you round myself. They're only a minute away from St Benet's. I'd like to meet the mother,' she added softly, almost to herself.

A few minutes later, Mrs Butler's mouth twitched. She had been thinking. 'So it doesn't look as though they are churchgoers,' she said.

Dr Butler smoothed his hair against his scalp with the palm of his hand. 'Plenty of people are churchgoers without going to church every week, Hilda. We're in the minority nowadays.'

His wife ignored him. Humming softly, she straightened Andrew's collar and tie and checked her lipstick in the hall mirror. 'Ready everyone?'

Then, as she did every Sunday morning at ten minutes to eleven, she opened the front door, ushered her family out before her, and set off up the road to pray.

Seraphina Valentine, *née* Wilkinson, was an identical twin. She and her sister Araminta had been recognised as the most beautiful girls of their generation at Oxford where they graced the corridors of St Hilda's. From their Spanish mother they had inherited their thick black hair and lustrous brown-black eyes. Both were scholars, and they were identical in almost every way, though Seraphina was left-handed and Araminta right-handed. In temperament, too, they differed. Araminta enjoyed the privileges of their diplomatic upbringing and was attracted to conservative young men in striped shirts who shared her father's conventional beliefs. Seraphina, on the other hand, suffered frissons of guilt about her family's wealth, and invariably drifted towards clever young men whose political beliefs were at odds with those of her father. It was inevitable that she should end up with Anthony Valentine, who was recognised as not only the cleverest student in his year but also an intelligent left-wing thinker. He took a First with little effort and was immediately offered an academic post at the London School of Economics, hotbed of the student politics that he relished so much.

Nowadays, Anthony Valentine was renowned as the students' friend and eloquent expert on popular youth culture, with weekly columns in the *New Statesman* and the

Guardian and frequent invitations to speak at demonstrations and rallies and to appear as a pundit of television talk shows.

So Seraphina married Anthony and, with two lots of twins, bore him eight children. They were part of the trendy set of young London intellectuals, and they were invited to every important happening and party in the capital, whether it was literary, artistic, political or social. They campaigned for everything that was fair and just. But they also loved and appreciated beautiful works of art, supported the underdog and were always outspoken in their views. They were also both talented in their own right. To the outside world, the Valentines seemed to be touched with magic.

Seraphina's twin sister, Araminta, meanwhile, married a weak-chinned young man in the Foreign Office. In spite of his feebleness in bed, he managed to sire four children within five years, after which Araminta was happy and relieved to move into her own bedroom and enjoy the life of a successful diplomat's wife. She devoted herself to a life of pleasure, her hospitality as famous as her infidelities.

When Vita Valentine opened the door to welcome Lucy, the rich smell of roasting meat and steamed pudding wafted out into the front porch.

Vita stood in the doorway smiling broadly. She put out her arm. 'How do you do, Mrs Butler? I'm so pleased that Lucy could come.' She beamed at Lucy.

Lucy smiled back shyly as her mother, somewhat ruffled, shook the child's hand. 'How do you do?'

'My mother says we'll bring Lucy home this afternoon,' continued Vita with the same tone of confidence. 'There's no need to collect her.'

As she spoke, a tall dark figure glided across the hall

towards them. Lucy recognised her immediately as the woman in the portrait – Seraphina Valentine. Although fifteen years older than her portrait, she was even more beautiful than her image, as though the bearing and births of eight children had, in some way, enhanced her physically. She was willowy and straight-backed, with thick black hair cascading halfway down her back and shoulders. She wore a long blue-and-white paisley skirt which brushed her ankles, and a sleeveless white bodice which was nipped at the waist and revealed firmly shaped sunburned arms.

Lucy bit her lip and stared in admiration. Mrs Valentine was so young! By comparison, her own mother seemed embarrassingly old and frumpy, with her church frock and hat, beige stockings and sensible shoes, not to mention her carefully permed hair (done every week at Daphne's Parlour down the road).

Lucy then noticed that Mrs Valentine wore no shoes. Under the flowing blue paisley, her bare tanned feet peeped out prettily.

Mrs Valentine held out her hand in welcome. 'I'm Seraphina Valentine,' she said with a charming smile. 'How do you do, Mrs Butler?'

Hilda Butler stammered out a response and again pushed out a stiff hand. Her daughter could see, with surprise, that her mother was nervous.

'Please call me Hilda,' she replied. 'It's very good of you to invite Lucy to play. Are you sure about having her stay for lunch? It's not too much trouble?'

Seraphina smiled. Her red lips parted. Her white teeth flashed. She seemed to have been put together without a fault.

'She can stay all day, if she wants. One more child around the place makes no difference at all. And she must stay for lunch, or there won't be time to settle in. Someone will bring her back this afternoon. We'll ring you if it's later than five.'

Lucy stepped into the house. She was aware of turning her back on the woman hovering in the porch. Lucy could not bring herself to turn back and say goodbye to the mother she was ashamed of.

To her relief, Dido, the dog, came bounding across the hall to greet her. She knelt down to pet it and concentrated on the brown spaniel until she heard the welcome click of the door latch.

That first Sunday lunch at the Valentine house changed Lucy's view of the world. It was the first time she realised that not everyone lived in the same way as her family.

First there was the scene in the sitting room, with the Sunday newspapers strewn around the room being read by various members of the family, small children kneeling on the floor around a game of *Monopoly* and two boys playing duets at the grand piano in the corner. Anthony Valentine sat back in a large armchair, one long leg crossed over the other, holding the newspaper up in front of him and laughing and commenting on things he was reading to nobody in particular. Mrs Valentine drifted in and out of the room in her bare feet and long skirt, carrying glasses of wine for her husband and herself and orange squash for the children. The delicious rich smell of roasting meat and vegetables seemed to float into every corner of the house.

When Vita introduced Lucy to her father, Anthony Valentine leaped to his feet and shook Lucy's hand vigorously.

'I hope you'll enjoy yourself,' he said with a broad grin. He was immensely tall and almost stooped to reach her hand. He was less like his portrait than his wife. He was broader and less blond, but still had fierce blue eyes and was very handsome. Before Lucy could force out an awkward reply, he sat down and disappeared behind the newspaper again.

'Come and play a game of *What*,' said Vita, 'we've just got time before lunch.'

They all sat down for lunch at two o'clock. Vita informed her that the whole family was together because the older boys were home from their boarding schools for the weekend. 'Mother loves to have us all around her,' she confided. 'We're her chicks.'

Indeed, Seraphina Valentine seemed in her element surrounded by her children, who clamoured for her attention and laughed and teased each other with a charming playfulness. To Lucy, so used to her frowning mother who was always worrying about whether things were going right, this smiling relaxed woman seemed like an angel.

'Now I want Lucy to come and sit next to me,' said Mrs Valentine, patting the chair next to her. 'I want to find out all about you.'

As Lucy slipped in beside her, Seraphina tossed back her hair and sighed happily. 'It is wonderful to have all our children here. It's not often that we're all together like this.'

Lucy looked around the table at the crowd of people. It was incredible to think that they were all one family. The parents at each end, the younger twins (Florian now quite recovered), the girls and the older boys who had travelled home from school for the weekend. And then there was the other little boy sitting in the middle. The one Vita had called the Brat.

He had straight brown hair which flopped down over his forehead. His watchful, closely spaced eyes and thin lips gave him a mean, pinched expression. Lucy noticed that he rarely smiled. He sat there hardly saying a word, humming quietly to himself and swinging his legs under the table. No one spoke to him in return.

Lucy scrutinised the older boys with care. The twins, both fourteen, had croaky voices on the verge of breaking. They were tall and blond like their father, and teased each other relentlessly, goosing each other every now and then with a poke in the ribs.

Anthony Valentine stood at one end of the long table sharpening the long carving knife. 'Remember now, all joints on the table will be carved!' He laughed and cast his sparkling blue eyes around the room as the children giggled guiltily and slipped their elbows down by their sides.

Mrs Valentine sat at the other end of the table. She looked relaxed and happy, occasionally pushing long wisps of black hair behind her long dangling Indian earrings. The table was laid casually with mismatched knives and forks placed haphazardly around the edge. Large jugs of water had been placed at each end and paper napkins in most of the places. Lucy took it all in with interest. What would her mother think of this, she with her perfect table settings and silver cutlery service – a wedding present from her own mother – all beautifully kept and polished and always put away after use in the teak canteen on the sideboard? Not much, she thought.

There was an empty place next to the Brat in the middle. Lucy eyed him discreetly. Who was this child?

Even as she wondered, Mrs Valentine reached over and touched her hand with her fingertips. 'Now, have you been introduced to everyone?' she asked. 'I hope Vita was polite enough to make sure you were . . .'

Vita looked up, caught out, a flush on her cheeks. 'I did, a bit . . .' Her voice tailed off.

Seraphina raised her head and tossed back her hair. The

sweet smile remained on her face. 'Now there's Constantine and Achilles, the elder twins, and Byron, all back from Bedales for a couple of days. Then you know Vita, of course, and Perdita and Lorelei, and Florian, now recovered, thank goodness, and our little baby Celestria. And then there's David, too, making it nine in all. He's one of the family, too. David is Olwyn's son. He's been here since he was three weeks old, haven't you, David?'

David nodded and said nothing.

Lucy could feel Vita shift in her seat and stiffen beside her. 'Everyone has such interesting names,' she said.

'Except the Brat,' Vita murmured so that only Lucy could hear.

Seraphina smiled. 'I adore interesting names,' she said. 'Probably because my own name was so unusual. It's from the Hebrew word *saraf* which means to burn. In the plural, *seraphim*, it means celestial beings.'

She looked around the table. 'Achilles, of course, was a hero in Greek mythology, and Constantine, which derives from the Latin which means constant, or firm, was the name of the first Christian Emperor. Celestria comes from the Latin *caelum*, which means heaven, or the home of gods and angels. Vita comes from the Latin, too, meaning life.' She tailed off as Olwyn entered the room carrying a large battered silver platter with a hefty roast leg of lamb.

It was the first time Lucy had looked at the housekeeper properly. Olwyn was short and heavy-set, with wide shoulders and hips, and thick legs. She wore a green knitted pullover and tight skirt which was pulled taut over her belly. Her short fair hair was cut in old-fashioned schoolgirl bangs, and her pale blue eyes were expressionless.

Olwyn placed the steaming meat before Anthony Valentine, who stood poised and ready with the freshly sharpened carving knife and fork.

Mrs Valentine clapped her hands lightly. 'Now, come now, children,' she exclaimed. 'Everyone help. Olwyn's not our servant, you know. Lucy, of course, is a guest, so she may stay seated.'

The children jumped to their feet and began to run in and out of the kitchen, carrying the bowls of potatoes, carrots, beans and steaming jugs of brown gravy. David joined in, too, but with a markedly slow reluctance.

Anthony Valentine stood at the end of the table and carved. He talked in a loud and passionate voice all the time, encouraging the children to talk, to tell him exactly what they thought about the week's events, and the exact reasons for their opinions. Anything and everything was analysed and discussed. No one had to agree. In fact, it was a good sign to disagree. 'What matters is that you have an opinion; it shows that you have thought about it properly and not just adopted some stupid received wisdom,' their father announced.

Lucy watched the scene with growing amazement. She listened to the older twins arguing with their parents not only about the tactics of students in Paris during the riots last May, or the graceful beauty of the Henry Moore exhibits at the new Hayward Gallery built on the South Bank, but also the merits of the Beatles. It astonished her. Her parents did not approve of the Beatles in any form. Her mother thought they were dirty and subversive, and her father thought they made a dreadful racket. The Valentines talked about the Beatles, the Rolling Stones and Bob Dylan as if they were as important as the opera her father liked to listen to on Sunday evenings.

In their mid-thirties, the Valentines made a striking couple. Eighteen years before, at Oxford, they had been a presence then. The impact they had on those who knew them now was just as strong, and Lucy was impressed.

The Valentine family had all settled down to the meal. 'I do like names,' Seraphina continued. She had a gentle singsong voice. 'It's important to have an unusual name, a name that means something interesting.

'Now, your name, Lucy, is the feminine form of Lucius, which comes from the Latin *lux*, meaning light. And what's your middle name?'

The dark eyes looked at her with interest.

'My middle name is Lorna. I'm Lucy Lorna.'

Seraphina nodded. 'How interesting. No doubt your mother named you after Lorna Doone, that romantic heroine of the book.'

Lucy stared at her blankly.

'The book, *Lorna Doone*,' Mrs Valentine repeated. She stared at the girl. 'No?'

Lucy shook her head slowly. 'I don't think so,' she said. 'I was just named after my Auntie Lorna, I think.'

Seraphina Valentine smiled, and squeezed Lucy's hand. 'I expect your aunt was named after Lorna Doone, then. A most popular book, it was, published in 1870, I believe. *Lorna Doone* was a great success and the name Lorna was just invented by the author. Then it became all the rage. It's a bit like the name Wendy. Did you know that Wendy is a made-up name? It was invented by a friend of James Barrie, who then used it in *Peter Pan*. Did you know that? So clever to make up a name that lasts. And, of course, Shakespeare invented the name Perdita, for the heroine of *The Winter's Tale*. It's derived from the Latin *perditus*, meaning lost . . .'

She looked over fondly at her second daughter who was reaching across the table for the bread.

'Don't reach, Perdita,' she called. 'Ask someone to pass you the bread.' She turned back to Lucy with a smile. 'Nobody could ever describe Perdita as lost,' she laughed lightly.

She scarcely paused as she quizzed Lucy about herself. 'Now, tell me what books you like to read – who is your favourite author?'

The conversation around the table turned to books and language. Olwyn and the children brought the food to the table, cleared the plates and brought the next course. Lucy noticed that David occasionally got to his feet to help but not often and certainly less often than the other children.

While the parents directed the conversation, Olwyn sat in the middle of the table watching the Valentine children eat, ticking them off quietly but sternly every now and then for talking with their mouths full or reaching across the table instead of asking for a dish to be passed. Every now and then, Anthony Valentine made some teasing remark to Olwyn, causing the housekeeper to laugh and reply quickly.

They talked of books and films and music. They laughed and argued and thumped the table. Lucy sat beside Seraphina Valentine feeling quite intoxicated by the atmosphere. Never had she seen adults behaving with such abandon or talking to their children as though their opinions mattered. By the end of the meal, she felt she had fallen in love with the Valentine parents and longed to be included in their brood.

'Now where do you live, Lucy?' Anthony Valentine asked.

'Falkland Road,' she replied shyly, aware that everyone was looking at her.

Anthony nodded. 'Where in Falkland Road?'

'Opposite the Wesleyan Chapel.'

'Ah,' he replied, 'the poor ignored Wesleyan Chapel. Built in such Gothic splendour a century ago, and regarded for so long as the most important free church in the district. Now it's hardly used at all. There used to be so many Methodists in Kentish Town. That's why Gospel Oak is called that – it's where the early Methodists taught the gospel, out in the open air. And that's where the council is now pulling down perfectly good houses to build those ghastly housing estates.'

'There's talk of the Methodists doing a straight swap with the Roman Catholics,' said Olwyn. 'The Catholic church in Fortess Road is much too small for them all.'

'I haven't noticed you going to chapel very often, Olwyn,' teased Anthony, helping himself to some more red wine.

Olwyn smirked. 'No, I don't think chapel and I mix too well nowadays. I spent too much time going to chapel as a young girl, I did, back in Cardigan when I was a child. I had enough chapel then to last for the rest of my life.'

Seraphina turned to Lucy. 'Did you know that the Welsh have traditionally run the dairies in north London for years?'

Olwyn nodded. 'That they did. I grew up on a farm in the wilds of Wales and came to London to seek my fame and fortune. In the early days I stayed with some relatives who ran a dairy in Finsbury Park. The milk came from the farms in my area of Cardigan. All the Welsh milk went to London and came back to Wales as English butter! In London, we used to speak Welsh all the time to each other. Once someone on the bus going down Holloway Road heard me and my cousin talking in Welsh and asked if we were Italian.'

Vita chimed in. 'Talking about the Catholics, they spill out into the street all day on Sundays, sometimes even out into the road.'

'Methodism saved this country from a serious popular revolt on the scale of the French Revolution,' said Anthony, getting into his stride. 'It really did make religion the opiate of the working class. But their membership has been plummeting over the past fifty years.' He lifted his glass of wine to his lips. 'They are partly to blame for this themselves because they will insist on teetotalism. Not much fun for anyone . . .'

As the conversation moved about from adult to child and back again, Lucy listened in awe. This was so different from the weekly Sunday lunches at home, where her mother fussed about the table settings and nagged her and Andrew incessantly about their manners.

After lunch, Vita led Lucy out into the garden where they lay on their backs in the long grass, the hazy sun warming their bare arms and legs.

Lucy watched the swallows swooping above them in the blue sky.

'You're lucky to have so many brothers and sisters,' she said. But she was thinking: You're so lucky, full stop. You're so lucky to be in a family where everyone is interested in books and ideas and life in the outside world beyond work and the neighbours. She did not speak these last thoughts out aloud but they spun in her head as she stared up at the blue sky above.

Vita had found a ladybird on the leaf of a shrub and was trying to persuade it to walk on her arm. 'Mmm,' she replied.

'It must be wonderful to have such a big family . . .'

'It's okay,' said Vita without enthusiasm. She did not seem interested in talking about it.

The girls fell into silence again and then Lucy's curiosity

grew. She wanted to know everything about this family
she wanted to be part of. Vita patiently answered her
questions.

'The twins and Byron go to Bedales School, and the rest
of us go to King Alfred's, another progressive school.'

'What's a progressive school?' Lucy had never heard of
such a thing.

'It's not as strict as the normal type of school,' explained
Vita. 'You don't wear uniform and the children are considered as important as the teachers. Even when we dance
on the desks and do other naughty things, the teachers
don't get really cross. It's great. And at Bedales the boys
have midnight feasts and do all sorts of things they're
not supposed to do. They're even allowed to smoke.' She
paused and then added, 'I don't think they're allowed to
smoke drugs, but I'm not sure.'

Lucy had never heard of people smoking drugs but her
interest was elsewhere. 'And what about Olwyn? How long
has Olwyn been your housekeeper?'

Vita rolled her eyes. 'She came when the Brat was
three weeks old. She was training to be a social worker
but she got pregnant. That meant that she had to give
up her training and look for work. She's been here ever
since.'

'So David's like another brother, in a way . . .'

Vita did not reply, and Lucy felt worried. She was
desperate to keep the conversation going, to find out about
all these people.

'Does David go to the same school as you or your
brothers?'

Vita shook her head. 'The Brat? No, he goes to the school
down the road. Olwyn couldn't afford to send him to our
school.' She paused and added, 'Thank goodness.'

Lucy watched the ladybird clambering with some difficulty on the fine hairs on Vita's arm. 'Why do you call David the Brat all the time?'

Vita rolled over and suddenly scrambled to her feet. 'Oh, I don't know,' she said casually. 'He just is one.' She did not want to elaborate. She flicked the ladybird into the air and jumped to her feet. 'Come on,' she said, 'let's find Perdita.'

CHAPTER 5

May, 1997

Life and Death

Lucy received a letter from the fertility clinic surprisingly quickly. They had a last-minute cancellation and could fit her in. At least she was not going to have to wait for months, as she had expected, but she was suddenly anxious about being sucked into the hospital system. She had been feeling under the weather recently, which she put down to her sadness about the condition of her brother Andrew.

The clinic was busy. There were only two doctors on duty, the consultant – a tall, handsome man with thick grey hair and a pinstriped suit under his white coat – and his senior registrar.

Women sat in rows along the corridor, some flicking through the old magazines on offer, some just staring sadly into space. The pain of their failed attempts to procreate was clearly evident on their faces.

A few women were accompanied by their husbands. These too were also sad-looking people who sat slumped in chairs next to their wives, turning the pages of the women's magazines with a terrible listlessness.

The queue moved slowly. It was humid. Every ten minutes or so the nurse would call out someone's name. A woman would get to her feet, be weighed in full view of everyone and then taken off to a cubicle to undress and await the arrival of the man who may or may not provide them with the answer to their dreams.

Lucy tried to read her book and fight off her growing impatience with the delay. She had already been waiting forty minutes after her appointment time. When her annoyance had grown particularly strong, she reminded herself that she was lucky to have got an appointment so quickly. She should be grateful that she was there at all, she told herself.

As she sat there staring at the pistachio green walls and the health posters Blu-Tacked to them, she thought about the night before when Vita had come over for a drink. Lucy had wanted Simon to meet her important friend from the past. Simon was not a particularly sociable man and Lucy was surprised and pleased by how well he and Vita had got on. Being journalists, they had a lot of common ground and acquaintances they both knew. They shared their opinions of stroppy editors, lazy writers and people who ripped off other people's work. The evening had been a success on all sides. Vita told Lucy that her sister Perdita wanted to see her again, too, and Lucy agreed to a day when the three of them could meet up again.

Another patient had been called. Lucy thought of Andrew in a ward two floors below her now. She was planning to visit him afterwards if she had time.

Andrew was back in the hospital again and very low in spirits. After his first attack of PCP, he had been discharged from hospital within a week. For a while he had been feeling fine again, though rather nauseous from the Septrin he was

taking for the pneumonia. Then just three days ago he had
started getting attacks of diarrhoea which did not stop.
He could not control it at home and had to go into the
hospital. There they told him he now had *cryptosporidium*,
a parasite that lives in the drinking water, which they
could not eliminate from his system. They also thought
he showed signs of pneumonia again. They admitted him
to try to control his gut and check again on the state of
his lungs.

'They all appear kind and well meaning,' Andrew had said
during his first stay, 'but I know better than most people that
to them I am basically only a case study. I'm a specimen
who can help them learn more about HIV. I'd do the same
in their position but I'm not. All I want is a bit of peace and
quiet at home.'

Now he had been hauled in again so that the doctors could
learn some more.

Upstairs at the infertility clinic, it was Lucy's turn at last.
She had waited an hour. Four years and one hour. She was
weighed and taken into a cubicle to get changed. Dressed in a
starched blue hospital gown, she smiled at the tall handsome
consultant as he came into the room.

'Good morning, Mrs Montague.' He had a friendly face
and an avuncular manner. His smile seemed genuine.

He studied Dr Kenny's letter of referral and then turned
to her. 'You've been trying to conceive for four years.'

'That's right.' Lucy tried to smile back and make her voice
sound bright and cheerful. She could not bear to be identified
with the sad team of women sitting outside in those chairs in
the corridor.

'And you've never been pregnant before? No accidents?
Abortions? Miscarriages?'

She knew he had to ask such a question. It was relevant for him to know if she had ever conceived in her life. It was not a nosey question about her sexual history.

She shook her head. 'No, nothing.'

'All right, pop yourself up on the bed and let's have a look at you.'

Lucy lay on her back with her legs bent while the doctor prodded and probed her body, gently, carefully. He felt her breasts and around under her arms. She was vaguely aware that her breasts felt heavy and tender to his touch.

The doctor's face was inscrutable but he seemed to be spending a long time feeling around her lower belly, gently and quietly.

'When did you say your last period was?'

She had to think for a moment. Normally she knew exactly when it was but since she had admitted that she needed help, she had stopped counting. 'About three weeks ago.'

'And it was a normal period.'

It came out as neither a statement nor a question. Lucy had no sense of what he meant.

'I think so.' Creeping up from deep inside her came a fear that something was wrong. Something very serious. She tried to remember. He had to know all the facts. 'But when I think about it, it was perhaps a little lighter than usual. It didn't last very long. But it was definitely a period. It came on the dot, on the twenty-seventh day of my cycle.'

She remembered her sorrow only too well. And she remembered thinking that perhaps her period was light because she was going into an early menopause, just to finish things off for her.

'Anyway, I think we missed the fertile days that month because my husband was away,' she added ruefully.

'And the period before that? That was normal?'

'As far as I remember, yes.'

All periods had become the same to Lucy, the bloody messenger of death. If not the death of a fertilised ovum, a death of another tiny part of her. Sometimes she felt as though there was not much left alive in her.

The consultant had finished. 'All right, sit up, Mrs Montague. I'm not going to do an internal examination today.'

Lucy stared at him. 'Why not?' Her throat tightened with fear. It was cancer. He was going to tell her that something was wrong, so dreadful that she should stop thinking about something as trivial as infertility. She clenched her fists over the edge of the bed.

The doctor turned to look at her. His eyes were kind and intelligent. 'I wouldn't say this if I weren't certain because I know how painful it is for you ladies when you cannot conceive.'

Lucy stared at him. This was not making sense. He did not look serious in a worried sort of way. But then doctors are used to conveying bad news.

'The fact is,' he continued, 'you appear to be pregnant. As soon as you can you should make an appointment on the other side of the building in the antenatal clinic.'

'Pregnant?' Lucy was dazed. She sat rigid in her position.

The doctor smiled at her and patted her hand. 'You have what we call a "waiting list" pregnancy. It's more common than you'd think. Sometimes just the very fact that you know your problem is going to be taken seriously at last can do something to the reproductive system. It's very mysterious. A little tender loving care can do all sorts of wonderful things.'

'But my periods . . . I've been having periods. How can I be pregnant? And how can I possibly be pregnant when we didn't even have sex at the right time last month?'

'My guess is that you conceived the month before, so you were already pregnant last month. Your last two periods have not been real periods, even though they seemed to be normal to you. As you said, the last one was a bit lighter. It's possible to have some breakthrough bleeding at the time when you would have had a period, which makes the woman think she's having periods. I've known of cases where the woman has had a monthly bleed throughout the nine months of her pregnancy.

'But by my examination I should think you are approximately ten weeks pregnant.'

Lucy began to laugh, suddenly and uncontrollably. Tears of joy filled her eyes. 'Thank you so much,' she said. She wanted to leap up and hug him. 'Thank you so much. I can't believe it. It's such a shock.'

She climbed down from the bed. Her legs were trembling. 'I can't thank you enough.'

The doctor smiled. 'You don't need to thank me, but I'll look forward to seeing you in the other clinic. You can get dressed now.' As he left the room, Lucy was too grateful to him for being the bearer of such good news to be annoyed by the patronising little pat he gave her on the knee.

Lucy dressed as quickly as her shaking hands would allow, fumbling with the buttons on her blouse and pulling her pants on backwards by mistake. She could not stop grinning and shaking her head in disbelief. Within a minute, she had gone from being miserable to a state of ecstasy. Everything about life had changed.

Not everything, of course. Lucy skipped out of the clinic, leaving all the sad women behind, joyful in her knowledge that she was no longer one of them. Avoiding the lift, she ran quickly down the stairs to visit Andrew.

The moment she stepped into the ward, she automatically

collected herself. Her ecstasy seemed inappropriate and insensitive in such a place.

Lucy was no longer bothered when she walked into AIDS wards at the hospital. Her first visit had been quite different. Before she went, just the thought of it had made her rigid with apprehension – afraid of what she might see but also even more afraid of how she might react, particularly at the sight of her brother.

It had indeed been a harrowing experience, seeing those rows of stricken young men, some blind, some constantly vomiting into buckets at their bedsides, wasted and anaemic, staring listlessly around them, all hope gone. But having visited him a few times at the hospital, Lucy had become used to it. It had become horribly unshocking.

Andrew was dozing when Lucy first arrived. She stood by his bed for a few minutes looking at him. As if he sensed her presence through his sleep, he stirred and opened his eyes. He smiled sleepily at her.

Lucy took his long bony fingers in her hand and leaned over to kiss him on the cheek. This was a gesture of greeting she had made herself do ostentatiously for four years, ever since Andrew had told her he was HIV-positive, but she was ashamed that even now, she avoided touching his lips. The AIDS virus cannot be passed on by social kissing – even deep French kissing, she knew that. HIV is a very fragile virus and it is difficult to become infected by it, she knew all that, too. She knew that it was impossible to get it from lavatory seats, sharing eating utensils, mosquitoes and, yes, kissing. But there was always that shameful little irrational uncertainty inside – and still she could not touch his lips. She did not want his saliva on hers.

Andrew had lost even more weight since her last visit. His six feet four inch frame had lost a lot of muscle and he was beginning to look like the skinny, stick-legged seven-year-old she knew as a child. As an adult, he had grown into a big strapping fellow, a brother a girl could be proud of.

But his skin was a good colour and, in fact, compared with some of the other patients in the ward, he looked quite robust. He was thin for him but not that thin.

While it was comforting to realise that, it was also worrying to think about how much further Andrew had to go before he looked like some of the other men in the ward, like his neighbour in the next bed, for instance. The poor man, who had a good job in a local authority, looked like somebody out of Belsen. His huge eyes had sunk into deep sockets and stared out at the world looking dazed and listless. His hair was dull and brittle, and the skin on his bony limbs was peeling.

He had been there when Andrew had first been admitted, three weeks before. Then he had had much more flesh on his bones and had been sitting up and chatting to a jolly group of friends who had come to visit him after work – clever, decent young people with good jobs and happy lives.

He had deteriorated a lot since Lucy had last seen him. There were many new faces in the ward, some looking remarkably healthy and normal, others evidently suffering from all sorts of opportunistic infections. One man opposite lay in bed, listless, his face covered with a mass of bluish red patches, the telltale signs of Kaposi's sarcoma, or KS, as those in the know called it.

Lucy had read up about KS, as she had about all sorts of AIDS illnesses. She knew that it was named after Moritz Kaposi, a professor of dermatology at the University of Vienna Medical School who in 1879 described an entity he called 'multiple pigment sarcoma', consisting of a group of reddish brown or bluish red nodules, usually a quarter of an inch in diameter, anywhere on the skin. In patients with HIV, KS is another AIDS-defining illness. Though not life-threatening in itself, it can be horribly disfiguring if it spreads across the face, and can cause serious problems if it spreads internally.

Lucy handed Andrew the giant Galaxy chocolate bar she had bought in the kiosk in the hospital lobby. He had always adored chocolate; she brought him some on every visit. 'This should keep you going.'

'The parents came to see me again,' Andrew said, tearing the paper off the chocolate and nibbling at a corner.

Lucy waited for more.

'Dad's fine but I think Mum finds it unbearable. She sits by my bed looking for an excuse to scarper.'

'At least she's visiting you,' said Lucy. 'I was afraid she might be too frightened to come into an AIDS ward.'

Andrew smiled ruefully. 'I think Dad managed to assert himself for the first time ever and gave her a talking to.' He sighed again. 'Still, we have nothing to say to each other, the parents and I. They sit here more or less in silence until it seems an acceptable time to leave.'

Remembering her dream-memory, Lucy asked, 'Do you recall a time when the parents were happy together?'

Andrew looked thoughtful. 'I think there was, a long long time ago, and so long ago that it doesn't matter. And I don't care, not after the way they've behaved towards me.

'I'm just a big disappointment to them, I suppose,' he continued. 'Not only did I not become a doctor, like a dutiful son, but I also turned out to be a faggot. Now I'm dying in such a way that all their friends will know that I am a faggot, that I have sex with men, when Mum's probably managed to keep it all a big secret up to now.'

It was not the first time that Andrew had talked like this. Over the past few weeks he had become somewhat obsessed with his parents' behaviour towards him. Lucy did not contradict him because much of what he said was true but she did wish that Andrew would stop tormenting himself about it. He had to let it go.

'Well, at least they came to see you,' she said. 'You know lots of people are rejected by their parents when they tell them they're HIV.'

'Yes, yes. I hardly need to be told that.'

'I do think Mother loves you, Andrew, she's just incapable of showing it.'

'If she can't show it, then she might as well not feel it.'

Andrew's voice was bitter. He turned away but at the angle, Lucy could see his eyes glistening. 'She doesn't kiss me when she comes,' he said softly. 'But then, what do I care?'

Lucy was silent for a moment, then she said, 'I think you do care, Andrew. I think you care quite a lot.'

Andrew turned back his head quickly as if to argue, but then he said softly, 'What day is it today? I lose track so quickly in here. What's the date?'

'It's May the thirtieth.'

Andrew looked up at the ceiling and sighed. 'It's odd to think I'm going to die. I know we all die at some point but it's a weird feeling knowing that it's imminent. It's weird to know that this time next year I'm probably not going to be here. It's odd to look at a calendar, and look at the days between now and Christmas and think that on one of those days, I shall probably die. One of those days will be my deathday. You will know that, and Patrick and Mum and Dad will know that date and you'll all remember it every year. It's a peculiar feeling to know that I'm definitely going to die young, that I shall never grow old. You will only remember me at this age or younger.'

Lucy grabbed his hand. 'That's not true, Andrew, you know that that's not true. Many people live for ten, fifteen years with HIV. There's no reason to suppose you'll die so soon. The advances they've made with drugs to treat all these things that go wrong mean that you can be treated.'

'Only until the next thing goes wrong.' Andrew's eyes were filling with tears as he fixed them on his sister.

'I've been thinking about this a lot, Lucy,' he said. 'I'm not interested in struggling on until the bitter end. I don't want to have my body giving up on me bit by bit. I'm very vain and I don't want to be covered with KS like that bloke over there. I'm terrified of going blind, and lots of people get this horrible virus in the eyes. Then lots of people get dementia. That would be even worse. But I couldn't bear any of these things happening. They're just not worth it.'

'What's not worth it?'

Andrew drew a quick breath. 'I'll kill myself before I get to that stage.' He spoke in a fierce hiss and stared at her defiantly.

Lucy stared back and nodded gently. 'I understand,' she said finally.

Andrew pushed himself up on his elbow. 'The problem with all this is knowing when to do it. It's a question of balance, of getting the timing right.' He was suddenly animated. 'I want to go on for as long as I can enjoy myself but if I leave it too late I may suddenly find myself trapped in hospital where I won't get the opportunity, or be too incapacitated to carry it out. That's my fear.'

He had obviously been thinking all this out for a long time. 'You will help me, won't you, Lucy? When the time comes, you'll be there for me?'

Lucy did not know exactly what her brother was saying. She assumed that through the gay network Andrew had the means to do away with himself. Surely he had been given specific instructions – like swallowing a handful of tranquillisers, drinking several large whiskies and placing a plastic bag over your head. If you breathe gently, you just gradually go to sleep. That was the way she remembered Bruno Bettelheim, the child psychiatrist, did himself in when he had had enough of life. Surely Andrew had done his homework. The thought of the act itself was too painful to think about in much detail and probably the less she knew, the better. He was right. She could not argue against him.

'You know I'll always be here for you,' she whispered. 'I've always supported whatever you've wanted to do.'

She swallowed hard. 'But, Andrew, you will tell me, won't you? You will tell me if you're going to do it, so I can say goodbye.'

He turned away and loosened his hold on her hand. 'I don't know if I can promise that,' he said flatly. 'In some ways I think it's better just to do it without a fuss, without telling anyone. Probably Patrick will be the only one to know. And perhaps I won't even tell him when the time comes . . .'

They sat in silence for a few minutes. Then Andrew spoke again. 'I've been doing a lot of reading about death lately. We know so little about it. Why should it be worse than sleep? Socrates said that, just before he died after taking poison. He said, "If it was an annihilation of our being, it is still an improvement to enter a long and peaceful night. We feel nothing sweeter in life than a deep and tranquil rest and sleep, without dreams."'

Lucy smiled. 'Good for Socrates,' she murmured.

There was no more to say about this. Then Lucy remembered her own good news. She smiled. 'By the way,' she said quietly, 'you're going to be an uncle. Believe it or not, I've just been told that I'm two and a half months pregnant. You're the first to know. The baby's due in January, so you'll just have to stick around until then.'

Her brother smiled. 'Well done,' he said. 'I'm very pleased for you and Simon. I know how much that means to you. I'd love to have had children myself . . .' His voice tailed off and then he said, 'I would love to stick around to see my nephew or niece, but it would be foolish of me to make any promises now. Mind you, there is one promise I'll make, and that is that the minute I get out of here – with any luck by the weekend – I'll buy a bottle of champagne and we'll drink a toast to the future member of the family.'

Andrew collapsed into the pillow, his eyelids drooped. 'I'm tired,' he said. 'This bloody tiredness sweeps over me and I can't fight it.'

Lucy got to her feet. 'I'll leave you to rest,' she said. 'By the way, I've been meaning to ask you if you remember the Valentine family when we lived in Kentish Town. I don't expect you do because they were my friends rather than yours, and you were only seven. I recently met one of the girls again . . .'

Andrew was smiling sleepily. 'I do remember them,' he murmured. 'There were lots of children . . . the girls were very powerful . . . there was a nanny with mean eyes . . .' His voice faded and suddenly he was silent with sleep.

Lucy tiptoed away from the bed and out of the ward. She left the hospital feeling closer to Andrew than she had since she was a child. Somehow the teenage years and then adulthood had conspired to force the two of them apart. They remained close in spirit but work and their respective relationships meant that they never had time alone together and so never had the chance to talk about their parents in any detail.

How she longed for them all to be friends! Lucy had the strongest urge to get Andrew and her parents reconciled – she only hoped it would be possible before it was too late.

Lucy told Simon the good news when he came home from work. His joy showed her that he had been more worried about their fertility problems than he had previously let on. He kissed her and hugged her tight. 'I'm so happy for you,' he said. But the sentimental shimmer in his eyes told her that he was happy for himself too.

They drove down to Lucy's parents' house in Dulwich, south London. Lucy had decided to surprise them with her news in person. Simon drove rather recklessly as the truth about Lucy's condition gradually sank in. He talked and joked incessantly.

'The responsibility! Now we really are grown-up! No more lie-ins on Sunday mornings, that's what they all say. No more hangovers. And if it's a boy I'll have every excuse to spend my Saturday afternoons watching cricket matches . . .'

Lucy smirked. 'You might have a cricket-mad daughter, you know. And you're jumping the gun a bit. It hasn't been born yet. Let's get there first.' She felt supremely content and contained in a way that she had not for many years. 'Besides,' she added, 'remember what Vita said the other day: with children, it's the first few years that are really hard. When they're old enough, you can bribe them with TV or treats if you want to get the occasional lie-in.'

Simon laughed. 'I hope she's right, I hope our kids don't turn out to be incorruptible. Oh, the joys of daytime television! Our parents never had anything like that when we were growing up.'

He fell silent and looked thoughtful. As they stopped at some traffic lights, Simon peered at Lucy. 'Does this mean that I have to get a more ambitious job?'

'I won't make you do that,' laughed Lucy, 'but you may have to limit your book collecting for a few years, or decades.'

Simon had only a few hobbies. He liked watching but not playing cricket, and he liked reading. Recently he had begun to collect first editions of modern crime novels, rummaging through second-hand bookshops and car boot sales, and poring over the catalogues of second-hand book dealers. He already had an impressive collection of Ruth Rendells, Patricia Highsmiths, P.D. Jameses and Elmore Leonards. He liked to boast about how little he paid for the books but Lucy suspected that he did not always reveal the true sum that he spent each month on this habit. It had become a joke between them.

'At least I don't bet on the horses like some of the blokes on the paper. The Features Editor loses forty quid a week, and at least my books should grow in value!'

Lucy smiled at Simon and placed her hand on his leg. She could feel the muscle in his thigh tense up as he shifted gear. A warm tingle ran through her. It seemed as if all their difficulties were over. 'And I'm pleased you liked Vita so much the other day. I was afraid you wouldn't. I thought you might find her too assertive.'

Vita had taken up Lucy's invitation to have a drink and meet Simon one evening. Simon was not keen on particularly confident, 'aggressive' women. Although he tolerated Rosie, he often found her uncomfortably over-bearing. 'I think it's interesting that you are attracted to assertive women as friends, when you're not overtly like that yourself.'

It made Lucy chuckle. 'Perhaps I choose them because you're less likely to run off with them.'

Simon smiled wryly. 'Yes, but I did like Vita. I thought she was interesting. I've noticed her byline in the nationals for some time. She's done some good campaigning pieces on various social issues which I like. And it may be that she could do some pieces for us – she's got a good eye for a story. I was pleased that she didn't seem to think it beneath her to write for a local rag.'

For all his apparent lack of ambition, Simon loved working on a local paper because a good local paper – as his was – could truly affect ordinary people's lives in a way that a national newspaper could not. A newspaper campaigning, for instance, for traffic-calming humps in the road outside the primary school, or rooting out dishonest landlords, could do far more good than any of the high-minded broadsheets some of his more ambitious mates had moved on to.

Lucy respected Simon for that and she never put pressure on him to go for more glamorous jobs on the nationals, where he would certainly have less influence in the world than he did now.

'I did like Vita,' Simon was saying. 'She's good-looking, too,' he added with a lascivious grin.

Lucy sat back in her seat and allowed her head to roll gently on the head rest behind her. Suddenly life seemed simple and sweet. When their prospects had seemed so grim before, now they suddenly had a future – at least, seven months ahead and beyond, they did. From bumping along the bottom, she had now shot up to the heights of ecstasy. She was excited about telling her parents and looked forward to seeing the look on their faces at the news. That should cheer them up, she thought. Again she hoped that the baby would give her mother something new to think about, so she would stop fussing about the house and bullying Lucy's father. But then, she hoped that Andrew's condition would have done that, too.

As if Simon had been reading this last thought of hers, he said, 'Well, now your father will really have to believe that Andrew is never going to follow in his footsteps. I've always felt that deep down Gordon still thinks that Andrew is suddenly going to decide to practise as a doctor, after all.'

Lucy nodded. 'Daddy's so proud of the family tradition – his grandfather, his father and then himself – and it was always expected of the sons of the family. All my childhood, my parents talked about Andrew going to medical school. No other options were ever considered. And they certainly never thought I should go to medical school. A nursing training would have been acceptable – like my mother's – but not medical school.'

'So Andrew conformed until he actually qualified,' said Simon. 'Then he turned his back on it all. That must have hurt your parents.'

'Yes, he turned his back on them, too, really. They've never properly forgiven him.' Lucy paused. 'Still, I would hope that they are no longer fretting about whether Andrew is going to continue the family tradition when Daddy retires next year. All they need to worry about now is how many months, or years, Andrew's got left.'

They drove on over Battersea Bridge and down through Brixton and Herne Hill towards Dulwich, where Lucy's parents still lived in the house they had moved to from Kentish Town at the end of the 1960s.

* * *

Lucy's announcement of her good news caused great rejoicing at her parents' home during the early part of the evening. Hilda hugged and kissed both her daughter and son-in-law and Dr Butler pulled out a bottle of champagne, given to him last Christmas by a grateful patient. They sat in the sitting room with the French doors open sipping the fizzy wine and talking animatedly about the little object buried deep inside Lucy, a little object that was part of all of them. It was now all right to talk about it. But as the evening wore on, the earlier levity and feeling of hope gradually fell away bit by bit as people switched their thoughts from the future of the unborn to the remaining life of the about-to-die. It was mostly unspoken, however, Andrew's name was hardly mentioned, though his presence hovered over the dinner table like Banquo's ghost.

When Lucy tried to ask her mother about Andrew, their conversation became a tangled mess.

'You saw Andrew,' Lucy said quietly.

Hilda had picked up the bowl of French beans and offered them to Simon. 'That's right,' she said quickly. 'Would you like some beans, Simon? They're from the garden.'

Lucy was used to her mother's evasiveness and was not ready to give up easily. 'How did you find him?'

Her mother glanced up at her sharply. Her expression was pinched and taut. 'What do you mean?'

'Andrew,' continued Lucy. 'When you saw him, how did you find him?'

'We found him in the ward.' Her mother pursed her lips and helped herself to some beans.

Now Lucy retreated. What was the point?

Her father cleared his throat. 'We thought Andrew had lost a lot of weight,' he said. 'A considerable amount.'

After that, Hilda made it impossible to try again. She began to talk incessantly, jumping from one topic to another as though a silence in the conversation would allow something nasty to creep in. And news about the baby had given her a great opportunity for such chatter. It was as if she had shoved Andrew's ghostly presence out into the cold and slammed the door behind him. She launched into a monologue: 'I can't wait to let everyone know,' she said. 'At last I'm going to be a grandmother. I shall start knitting straight away. Now, where are you going to have the baby? I hope you're not thinking of having it at home, not at your age. I wonder what it'll be. I suppose you'll be able to find out, with all the tests they do nowadays, but I think it's fun not to know, it's far more exciting to find out at the birth.'

Lucy endured the rest of the meal in silence. Then she cleared the table and left her mother talking rapidly to a tolerant Simon in the sitting room while she and her father washed the dishes.

'Does Mother care about Andrew at all?' Lucy did not look at her father as she spoke. 'She's hardly mentioned him all evening. In fact, she's positively avoided talking about him.'

Dr Butler dried the glasses with the checked dishcloth and placed them carefully in the sideboard. 'Yes, she does, of course,' he said. 'But she's very excited by your news, as you can tell, and so am I.' He paused. 'But your mother has had a big shock, you know, and it will take a while for her to get over it.'

Lucy sniffed. 'Well, she'd better hurry up before it's too late.'

'You know it's difficult for a religious woman like your mother to get a grip on homosexuality.'

Lucy turned to look at her father. 'Why don't you tell her to stop being so ridiculous, then? Why can't you make her see sense?'

Her father looked away. 'I've done my best,' he said. 'I don't think I can do any more.'

Lucy sniffed again dismissively, causing her father to look up quickly.

'Don't judge her too harshly,' he said quietly. 'Your mother's not perfect, just as none of us is perfect. She's had a few blows in her life and it takes a while to recover each time.' He paused and then continued. 'Sometimes it's not possible to recover completely. But I do believe she'll come through this all right.'

Lucy looked up. 'What blows? What blows has she had?' Her mother had always seemed so simple, her life so straightforward, it seemed to her, a housewife and mother, the wife of a doctor. She looked straight at her father, challenging him to explain.

Dr Butler stared back, tempted to explain about the tragedies and disappointments that had become the barnacles of their married life. But now was not the time.

'One day I'll tell you about it,' he said. 'Not now. Pass me that pot. It needs a good rub.'

Lucy handed him the orange Le Creuset dish and turned to finish washing the plates in silence, making a conscious decision to think about something other than Andrew. She switched her thoughts to the drink she had arranged to have with the Valentine sisters later that week, and she realised that she felt oddly nervous about meeting up with Perdita again.

Lucy had arranged to meet the Valentine sisters in a bar in Covent Garden. Vita had been adamant about getting Lucy

and Perdita together when she had been for a drink to meet
Simon. 'Perdita wants to see you,' she said.

Lucy had been surprised. She did not remember having
a particularly strong attachment to Perdita. In fact, when
she thought about Perdita, or tried to remember what she
had been like, all she could recall was a strange feeling of
wariness, an odd feeling of unease.

Lucy strode across a busy Covent Garden and found the
two sisters were already at the bar. They were sitting at a
table, three glasses and a bottle of white wine on the table
between them.

Vita jumped to her feet when she saw Lucy and greeted
her with a broad smile. 'There you are! And this is Perdita.'

Perdita rose to her feet, too, and reached out to shake
hands. Lucy recognised her straight away, the same pretty,
round face, the pale blue eyes, the dark mole on her cheek
and the glossy black hair. Straight from a day in court, she
looked severely smart in the dark clothes of her trade.

Perdita was smiling, but Lucy felt the pale eyes lacked
sincerity. She did not feel at ease.

'Have a drink,' Perdita said, pouring some of the wine
into the empty glass on the table.

It was a curious meeting and afterwards Lucy was not at
all sure what its purpose was. If Perdita had been keen to
see her, she still did not know why. It was almost as though
Perdita – now a successful barrister specialising in family
law and child abuse cases – had wanted to check her out,
to have a look at her twenty-eight years later.

No real contact was made between them that evening.
While Vita was friendly and talkative, and kept the conversation going, Perdita was closed and unforthcoming. Lucy
felt she was being inspected.

There was just one moment when Perdita turned her

impenetrable pale eyes on to Lucy and said abruptly, 'I suppose we only actually knew you for a few weeks one summer, didn't we?'

Lucy was eager to talk about their shared experience. 'Yes, that's right, though to me it seems much longer than that. I came to your house almost every day, as I remember, and I came to stay with you all at your grandmother's house, too. I was so amazed by the size of your family. There were so many of you, and your parents seemed so lovely and easygoing.' She laughed. 'They were such a contrast to mine!'

The sisters smiled and said nothing. Lucy suddenly remembered something. 'Didn't you have a nanny or housekeeper?'

It suddenly came to her, a vivid image of the housekeeper. She had a picture in her head of a stocky woman with plump knees serving up sausages and mashed potatoes to a crowd of noisy Valentine children around the table. 'And didn't she have a child, too? A boy. What was he called?'

A silence hung suspended in the space between them. Perdita sipped from her glass. 'David,' she said quietly. 'He was called David.'

There was something else, nagging in Lucy's brain. She tried to tease it out, but it stayed there. 'Yes, David, that's right. I'd forgotten. I only vaguely remember how he looked . . .'

Vita reached over and poured more wine into her glass. 'I'll get some peanuts,' she said, waving her arm to catch the waiter's attention.

'David,' Lucy repeated the name, trying to force an image of the boy into her head. 'He was about our age, wasn't he? And he got very ill . . .' Now it was coming back. She was shocked as the recollection came back with a jolt. 'Why, he died, didn't he?'

The sisters glanced at each other in a way that sent Lucy flying back to that summer. She remembered how they used to glance at each other like that in front of her, often when she had asked them something. It was a disturbingly familiar gesture.

Then Perdita nodded. 'That's right. He did die. He got very ill and died.'

Lucy was frowning. 'Yes, I remember that now. But what happened then? What happened to his mother? It must have been awful for her.'

Perdita and Vita nodded slowly and thoughtfully, in unison.

'Olwyn left us soon after David died,' said Vita. 'We did not keep in touch. I think she went back to her family in Wales.'

'And my family moved away, too,' said Lucy. She twisted the stem of her glass.

'That's right, you did,' replied Perdita. She spoke quietly, her eyes fixed on Lucy all the time.

Suddenly she smiled, revealing beautiful, even white teeth. 'Now, I understand that you are going to have a baby. That's wonderful news.'

Lucy nodded and smiled coyly. 'Yes,' she said. 'I'd almost given up hope.'

The topic was changed and the rest of the short evening was an odd and unexpected hour of small talk. Lucy sensed that Perdita had almost lost interest in her. She was certainly distracted.

The wine was finished and it was time to go. Lucy went home feeling quite dejected. Vita had been effusively friendly still, but Lucy left puzzling about why Perdita had been keen to see her in the first place. Perhaps it was just to be polite, but why? Perdita was a busy woman and they had not had the same strong bond between them that existed between Lucy and Vita. So why should she bother to fix up such a meeting? Lucy knew that there had to be some reason for it.

Lucy sat on the bus home feeling most peculiar. It was silly but it was almost as if Perdita had been checking her out in some way. But why and for what reason, she had no idea.

She was also bothered by the exchange about the house-keeper's boy, David. It was amazing that she had completely forgotten that he had died, and the discussion about him had just fizzled out like a dying sparkler. But there was something more; her gut feeling told her that. As she struggled to recall that ninth summer of her life, she was aware of an unsettling feeling in the pit of her stomach. She had no idea why; however hard she tried to catch the uneasiness and lay it out to dissect it, it remained elusive inside her, taunting her from a distance like some cruel school bully long ago.

That night the childmares returned. She dreamed that she gave birth to a perfect baby. She was ecstatic, filled with intense pleasure. The baby lay in her arms but as she gazed down at it she noticed that it had stopped breathing. In fact, it had never been breathing. The baby had been born dead but no one had noticed.

Lucy woke up crying. Why was she still having these dreams? She was pregnant. She was going to have a baby. Why was she still having these horrible dreams when there was no reason?

CHAPTER 6

July, 1968

Freedom

As she absorbed the first impressions of the Valentine family, Lucy realised that her experience of the Sunday lunch was unusual because the family was very rarely gathered all together in that way. The normal state of affairs was for everyone to be dashing one way or another, pursuing their own interests.

The next thing that struck her was the loving way in which Mr and Mrs Valentine behaved towards each other. They were very absorbed with each other, and clearly loved one another. They did not converse in the way her own parents did, in tight, barking outbursts with undercurrents that flowed on through the days and months without ever coming to the surface.

No, Anthony and Seraphina seemed openly to like one another, always attentive, listening to what the other had to say, laughing at each other's little ironies and engaging in rigorous playful arguments. It was a form of communication she had never seen before and it made her feel safe. They never seemed to argue about their children or drag their children into battles of will between them. It was always just the two of them.

She was equally impressed (the first time she witnessed it) by the way they touched in front of others. Although Lucy, of course, knew the facts of life, she could not even think that her parents ever had sex, ever mated like the dogs in the street. Her own and Andrew's existence proved that they had done it, twice, at least. But since then, surely, they had never touched each other in that way.

The Valentines, on the other hand, were like the young hippy couples she sometimes saw on Hampstead Heath or in Regent's Park where she would walk with her parents and brother on Sunday afternoons. They touched each other playfully, to interrupt a remark or catch each other's attention. They complimented each other on their looks or ideas. Once, Lucy watched on with astonishment while Anthony Valentine ran his hand over Seraphina's hip and the round of her buttock under her skirt. She was confused by a strange *frisson* of excitement that tugged at her chest.

The Valentines were indeed as sexually attracted to each other as they had ever been. Fortunately, Anthony's feelings for his wife were if anything enhanced throughout her six pregnancies. Many men are frightened by the physical manifestation of feminine fecundity but Anthony was drawn to it every time.

The children often witnessed their parents' day-to-day affection for each other but they did not see their father run his hand up their mother's leg while she was reaching up for a reference book from a high bookshelf, or see her turn around and thrust her leg between his as she reached up her arms and pressed her tongue deep into his mouth. They did not see the tussling and rolling on the bed, the sucking and licking, the stroking and the squeezing, arms and legs entwined, groaning and clinging to each other in joyful nympholepsy.

Anthony and Seraphina knew that they were lucky. In each other they had found a mate for life, someone each had grown with at the same pace. Their sexual energy and enthusiasm simply reflected the other mental and physical energy they shared. They each saw parts of themselves in the other. They were two halves who together made the whole.

To outsiders they were the perfect couple. To their children, they were ideal. Everyone told the young Valentines how clever and handsome and attractive their parents were. They had kudos at school for having famous parents, parents who stood up for their beliefs and made speeches against the Vietnam War and defended the rights of young students to have a voice of their own. And parents they called by their first names, Anthony and Seraphina, rather than Mummy and Daddy, or Mum and Dad, like the rest of the world.

Anthony Valentine was frequently seen on television with well-known people in, say, a delegation which included the philosopher A.J. Ayer, going to the American Embassy to protest against the trial of the famous Dr Spock in America. And Anthony Valentine was often there on the news and talk shows, having visited Paris during the May riots and being on friendly terms with the big student leaders in France and America.

Young people often admired him for saying things they felt but had never articulated before, while older members of the Establishment thought he was clever but probably in the pay of the Russians. Ordinary people who did not have very strong political views, such as Dr and Mrs Butler, thought that the Valentines were very clever but probably a bit too idealistic with it.

At the Valentine home, the parents were often there in the background – Seraphina in her study, painting or writing, and Anthony, if he wasn't at the LSE, would be holed up in his study too. Then they were not to be disturbed at any time, and children were not allowed to make noise outside their doors. The only time Lucy ever heard either Seraphina or Anthony Valentine get angry with their children was when one of them made too much noise outside their studies when they were trying to work.

Apart from that, there appeared to be no rules in the house. So, free in the day, the Valentine children, it seemed to Lucy, had the greatest fun. They rode their bikes all over the neighbourhood, through the wide leafy streets of Tufnell Park and Holloway, and through the rough estates of Somers Town and Kentish Town. They did not have to tell anyone where they were going or what they were doing. They simply knew that if they wanted to eat lunch or tea they had to be at the dining room table at certain times of the day.

In fact, the Valentine children saw very little of their parents. Anthony and Seraphina would emerge at six every evening for drinks after the children had eaten their high tea in the dining room. Olwyn prepared this meal each day, serving up enormous steaming dishes of shepherd's pie or Irish stew with Brussels sprouts and boiled potatoes.

There was a work rota written up and pinned to the wall in the kitchen. The tasks were all written down one side – the setting of the table, the clearing up, washing and drying – and the children's names were carefully written beside them. Everyone knew what to do and Lucy was impressed to see that they all did it, too, without complaining. For they seemed to know that once they had carried out their tasks, they were free from adult control.

David's name was also on the rota, though Lucy rarely saw the boy doing his jobs with the same diligence shown by the Valentines.

After tea, while Anthony and Seraphina sipped their cocktails in the sitting room, the children milled around them, playing the piano, arguing or playing cards. Half an hour was all the children had. Then it was time for the parents to go out, or simply to retire to their studies again while the children were marched off for their baths.

Those summer weeks seemed to go on for ever. Lucy had an open invitation to play at the Valentines' house whenever she wished. At first Hilda Butler worried that it was an intrusion for Lucy to go every day but after Seraphina Valentine had assured her for the fourth time that Lucy was genuinely welcome, Hilda Butler allowed herself to believe it. She also allowed Lucy to walk up the road on her own, which had never happened before. Perhaps seeing the Valentine children dashing unchaperoned around the neighbourhood had made her think that really it was safe to let Lucy out on her own to walk five hundred yards up the road. Or perhaps she was simply unable to reveal that until now she had accompanied Lucy everywhere. The reason did not matter; Lucy was ecstatic at her newfound freedom.

Gradually Lucy saw how the Valentine house operated. Although Seraphina and Anthony were often around in the day, they were also frequently out, either at work or attending concerts, poetry readings, art previews, the theatre or literary parties.

The person who really ran the household was Olwyn. She was the centre of the entire operation, organising the food and meal times, and the children's work rota, managing the two cleaning ladies, buying clothes for the children, dressing, washing and feeding them.

When Olwyn was not washing or feeding them, the children were free to run wild. That first week of the holidays, the older boys initiated a project to build a tree house in the garden. It was a tremendous effort and all the children became involved. They drew up the plans, carried the planks home from the wood merchant in Kentish Town Road (bought with money handed out by Anthony before he left to go to a meeting one morning), and hauled each plank up with a rope, positioning it and hammering in the nails.

The twins were big and strong and clever with their hands. In no time the shell of the little house was ready – reached by a ladder set against the trunk of the old horse chestnut tree.

'Now we need to make it comfortable,' declared Vita. 'And we need food for our meals.'

'Can we sleep up here?' asked Florian.

'Girls only,' said Perdita firmly.

Once the tree house had been erected, the elder boys lost interest and disappeared to concentrate on some other project. Now the interesting part started for the girls. They had spent the morning swimming at the Lido on Parliament Hill, Lucy included, and then returned for an afternoon in the garden at home. With the older boys out of the way, the tree house was theirs.

They dashed in and out of the house, carrying cushions and dragging blankets and rugs from the playroom. They carted out orange crates to sit on and kitchen towels to hang across the windows as curtains.

Slowly the house in the tree took on a rough look of comfort. It was finished. The girls looked at each other, wondering what to do next.

'I'm hungry,' Celestria whined miserably, clutching her belly.

'Olwyn said she'd bring us out a snack.'

Within five minutes, while the girls were settling themselves cross-legged on the tree house floor, Olwyn came out of the house carrying a wicker basket. David trailed along behind her.

'David wants to join you,' Olwyn said, as Vita let down a rope to be tied around the handle of the basket.

Perdita grimaced, though Olwyn could not see her.

The basket was hoisted up into the tree house and David clambered up the ladder to join them.

Perdita was silent as she divided up between them the egg mayonnaise sandwiches and freshly baked butterfly cakes and chocolate fingers.

David sat down opposite Lucy. He did not say a word but tucked into his pile of food with a cheerful smile on his face. Lucy felt sorry for him. It was so obvious that he wanted to be included all the time, and it just wasn't that easy.

She watched him as he ate. He was stockily built and had floppy brown hair which fell over his eyes, and wide gaps between his teeth.

He rarely spoke but ate his sandwiches slowly, chewing each mouthful with deep concentration.

'I'm still hungry,' said Perdita, licking the crumbs off her lips and eyeing the empty basket. 'I wonder if we can get anything else.'

Vita looked doubtful. 'Olwyn said we couldn't have any more or we'd ruin our appetites for tea later on.'

Perdita rolled her eyes impatiently and pushed herself to her feet. 'We'll see about that,' she said. With the basket swinging on her arm, she climbed down the ladder and disappeared into the house.

It was cool in the tree house under the waving green leaves of the horse chestnut tree. Conkers were appearing between the leaves. The children did not say much as they waited for Perdita to return. Lucy watched a ladybird walking slowly up the side of the tree house, carefully negotiating the rough splinters in the wooden plank as though each one were a tricky hill. At one point she caught Vita's eye. Vita smiled at her, causing a warm rush of pleasure to flow through Lucy's veins. Lucy smiled back.

The younger children had started a clapping game and then they began to play scissors – 'One, two, three . . .' – each time, forming the shape of paper, stone, pencil or scissors with their hands.

At last Perdita ran from the house carrying the basket. She climbed breathlessly up the ladder.

'Great!' Vita began to unpack the basket to reveal apples and pears and a packet of biscuits.

'There's some cold chicken, too,' said Perdita with some pride. 'Probably enough for a bite for everyone.'

'It's a lot,' commented Vita, sharing out the biscuits. 'Did Olwyn give you all this?'

Perdita laughed. 'Of course not! She wouldn't give me anything more. I just took it from the larder. There's so much food in there, no one will know . . .'

She stopped abruptly. Lucy noticed Vita roll her eyes. Perdita turned to David who was looking intently at the biscuits in his hands. Her eyes narrowed. 'Don't you dare say anything, David. Do you hear? You'll get it if you do . . .'

David looked at her, his mouth working slowly at the biscuit crumbs inside his mouth. Raising his eyebrows in an expression of innocence, he shook his head. 'No, of course I won't tell,' he said simply.

After a while the tree house lost its appeal so they climbed down to do other things. The younger children cooled off with water from the hosepipe, chasing each other around the lawn and shrieking with laughter, while Lucy, Vita and Perdita played a game of *Monopoly* with the older boys.

Lucy left the Valentines' house in the early evening after high tea of fried sausages, chips and peas. She felt happy and content. To her irritation, when she was halfway down Lady Margaret Road, she realised that she had left her swimming bag behind. After their swim at the Lido, she had stuffed her wet towel and costume into the duffel bag which she now realised she had left behind in the Valentines' house. Her mother had already scolded her twice that week for coming home without her cardigan and for getting filthy dirty while playing in the Valentines' garden. Lucy was half-tempted to leave the bag at the house, to say nothing and to hope that her mother would not notice. But there was always the risk of her mother asking where her swimming things were (she had the habit of remembering things like that). Also, she had arranged to go back to the Valentines the next morning for another swim, and the thought of having to wear a cold, clammy swimming costume was intolerable.

No, she had to go back, even if it meant getting home a bit late. Her mother would be cross but it would be too bad. Her newfound bravado surprised her. She must have caught it off the Valentine girls, she thought with some pride.

At the Valentine house, she let herself in through the gate and walked round the side to the back of the house, the route she always took nowadays.

There was the sound of water upstairs as the bath was being run for the younger children. Shouts of youngsters running around wildly upstairs rang out into the evening air.

Lucy stepped in through the back door. In the small hall outside the kitchen, she was stopped by the sound of Olwyn's raised voice. It was angry and threatening.

'Don't you dare do that again,' she was saying.

Nobody answered. Lucy edged forward to peer through the gap between the door and the wall. She could see Perdita standing before Olwyn, her head held high, her arms hanging straight down her sides. Her hands were clenched in tight little fists of defiance. Her chin jutted out.

Over by the far wall, Lucy could see David leaning nonchalantly against the Aga, a smirk spread across his face.

Oh dear, thought Lucy, Perdita's in trouble for stealing that food. And now she's being told off . . .

She watched with horror as Olwyn's arm came up and, as if in slow motion, whacked Perdita hard across the side of her head. Perdita staggered several feet across the room, crashing into the kitchen table. Her hand flew up to her ear.

Lucy's hand flew up to her mouth as she stifled a gasp. Stepping back, she quickly retreated from the house. She could leave her bag until the morning, after all.

She let herself out of the garden and ran down Lady Margaret Road. Her heart was racing, not from exertion but from shock, from the image which now swirled in her head of Perdita standing there challenging Olwyn to hit her again, and from the startling fact that during the entire incident, Perdita never once uttered a sound.

Lucy did not say anything to her parents about Olwyn hitting Perdita. She wanted to but she was afraid that if she did her mother would immediately stop her going to play with the Valentines. She could not bear the thought of that happening, so she said nothing, neither that evening, nor ever.

CHAPTER 7

June, 1997

Family Life

Lucy was in a buoyant mood on the day she went down to the market in Hammersmith to buy food for supper. There was an unfamiliar spring in her step, her shoulders were squared, her head held high. It was a long time since she had felt so good. With a life inside her, she felt consciously alive. It was also true that the early panic about Andrew had subsided after he had recovered from his early attacks of pneumonia remarkably well.

Andrew had been out of hospital for ten days now. His first evening out, at the small house he shared with Patrick in Notting Hill Gate, Lucy, Andrew and Patrick had drunk the champagne to celebrate the existence of Lucy's unborn baby.

The celebration was slightly subdued by the unexpressed acknowledgement that much of Andrew's life from now on was likely to be taken up with visits to and from hospital.

Andrew was sanguine about it. 'We'll take it slowly,' he said.

Now Lucy was shopping because she had invited Andrew and Patrick to supper that evening, along with her parents.

Andrew was loath to invite his parents to his own home, afraid that they might turn down the invitation. So Lucy had taken the matter in hand and invited everyone to her house with her and Simon. 'Neutral ground for everyone,' she said.

Simon was not pleased about the arrangements. 'You can't be the peacemaker, Lucy,' he said. 'You mustn't try to make people be what they aren't. Your mother has rejected Andrew up until now and it's highly unlikely that she's suddenly going to change in any fundamental way.'

Lucy frowned and said nothing. She was annoyed to be ticked off but she knew that Simon was probably right. She just could not help herself, so desperate was she for everyone to get on without friction.

Ignoring Simon's criticism, she focused on her fear that Andrew might cancel at the last minute. He had been cancelling on her a lot recently. Since being discharged from hospital, he had called off two lunch dates with her because he had not felt well enough to drag himself out of the house. He could only make plans on a daily basis because he was so chronically tired that he could never anticipate how much energy he might have in any one hour. He had oral thrush, with nasty white curds in his mouth, and he felt nauseous for much of the time.

As she wandered around the market, she tried not to think about Andrew's physical condition and switched her thoughts to the busy life of the street market around her.

She had always liked the noise and bustle of the market and the chirpy veneer of rudeness from the stallholders. There was one in particular she liked, because he was happy to let her pick out her own fruit and vegetables, so she always gave him her custom. Today she examined the glossy green peppers, and blue-black aubergines, gently squeezing the courgettes, testing them for firmness.

As she paid and waited for her change, she found herself staring at the green grapes nestling in blue tissue paper on the fake grass matting underneath. She had once seen a photograph in a magazine (probably Rosie's rag) which showed the female reproductive organs as represented by various fruits and vegetables – grapes for the ovaries, a pear for the uterus, a courgette for the vagina.

She remembered it because it had been a striking image, and a warm one. It was unusual and rather pleasant to think of one's reproductive organs as familiar objects and not alien bits of flesh and tissue hidden inside her belly.

Now she was pregnant, Lucy felt able to like her body again and to feel affectionate towards her reproductive organs in a way that she had not before. For all the time she had been trying to conceive, she had perceived her body as alien and hostile, as something separate from her real self, month after month rejecting her and her deep longing to start a life inside her.

'There you are, darling.' The stallholder handed Lucy her change.

She smiled broadly. 'Thank you,' she said gaily. She did feel good today. It was still difficult to believe that she was truly pregnant. It made her feel like a different person, as if she were empowered with a special strength. Such fortitude made the prospect of an evening with her parents and Andrew together more bearable. Perhaps it would all go well. Perhaps everyone would make up and forget their years of differences and there would be love and reconciliation. Then Simon would see that Lucy's efforts were right, rather than foolish and naïve, after all.

At least she would enjoy cooking the meal, listening to the

radio as she chopped the vegetables and softened the onions in the frying pan. She felt omnipotent with this little life inside her. No, the evening was bound to be a success . . .

Lucy's parents arrived first, and flustered, after a traumatic journey from Dulwich up to Lucy and Simon's house. Hilda Butler hated having to drive into town at the best of times but this trip confirmed her view that living north of the Thames was a dire mistake on Lucy's part.

She and Gordon had set off with plenty of time, as always, and had made good progress until they reached Clapham, where road works had caused long traffic jams all along the road. Young men and women were walking up and down the lines of cars offering bunches of roses or the latest edition of the *Evening Standard* for frustrated commuters on their way home from work. A couple of young girls were waving wet sponges and occasionally washing the windscreens of those drivers who allowed them. They could not have been much older than seventeen. One, with bright orange hair which stuck straight up in the air, began to wash the windscreen of Dr Butler's car.

'No, thank you,' he called out of the window. Dr Butler washed his car every two weeks with water considerably cleaner than what was being splashed on to it at that moment. 'No, thank you,' he repeated.

The girl ignored him and reached across the windscreen with a rubber wiper, revealing a sinewy, unshaven arm-pit.

'Go away!' Dr Butler stuck his head out of the window. 'Go away, I said no!'

His wife shrank back into the back of her seat. She was frightened of young people.

The girl stepped back and stared at him with a hostile

expression. She chewed gum slowly. 'I'm just trying to earn a bob or two,' she hissed. 'You stupid old gits.'

Fortunately the traffic had started to move again. Dr Butler wound up his window and put his foot down on the accelerator. 'I suppose we are old,' he said quietly.

Hilda pursed her lips and sucked in air. 'I think you might have been a bit firmer with them,' she snapped. 'You didn't sound very authoritative.'

Gordon kept quiet. He was used to his wife's digs by now and knew better than to respond.

At last they were moving and escaped the worst of the jams. But then, going over Chelsea Bridge, a young boy in the car in front had stuck his head out of the window and let out a stream of vomit which flew straight back towards the Butlers' car and splattered all over the windscreen.

It took Dr Butler ten minutes to clean up the mess before they could set off again. As he wiped the vomit off the windscreen, his wife sat tensely in the front seat, her fingers twisting around each other, her lips tight.

Andrew and Patrick had not yet arrived. Dr Butler paced around the sitting room while his wife perched on the edge of the sofa, her knees pressed together, her neck taut.

Simon offered them drinks while Lucy put on the water for the pasta. Seven minutes later, the doorbell rang. Mrs Butler jumped, her nervousness apparent to everyone. Hilda and Gordon had seen Andrew several times in hospital, but this was the first time in four years that they had met socially.

Lucy opened the door, wondering, as always, what Andrew would look like now. She had not seen him for a week and he had mentioned over the telephone that he had lost a lot more weight.

Indeed, he had. Now the skin was taut over his face so

that the outline of his skull was becoming clear to see. His eyes were large and staring, giving off an expression of deep sorrow. His fingertips were bluish, as though he had come in from the cold.

Andrew and Patrick walked into the sitting room behind Lucy, who watched Patrick walk over to her mother and hold out his hand. Mrs Butler pushed herself off the sofa to her feet. She shook Patrick's hand and tried to smile as she mumbled a greeting. A look of confusion spread across her face as she turned to Andrew, who was standing behind Patrick, waiting for her to make the first move.

For a brief moment, Lucy's spirits rose as she thought her mother was moving towards him as if she were going to kiss him. But then Hilda hesitated, she held back and the opportunity was lost. She hesitated for another second. Andrew had been poised to respond. Now he stepped back and nodded. 'Hello, Mother,' he said. 'Hi, Dad.'

Lucy felt Simon's critical gaze on her face. She looked away; it was excruciating.

As the evening progressed, Lucy was filled with a growing sense of hopelessness. She watched her mother's nervous and undemonstrative greeting, and she saw Andrew, after an initial look of hope, back off, hurt by his mother's inability to gather him in her arms and hug him. Her father's inept attempts to humour everyone made her squirm, and she was annoyed by the way he talked too loudly about the cricket score with Simon. Every now and then Lucy tried in vain to shut Simon up by glaring at him. Dr Butler loved cricket and followed it enthusiastically at every opportunity. When he discovered that Simon was a fellow fan, he had been delighted. That made up for the fact that his own son had never shown any interest in sport of any kind, ever.

Dr Butler did, however, talk to Andrew, asking about his

health. As a doctor, he was genuinely interested in hearing
the latest developments in treatment and what was being
done by the doctors to help him, and this was a language
he shared with Andrew.

Gordon also talked to Patrick, who was a personable
young man, a solicitor, sociable and friendly, and easy
company.

Lucy watched and listened. She watched her mother
sitting anxiously in her place at table sipping at her soup
and nibbling at her pasta. As the men talked, Hilda said
nothing, retreating into a troubled silence at the end of the
table. The whole situation clearly made her uncomfortable.
Lucy's heart was thumping with frustration and anxiety. If
her mother could not talk to Andrew, her own son, now,
she thought, she never would.

Gripped by an urge to inject some life into the conversation, Lucy was keen to pump Andrew for more memories
about the Valentine family. Placing a bowl of green salad
on the table, she jumped in. 'What else can you remember, Andrew, about the Valentines? I want to know your
impression of them.'

Andrew was looking uncomfortable but he managed a
smile. 'I remember that you were besotted with them. You
would do anything they asked you to do . . .'

Lucy was aware of her father's own discomfort at the
other end of the table. He was frowning and fiddling with
his napkin. Her mother, meanwhile, looked cross. Lucy was
not going to be deterred from grabbing this opportunity to
learn more from Andrew. Ignoring her parents, she pushed
on. 'Like what? What sort of thing did I do for them?'
She was excited that Andrew did seem to remember the
Valentines so well. He would be able to help reconstruct
that summer.

But Andrew's face had become twisted with pain. He winced as his body hunched over the table and he clutched at his chest.

'Are you all right?' Lucy stared at her brother.

Patrick was instantly solicitous. 'Is your chest hurting again?' He jumped to his feet and moved over to stand behind Andrew, whose eyes had filled with tears from the pain.

Perhaps it was more than the pain, which came and went in an erratic way, and the doctors never knew for sure what it was. Perhaps this time it was just the stress and strain of such an evening with his parents, but Andrew finally broke down. His attempt to hold back his feelings failed as his thirty-five-year-old face crumpled like a five-year-old's, and he dropped his head in his hands.

Patrick massaged Andrew's shoulders affectionately, rubbing them rhythmically and firmly.

Lucy watched her mother frown in embarrassed confusion as Patrick then bent down and kissed Andrew on the neck, murmuring reassurances into his ear. 'You're going to be all right, darling,' he whispered. 'Do you want to go home?'

Everyone else was silent. Dr Butler and Simon looked away, uneasy with this display of affection from one man to another.

Hilda sat rigid in her chair. The sinews of her neck were visibly taut. Was it disapproval she felt? Or was it disgust? She had always been too scared to imagine fully what homosexual men got up to when they were on their own, and this display simply confirmed that she was right not to think about it. She just knew it was wrong.

But as she watched her son crying, she remembered him as a little boy wailing because he had fallen over and hurt his knee. She saw her boy, her only son, who now, in his thinness, looked more like that little boy than a grown man.

Something inside her made her react now. She quietly reached out over the table and took Andrew's fingers in her hand. His fingers were cold and bluish, and she saw how skeletal they were. For a second she wondered if she was risking infection this way, even though she knew rationally that she could not. But just for that moment, her instincts as a mother were stronger than the prejudices and beliefs that normally ruled her life. As Andrew's fingers closed on hers, she took a sharp breath and tears filled the corners of her eyes.

Patrick took Andrew home before Lucy could serve up the chocolate mousse she had made for pudding. Andrew's pains had subsided but it was agreed that he was tired and that perhaps he should get a good night's sleep. Perhaps, too, he could go to the hospital again the next day, just for a quick check-up and reassurance, for what that was worth.

After they had left, Lucy's parents decided to leave, too. They had been traumatised enough by the evening and were anxious to get back to the safety of south London before it became too late. As they said their goodbyes, Lucy and her mother clung to each other for a second longer than usual, as if in recognition of what had happened that evening.

It was still quite early as Simon and Lucy washed the dishes in silence. The evening had been a sort of disaster but also a kind of triumph. And Lucy still felt relieved by the fact that her mother had been able to reach out and hold Andrew's hand. She was also intrigued by Andrew's remark about her being besotted with the Valentines and that she would do anything for them. Lucy hoped desperately that she was going to get the chance to ask Andrew more before it was too late. She was becoming very aware of how their time together was running out.

Lucy and Simon snuggled up together on the sofa to watch the news on television. Afterwards, Lucy took herself off to bed. She was exhausted. She had been feeling quite tired from the pregnancy anyway but as she undressed she was suddenly hit by a strong dragging feeling pulling her down.

That was the first sign.

The brown spots of blood on her pants were the second.

The pains, first nagging throbs and then what felt like deep stabbing period pains, began within half an hour.

Her own doctor was on call that night. Dr Kenny arrived at around midnight. By this time, Lucy knew that she was about to miscarry.

After a brief internal examination, Dr Kenny confirmed that the miscarriage could not be stopped. Lucy's cervix was dilating.

'I'll call an ambulance for you now.'

Lying in bed, her face pale, Lucy grimaced. 'What's the point of that? If I'm going to lose the baby, I don't need to go to hospital. It doesn't matter where I am.'

The doctor looked down at her for a moment and nodded. She reached over and squeezed her hand. 'That's true. But they could make you feel more comfortable in hospital.'

Lucy turned her face to the wall. 'I'd rather be in my own home,' she muttered.

The doctor left after Lucy had listlessly turned down her offer of an injection of pethidine. 'I'd rather feel the pain,' she murmured.

And feel the pain she did. She regretted turning down the doctor's offer of pain relief. The first few stabbing cramps seemed to come from a deep dark hole inside her.

They came in waves, each time preceding the expulsion of blood and foetal matter. An hour later, Lucy miscarried the ten-week-old foetus. It was two in the morning.

Simon held her hand throughout, and cried with her as they watched the tiny baby and livery placental tissue flush down the lavatory.

Lucy only managed to get a few hours' sleep that night. She was half-conscious throughout. She dreamed of a crowd of tiny children, their arms outstretched to the sky. 'Mama! Mama!' Their wail was high-pitched and sad. Lucy was walking towards them but they shied away from her with wide, frightened eyes. She stopped to stare at them and the children began to shrink in size and fade into the darkness that was creeping up behind them. Their images melted into the blackness, their wails lost in the wind. Then they were gone.

Dr Kenny telephoned the next morning and sounded genuinely sad for Lucy. 'I think it might be a good idea for you to come down to the surgery so that I can check that everything's all right. And we can have a chat,' she added.

'Yes,' replied Lucy in a flat voice. 'I shall.'

But she knew she would not. Why bother? The baby had gone. Nothing could be done to save it now, as it made its way down through London's sewerage system. What was the point of anything?

CHAPTER 8

July, 1968
Larking About

The day after Lucy had seen Olwyn swiping Perdita across the head, Lucy came up to play at the Valentine house. She had said nothing to her own parents about the incident she had witnessed the night before, but she was certainly expecting some comments from her friends. Indeed, she expected the house to be in an uproar about such a terrible event!

Oddly, when she arrived there was no reference to the previous evening from anyone. Odder still, she found Perdita sitting at the kitchen table using the old Singer sewing machine while Olwyn stood beside, guiding Perdita's fingers as she manipulated the soft fabric. 'Olwyn's been showing me how to make clothes with the machine. I've made a pair of shorts.' With obvious pride, she held up a pair of simple, red cotton shorts.

Perdita looked quite cheerful and happy, and acted as though nothing had happened between her and Olwyn the evening before. Lucy was puzzled and she even began to doubt her own memory. Perhaps that scene had not happened at all. Perhaps she had just had a vivid dream about it.

'You left your swimming things,' Olwyn said. 'I hung them out to dry for you.'

'Thank you,' whispered Lucy, feeling even more confused by Olwyn's apparent thoughtfulness. Lucy had to ask Vita about it. Surely she would have something to say about Olwyn's unkindness.

Waiting until they were alone in Vita's room, she said, 'When I was going home yesterday I saw Olwyn hit Perdita.'

She said it and stopped, watching the other girl, waiting for a reaction.

Vita looked up and stared at her, her face strangely blank. Lucy wondered if she had been listening. 'I saw Olwyn hit Perdita,' she repeated. 'On the head, hard.'

There was another moment's silence. Vita turned to look out of the window and up at the sky. Then she turned back and shrugged. 'Well,' she said casually, 'Perdita didn't say anything about it so it was probably nothing.'

So that was it. It was probably nothing. Vita's words wormed their way inside Lucy. Now she felt silly for even mentioning it. It was probably nothing. There was something wrong with her, Lucy, for making a fuss, for thinking that what happened was unusual.

From that moment she resolved never again to ask about anything that seemed out of the ordinary. Such naïveté would expose her as an outsider. When you were at the Valentines', you should never be surprised by anything, she told herself. Nothing was strange.

Lucy went up to play at the Valentines' house every day that week. While her mother was glad that Lucy was being entertained during the long summer holidays before they set off for their own family trip, she was not delighted when Lucy came home all grubby from her games with the Valentine children. Sometimes it was just her hands and fingernails that were dirty but occasionally, if the children had staged, say, a wrestling match in the garden, her clothes were muddy, wet or grass-stained, too.

'What does it matter, Mother?' Lucy asked one day as her mother pulled her T-shirt off over her head. 'You wash the clothes every day anyway.'

Her mother gave her an annoyed frown. 'That's not the point,' she said. 'I don't like you wandering home looking as if you haven't had a bath for weeks. What will people say? Anyone would think that you were from one of the estates . . .'

Lucy was too young to grasp the extent of her mother's snobbery but she did sense Hilda's continuing confusion about the Valentine family. They were rich enough for her to approve of her daughter's friendship but she was clearly upset that they did not act rich, or in the way she thought wealthy people should act.

In fact, the Valentine parents did not act like anyone Lucy had ever met before. They said rude things about the Queen (Mr Valentine once referred to her as 'an old trout'), and made jokes about God – things she would never have dared tell her mother about. They talked a lot about politics and books and art and every week another pile of new hardback books would appear on the hall table.

It seemed to Lucy that the Valentines approved of everything her mother disapproved of, and disapproved of everything her mother believed good and right. They approved of children arguing with them, stating their position and defending it, when her mother could not abide what she called 'back talk' in a child. They approved of student demonstrations and rock music and long hair on men, while Hilda thought that all such matters were disgraceful.

They liked spicy food and lots of garlic, and wine with their meals every night, a sharp contrast to Hilda's diet of plain food, meals of well-cooked meat and boiled vegetables, and total abstinence, except for a medium dry sherry on Christmas Day, which she never finished because it made her tiddly.

The Valentines allowed their children to read comics and Enid Blyton stories – what Mrs Butler called 'trashy' books. And they never criticised their children's choice of reading, for they believed, Vita explained, that children discover for themselves the difference between difficult and easy literature.

Lucy was deeply impressed and envious. At home she was never allowed to read comics and only allowed to read an Enid Blyton story after she had read ten 'good' books, chosen by her mother. The Valentines were also allowed to watch whatever they liked on television – though they were only allowed an hour a day. They could choose what they wanted. Lucy had no choice. The only thing she and Andrew were ever allowed to watch was *Blue Peter*. And they never watched commercial television. Her parents could only get the two BBC channels on their television.

The more she saw of the Valentine family, the more she wanted to be part of it. They despised all conventions and loathed any kind of conformism. They thought it was good to be different. How Lucy longed to have parents who encouraged her to question everything that the rest of the world took for granted. And how shocked her mother would be if she knew exactly how much the Valentine parents cocked a snook at everything in life!

One day, Lucy was invited to stay the night at the Valentines'. She had spent the whole day there, having arrived at nine in the morning. She and Vita had gone swimming at the Lido and then cycled all the way across Hampstead Heath to Whitestone Pond and back, ignoring the shouts of the occasional official who yelled that bikes were not allowed on the Heath. The girls just laughed cheekily and pedalled faster. They climbed trees and scratched their initials in the bark. They tried to catch some ducklings until a woman shouted at them to stop. Coming home, they left their footprints in the wet cement floor on a building site near Little Green Street, and threw thick blocks of wood on to the railway line.

In the afternoon the older boys were around, and they all played noisy games of rummy until tea time. By six o'clock, after tea, it was agreed that Lucy should stay the night. Since she had been there all day, she might as well stay the night, too. 'You can borrow my pyjamas,' Vita offered.

The Valentine parents were going out to a dinner party. The elder girls sat in their mother's room while Seraphina sat at her dressing table and made up her face. Dressed in a kingfisher blue silk kaftan, she combed her lustrous black hair until it gleamed in the evening light. Leaning forward, and with the tip of her tongue peeping between her lips as she concentrated, with extraordinary precision, she applied a black kohl pencil over the edge of her eyelids. Then she painted her lips with a beige lipstick.

The girls hovered behind her, fingering the black boxes of Mary Quant make-up and watching to see exactly how Seraphina ran the liner over her eyelids. 'You need a steady hand,' she said with a light laugh.

In the bathroom next door, Anthony Valentine was listening to Bob Dylan's latest album while he lay in the soapy water. There was a speaker from the stereo system placed in the room above the door. He lay down on his back, his long legs bent at the knees. He closed his eyes and sighed with satisfaction.

Directly above, in the children's bathroom on the top floor, Olwyn was bathing the younger children. She scrubbed their faces until they were bright pink and quickly and thoroughly soaped and rinsed their bodies. She yanked each child out of the bath and rubbed it dry with a towel. She pulled their night clothes on. 'Into bed, now!' And she turned to the next one.

Downstairs Lucy sat shyly on the edge of the large double bed and watched Vita and Perdita crowd around their mother. They chatted to each other in the playful banter that characterised the way the Valentines spoke to each other. It was teasing and clever and, most peculiar to Lucy's ears, it seemed equal. Her own mother would have been shocked to hear children speaking to their parents in such a way; to Hilda Butler, such informality would signify a certain lack of respect for their elders.

Anthony Valentine had finished his bath. He dried his large hirsute body with a wide red towel and wandered into the bedroom, unaware of the nine-year-old blushing on the bed.

Lucy had never seen a full-grown penis before. She felt a weird thrill run through her at the sight of this long thick piece of flesh emerging from a dense crop of curly blond hair and hanging down to swing like an elephant's trunk between Mr Valentine's legs. It was both attractive and repulsive.

She tried to avert her eyes but they kept wandering back to peep at this strange piece of anatomy, so different from her brother's hairless little specimen. She had never seen her father naked, ever. Modesty was encouraged in the Butler household. She had never imagined that a man's willy could get so big. It was scary. She felt a mix of awe and excitement every time she glanced at it.

Anthony Valentine moved about the room, picking up clean socks and underpants. At last he had covered up his lower half and Lucy could relax again. She felt oddly exhausted by what she had just seen, and hoped that no one had noticed her embarrassment.

Seraphina's dazzling blue kaftan clung pleasingly to her soft curves as she slipped her feet into flat gold sandals. Finally, she sprayed a blast of scent into the air and walked through it.

Anthony had slipped on a white cotton turtle-necked sweater and a pair of well-cut navy blue hipster bell-bottoms. Pulling in his stomach, he did up the belt and inspected himself in the mirror. Then, smoothing down his thick blond hair, he rubbed his jaw to check the smoothness of his shave and thought about the evening ahead.

He was looking forward to the evening, which entailed dinner with some nicely argumentative friends. They were going to eat in a Greek restaurant in Camden Town where they would no doubt tussle over political matters as they ate their taramasalata and kleftikon. Then afterwards they would go back to their friends' flat in Gloucester Crescent for coffee and a few joints.

Anthony enjoyed smoking dope, though he tried not to smoke it too often because it had a tendency to make him sleepy in the mornings. He did love it, though. He relished the slow onset and the feeling of wellbeing it brought with it. And he liked the way various types of hash or grass affected him in different ways – from the giggly mellowness he got from his American friends' grass, to the intense buzz from the more refined Lebanese Gold. What he enjoyed most of all, however, was the ritual of rolling the joint itself. He loved the plucking out of the three Rizla papers from the red packet, the gluing together of two and then the third across the top. He loved running the tip of his tongue along the length of a No. 6 cigarette and pulling it open to allow the dry line of tobacco to drop quietly on to the papers, slightly to the right. Then, if it was resin, the heating of a corner of the sticky block and then the careful crumbling of hash over the tobacco, spaced evenly and fairly, making sure it was all the way through. The skilled rolling, tight and clean, followed by a quick lick of the glue to seal it. The roach. Tearing up some thin card – a postcard, or the Rizla packet itself – to roll up and push into one end. A swift twist of the other end, and the joint was ready to smoke.

Rummaging around at the back of the sock drawer, he found the little packet wrapped in silver foil and slipped it into his pocket. It was Friday night. He had worked hard all week. He deserved a night of indulgence.

He caught Seraphina's eye and winked. Smoking marijuana made his wife delightfully lustful, and he looked forward to sex with her later that night. Her quick smile in return told him that she would be in the mood for some good loving when the time came. He almost shuddered with pleasure at the thought.

Seraphina and Anthony finally left after a noisy departure of kisses and hugs for all the children. From upstairs, Olwyn called the elder girls to have a bath.

Perdita groaned. 'Friday night is hair-wash night. Torture!'

'I'll do yours as well, Lucy, while you're here,' Olwyn said in her soft Welsh brogue. Watching Olwyn's thick-set frame and square face, Lucy realised that she had never seen the housekeeper smile.

The bath had been run again and was filled with deep, hot

water. Vita stripped off and climbed in. It was a particularly long bath, installed to accommodate Anthony Valentine's tall frame, and it was ideal for bathing several children at the same time.

Lucy waited for her turn.

The younger children were playing in their bedrooms. From down below, whoops of joy and shrill laughter could be heard as they bounced on the beds and threw pillows at each other.

David appeared in the doorway. 'Shall I tell them to be quiet, Mother?'

Olwyn glanced up at him as she sprayed water on Vita's head through the steel nozzle of the spray. 'No,' she said quietly. 'I'll sort them out in a minute.'

The noise grew louder and shriller as the children became more excited.

Olwyn poured shampoo on to Vita's scalp, scrubbed it hard and then rinsed out the soap.

Then she turned to Lucy.

Lucy was used to her mother washing her hair, which she did as a weekly ritual, with jugs of water in the bath. Unlike the Valentines, the Butlers did not have fitted spray attachments in their bath. Lucy was often irritated by her mother's slowness but at least Hilda was always gentle.

Lucy only realised this as she felt Olwyn's long nails dig into the skin of her scalp, clamping it like the claws of an eagle. Her head was manipulated roughly from side to side. She tried not to cry out as the nails felt as if they were ripping her skin. She shut her eyes as Olwyn began to rinse the shampoo out, allowing the water to fall over Lucy's face, regardless of whether the soap ran into Lucy's eyes. By the time the hair wash was finished, Lucy was on the verge of tears, her eyes were stinging from the sharpness of the shampoo and her scalp throbbed from the rough scrubbing. She felt quite dazed.

Olwyn turned off the tap and replaced the spray. Gripping Lucy's upper arm, she pulled her out of the water. 'That's you done,' she said with satisfaction. 'Perdita, now you get in!'

As Perdita slipped her naked body into the bath, the noise in the children's bedroom grew. There were bangs and shouts. Olwyn handed Lucy a towel, then she marched quickly down the corridor and disappeared into the little ones' bedroom.

Immediately there was silence. Lucy could hear the sound of scuffling and a muffled thump. David was standing in the corridor looking into the bedroom. Then there was no more sound, just a silence.

Two minutes later, Olwyn returned to the bathroom, pushing the sleeves of her cardigan up her plump forearms to finish the hair washing. Lucy tried to catch Vita's attention but Vita was busy drying her toes with great concentration, biting the corner of her upper lip.

Olwyn turned on the spray and began to scrub Perdita's head. Lucy missed the look between the two sisters, a look through narrowed eyes.

After the bath, Olwyn put the other children to bed while the older girls went downstairs to have mugs of hot milk. As they sat in the kitchen, the three older brothers arrived home, triumphant from a tennis tournament where they had been playing all week. They had won everything. 'We cleaned up,' said Achilles. The twins had won the doubles together, and Achilles and Constantine were singles winner and runner-up respectively in their age-group class. Byron had won his class, too, in straight sets. They carried silver-plated cups and medals which they dropped carelessly on the sideboard as they rummaged around in the kitchen for something to eat.

In his pyjamas, David slipped into the kitchen and sat at the table with them. Elbows on the table, he rested his chin in the palms of his hands and watched with darting eyes, a nervous smile on his lips.

Scrutinising him, Lucy was surprised to feel a soft tug of pity for the boy. He seemed to regard the older boys with some admiration, and she felt sad for him. David was always trying to be accepted, in his way, even though he also always behaved in such sneaky ways.

'I think I'd like something stronger,' laughed Achilles, squatting down to reach into the lower part of the sideboard. The boys' striking good looks were further enhanced by their tennis whites, which showed off their strong tanned limbs, glistening with golden hairs.

Constantine grinned. 'You mean the gin?'

'Yup.'

Achilles glanced at Vita. 'Where is she?' he asked quietly.

Vita smiled. 'Putting the babies to bed.'

Achilles pulled the large green bottle from the shelf and held it up to examine it in the light. 'It's half full now.'

He glanced over his shoulder at the girls and winked. Then, seeing David, he walked over and grasped his shoulder. 'See this?' he said, holding the bottle threateningly by the neck.

David looked up and nodded meekly.

'You say a word to anyone and you get this smashed on your head. Understand?'

David nodded earnestly.

'I mean it.'

Achilles unscrewed the cap on the bottle, grabbed two glass tumblers from the sideboard and poured an inch of gin into each one. Then he turned on the cold tap and carefully ran water into the bottle, measuring it up to the point where the level had been before.

He handed Constantine his glass and replaced the bottle in the cupboard. 'No one will ever know,' he said with satisfaction. He tipped back his head and drank the gin in one go.

'Mmm,' he murmured. 'God, I love the way it burns my throat.'

Constantine took a sip of his drink and grimaced. 'I'm not sure that I like it straight,' he said. 'I think I need some tonic in it.'

'You drip,' laughed Achilles. 'Can't take it, eh?'

Lucy slept on a camp bed on Vita's bedroom floor. For a while, the girls talked in the dark. Every now and then Vita would let out a sharp hiss. 'Ssssh!' She would listen carefully. 'We've got to keep our voices down,' she whispered.

Lucy wanted to ask why, and what would happen if Olwyn heard them but she sensed an unspoken warning coming from Vita's bed. It was better not to enquire.

She lay in the dark, aware of the delicious warmth of her bedding. An intense feeling of happiness built up inside her as she pretended that she was part of the Valentine family herself.

'You're my best friend, Vita,' she whispered shyly, praying as the words came out of her mouth that Vita would not laugh at her. Was it a foolish thing to say? Something made her feel it necessary to stake her claim, to let Vita know how she felt.

There was a pause in the darkness. Then she could hear Vita turn over in bed. 'That's nice,' Vita said at last. 'I suppose you're my best friend, too.' There was silence. Then Vita added, 'I've never really had any friends. Our mother always says that when you have so many brothers and sisters you don't need friends because you always have someone to play with.'

Lucy took in Vita's words and felt wounded that she meant so little to this girl. She knew that friends were more than simply people to play with. Surely Vita knew that too!

In her sleepiness, she vowed to make Vita need her as a friend. More than anything in the world, she wanted Vita to need her, and for her to acknowledge it.

Vita woke Lucy up at five o'clock the next morning. 'Quick,' she whispered. 'Get dressed but be very quiet. We don't want the Brat to wake up and see us . . .'

It was a clear morning with a cloudless pale blue sky and a weakly yellow but promising early sun.

Perdita was waiting downstairs in the kitchen. She held three buttered bagels in her hand. 'Breakfast,' she said, handing one each to Lucy and Vita. 'We need plenty of energy for the slalom.'

Dido, the dog, stood by the door wagging her tail excitedly in anticipation of a good run outside.

They let themselves out into the garden and went to the shed from which they pulled a long home-made go-cart constructed by the twins from some old pram wheels and planks of wood.

Lucy followed behind as Vita and Perdita pulled the contraption out to the front gate.

'The timing's perfect,' said Perdita, her eyes shining with excitement.

Outside in Lady Margaret Road, the day was quiet. The girls pulled the go-cart up to the top of the road just where it turned into the steep, tree-lined avenue that led into Leighton Road at the bottom.

Vita dragged the vehicle into the middle of the road and positioned it over the white line. 'Get in, Lucy!' she ordered. 'Put your arms around my waist. Perdita's got the stop watch. She'll sit behind you and time it.'

Lucy looked around her. The streets were deserted but she felt nervous standing poised in the middle of a road like this. 'Isn't it rather dangerous?' she stammered.

Vita laughed. 'That's why it's such fun. Now, jump in so that we can get off.'

Lucy clambered into the wooden box. 'But what happens if a car comes along?'

Vita and Perdita sprang nimbly into the box at the same time. 'Then we die!' they shrieked, their reckless laughter blowing away in the wind behind them as the go-cart shot down the hill towards Leighton Road.

It was undoubtedly fun. With Dido running alongside them, her tongue hanging out, Vita steered the go-cart with great skill, cutting diagonally across the road from left to right and then to the left again, like a skier doing the slalom in the snow. With the fresh wind in their faces, they shot past Ospringe Road, Countess Road and Ascham Street. As they passed Falkland Road, and the enormous Gothic Wesleyan Chapel on the corner, Lucy thought of her family asleep in bed and the horror on her mother's face if she saw what her daughter was up to just a few hundred yards away.

They zipped past the council flats at the end of the road, and finally came to a graceful stop at the bottom of the hill. The girls stepped out of their chariot, laughing and panting in exhilaration.

'Two minutes and fifty-nine seconds!' shouted Perdita, checking her stopwatch.

'Our best time ever. You must bring us luck,' Vita grinned at Lucy who blushed with pride.

Then just as they pulled the go-cart on to the pavement, a car driven by a young man with shoulder-length hair screeched around the corner and roared up Lady Margaret Road at about fifty miles an hour.

Vita smirked. 'Glad we didn't meet him on our way down . . .'

Lucy watched the car disappear up the road and wondered how close they had been to being hit by it.

Pulling the go-cart behind them, the girls ambled along the pavement towards Kentish Town Road.

'There're the twins!' Vita stopped and pointed across the road junction where Constantine and Achilles had leaned their bicycles against the iron railings.

Perdita scowled. 'Those pigs!' she said crossly.

The boys themselves were straddled across the top of the railing over the railway bridge.

'What are they doing?' Lucy was mystified.

'They're up to something,' said Vita. She let out a low shout: 'Hey!'

The boys looked up, startled. Seeing that it was only their little sisters and friend, they turned back to concentrate on what they were doing before. They glanced briefly around them. The road was still empty, not a soul in sight.

Achilles looked at his watch. 'Any minute now,' he said.

'I can hear it,' said Constantine. In the distance the rumbling of a train echoed along the tracks. 'It's coming!'

It was then that Lucy saw that the boys each held a large rock in their hands.

The train was close now. They could hear the loud clackety-clack on the line.

The boys turned to look at the railway track below.

'When I say,' whispered Achilles. As the train appeared from out of the tunnel, the boys raised their arms. 'Now!'

They dropped the rocks at the same time. The sound of their crashing on to the roof of the morning train resounded across the road.

'Now scram!' The boys jumped down from the wall, grabbed their bicycles and rode off up Fortess Road, leaving the three girls watching them from the junction.

'They think they're so clever,' grumbled Vita.

'Why did they do that?' Lucy was watching the boys disappearing up the hill.

'Because they're pigs,' snapped Perdita.

'They might hurt somebody or cause the train to crash.' Lucy was unnerved. It seemed so wrong, so *bad*.

But that was not Perdita's concern. 'Oh, it won't hurt anyone,' she said casually. 'They said they'd take me with them the next time they did it, and they didn't. They deliberately left me behind. They didn't wake me up. Pigs.'

'They never keep their word,' complained Vita. 'You can't trust them, ever. They're about as bad as the Brat sometimes,' she added, her voice loaded with scorn.

It was still only six o'clock. Kentish Town was quiet, though there were now a few more cars on the road and the occasional pedestrian walking by.

Lucy's stomach rumbled with hunger. She was pleased when Perdita suggested they get something to eat. 'Let's get some raspberries on the way home,' she said. 'The Wilsons have got a lot and I know they're away this weekend.'

Hauling the go-cart up the hill behind them, and with Dido padding quietly alongside, the girls walked up Leverton Street to the wall at the corner of Falkland Road. Perdita looked around her. 'I'll go over and get some. You be the lookouts. If you see someone, give me a low whistle and scram. Then I'll make my own way back.'

Perdita pulled herself up on the wall and dropped down over the other side. Lucy's heart pounded in her chest as she stood with Vita on the corner. The dog sat panting by her feet. Lucy was frightened. She felt like a criminal. They were stealing. Her heart jumped in her throat. It seemed that they were waiting an age before Perdita finally reappeared, jumping back over the wall with her cardigan crammed full of plump red raspberries. No one had seen them. Now they could get home quickly!

They walked slowly back up Leverton Street, along Ascham Street and Lady Margaret Road, gorging themselves on the ripe fruit. Wiping the juice from their chins, they arrived home to find the twins cooking up a fine breakfast of bacon, eggs, mushrooms and fried bread. 'There's enough for you girls, if you want some,' declared Achilles generously. 'I'll stick some in for you, too.'

All friends again, Lucy sat down with the elder Valentine children and ate the tasty food long before the rest of the household had woken up. Cooking and eating their own breakfast as if they were grown-ups!

CHAPTER 9

June, 1997

Mother Love

The day after Lucy's miscarriage, her doctor telephoned to see how she was. She suggested that Lucy come in for a check-up but she did not push her. 'Just come down to the surgery if you have any worries about it. It's normal to bleed quite heavily after a miscarriage, so you shouldn't worry needlessly about that. But you know I'm here if you need to talk.'

'Thank you,' replied Lucy, half touched by Dr Kenny's concern and half annoyed by the intrusion. She felt exhausted and defeated by the events of the night before. There was no knowing how she could survive any more blows.

'Wait a while before you try again,' continued the doctor. 'Three months is the recommended period.'

'Three months! I can't wait that long,' exclaimed Lucy. 'I'm thirty-seven, I'm running out of time.'

Dr Kenny paused. 'Well, wait until the bleeding has stopped. It probably doesn't really make much difference physiologically. But you shouldn't be downhearted. Looking on the bright side, you now know you can conceive . . . That's very important. Now that we know you have done it once, there's no reason why you shouldn't be able to do it again. Conceiving is the most difficult part.'

Lucy listened to the doctor's cheerful pep talk with mixed feelings. She wanted to be hopeful, to believe what the doctor said but she also wanted to protect herself, not to raise her hopes again for fear of having them dashed and of laying herself open to more wounds in the future. Although she could not put it into words, she felt that where her baby had been, an anger now raged inside her, a fury at the unfairness of what had happened, of losing the baby she had waited so long to conceive. She burned with a fury that frightened her. And at the same time she felt defeated. They were back to where they had started, back to fertile days and soul-destroying periods. Could she bear it? Lucy was not sure if she had the strength to go through it all again.

In fact, the issue of how long to wait until trying again was irrelevant. After the loss of their baby, Simon unexpectedly sank into his own kind of gloom. Lucy had not realised how affected he would be but she was surprised and shocked to see how badly he took it. He was short-tempered and grumpy for most of the time. He rarely shaved and he stayed late at work, only returning home after midnight, often stinking of beer.

Sex was out of the question. He and Lucy barely spoke to each other, each incapable of comforting the other. They saw each other occasionally at breakfast, before Simon dashed out to work.

Then, after a while, Simon appeared to cheer up. He began to shave properly again and wear freshly laundered clothes. While he still worked late at night, he did occasionally suggest that they go to the cinema or down to the pub for a drink. But Lucy did not feel they were together as they had been, they did not engage as they used to. Babies and conception were not mentioned. They did not touch each other in bed or out of it. Neither seemed to have a spark of passion inside them.

Lucy was not very bothered by this because for her there was another profound reason for not rushing into trying to get pregnant again.

Andrew was fading faster now. It seemed that almost every other day there was another development with his health – another part of his body had broken down or given up on him. She spoke to him or Patrick on the telephone most days. The conversation was exclusively about Andrew's health.

She knew she could not cope with trying to bring another person into the world while this one was about to leave it, and she realised that she did not want to get pregnant until Andrew had died. She knew that she had to wait until she had buried him, until she had stopped worrying about him, before she could concentrate on herself again. So she was not sorry that Simon seemed willing to avoid sexual contact with her in bed. The question of how long the wait would be remained unanswered.

Andrew's appearance was now quite disturbing. To anyone who had visited an AIDS ward it was fairly obvious that he was close to the final stage of his life. To an innocent onlooker he simply looked ill and very undernourished.

Today Lucy was meeting Andrew in a small café in Notting Hill Gate. He had just come from a check-up at the hospital. He looked tired as he walked in through the door. He wore a blue Yankees baseball cap on his short cropped hair. His jeans were baggy over his thin legs. Unsteady on his feet, he came across the room and sat down opposite her.

Lucy ordered a cappuccino for him and waited. She was hoping to ask him again about the Valentines, to see what else he could remember but it was difficult to get him to talk about anything other than himself nowadays, and it seemed selfish, if not cruel, to force other subjects on him when he was preoccupied with his own problems. First she had to judge his mood.

'How was the hospital?'

Her brother turned his face towards her and shrugged. 'I've got a virus in my eyes, something called CMV. I noticed something was wrong with my right eye recently. I've been getting tunnel vision in it. Apparently, both eyes are infected now, though the left seems okay at the moment.'

'What does that mean?'

Andrew gave a small shrug. 'It means that I'm going blind. If I'm not treated, I'll go blind very quickly. If I am treated, I'll retain my sight for a few more months. It's very serious.'

'What's the treatment?'

'I have to have a catheter put into my chest so they can give me antibiotics intravenously every day.'

'How many more months will that give you?'

'Nine. Then I'll be blind.'

Lucy nodded. 'That's what happened to Derek Jarman.'

'Yup.'

Andrew toyed with the milky froth on his cappuccino. 'Going blind is my greatest fear.' He corrected himself. 'One of my greatest fears – losing my mind is the other.' His voice had dropped to a forceful whisper. 'I'm not going to let that happen . . .'

They sat in silence and, not knowing what else to do, Lucy reached over and squeezed Andrew's hand. As she did so, he bit his lip. Then he could not hold himself together. He began to sob, his mouth pulled back in a grimace. He looked at her with his big blue damaged eyes. 'I'm frightened, Lucy,' he whispered. 'I'm scared . . .'

Lucy glanced around to see if anyone was watching, but the other customers were concentrating on their own thoughts and worries.

Suddenly Andrew pulled himself to his feet. 'I think I'm going to be sick.' He looked around for the sign for the lavatories and disappeared, stumbling against a table as he went.

He reappeared five minutes later. He was dry-eyed.

The manager of the café – a fashionable place with classical music and designer sandwiches – had been watching Andrew. As Andrew settled down in his chair again, the man came over. 'Is everything all right?' he asked, looking closely at Andrew.

'Yes, fine,' Lucy said sharply. She sensed that the manager guessed what was wrong with Andrew. She also guessed that he probably did not want a person with AIDS on his premises. 'Everything's fine, thank you,' she insisted, her chest tightening with protective aggression.

They stayed for another ten minutes, if only to prove to the beady-eyed manager that they would leave when they chose rather than he. As they left, Lucy glared at the manager. 'I shan't be coming back here in a hurry,' she said loudly.

But her thoughts were no longer on their treatment in the café. The words 'Nine months' circled in her head. Nine months. No more than nine months left. And probably not even that.

Hilda Butler had laid on a delicious lunch for her daughter, which they now ate on the terrace in the garden of her Dulwich home.

It was a hot day so they had to put up the sun umbrella,

which now cast plenty of welcome shade across Hilda and Lucy while they sipped elderflower cordial and ate chicken salad with cold rice, followed by summer pudding and cream.

'What a feast!' Lucy sat back in her chair feeling bloated.

'Well, I thought you needed a bit of cheering up.'

Lucy glanced up at her mother, surprised by her sudden thoughtfulness. For once her mother was sitting still. Usually by this time she would be clearing the plates and wiping the table.

Hilda continued. 'It must be hard for you to lose a baby, especially after trying for so long. That must have made it feel like a double blow.'

Lucy felt her throat constricting. 'Yes, but I'm okay now, Mother.' She did not want to cry in front of her mother; she did not want a heart-to-heart. 'We'll just try again soon.'

'Don't try too soon,' Hilda said in a quiet but earnest voice. 'Let yourself grieve first.'

Lucy shrugged. She was beginning to feel embarrassed.

Hilda was still talking. 'I've never told you this before but I lost a baby once, too.'

Lucy looked up in surprise. 'You did?'

'You were too young to remember. You were a toddler. I had a little boy but there were so many things wrong with him, he didn't have a chance. He died almost immediately.'

Her face had become distorted and twisted at the painful memory she had pushed deep inside her for so long. 'And I don't think I gave myself long enough to get over it properly at the time. I got pregnant with Andrew almost straight away.' She sighed softly. 'That was probably a mistake, though it seemed right at the time.'

Lucy stared at her mother. 'But why haven't you told

me before? Why did you keep it a secret for all this time?'

Hilda shook her head. Her eyes and the tips of her nose were red. 'It was too painful, I suppose. It was easier not to talk about it. You never saw the baby because he never came home from the hospital, and I don't think you were even aware that I was pregnant, or what that meant, anyway.

'Your father was terribly upset at the time. I think being a doctor, he felt a failure because he couldn't do anything to save him. But nothing could have saved him, no doctor could have helped. He wasn't even properly formed – he had the worst hare lip and cleft palate that the doctors had ever seen and he also had the most severe form of spina bifida. If he had lived, he would have been severely handicapped.'

Hilda's voice had dropped to a whisper as Lucy suddenly began to recall the photographs of damaged babies she used to pore over as a child in her father's surgery.

'They say that miscarriages can be Nature's way of making sure imperfect babies are not born. I'm very sad that you had a miscarriage but if there was something wrong with the baby, if that was why you lost it, then perhaps it was better to lose it then rather than later. They also say that sometimes the body has to have a practice run with pregnancy before being able to go ahead. Next time you'll conceive and hold the baby with no trouble at all.' She smiled.

Lucy looked at her mother and saw a woman trying her best to make contact with her for the first time in years. She smiled back.

'I hope you're right, Mother.'

Lucy got to her feet. 'Let's clear away this lot and go for a walk in the park.' She began to stack the dishes and cutlery.

Her mother sat still. 'Oh, let's stay here. It's so pleasant just sitting in the garden.'

'But it'd be good to stretch our legs, and it's not too hot now, there's a lovely breeze. And since it's a week day, the park won't be crowded.'

She looked up at her mother and frowned.

Hilda was sitting rigid on the edge of her chair. Her neck was tight and strained. 'I really don't want to go,' she said, her lower lip wobbling like a child's.

Lucy looked at her mother in dismay. Instead of the strong, directed, busy woman she had known all her life, she saw a person on the point of collapse. Her mother seemed to have shrunk in size as she looked up plaintively at her daughter with watery eyes. Lucy waited. She knew that her mother was going to say something, and make a link with her.

Hilda's strength had gone. Her lower lip dropped as she spoke, her voice cracked. 'I'm so frightened for Andrew,' she whispered. 'I lie awake every night thinking about him and what's going to happen to him.'

'He's going to die soon,' Lucy said firmly. 'And there's nothing we can do about it, except love him.'

'I do love him,' whispered Hilda. 'Of course I love him, he's my son.

'What I think about every night is how he's going to be punished. He's going to be going to Hell . . .'

Lucy looked down at her. 'Fortunately, I don't believe in an afterlife,' she snapped, suddenly struck by the brutal thought that her mother had only herself – and her beliefs – to blame for such fears. Underneath, she felt angry that her mother's religious faith was now making her concentrate on Andrew's death rather than his life.

Hilda cleared her throat and collected herself. Perhaps she

had sensed her daughter's lack of sympathy. She blew her nose and shook her head. 'I want to give you something while you're here.'

She got up and went into the house. A moment later she returned and handed Lucy a Jiffy bag. 'I want you to have these now,' she said. 'I find them too painful to look at, and I'd rather not have them in the house. I may want to see them again in years to come but, for the time being, I'd rather they were in your safe keeping.'

Lucy reached into the bag and pulled out four leatherbound volumes. She recognised them immediately. They were familiar from her childhood when she used to help her mother put in the carefully edited pictures her father had taken of the family.

Holding one in her lap, she opened it up and turned the pages with care. This covered the late Sixties. Most of the pictures were grainy black-and-white shots of herself and Andrew as young children running around the garden of their old house in Kentish Town. Flicking through, she stopped at one striking close-up of Andrew, aged about six, fast asleep in bed. He looked like an angel, with pure features and unblemished skin, his arm thrown behind him on the pillow, his mouth slightly open.

Noticing Lucy pause, Hilda looked over her shoulder. 'That's my favourite picture of Andrew,' she said. 'I used to sit on his bed and stroke the hair off his forehead as he slept. I used to sit there, as I did with you, looking at that innocent face and imagine his life ahead. I'd imagine him at school, at university, becoming a doctor, getting married and having children. I used to have his whole life in my head.' She sighed deeply. 'But it was not to be,' she said wearily. 'And it never will be . . . now.'

Lucy chewed her lip and nodded. 'No,' she said, closing the album and hugging it to her chest.

Hilda had not finished. Her eyes had a glazed look as she talked. 'That's been one of my faults in life,' she said, 'planning other people's careers for them. Then it doesn't work out. Something goes wrong and it all gets ruined.' Hilda turned to look at her daughter. 'I did it to your father,' she whispered, 'and in a terrible way . . .'

Lucy looked at her mother in discomfort. This unfamiliar openness was almost too much for her. She absorbed the words about her father but her thoughts were on Andrew. For as she hugged the photograph album to her chest, she was reminded of an odd occasion when she had been mean to her little brother. It had been completely out of character, really, for Lucy adored Andrew, who had returned her feelings. But for some reason she had decided to assert herself as his older sister.

She could remember it now. She came home from the Valentines' one afternoon and Andrew had asked her in his usual way if she would play *Snakes and Ladders* with him.

'Shove off!' Lucy snapped brutally at him.

She reddened with shame as she recalled the unkindness in her voice. It was an experiment, she remembered. She was trying something out, an attitude, a sense of power, that she had picked up at her friends' house.

Andrew had looked at her with bewildered eyes, his lower lip trembled with confusion. Lucy had never spoken sharply to him like that before. It made no sense of what he knew of his kind big sister.

'Why are you being horrid to me?' he wailed.

Lucy stared back at him, waiting to see what would happen.

Andrew looked at her for a second more, and then ran off crying, leaving Lucy to turn away with surprise at her power. But she felt uneasy about it, too.

Now Lucy smiled tearfully at her mother. 'Andrew's life hasn't been what you wanted, Mother, but it has been closer to what he wanted. No one would ask for this kind of ending but he has enjoyed himself, too. That's important.'

Hilda nodded ruefully. 'If you say so, Lucy. It gives me some comfort to hear that, I suppose, but I don't think one can say the same for your poor father. I've been very hard on him, I'm afraid.'

For a moment they were close. Mother and daughter hugged each other tight, joined in their sadness for lost lives.

That night Lucy dreamed that she and Simon were walking along a river bank, hand in hand. Then they saw a child floating by in the water. It stared up at them with pleading eyes. Lucy reached out to grab the baby, but just before she could touch its fingers, it sank with a soft gurgle down into the fast-flowing black water.

CHAPTER 10

August, 1968
Sussex

Lucy was thrilled to be invited to spend a week with Vita and her siblings at their grandmother's house in west Sussex. She could never have imagined such a place existed.

Daphne Valentine lived in Graffham, a small village which nestles snugly at the foot of the South Downs. It is on no main roads and the quiet lane through the village itself leads into the private track cutting through Lavington Stud to a boys' boarding school called Seaford College.

The village itself lacks charm, with the church and the school at one end at the top of a hill, and the rest of the village sprawling along the road, with the sports ground and the war memorial at least half a mile away from the village shop.

Farther down the road, towards Midhurst, two white stone cones mark the gravel entrance to Glasses, a large house built on the site of a medieval glass factory. Originally the house had been named Brook House by its wealthy and unimaginative owner. Years later, after the war, when Anthony Valentine's parents bought it, his lively and inventive mother renamed it Glasses.

Daphne Valentine was well known in the area as the woman who not only hunted with the hounds twice a week but also rode side-saddle, dressed in an elegant bottle-green habit. She was rich, generous and gregarious. Her parties were famous and she enjoyed all company – old and young. She loved nothing more than having her grandchildren to stay though, of course, when they did come, she employed extra help – usually a woman from the village – for her housekeeper, Mrs Peters. And when Anthony's children came down – goodness, there were so many of them – their nanny, Olwyn, had to come too, to feed and bath them, and to put them to bed.

Daphne had been widowed ten years before, when her husband died soon after a hunting accident. Tackling a massive gate on Lord Cowdray's estate, his big chestnut hunter just caught his back legs on the top bar. The horse twisted in mid-air, sending Jasper Valentine crashing to the ground. It then rolled over on to its rider, pulverising his ribcage and bursting his spleen. Jasper Valentine never really recovered. After six months he had two strokes in rapid succession and died.

Daphne was sad not to have Jasper around, for she had been fond of the old boy. But in some ways she was also quite relieved. Fifteen years her senior, as he had become older, his demands had become increasingly irritating to her. He insisted on having two cooked meals a day and since he never learned to drive, and refused to pay for a chauffeur, she had to ferry him around everywhere. In fact, although she would never have admitted it, her husband's death brought her an unexpected and delightful sense of liberation.

Daphne enjoyed her grandchildren's company. She loved the way they were so bright and amusing, brought up not to be afraid of adults. They were also rather unruly. 'Anthony has already instilled in them his utter lack of respect for authority,' she told her friend Margery as they rode across the South Downs together on their hacks. 'It's all very well, cocking a snook at the system, but you have to be very clever and talented to get away with that much of the time . . .' She laughed. 'Anthony's bolshiness used to drive Jasper mad.' She urged her horse into a trot. 'I've always rather admired it myself!'

Daphne was pleased that Vita had brought a little friend along. Lucy seemed a well-bred girl, polite and quiet. 'It's good to have someone from outside the family,' she said. 'It changes the way the children behave towards each other. Sometimes I think they are too close.'

Margery nodded and waved the fly swat above her horse's thick black mane. The flies were bad that morning on the Downs. 'Anthony and his wife are lucky to have you to take all their children for a whole week,' she said. 'I'd never do that for my grandchildren, and I've only got three of them!'

Daphne laughed. Her horse had slowed down to a walk again. It was pleasant up on the Downs, with nobody around for miles. 'I suppose I'd do anything for Anthony. Anthony is my weak spot. And of course, Olwyn comes along with the children. She's marvellous – so organised and efficient. I don't know how any of us would manage without her.'

With that, she kicked her horse into a gallop and set off up a vast green firebreak which cut through the pine woods. Margery followed along behind on her ancient bay cob.

Anthony and Seraphina had gone to the United States for a week, so it was convenient for them to send all the children down, as they often did in the summer. They hated the country and rarely came to Sussex for longer than a day, but they were grateful enough to Daphne for having the children whenever necessary.

Daphne Valentine's house offered everything a child could want. Apart from the attics and nooks and crannies for playing hide-and-seek in, there was also a large games room with table tennis permanently set up in the middle, and an exquisitely carved wooden rocking horse (bought from Heal's for Anthony's third birthday), and cupboards bursting with games – *Monopoly*, *Risk*, *Cluedo*, cards, jigsaws, chess. Everything anyone could possibly want for a rainy day.

Outside, there was a huge, sprawling garden, with rockeries and lawns and long herbaceous borders, shrubberies, bluebell woods and streams. Behind the house up the hill was a large kitchen garden, a wide chicken run, and two long greenhouses. To the side of the kitchen garden was a large blue swimming pool with an uninterrupted view of the South Downs, and beyond that a hard tennis court. Beyond that still, there were the stables and twelve acres of fields for the many horses and ponies Daphne had collected over the years.

Quite apart from her two grey hunters there were her daughters' two New Forest ponies, now ancient and sagging in the middle but too well loved to let go anywhere, and three reliable ponies for the grandchildren to ride, as well as Tweety, the fat chestnut Shetland she had bought when Anthony was two, and just old enough to sit in a saddle.

Daphne always cherished having her grandchildren. When they were staying, every day began with the tiny ones piling into her high four-poster bed at an early hour, carrying their picture books for her to read as they snuggled up to her. They all loved this practice and continued to do it even when they could read perfectly well on their own.

Daphne did not devote all her time to the children,

however. She had her own commitments and timetables. In addition to riding with her friends every day, there was the committee for the village fête, as well as the hunt committee and the local pony club, with which she was still involved. She did not disrupt her schedule because of the children but she still had plenty of time to see them at breakfast and lunch, and to have wild games of racing demon after their high tea before they went off to bed. Once or twice she ate supper with the older boys if they weren't too busy watching something on TV. Everyone came and went, free to choose what they did without interference from anyone.

The week that Lucy went to stay with the Valentines would remain vivid in her head for a long time afterwards. The early August weather was hot and clear, with cloudless blue skies from the sharp early dawn to drowsy dusk.

The children spent their days outside, swimming in the pool, riding the ponies around the fields, running through the woods, climbing trees and playing hide-and-seek in the huge garden. The older boys often went rafting on the river, which the girls were not allowed to do, their grandmother had dictated, until they were twelve.

The girls did not mind. The sun was hot and there was always the pool to swim in, which they did five or six times a day. All the Valentine children could swim like fish – even little Celestria was nimble and confident without armbands. Lucy felt clumsy and nervous, and hovered around the shallow end practising her breaststroke, but it gave her some pleasure to see that David was even less accomplished than she.

One afternoon the older children decided to play a game of hide-and-seek while the very young ones were having a postprandial nap. There was a raised rockery near the drawing room with a curious wooden door at the bottom.

'The house was taken over by the army during the war,' explained Vita. 'We think they dug these corridors under the rockery but we're not sure why. Grandmother thinks it may have been for storing their wine.' She pulled the door open and the girls stepped into a cold dark corridor carved out of the sandy soil. Lucy shivered. The air was chilled. A short walk round brought them back to where they had started from. 'It's great, don't you think?' asked Vita.

The game began. Perdita was It, and stood in the front of the house, her hands over her eyes, counting up to a hundred. Vita and Lucy began to run.

'Oh no,' groaned Vita as she saw David coming up. 'Find your own hiding place,' she snapped.

David's face puckered. 'Why can't I come with you?' he complained. 'You're better at finding places to hide than me.'

Vita hesitated for a moment, then she relented. 'Okay, come with us this way. I know where you can hide.' She ran quickly round to the back of the house, with David and Lucy following.

'Quick! In here!' Vita pulled away the wooden door to the underground chamber. 'You hide in here, it's the best place ever!'

'Thanks!' David beamed and crept inside.

'You sit down and I'll shut the door,' Vita ordered. She pushed the heavy door firmly back into place, then turned to Lucy.

'Let's go up to the stables – she'll never find us there.'

The game went on for half an hour. Perdita found Lucy and Vita hiding in the hay barn, covered with newly cut hay from the garden and giggling uncontrollably. She also found

Celestria and Florian crouching down in the greenhouse. Then someone else was It and the hiding places shifted to another part of the garden.

At five o'clock the gong rang out across the garden, signalling that tea was ready. The children ran back to the house, washed their hands and settled themselves at the table, where Olwyn and fat, jolly Mrs Peters had laid out plates of steaming shepherd's pie and baked beans.

'Where's David?' Olwyn asked. 'Wasn't he playing with you?'

Lucy had forgotten about him completely. She looked at Vita, who was about to place a forkful of mince and potatoes in her mouth.

'Oh,' she said. 'I forgot.' Placing her napkin on the table, she said, 'I think I might know where he is.' She signalled to Lucy to follow. Lucy glanced at Olwyn, who was watching them keenly.

'We won't be a minute,' Vita called breezily as the girls ran outside towards the rockery. When they reached it they stopped outside.

'Ssh,' whispered Vita. 'Listen.' Vita placed her ear to the door with a light smile on her lips. Lucy could just hear a feeble banging and a faint cry from inside.

'David!' Vita called, pulling back the door. 'Are you still in there?'

David emerged from the darkness, his small face swollen from crying. His fingernails were broken and torn from his frantic scratching at the door.

'You left me here!' he sobbed. 'You left me here on purpose!'

'No I didn't, David. I swear.' Vita rubbed his back with a show of affection. 'I didn't do it on purpose, I swear. It was an accident, David, I promise,' she kept saying. 'I forgot all about you, I thought you'd be discovered. I didn't know you'd stay in there all this time, it's true, I promise.'

David had stopped crying and was staring at Vita with narrowed eyes. 'I don't believe you, and I'm going to tell Olwyn what you did. Then you'll be sorry . . .'

Vita put her arm around his shoulders. 'Please don't tell Olwyn,' she said. She was trying to sound cheerful. 'Because it wouldn't be true, you see, so it wouldn't be fair . . .'

But David started walking ahead, on his own. 'We'll see,' he said. 'I'll think about it.'

Later that evening, Olwyn called Vita into her room. Lucy hung around in the corridor outside and Perdita joined her, pressing her ear to the door. But Lucy could hear well enough the low, threatening voice, followed by Vita's bright voice answering back. Then there was silence, followed by footsteps coming to the door.

'Quick, run!' said Perdita. She grabbed Lucy's hand and ran down the corridor, down the back stairs to the kitchen where kind Mrs Peters was heating up a saucepan of milk so that everyone could have hot chocolate before going to bed.

As Lucy and Perdita sipped their steaming chocolate with the others, Vita appeared down the stairs. She seemed subdued. Her eyes had a dull, glazed look.

David toyed with his drink, commenting on the Peter Rabbit design on his china mug. The other children glanced at Vita but then looked away as Olwyn herself appeared in the door.

As Vita lowered her head to drink, Lucy saw a tear glittering in the corner of her eye. She also thought her left ear was glowing an angry red, though that might just be the warm light in the kitchen.

Later, after supper, Lucy tried to get Vita to tell her what happened. It seemed different from when Perdita was hit. After that, Lucy had decided not to comment on unusual things happening. But this was different. She had seen Vita in pain. It would be wrong not to mention it.

'Are you okay, Vita?' she asked gently as they walked outside in the evening dusk.

Vita scratched her head and squinted up at the Downs in the distance. 'I'm fine,' she said quickly. 'Look!' She pointed to the hill directly in front of them. 'They've started to bring in the harvest. You can see the combine harvesters.'

Lucy peered into the far distance. She could see the soft rounded hill, yellow on one side and a deep ochre colour on the other, where the corn had already been cut. At the side of the huge field were parked two machines, ready to finish the job the next day.

'I like to see that every year,' said Vita. 'It's a week earlier this year. I suppose the weather's been so good. It's funny I didn't notice them doing it earlier,' she added, more to herself than to Lucy.

As the girls walked on back to the house, Lucy realised that it was pointless trying to get Vita to talk about Olwyn, and nothing more was said.

The Valentine children were remarkably knowledgeable about nature and wildlife. They knew many of the different types of birds and flowers and butterflies. Taught by their grandmother, who was a great naturalist, their knowledge about the countryside made Lucy feel quite inadequate. Daphne had passed her enthusiasm on to her grandchildren, making sure that they could tell the difference between the song of a thrush and a blackbird, and the call of a nightingale and a nightjar.

One morning Achilles called Lucy. 'Quick! I've got something to show you,' he whispered.

Lucy was flattered that he wanted to show her something alone, without any of the others around.

Feeling a thrill of smug pleasure, she followed him down the garden, past the colourful herbaceous borders and rockeries, under the old yew hedge and down to the outbuildings near the end of the drive. These were the old stables, now converted into garages for the cars, storerooms with slatted shelves for housing the apple harvest, and a large room where logs from the woods could be stored to dry before being chopped for the open fires in the house.

Achilles guided Lucy into the wood store. 'Look!' He pointed up above the thick oak beams which stretched across the width of the building. The roof rose a good thirty feet above them. 'Do you see?'

He kept his voice low.

Lucy looked up into the grey darkness. She could see the sky through several of the red roof tiles. Scanning the space above them, she could just make out two small dark bags hanging from one of the beams in the corner.

'What are they?'

Achilles smiled. 'Bats – bats roosting in the beams. They sleep in the day and in the night they go out to catch insects. I think those are noctule bats – they're the largest and most common. You sometimes see them in the evening because they come out so early after sunset. People often think they're swifts.'

Lucy stood still and shuddered. A horrible clammy sweat crept down her back as Achilles continued to display his considerable knowledge about bats. He told her that there were fourteen species of bat in Britain, that all types were found on the south coast of England, where the warmer climate meant that there were plenty of insects, and fewer and fewer species found as you go north.

She nodded and smiled as he continued. 'They're really just flying mice. They feed on insects, from tiny gnats to large beetles. It's reckoned that they can eat up to three and a half thousand insects in one night . . .'

'That's a lot of insects,' murmured Lucy, anxious to escape. The very thought of mice, particularly flying mice, made her shudder. She was convinced that the ones up above her would be woken by their voices and fly down and get caught in her hair. It was too sickening to think about.

She did not dare say anything to Achilles who was staring up so fondly at his find, so she was relieved to hear Vita calling for her to go riding.

She backed out of the barn and into the bright sunshine.

Achilles followed her but was still talking enthusiastically. 'There's lots of folklore about bats. It's supposed to be lucky to see bats flying in daylight but it's bad luck to wake them up to make them fly – so you mustn't disturb them.

'There are also a lot of silly myths about bats,' Achilles continued. 'That saying "as blind as a bat" is daft because bats have very good eyesight. They also never get caught up in people's hair, in the way some idiots think, because they have a sort of radar system which helps them locate objects in the dark so they never bang into anything.'

Lucy backed away, smiling. Her face was red with shame and she prayed that Achilles would not know that she was one of those idiots who thought bats would get tangled up in her hair. She was afraid he could tell from her expression.

'I'll see you later,' she called. 'Thanks for showing me the bats.'

'Perhaps we'll see them flying later this evening. That'll be good . . .'

Lucy ran to join Vita as Achilles went back into the barn to study his flying rodents more closely.

Even though she could do without his bats, Lucy was aware that she was developing a crush on Achilles. He was so funny, and he made her laugh with his endless stream of irreverent jokes and remarks. She thought he liked her, too (why else might he have taken her to see his bats?), but she was worried that she might appear drippy to him.

There was an excruciating moment at breakfast one morning. Lucy was just beginning to dare to join in with the normal banter between the Valentine children with a confidence that impressed even herself. They were eating delicious salty kippers, fresh eggs from the hens, and crisp fried potatoes. Celestria was looking sleepy and she rubbed her eye slowly.

'I've got a crust on my eye,' she lisped, picking something out and holding it up between her thumb and forefinger.

Lucy laughed affectionately. She liked Celestria, whom she regarded like a cuddly puppy. 'Oh, that's sleep in your eye. We call it fairy dust at our house.'

As she said it, she knew it was a mistake. Perdita smirked and looked down into her plate.

'Hah!' Achilles waved his arms around. 'Well, in our house, we call it eye crap!' He threw back his head and laughed while his brothers and sisters giggled into their kippers and eggs.

Lucy tried to smile but her mouth refused to form the right shape. A pink blush crept up her neck and cheeks. How humiliated she felt, how feeble they must all think she was! Suddenly she wished she were not there, that she was back home with her little brother Andrew who never made fun of her or tried to catch her out.

Her shame did not last long, for later that day Achilles asked her if she wanted to come swimming with him and Constantine that afternoon in the swimming hole they had discovered the day before while out rafting. 'You have to walk across three fields to get there,' he said, 'but once you're there it's great.'

The boys assured their grandmother that the swimming hole was not on part of the main river and that there were no currents. 'It's very safe to swim,' Achilles said.

'I want to come,' said Perdita.

'And me,' added Vita.

Achilles rolled his eyes. 'Do you have to?' he asked with a groan.

Daphne heard this last remark and decided to intervene.

'You can all go, you older ones; the babies have to stay behind with Olwyn and Mrs Peters. But I want you older boys to be in charge. The currents in that river can be very strong, and the water can look deceptively calm.'

'All right,' grumbled Achilles. Looking at Lucy, he added, 'We have to go through the field with the bull in it, you know.'

Lucy was thrilled to be invited by the older boys and she decided not to mention the river or the bull in her daily letter home. Because it was Lucy's first time away from home for more than one night, her mother had made letter writing a condition of her going. The Valentines all knew she had to do it but she did it as surreptitiously as she could, handing the daily envelope to the postman when he arrived with the delivery to the house each morning.

The letters were bland and flat and contained nothing of the truth about Lucy's stay. She described the house and the grounds and the animals, and assured her mother that she was eating at least one hot meal a day (a requirement

Hilda insisted on in spite of Gordon's assurance that hot meals were not essential for good health), washing behind her ears and brushing her teeth.

What Lucy did not write about was the exciting bits – how they stole the plums from the trees and gorged themselves on strawberries straight from the kitchen garden, or chased the chickens around the run, or how they jumped on to the ponies without saddles or bridles and trotted around the field until the ponies bucked them off. Nor did she write about pinching food from the larder for picnics in their secret hiding places in hedges and the tree house in the old beech tree in the wood. And she certainly said nothing about the boys shooting the local farmer's white ducks with their air guns and then cooking them over a campfire by the stream.

How her mother would have been shocked by her daily activities. And how much fun she was having! Rivers and bulls would certainly not be mentioned in the next letter.

That afternoon the three boys and three girls set off for the river. They were halfway down the drive when Olwyn called after them. 'David's coming too!'

Vita groaned.

'Trust the Brat to get his own way. He has to spoil everything.'

Achilles shrugged. 'Just ignore him,' he muttered.

The group set off, with Lucy trying to walk as close to Achilles as possible. She liked the shape of his bare arms below the sleeves of his T-shirt and his tanned legs with their curly golden hairs below his shorts. Even though he and Constantine were identical twins, and equally handsome and tall, she saw tremendous differences between the two boys now: Constantine was abrasive and nervy while Achilles seemed wonderfully relaxed about everything. He took life in his stride.

When they reached the field with the bull, they stopped to hang over the gate for a few minutes. The heavy black beast was grazing in a far corner. Occasionally the sun glinted on the ring in its nose.

'If we head over that way,' said Vita, 'it probably won't see us.'

'It probably doesn't care much about us anyway,' replied Perdita.

They climbed over, one by one. Lucy was nervous but she stuck close to Achilles, reassured by his look of quiet calm. As long as Achilles was not afraid, she thought, she would not be either.

They were halfway across the field when the bull saw them. It lifted its head and studied them intently.

David panicked.

'It's seen us!' he screamed. 'It's going to charge!'

The boy began to run but Constantine grabbed the neck of his sweatshirt and yanked him back.

'Don't be so stupid, David! If you run, you make yourself the perfect target. Just walk slowly and calmly and it'll probably forget about us.'

The children continued their walk across the field, each keeping their eyes on the bull, which had raised its head higher and was scrutinising them with more interest now. It did look as if it were trying to decide whether it could muster up the energy to investigate this movement on its territory.

One hundred yards from the gate, David let out a little cry and started to run again. This time they all caught the panic and they all ran. David wailed and whimpered in fear, convinced that the bull had begun his charge.

They got to the gate and clambered over, puffing and panting as they looked back to see where the bull was.

The animal had not moved. The sun still glinted on the brass ring in his nose as he stood in that same far corner. He was not bothered by them at all.

'Can we go back a different way?' asked Vita.

There had been a fair bit of rain earlier in the month, so the river was swollen and flowing fast in places. The older boys quickly led the others down to the water hole they had found the day before. It was a pretty spot, in a clearing under beech trees. A kingfisher darted from the mossy bank as they approached the large round pool that was fed by the river.

'Last one in's a drip!' yelled Achilles, pulling off his clothes and plunging his strong naked body into the cold water.

Lucy was riveted by the sight of Achilles' long penis and bush of blond pubic hair. She was then alarmed to see the other boys stripping off in the same way. Then Vita and Perdita were doing the same. There was no time for hesitation. She took off her skirt and blouse, but modesty made her keep her pants on. David too had stripped off but kept on his underpants.

'Come on in!' called Achilles. 'The water's great!' He swam powerfully into the middle of the pool, then disappeared underwater with a great kick. Vita dived in, followed by Constantine and Perdita.

The Valentine children took to the water with the graceful ease of otters. Lucy did not feel so sure of herself. And she knew that David did not feel particularly confident either. Unlike the Valentine children, who had regular swimming tuition at their private schools, David didn't get lessons at the local primary and could barely swim at all.

Lucy sat on the bank and dipped her feet in the water. It

was cold, but the sun shining on her back was pleasantly warm. The Valentine children gradually emerged from the water, dripping wet and panting from the exertion, then flopped down on the grass. Lucy could not stop herself peering furtively at the twins' large penises nestling in thick beds of curly pubic hair.

David stood on the bank, chucking stones into the water. Lucy noticed Perdita sidling up to him.

'Look up there, David,' she said, 'there's a squirrel.' She pointed at the top of a massive beech tree which spread its boughs gracefully over the water.

As David looked up, Perdita stepped closer to him and shoved him sideways, sending him toppling into the water with a great splash.

David dropped without a sound under the surface of the pool, then emerged seconds later gasping for breath, his arms flailing.

'Help!' he shouted, gulping at the air. 'It's too deep, I can't swim!' His head disappeared under the water again, and then reappeared again, gasping and spluttering.

Lucy watched in horror as David started moving down-stream with the current. She glanced at the other children, who all stood transfixed by the sight of the helpless boy moving slowly away from them. Lucy looked over at Perdita. No one moved; no one looked worried; in fact, it was as if they were thinking of something other than the danger the boy was in. Lucy heard the words bellowing from her lips: 'Do something! Quick! Save him!'

A moment later there was a loud splash as Achilles dived in and swam expertly to David. He grabbed him in the special way he had been taught in life-saving lessons at school, swam to the bank, and dragged the exhausted boy on to the grass.

David lay panting for a few moments, then he turned to Perdita. 'You did that on purpose, didn't you! You pushed me in.'

Perdita raised her head and smiled. 'No I didn't,' she said. 'I bumped into you by mistake and you lost your footing. It was an accident, anyone will tell you that. Won't they, Lucy?'

She stared hard at Lucy as she spoke the last words.

'And besides,' she added as she turned back to David, 'you were rescued. You're safe. And you haven't even said thank you to Achilles.'

As they set off home for their tea, the children once again crossed the field with the bull. This time they had no fear. The bull was too lazy to budge from its position, they knew that now.

The Valentine boys walked ahead, their long legs covering the ground with ease. Perdita and Vita ran along behind them, their eyes shining, their heads held high. Coming along behind, Lucy walked with David. She did not say anything to him but she felt she ought to stay close to him, to make him feel a little safer after his shock. He was a brat, she thought, but he did not deserve the treatment he had got that afternoon. Lucy was unsettled by what had happened. Watching Perdita's purposeful step and proud posture, she wondered about her. Nothing would ever be said about what had happened, of course, but Lucy had finally come to realise that Perdita's feelings about David were not simply those of irritation. They ran far deeper than that. Lucy felt she had had a glimpse of something terrible and ruthless about Perdita, about all the Valentines. And for a brief moment, it scared her.

CHAPTER 11

June, 1997
Betrayal

It was still June, and four weeks since Lucy's miscarriage. For several days now Lucy had been convinced that Simon was having an affair. She had been aware of a distance between them for some time. They used to be so close, so attuned to each other's thoughts and moods. Now she felt they were miles apart, and with this feeling came a profound sense of loneliness.

Several nights a week Simon had been coming home later than usual. The gloominess that he had shown immediately after the loss of the baby had been replaced by a cheery consideration towards Lucy that was not entirely convincing.

On the rare occasions they made love, it was initiated by him. And now that she was suspicious, she felt there was a difference in his technique, an urgent pushing, new ways of stimulating her, even more solicitude. Even the way he kissed had changed.

Lucy's own days were grim. Her baby was dead and her time was taken up with worrying about Andrew and the few bits of copy-editing she was doing for a publisher. There was nothing to look forward to; it seemed that

life could not be worse. She felt enveloped by gloominess.

Despite her suspicions she knew she couldn't accuse
Simon of having an affair on the basis of his kissing
technique. It was only when she was clearing out his
pockets before doing the weekly wash and found a receipt
for a restaurant bill for two – on a night when he had told her
he'd been working late – that she felt she had some concrete
evidence to go on. She remembered that he had come home
particularly late that night.

It terrified her to confront him about it; she was trembling
with nervousness. But telling herself she had nothing to lose,
she braced herself and accused him, presenting the restaurant
bill as evidence.

Simon denied it at first. 'I just had a bite to eat with
Tom Edwards, the Features Editor. His wife's away and
we decided to eat together.'

But the bill was itemised. Lucy knew that Tom Edwards
was a rugby playing beer drinker. 'I suppose it was Tom
who ordered the spritzer,' Lucy said coldly.

Simon never drank white wine, and certainly never messed
around with mineral water.

'Please don't lie to me, Simon. Things are bad enough
without this happening.' She covered her eyes with her
hands to hide her tears.

Simon got up and put his arms around her.

'I'm sorry, my darling. I'm really sorry.' He nuzzled her
hair. 'I'm sorry I lied. I'm sorry I thought I could get away
with it. I have had a little affair but it wasn't anything, hardly
an affair even. It was with one of the subs, one who's leaving
next week anyway. Perhaps because I knew she was leaving,
I knew it wasn't important. I thought I could get away with
it. You know, it's really not serious. I'm truly sorry this has

happened. It was insensitive and cruel of me to do this to you at such a time . . .'

He ran his hand through his hair and then added, 'But I suppose it's probably why I did it, too.'

'Well I hope you bloody well used a condom,' Lucy snapped.

Simon pulled her to him tight. 'Of course I did, my darling. I'd never do anything that would put either of us at risk.'

It was unfortunate that Rosie was away that weekend. She was the only person Lucy felt she could (or wanted to) talk to about the situation in which she now found herself. She knew it was all typical – the five years of marriage, the strain of trying to start a family, the grieving for a child never born. She felt all these things but she could not say them out loud to anyone except Rosie. Only Rosie was allowed to see the defences let down.

But Rosie was up in Scotland with a new boyfriend. She would not be back for another two days. Lucy would have to endure her problems alone until Rosie got back.

A couple of days after her confrontation with Simon, Lucy had Andrew and Patrick coming to supper. It had been arranged for a while now, that if Andrew was well enough the two of them would come round for a Chinese takeaway.

Lucy felt so angry with Simon that she wanted someone else to mix up the dynamics of the group. Normally she would invite Rosie but she decided, in her friend's absence, to invite Vita instead. When she phoned her, Vita was delighted.

'I'd love to come,' she said. 'I should be able to organise a babysitter. See you then!'

Lucy had barely said a word to Simon and they stepped around each other politely. Andrew and Patrick arrived first. It was a warm summer evening, so they decided to eat outside.

They sat out on the terrace at the back of the house. The dwarf sunflowers in their pots looked bright and cheerful, so different from Lucy's mood.

Andrew was very keen to see the photograph albums that Lucy had been given by their mother.

'I haven't looked at them for years,' he said.

Patrick squeezed him and said in his campiest voice, 'And I can't wait to see you as a little boy in shorts.'

They pored over the albums – baby photos of Lucy first, then Andrew going through the stages of infancy, babyhood, little-childhood.

The photo albums had been lovingly cared for and carefully edited by Hilda over the years. They showed only happy, smiling children and laughing, doting adults. None of the tears and screams and tantrums of childhood had been allowed on to the pages. The out-takes had been discarded years before.

Looking at them now, Lucy was struck by how happy her father looked in those early photographs. Since her mother was the photographer, she rarely appeared in the pictures herself, but there were several shots of Gordon holding his children by the hand and smiling proudly at the camera. He looked like a happy man. What on earth happened to make him the downtrodden faded creature he now was? And what had her mother meant when she said she had been hard on him?

Andrew and Patrick bent over the album together and turned the pages with fascination. They kept laughing and pointing at a funny expression, a ridiculous outfit, a bizarre bit of cropping by an inexperienced or harried photographer. As Lucy watched them she realised she had not seen Andrew laugh like that, seemingly forgetting about himself and his condition, for a long time.

The doorbell rang and Lucy went to let in Vita, who was looking very attractive with her hair pulled back off her face and arranged in a loose bun at the nape of her neck. Her dark eyes were accentuated by subtle make-up which made them seem even bigger and sharper than usual. Her skin was smooth and clear and her lips were highlighted by a rich plum lipstick.

Vita stepped up and kissed Lucy on the cheek.

Simon came up behind and greeted Vita in a friendly fashion, too. 'We've just been looking at old family photos,' he said. 'Come and join the party.'

He led her into the garden and introduced her to Andrew and Patrick.

As Vita shook Andrew's hand, he smiled. 'Well, Vita Valentine,' he said, 'Lucy's been telling me about how you've met up again. I don't suppose you remember me. I was probably just Lucy's irritating little brother.'

Vita smiled broadly. 'Of course I remember you,' she replied. 'I always thought you were rather cute. You were such a serious little boy, very observant, always watching . . .'

Andrew nodded and smiled. 'That's true,' he said. 'I noticed a lot that went on,' he added cryptically.

Patrick hugged Andrew to him. 'He's still observant and he's still cute,' he laughed.

Lucy showed Vita one of the albums. 'We're looking at these pictures that were taken while we were still living in Kentish Town, and I think there may even be some of you in here, when you came on holiday to Norfolk,'

said Lucy. 'Let's have a look.' She handed Vita a glass
of wine and settled down beside her with the album marked
'1967–68'.

There she was herself, a bright-eyed nine-year-old standing with seven-year-old Andrew. There she was on her
skates outside their terraced house in Kentish Town. Here
they were, feeding the ducks at Highgate Ponds, and here
was Lucy skipping on Hampstead Heath.

'Yes, look! These were in Norfolk, on that holiday.'

There was a collection of photographs of the holiday home
with Lucy, Andrew and Vita running around in swimsuits
in the garden, or playing in the sand on the beach. There
was one picture of Vita on her own, looking straight into
the camera with a grave expression on her face.

Seeing this now, Lucy was struck by how adult Vita had
looked, with that deep, penetrating gaze. It was not cold but
there was something unnatural about it. Lucy gave a peculiar
shudder.

She turned the page to another picture of herself dressed
in her favourite summer frock and Clarks sandals. She was
smiling cheerfully at the camera.

Patrick peered over her shoulder. 'You were a stunner
even then,' he said. 'Look at that smile!'

Lucy laughed and kissed him on the cheek. 'You're so
kind,' she said. 'You can come to supper any time.'

While the others continued looking at the edited history
of the Butler family, Lucy went into the kitchen to get plates
and cutlery for their Chinese food. It was a good spread
– hot-and-sour soup, Singapore fried noodles, deep-fried
squid, stuffed tofu, pork spare ribs, seasonal vegetables
and steamed rice. There were cans of beer and a couple
of bottles of cheap but decent Chilean white wine.

Vita came in behind her to help.

'How are you, Lucy?' she asked, taking the tops off the cups of soup. 'How've you been? I haven't seen you since the miscarriage, but I've been thinking about you.'

Lucy shrugged. 'I'm all right, thanks. And thank you for your card, by the way. I meant to write to thank you properly . . . It was kind of you, I appreciated the thought.'

Vita smiled. 'You don't need to thank me. I felt bad that I couldn't do anything more.'

Lucy had not been meaning to say anything about Simon's affair but the warmth in Vita's voice gave her an urge to spill it out, to tell her new friend about this devastating event in her hitherto happy marriage.

'Well, since you ask,' she said quietly, 'I'm not really very all right . . .'

Vita looked at her so quizzically that Lucy could not stop herself blurting out her thoughts.

'Simon's been having an affair. He told me the other night.'

There, she had said it.

Vita continued looking at her. 'Did he tell you whom with?'

'Someone at work. A temporary sub on the paper. He promised me it was over.'

She looked at Vita, waiting for some advice. 'I don't know what to do. I don't even know what to think.'

Lucy felt tears rising up inside her and quickly went back to placing the cartons of food on to trays to carry out.

Vita was silent for a few seconds. Then she dropped the meat and stepped over to put her arms around Lucy. She gave her a big hug. 'I wouldn't worry about it too much,' she said. 'Lots of men have affairs, and most mean nothing. Simon really loves you. I know that. It's obvious to everyone.'

Lucy looked up at her friend. She sniffed and quickly blew her nose. 'Do you really think so?'

'I'm sure of it,' replied Vita. 'I think your marriage is very solid and strong.'

Lucy tore a paper towel off the roll and blew her nose. 'I'm sorry for being silly. Thanks for being so understanding.' She wiped her eyes.

'Come on,' said Vita, 'let's get this food out. I'm starving.'

As the women began to carry out the trays, Patrick called out, 'Quick! Something's wrong! Something's happened to Andrew.'

They all turned to look at Andrew in the chair. He had dropped the album he'd been holding and was trying to speak, but couldn't. He mumbled and lifted one hand feebly; his eyes looked up at them, frightened.

'What's the matter?' asked Lucy. 'Can't you speak?'

Andrew shook his head. He tried to open his mouth but only a few clumsy grunts escaped from his throat.

There was silence for a few moments, then Simon said: 'We'd better call an ambulance, quick.'

Andrew raised an arm and shook his head again. He did not want an ambulance.

'Do you want us to wait?' Lucy almost shouted, panic rising quickly in her.

'You don't need to shout,' snapped Patrick. 'He's not deaf!'

Tears had filled Andrew's eyes as he nodded at his sister, a look of pathetic helplessness in his face. He was pleading to her to help him. With a sense of impotence, Lucy stared back at him, like him unable to move. She knew what he was thinking. He was thinking that it was too late. If they called the ambulance he would be whisked away into the clutches of the hospital, where he would never get the chance to do what he had planned.

'Wunh-wunh-*wait*.' He just managed to get the words out, sounding like someone who had just emerged from the dentist with a mouth paralysed by the local anaesthetic.

Everyone stood quietly, glancing at each other, waiting, not knowing what to do or say. Two minutes, three minutes, four . . . Finally, Simon broke the silence.

'Are you sure we should be leaving him this long? Surely it'd be best to get some medical help – and sooner rather than later.'

Lucy glared at him. 'I'll take him to the hospital if he *wants* to go, and not before then.'

Patrick nodded. 'We'll wait.'

About half an hour later the effects of the stroke were wearing off. Slowly Andrew began to be able to move his arm, and talk more easily. The sense of relief was palpable, and enormous. It was as if he had risen from the dead.

Patrick, who had not left Andrew's side, began speaking to him quietly, urging him now to go to the hospital. 'I'll make sure you don't stay under their control,' he assured Andrew. 'I promise.'

Lucy offered to drive them. She and Patrick helped Andrew into the back of her car. She drove as fast as she dared, looking constantly in her rear-view mirror at the two frightened young men in the back seat.

At the hospital she helped Patrick get Andrew out, then saw them in and drove off. As she left them she made Patrick promise to keep her informed about what was going on.

Lucy got home about an hour later, and let herself in quietly. Simon and Vita were sitting on the sofa together, laughing and talking in the sitting room, their backs to her. They had eaten their supper. Half-empty cartons of Chinese food and a drained bottle of wine stood on the table in front of them. They had not heard Lucy come in, and for a few minutes she stood in the kitchen watching them in the semi-darkness. After all that had happened this evening, it seemed strange to hear them laughing and talking so gaily.

Lucy looked at them again, and then she knew. From the way they leaned their dark heads close together so that Vita's sleek hair almost touched Simon's wild curls, from the way Simon's arm reached across the sofa behind Vita's back, Lucy knew.

Putting her bag on the floor, she coughed.

'I'm back,' she announced loudly.

Vita and Simon rose simultaneously, turning to face her. Their faces were bright and flushed from the alcohol. Lucy knew for certain. Vita's face was expressionless but Simon's was covered with guilt.

'What happened at the hospital? How's Andrew?' Simon was talking unnaturally fast. He was red-faced.

'Patrick said he'd let me know what happens,' Lucy replied wearily. Picking up her bag, she added: 'If you'll forgive me, I'm going up to bed. I'm terribly tired. Goodnight, Vita.' Her voice was cold. They knew she knew.

Without giving either of the lovers a chance to say more, she walked quickly upstairs to the bedroom, and pulled the door shut with a loud bang.

That night Lucy slept badly, unable to find a comfortable position in bed. When she did finally sleep for more than an hour, she dreamed that she had given birth to a baby boy. He had black curly hair and smiling red lips. She was very happy, swinging him in her arms and dancing around the room. Then a woman, the district nurse, came to see him. After examining the baby, she told Lucy that she was not looking after him properly. The nurse then placed the baby in a wicker basket and carried him away.

CHAPTER 12

August, 1968

Perdita's Problem

The summer weeks passed slowly. Looking back Lucy would remember those weeks as permanently sunny but of course there were cool and grey days when a fine drizzle settled on the surfaces of Kentish Town all day long, or when the rain pelted down endlessly all morning making outdoor play impossible until the skies brightened in the afternoon as the sun's rays pierced their way like arrows through the clouds to earth.

Whatever the weather, there was never a shortage of things to do at the Valentines' house. With so many people, there was always lively activity going on somewhere in the house or garden.

Soon after their return from their grandmother's house, the three older boys were preparing for their annual trip with Forest School Camps, where they pitched tents on the Welsh border and learned how to chop wood with an axe, make fires with two sticks, and catch crayfish in the cold mountain streams.

Later in the summer it had been arranged for Vita to join the Butlers on their seaside holiday in Norfolk, where they had rented a small house. They had taken the same house for three years running now. But that was not for a while yet. The summer was gloriously long.

The Valentines still regularly welcomed Lucy into their home. Lucy and Vita had become very close friends but Lucy was relieved that Achilles was no longer around. Her crush was shattered after what he did to her and Vita the night before he set off for camp.

Lucy, Vita and Achilles had had an active day on Hampstead Heath together, swimming in the ponds and watching a large group of hippies rolling a big, brightly coloured balloon up Parliament Hill and down again.

The children watched in wonder as these child-adults then all sat on the pretty balloon and performed an eerie, silent ballet before carefully packing up their toy and drifting out of the park.

Lucy and Achilles had had a good laugh at a couple of young women who had attached strings to the ground with little sticks.

'What are you doing?' asked Achilles with, Lucy thought, impressive boldness.

One of the women, a waif-like creature with thin white-blonde hair, smiled. 'We're talking to the worms,' she said in all seriousness.

Achilles nodded conspiratorially at Lucy and she could tell he was suppressing a laugh. How close she felt to him at that moment. So how betrayed she felt by his behaviour only a few hours later!

It happened that evening. Vita and Lucy were having a bath together in the children's bathroom. Seraphina had allowed the girls to use her expensive, intoxicating scented green bubble bath, which they had poured liberally into the water flowing out of the tap. White froth came up to the top of the bath, right to the curve of their soft pink shoulders.

The girls were squeezed into the bath together and rubbed their hot limbs with pleasure. Every now and then Vita turned on the hot tap to maintain the deliciously tropical atmosphere (something Lucy was never allowed to do at home where her mother did not believe that the bath was for anything other than getting clean).

They were in the top bathroom, which was built into the roof. There was no window, just a grate to let in the fresh air. Light shone from a pretty lamp set into the wall, casting a soft sheen on the William Morris willow pattern wallpaper.

'Look at you two, then!'

The girls turned and laughed to see Achilles standing in the doorway. Lucy blushed and hugged her knees to her chest under the white foam. She liked the look of this big blond boy, standing tough and brazen in the doorway as he looked down on the little mermaids.

Her smile froze as she noted the cruel teasing in his voice.

'Bet you're afraid of the dark.'

'No, we're not,' giggled Vita. 'Go away and leave us alone.' She picked up a soaking wet flannel and threw it at her brother. The flannel landed against the door with a loud slap and dropped heavily to the ground, spraying water everywhere.

Achilles switched off the light. With no window, the room was pitch-black.

'Stop it! Turn it back on.' Vita was laughing.

Lucy laughed too, but nervously.

The room was suddenly quiet. They could not see anything in the still blackout.

'Achilles?'

'Is he still there?' Lucy whispered.

Vita began to get cross. 'Achilles, stop being so stupid. Turn the light on now. You're being silly.'

Silence.

Lucy sat in the dark, huddled in the frothy bubbles. It was so quiet and dark. She rather liked it. She wondered whether she should get out and turn the light back on but she did not want to do that until she was sure Achilles had gone. She did not want him to suddenly switch on the light and see her naked.

'Oh, honestly,' Vita said crossly. She began to get to her feet.

Just at that moment, Lucy felt something. It felt like a stream of warm liquid running down her neck and shoulders. 'What's that?'

'What? What's going on?' Vita sounded annoyed. Then she shrieked. 'Oh, for Christ's sake, Achilles, you're disgusting! He's peeing on us. Get away, you horrible pig!'

Lucy opened her mouth to scream and a warm stream of urine hit her tongue, making her gag. 'Ugh, that's horrible!'

'Ha ha!' Achilles laughed into the dark room. 'Bye,' he called.

The girls heard the door click shut behind him and the sound of his heavy shoes clumping down the stairs.

Vita was furious. Dripping with water she got out of the bath and pulled the light cord. 'What a pig! We'll have to run the bath again and really scrub ourselves now.'

Lucy was shocked. She had the taste of human urine in her mouth. It revolted her. She grabbed the soap and began to scrub her neck and shoulders and arms, where the liquid had touched her.

She felt a combination of revulsion and fear. Why had he done it? What a horrid thing to do! And her mother would never let her come here again if she ever heard about it. Yet there was also something thrilling about such a naughty thing.

With the older boys no longer around to tease or trouble them, the girls developed an even stronger bond between them. The friendship was based on their common interests. Both girls were bookish and enjoyed the same writers – Noel Streatfield, E. Nesbit and Joan Aiken. They liked to walk around the streets of Kentish Town together in a pair, sometimes, to Lucy's thrill, holding hands, if Vita suggested it.

Lucy's infatuation with the Valentine family grew endlessly. She felt so at ease with them all, so free of adult supervision. And not very far below the surface (though she would never admit it to anyone), she preferred the big house in Lady Margaret Road to her own home. Secretly, and most shamefully, she wished that her name was Valentine, too.

Lucy was particularly close to Vita, though she also enjoyed Perdita's company. Perdita had a hard, caustic sense of humour and seemed to have no fear of anyone or anything. However, she could be cold and cruel, too, and got pleasure from showing people up.

This was never clearer than the day they were playing *Monopoly* in Vita's bedroom, and a pungent smell suddenly curled around Lucy's nostrils. She looked at Perdita, sure that it came from her direction, and Perdita's eyes flashed. 'Ugh,' she said, wrinkling her nose and waving her hand in front of her face. 'Someone's farted! I bet it's you, Lucy, it's coming from your part of the room.'

Lucy shook her head. 'No, it wasn't me,' she protested,

but the other children staring at her made her begin to blush. The heat crept up her neck and cheeks.

'Then why are you going red?' Perdita laughed unkindly with a toss of her head. 'It must have been those baked beans at lunch . . .' As she said it, Vita and Celestria started to chant:

> Beans, Beans,
> The musical fruit,
> The more you guzzle
> The more you toot.

They fell about on the floor, kicking their legs in the air and laughing.

Lucy tried to laugh, too, but she was embarrassed and annoyed at herself. She was pretty sure that it was Perdita who had made the smell and then openly accused Lucy to cover up. But she would never have dared suggest such a thing.

One week, Perdita began to act out of character. Her confident, cocksure manner had gone and she had become unusually snappish and irritable. Reluctant to play with the others, she spent much of her time in her own bedroom, reading or painting large gloomy paintings in dark colours.

'What's wrong with Perdita?' Lucy asked one day. She had been afraid to ask but she wondered if it had something to do with her friendship with Vita. Perhaps Perdita was jealous.

'Oh, nothing's wrong.'

Vita's voice was casual but Lucy could tell that the query had bothered her friend. She tentatively pursued it further.

'I sometimes get the feeling that she doesn't like me. She seems so cross all the time . . .'

Vita smiled and shook her head. 'It has nothing to do with you,' she said. 'Perdita likes you a lot.' She paused. 'No, she's upset because something's happening and she doesn't know what to do.'

'What's happening?'

Vita studied her carefully. 'Promise you won't say anything about it if I tell you?'

'Promise.'

Vita glanced around quickly and lowered her voice. 'She's started wetting her bed again. It's odd because Seraphina says she was dry at night when she was two. Anthony says there must be something she's upset about to make her wet her bed but whatever it is, Perdita is very embarrassed. It's horrid for her.'

Lucy was silent, imagining only too easily how embarrassing it must be for Perdita. 'Perhaps she drinks too much water before she goes to bed,' she offered.

Vita shrugged. 'I don't think so,' she said.

Secret or not, Perdita's problem was open for discussion at the children's tea that afternoon. The Valentine parents were out, having gone to an emergency meeting at the Camden Arts Centre. Lucy learned that because the Russians had invaded Czechoslovakia the week before, the exhibition of an East German artist called John Hartfield had been called off by the Conservative councillor, Geoffrey Finsburg. Along with many of their friends, Anthony and Seraphina were outraged, pointing out that Hartfield had been a wartime refugee who escaped from the Nazis, returning to East Germany in 1950. Much of his work was anti-Fascist in character and it was absurd to react to the Russian invasion in such a way.

Meanwhile, at tea, Perdita asked for a glass of milk and Olwyn shook her head. 'I'm sick of changing your sheets,' she said sharply. 'You're not to drink anything between now and bedtime. You've got to get over this problem.' Her voice was flat and firm, with no sense of concern.

David looked up with interest. 'What problem?' he asked in a loud voice. 'You mean, the bedwetting?' He looked at Perdita and grinned. 'I stopped wetting my bed when I was three,' he said.

Perdita was sitting at the end of the table, her shoulders hunched, her face stricken. She was biting her lips and fighting back tears. 'Please may I get down?' she asked quietly. 'I'm not hungry.'

Olwyn shot her a quick glance. 'You may get down but you won't be getting any tea later if you suddenly decide that you're hungry.'

Lucy stayed the night, at Vita's insistence. After the unpleasantness of tea time, the evening was blissful, when the Valentine parents returned from their emergency meeting about the art exhibition and sat down in the sitting room for drinks and to play with their children before going out to see *The Odd Couple* at the ABC cinema in Kentish Town Road. They laughed and teased and ruffled hair. Seraphina was so elegant and gentle. Lucy often scrutinised her from a distance. She just could not imagine having a mother like that, so clever, so perfect, so beautiful. And Anthony was wonderfully jovial and loud, his quick mind probing, provoking and stimulating his children so that they laughed and made him laugh, throwing back his head with carefree enthusiasm and pride at his clever offspring.

Even Perdita cheered up, especially after Vita had managed to sneak her a ham sandwich and apple from the kitchen while Olwyn was putting the babies to bed before settling down to watch *Coronation Street* on the television.

With the little ones out of the way, the atmosphere was calmer, and after a few rounds of *Beggar My Neighbour* and rummy, at which Anthony was fiendishly good, the girls were beginning to yawn.

'Goodnight, my darlings,' Seraphina said to them, embracing them with a kiss and a scented hug before they trooped off to bed.

Then she spoiled it.

'Perdita,' she called. 'Don't forget to go to the lavatory before you go to sleep. Olwyn says she thinks that may do the trick. Perhaps you just get too excited by your reading and forget to go.'

Perdita did not reply. She turned, her cheeks flushed a bright pink, her eyes watery.

After brushing her teeth, she went to her room and said no more.

Vita and Lucy lay in bed talking in the dark. 'I feel so sorry for Perdita,' said Vita. 'I just don't know what to do to help her.'

'No, me neither,' murmured Lucy, as sleep overwhelmed her.

Lucy was woken several hours later by pressure on her own bladder, pressure no doubt caused by the large mug of hot chocolate she had drunk at tea time.

The hall light was on, as it always was, and she slipped out of bed and walked down the landing to the lavatory at the end. She heard a noise and stopped by the doorway, stepping back into the darkness as she saw Olwyn walk past.

Olwyn's bedroom was on the next floor, yet she was heading for Perdita's room at the end of the landing. Lucy's heart pounded as she watched the housekeeper walk into Perdita's room. Olwyn bent briefly over the sleeping child's bed and then straightened up and came back out.

Lucy tried to hold her breath, praying that she would not be seen. The housekeeper walked past and continued up the stairs to her room.

Peering at the short dumpy figure going up the stairs, Lucy noticed that in her right hand, Olwyn was carrying a white enamel jug.

Lucy stood in the darkness for a few minutes, her heart still thumping. A decent time had elapsed. Now it was perfectly reasonable for her to go innocently to relieve her painfully full bladder. She was nervous, but she told herself that there was no reason to be afraid to cross the landing to go to the lavatory at two in the morning.

She scuttled across the hall to the small lavatory, where her urine poured out of her. The relief was enormous, the discomfort gone.

The exquisite pleasure of relieving herself had almost made her forget what she had just witnessed, but as she flushed the lavatory and emerged from the little room, she jumped in panic.

At the bottom of the stairs stood Olwyn, dressed as before. She nodded and looked at her with narrowed eyes. 'Oh, it's you, Lucy,' she said.

For a moment, Lucy thought she saw relief in Olwyn's expression. 'I heard a noise and I wondered who was wandering around.' She looked directly into Lucy's eyes. Her eyes were a pale icy blue. She smiled. 'And it's you.'

Lucy stared back at her. Her heart was pounding in her throat. 'I was up earlier,' she said simply. 'I got up earlier.'

Olwyn's eyes were boring into her.

Lucy stared back at the woman defiantly, half wanting to run away, half wanting to see what Olwyn would say.

Olwyn did not respond. She stared back at her, and turned back up the stairs. 'Good night, child,' she said.

Nothing more was ever said about the incident. Lucy did not mention it to anyone. She did not dare. There was something about the way Olwyn had looked at her that made her feel that she should not say a word to anyone, not even her friend Vita. After all, she did not know what she had seen. Olwyn may have had a perfectly good reason for being in Perdita's room at that hour of the morning. But why with a jug?

But she had to be careful. She had no proof. If she was wrong to think ill of Olwyn then an innocent person would be accused. If she was right then by telling the truth she might jeopardise her own position in the household. She might not be able to come any more.

Thus Lucy rationalised her decision to remain silent. And there the matter rested.

That night was the last time Perdita Valentine wet her bed.

Vita occasionally came to tea at Lucy's house. Hilda Butler was always anxious to ensure that the social contributions were equally balanced.

'Oh, the Valentines don't care,' said Lucy breezily. 'They don't keep a check on how many times I've been there.'

'Perhaps not,' replied her mother briskly, 'but it's important to return hospitality and kindness in whatever way we can.'

The truth was that Lucy still preferred going to the Valentines' house to her own because there was always more activity and excitement there.

It was evident that Vita thought that too.

There was not a great deal to do at the Butlers' house, apart from play cards or *Monopoly*. They were not allowed to do handstands and somersaults on the beds in case they ruined the mattresses. They were banned from playing ball in the garden in case they damaged the flowers. And inside the house, it was so pristine and neat that any idea of romping was out of the question. The very atmosphere inhibited such behaviour.

Andrew, being only seven, was not much fun, either, particularly since he was unusually self-contained for a boy of that age and preferred to sit in his room drawing pictures to taking part in any active games.

In Vita's presence, Lucy found herself becoming self-conscious about her home. Her mother kept it so clean, not a speck of dust, not a ball of fluff was to be seen lurking anywhere. Nothing was out of place. The family photographs were lined up on the mantelpiece at exactly the same angles year after year. Carefully paid bills were laid neatly on the hall table waiting to be posted the next day. Everything was under control, at all times. It could not have been more different from the warm chaos of the Valentine house.

Lucy became aware of things she had never noticed before – the way the lavatory paper matched the pink surround to the lavatory itself, and the bath mat and soap, too. Once she had put a roll of blue lavatory paper in there and her mother had been very cross. That was only for the blue lavatory on the top floor.

But most of the time it was simply boring being at home, and it seemed ridiculous to have Vita to tea simply for the sake of it when both girls knew that there was more fun to be had up the road.

On one such occasion, Vita was looking particularly bored. She sighed repeatedly and kept looking at her watch. In desperation, Lucy suddenly had an idea.

Her father was out on his rounds visiting patients at home and her mother was cooking tea in the kitchen. Now was the time.

'Come with me, I want to show you something,' she said, leading Vita downstairs to the ground floor and her father's surgery.

There was the sharp antiseptic smell in the room. Some patients' notes were lying on the large wooden desk.

'Now, look at these . . .'

Lucy pulled down some medical textbooks from the shelves and showed a wide-eyed Vita the grotesque photos of Nature's mistakes, the medical curiosities that made it to the text books. Vita was indeed impressed. She stared at the pictures of the Siamese twins and Down's syndrome babies, and children born with six toes on each foot. Then her eyes strayed along the shelves, and she walked beside them, running her fingers along the books and peering at their titles.

Lucy felt pleased. With growing confidence she went over to her father's desk and pulled out the lowest right-hand drawer. 'Look at these!' She watched her friend come over to look and felt a rush of pleasure as she saw Vita's eyes open with sudden interest at the jumbled stash of drugs.

'Hey, that's cool! Are they all medicines?'

Lucy nodded and began to pick out some of them. 'They're mostly old pills handed in by patients who don't need them any more, but lots are samples sent to my father by the drug companies. He's a bit careless with them, really. He says they should be locked up but I suppose since his surgery is in his own home, he never gets round to it.

The main drugs are locked up, in that cupboard there.' She pointed to the large cabinet behind the desk.

Vita knelt down by the drawer and looked through its contents, carefully picking up each metal container and reading the labels. 'Drinamyl, dexedrine, sodium amytal . . . There are so many of them,' she said. 'How on earth does a doctor know what all these drugs are, and what they're for?'

Lucy smiled. She was pleased that Vita had asked this question because she was able to give her the answer.

She reached over to the bookshelf and pulled out a red booklet. 'This is what they use. They look up the drugs in here. It tells them what to use them for and they can use it to check when they shouldn't give someone a certain drug. She repeated with care the lesson her father had taught her about looking up drugs and watching out for side effects.

'Mmmm.' Vita took the softback book and flicked through it, back and forth. Then she looked something up in the index and studied it for a few minutes. 'This is great,' she said, 'very interesting.'

Lucy felt a joyful pride spread through her at Vita's words. At least a doctor's surgery was one thing the Valentines were not able to offer her.

'It's really great,' said Vita, nodding her head thoughtfully as she fingered the book and looked back at the drawer. 'It's like a treasure trove . . .'

Lucy was puzzled but she laughed. 'Well, sort of, and we could play Doctors, or something.'

Suddenly they could hear Lucy's mother calling them from the kitchen upstairs. It was time for tea.

Making sure they put everything back in its place, the girls carefully closed the surgery door and went upstairs to enjoy a tasty tea of Lancashire hotpot and peas, followed by deliciously sweet caramel custard, a Hilda Butler special.

CHAPTER 13

June, 1997

Sex and Pleasure

Lucy woke up feeling numb. For a few moments she lay in bed trying to remember what bad thing had happened the night before to make her wake up with such a strong feeling of unease.

Slowly the events of the previous evening came back. She remembered the laughter as they looked over the photograph albums, then the shock of Andrew's stroke, watching him struggle to speak and move. But there was more than that. She recalled coming home after taking Andrew and Patrick to the hospital, exhausted and drained, to see Simon and Vita leaning against each other on the sofa and laughing the conspiratorial laugh of new lovers. Finally, she remembered stumbling into the bedroom and slamming the door, shutting out the world on her misery.

Lucy turned to look at Simon. His side of the bed was empty, but it was rumpled so he had obviously slept there, creeping into bed after Lucy had fallen asleep. But now he had already left for work, rising early as he always did, and for once not turning on the *Today* programme to listen to while he dressed. Presumably he had wanted to get out of the house without a confrontation with Lucy that morning.

That suited Lucy fine. She did not want to see Simon, either. She felt so angry about his lies and deceit that every time she thought about it her chest tightened as if someone were pulling a leather belt around it tighter and tighter.

She showered and dressed and ate a breakfast of toast and black coffee. Without concentrating much on the copy, she read the newspaper until it was time to settle down to finish editing the book she was working on. Her heart was not in it; her heart was not in anything.

Halfway through the morning, she had an urge to go through the drawers of her desk, to look at the old love letters Simon had written to her all those years before when he was pursuing her. Gingerly, she pulled out each letter from its envelope and read it, rebuilding their courtship in her head: 'I couldn't sleep last night after being with you . . .'; 'You looked so radiant when I saw you from across the road . . .'; 'Your laughter still rings in my head . . .'

It seemed astonishing to her now that Simon could once have been so besotted with her, had spent so much time thinking about her and writing to her. All these references to loving her stung her sharply. Turning the letters over in her hands, she felt a rage roar through her. How dare he make her fall in love with him and then betray her like this! She bit her lip and did not bother to hold back the tears as she read on, picking through the letters one by one. They revealed Simon as a sensitive man with powerful feelings, so different from the taciturn fellow he appeared to the world. 'I have never felt so obsessed with anyone before . . .'

Now Simon had left her, gone and slept with another woman, casually, as if Lucy did not exist, as if her feelings did not matter. And it was not just any woman either; it was Lucy's own friend.

As she sat clutching the letters in her hand and tears trickled down her cheeks, Lucy realised that Simon's behaviour had certainly made her angry (how could it not?), but it had also touched on something else, something more primitive than hurt pride. He had touched on the fear of all little children, that of being abandoned and alone. They feel it with their parents, they feel it at school.

But the hurt was complex. Lucy knew that she was not just upset about Simon abandoning her; she was upset about Vita, too. Vita had transferred her loyalty from Lucy to Simon, and this sense that she was losing Vita's friendship as well stirred up old feelings from the past. As a child she was desperate to be Vita's friend. And as an adult, nothing had changed.

Lucy sat on the sofa for a good hour, wallowing in her torment, her chest tight with anger and self-pity.

After a while, she calmed down. She was tempted to throw Simon's letters away but thinking (and hoping) that she might regret such an act in the future, she replaced them in her desk drawer. Thought of the future made her think about Andrew. She should ring the hospital to see how he was.

When she rang the ward, she was informed by a nurse with a soft Irish brogue that Andrew had fully recovered from the stroke but was now sleeping. Would she like to ring again later?

Rosie telephoned at about midday. She had got back from her Scottish trip late the night before and was now back at work. The new boyfriend had turned out to be rather uninteresting. 'He wasn't a complete bore but, let's put it this way, I spent much of the weekend reading novels,' Rosie said wearily.

'That's too bad,' said Lucy. 'I'm sorry he didn't turn out right for you.'

'You sound a bit gloomy.' Rosie could always pick up on Lucy's moods.

Lucy poured out her troubles to her friend, first about Andrew, and then about Simon and Vita.

Rosie listened in silence and then said, 'The little shit. And how dare she!'

'I haven't even begun to work out what I think about Vita,' said Lucy. 'I'm still fuming about Simon. At the moment I just don't even want to see him.'

She had a sudden longing to see Rosie, her dear loyal friend Rosie. 'What are you doing tonight? You're not by any chance free, are you? Do you fancy going to see a film?'

'I can't. I've got a ghastly awards dinner for the magazine industry at Grosvenor House. I have to go. The tickets cost ninety pounds each and it's a glitzy black-tie nonsense with everyone getting gongs for this and that. Last year we won the best women's magazine award but this year we're not even short-listed, so it's not very interesting. Still,' she added, 'it's actually always quite useful for networking . . .'

'Oh.' Lucy was disappointed.

'Actually, Lucy, maybe you'd like to come. I was meant to take this so-called boyfriend of mine but I don't feel like being in his company for another night. You could come along as my date, if you like. You might enjoy it as an outsider. The food's usually okay and there's always lots of wine.'

'But what about the boyfriend? Isn't he expecting to go?'

Rosie laughed. 'Ha, I'm sure he'll be relieved not to have

to spend another evening with me. I'll tell him he's off the hook.'

Lucy was surprised that she was interested in the invitation. 'Well, if it's really okay, I might rather like to come . . .'

'We're actually sharing a table with *Mate*, the men's magazine in our company. They're not a bad lot, in fact they're quite fun. Thinking about it, Lucy, you *must* come . . .'

It was not the sort of event Lucy normally liked but now she found the idea distinctly appealing.

'And one thing's for sure,' Rosie was saying, 'the awards dinner is always a pretty good occasion for getting laid . . .'

Lucy laughed. 'Well that settles it, then, doesn't it! Yes, I'd love to be your date for the evening.'

'By the way,' Rosie said, 'I don't know if you're interested in getting a full-time job, or whether you even want to work on a woman's magazine, but there is a sub-editor's job open here. I'm sure you could get it if you applied. My recommendation would go a long way.'

Lucy was taken aback by the suggestion. 'I'll have to think about that one,' she said. 'We can talk about it tonight . . . Now I have to make the agonising decision about what I'm going to wear.'

Lucy spent a lot of time dressing up for the evening, choosing a long Chinese jade silk dress and silver jacket. It was a long time since she had dressed up for any occasion, in the way she used to as a child. Whatever the event, in those days – staying up for supper, going to the theatre, visiting Granny, she was always dressed in her best.

Life was just not as formal any more now but she and Simon rarely, if ever, went anywhere that required such dressing up.

So it was fun to soak in deep bath water smelling of Floris limes and to wash and blow-dry her hair so that it stayed in a rather attractive sweep off her forehead. She did her face meticulously, using the make-up that usually sat untouched in the cupboard – light foundation, rouge tint, mascara. There seemed to be a lot of it for what was essentially a natural, no-make-up look.

Every now and then Lucy realised that her teeth were grinding as she set about her task, her jaw stiff with rage at Simon and a desire to get her own back at him. Rosie's support had galvanised her. She was going to have a good time tonight, whatever. And maybe she would get laid . . .

She left the house before Simon had returned from work. She left a note on the kitchen table telling him that she had gone out with Rosie for the evening. She signed it 'L', with no 'love' or 'x'. A cold, matter-of-fact note.

The awards dinner was held in a long room at the Grosvenor House Hotel in Park Lane. Rosie was already at the door waiting for her when she arrived. She had spent some time getting ready in a glamorous skin-tight black body and a crinkly plum-coloured silk skirt. Long silver earrings dangled from her ears. Her perpetually smiling lips were also a deep plum colour. 'Come and have some champagne,' she laughed. 'I'll introduce you to someone interesting.'

Hundreds of people – editors, designers and publishers – dressed in silks and sequins, unique Jacques Azagury outfits or demure Jean Muir, milled about in the anteroom, greeting each other with ostentatious kisses or gossiping more quietly in corners.

The excited buzz of conversation was broken every now and then by shrieked greetings as old friends and work colleagues met up again, not having seen each other since the year before. Glamorous, confident people, Lucy thought, successful in life, and pleased with it. So unlike her, she thought with wobbly confidence.

But Lucy kept her nerve. She was determined to enjoy herself. She knocked back several glasses of champagne and accepted a top-up every time the waiters came round. She smiled and laughed and thrust out her chest in the way she had seen Rosie do.

Rosie introduced Lucy to several of her colleagues from the magazine and many other people passing by. When the Master of Ceremonies announced the serving of dinner, they made their way to their table in the main room.

The dining room seated one thousand people, all from the magazine world, from the glossy women's monthlies to the specialist trade publications. They all sat at tables of twelve. There were six people from Rosie's magazine, including Lucy, all women, and six from *Mate*, all men.

Lucy was seated next to *Mate*'s Features Editor, a tall, good-looking blond man called Giles. He had a broad face, a pleasant smile and warm brown eyes.

'Don't you think we journalists are a ghastly lot?' he asked Lucy as he offered her the bread. 'So self-satisfied, as if we had any influence in the world at all. We don't matter one bit, not in magazines, anyway.'

Lucy smiled. She was feeling drunk already but did not stop Giles filling her wine glass again. 'Why don't you get out of magazines then and work on a newspaper if you feel that way?' She grinned charmingly at him.

Giles looked steadily at her and raised his glass to his lips. 'Who said I want to influence anyone? I'd be crazy to move. No, I like magazines, it's an easy life. Newspapers are too much like hard work.'

Giles was fun and good company. He asked Lucy about

herself and was interested without being intrusive. He informed her that his girlfriend was away on business but she never wanted to come to these things anyway. 'And I don't blame her,' he added. 'She's an economist. She works for the Treasury. She thinks I'm frivolous.' He drained his glass. 'Frankly, it's just as well that one of us is frivolous, don't you think?'

The wine was going to Lucy's head. She was not used to drinking very much and she was aware of a delicious tingling in her legs. Inside her chest she could feel a rising excitement at the conversation. The teasing tone in Giles's voice was clearly flirtatious, and Lucy, with her half-open mouth and her quick laughter, was flirtatious back.

Halfway through the meal, she realised that Giles's leg was pressing against her thigh under the table. Her heart beat fast. What was she to do about it? She knew she had a choice. She could withdraw it priggishly and make it clear that she was not available, that she was a married woman, and remind him that he had a girlfriend. Or she could allow it to continue and see how far it went. But how flattering, how exciting it was!

Did it really matter if she went off to sleep with this man? Would it be a bad thing to do? The fact that he was flirting with her gave her a boost, and if he fancied her enough to take her home to bed, then that would be a help, too. Simon had damaged her confidence at a time when she was already low. Surely she was allowed to make herself feel better in any way she could?

Lucy had only had a couple of boyfriends before she met Simon, and (unlike Rosie) she had been rather scared of going to bed with people she did not know well. She had always rather regretted this limited sexual experience, wondering if she had missed out in some way. Giles was clearly offering her an opportunity. Why should she not take this chance to get her own back at Simon and satisfy this secret need of hers to sleep with a stranger? She did not have to rub Simon's nose in it. It would be for her own sake, and satisfy her own curiosity.

Draining her glass, she decided to go for it . . .

After the chicken liver parfait, they ate their way through the roast lamb and baby vegetables, then an assortment of sorbets, coffee and chocolates. The awards were announced during coffee, and the winners trooped up to the stage to collect their prizes amidst loud clapping and cheers, or jeers from rival magazines.

Lucy was aware that the pressure of Giles's leg under the table was growing stronger. Now she gave in and allowed her foot to rub against his without protest. She hoped the economist girlfriend was a long way away.

'Let's get out of here,' Giles bent over and whispered into her ear. She could feel his breath on her neck. The final awards had been announced and now the raffle tickets – five-pound notes with people's names written on them – were being drawn from a black moleskin top hat.

Giles got to his feet and stood behind Lucy's chair to pull it out for her. Without a word, Lucy got up from the table, waved goodbye to a grinning Rosie, and followed Giles out of the room.

Giles hailed a taxi and took her to his flat, a comfortable place in Holland Park. They had kissed in the taxi and their hearts were pounding as he paid the driver and fumbled to find the keys in his pocket.

Once inside the flat, they fell on one another, pulling off their clothes and dropping them on the floor.

Lucy had not felt such excitement since the early days of

her courtship with Simon. She did not hold herself back; she wanted to enjoy every bit of it.

Giles was as skilled a lover as he was conversationalist. He removed Lucy's remaining garments and led her to his large double bed. 'Take off your jewellery,' he ordered.

Lucy took off her earrings.

'And all your rings.'

Her engagement and wedding rings lay on the bedside table beside the alarm clock as Giles began to massage her body, rubbing in baby lotion he had brought from the bathroom. His touch was light and skilful. He knew what he was doing; he had done it many times before and he evidently prided himself on his sensitivity and dexterity.

'Lie still,' he whispered. 'I don't want you to do anything.'

He rubbed Lucy's back and shoulders, her buttocks and legs. He rolled her over and rubbed her neck and breasts, and on down her belly.

His hands were firm and tender. Gradually Lucy felt the tension building up inside her. She let out a dreamy groan. Giles smiled and put his arms around her. He kissed her and held her tight as the exquisite spasm ran through her.

They lay quietly together for a few minutes. For a moment Lucy thought that that would be it. Perhaps this great lover was in fact impotent, capable of satisfying her but not himself. She was wrong.

Now Giles began to stroke her belly and thigh, and rose over her, kissing her hard.

She was just about to push him away and say something about safe sex (she was not so drunk as to be stupid), when he reached over to the bedside table drawer and pulled out a packet of condoms.

'Do you want to put it on for me?' He smiled lazily.

Thus it began again. He pushed hard inside her but his lovemaking was gentle and skilled. He varied the pace, always in control.

Lucy had never had more than one orgasm during a lovemaking session so she was surprised to feel the delicious tension building up again deep inside her pelvis.

Giles pushed and pulled back, he waited, he teased. He was very efficient, very effectual. He stroked her breasts and ran his hands around under her back.

Lucy arched her spine as she felt herself begin to rise again. As she let out another light groan, Giles pushed himself hard into her and let himself go. They collapsed in the warm groans of their synchronous orgasm.

Giles kissed her gently on the cheek and moved a tendril of damp hair off her forehead. 'Well done,' he murmured. 'That was good.' Lucy felt as though she had been given a gold star by the gym teacher, but she was pleased with herself all the same.

He rolled off and they lay together, she on his chest, his arm around her shoulder. Lucy felt eerily distanced from herself, as if she were taking part in a film and watching herself on the screen. This is the sex scene, the long naked intertwined limbs, the large double bed, the rumpled white sheets.

She began to doze. It was very late but Lucy did not care to know how late. She sighed happily. Whatever the consequences of this evening, she thought, she vowed that she would never regret these moments.

Sleep had almost overtaken her when she felt Giles's hand again running over her body. Was he really up to it again? More to the point, was she?

His touch ran over her upper arm again, rhythmically, then he shifted position and ran his fingers down her belly.

He did not seem at all tired as he kissed her again, softly, gently. Again, and again to her surprise, her body began to respond.

There was something different about his lead this time. His hands touched her thighs lightly, ran over her lower back and down between her buttocks.

She stiffened as she felt him press his finger against her.

'No!' she whispered, pulling away.

Giles kissed her. 'Have you never been buggered?'

She shook her head, embarrassed by his bluntness and by her own self-consciousness.

'Do you want to try?'

She looked up into his calm dark eyes.

'Won't it hurt?'

'I won't hurt you, I promise,' he said. 'It doesn't have to hurt.'

Lucy hesitated. She was tempted. It was something she had wondered about and now was surprised to feel an eagerness, almost an urge, in herself to try. Certainly it was not anything Simon would ever have suggested.

'Okay,' she said warily, 'I'll try. But you must stop if it hurts at all,' she added quickly.

She had to trust him.

Giles reached over to the drawer again. She had her face in the pillow but she heard the soft tearing of the condom packet. He was responsible. Then she heard him fiddling with something else, and then felt him rub the cold liquid jelly on her skin.

Positioning himself above her, he pushed against her gently and very slowly.

It did not hurt. It was strange, singularly exciting and sensuous. Giles was as careful as he said he would be. He came with a shuddering groan and then stayed inside her until he could slip out of her gently as their bodies relaxed.

Lucy smiled and kissed him. She felt almost proud of herself and she knew now why she had felt a need to try it. It was not just the erotic thrill of doing something that was a taboo but it was also that in some odd way it made her feel closer to Andrew. This must be what her homosexual brother did with his lovers, the act that was now killing him.

Giles climbed off her and rolled over on to his back beside her. 'Did you enjoy that?' he asked.

Lucy ran her hand over his strong chest. 'I did. I was surprised, but I did.'

Giles smiled. 'My girlfriend likes to be buggered,' he said. 'She says it's the only time she ever feels really vulnerable.'

Lucy swallowed hard. 'I suppose that says a lot about her,' she replied faintly.

'Yes, it does,' said Giles. 'But we get on fine. And don't you worry – she's at a conference in Washington until next week. Now, let's get some sleep. We have to go to work in the morning.'

Lucy's eyelids flickered. What an evening! She listened to Giles's breathing as he fell asleep. She knew that she would probably never sleep with him again. The likelihood was that she would never even see him again. And she would not care. It did not matter. That night had been enough.

Sex that night had been like playing a long and exciting game of tennis with a complete stranger. Sex with a stranger. What a boost! Rosie had been right. She sighed deeply. As she fell asleep she found herself wondering briefly if sex with economists was so varied. But before she could even think further about Giles's high-powered girlfriend, she was slipping into the mattress, slipping off into a deep and almost blissful sleep, without dreams.

CHAPTER 14

August, 1968
Norfolk

It had been Hilda Butler's idea to invite Vita Valentine to join the Butler family for a week in the house they were renting for a fortnight on the north coast of Norfolk.

'After all the time you've spent at the Valentines' house, being looked after and fed, it's the least we can do,' she told Lucy. 'And it'll be nice for you to have a companion for some of the time, too.'

Lucy was afraid that Vita would think a holiday with her family boring and would not want to come, so she was relieved and delighted when the invitation was accepted. It was wonderful to have Vita along, for as much as she loved her little brother, Andrew was no fun at all as a playmate. He spent all his time drawing pictures and reading books and had no interest in the seaside or the woods that Norfolk had to offer.

The small cottage they rented was on a farm, quite close to the seaside, and surrounded by fields and copses. The girls spent their time wandering bare-legged through the meadows and watching the animals and insects in the woods. Again, Vita revealed her extensive knowledge of the natural world, pointing out interesting beetles and butterflies, and identifying the songs of birds in the trees.

After all that time on the Valentine turf, it was interesting for Lucy to see Vita in a different setting. She was what her mother would describe as 'well brought up', always good about saying please and thank you, and greeting people with good mornings and good nights, and offering to help at appropriate moments.

But she also had opinions that shocked Hilda because they were about matters Hilda thought should not concern children. When Vita stated that the Vietnam War was morally wrong, Hilda reddened with annoyance and muttered to her husband that the child was simply mouthing what she had heard at home, which was probably true, thought Lucy. However, when on Saturday evening there was a discussion about going to church the next day, Hilda was truly shocked.

'Does your family normally go to church on Sundays, Vita?' she asked as innocently as she could sound. She did remember Lucy once telling her that the Valentines were atheists, but she could not quite believe it.

Vita shook her head vigorously. 'No, we never go to church.'

Hilda looked at her quizzically. 'What? Never? Not even at Christmas or Easter?'

Vita shrugged. 'My father said he might take us to Midnight Mass at Westminster Abbey one day.' She paused. 'But I don't think that really counts.'

'No,' agreed Hilda, her brow crossed in a vexed frown.

'Actually,' Vita continued, 'I'm not even christened. None of us is. My parents don't believe in God. And neither do I,' she added.

'Oh,' Hilda did not quite know what to say. She had

never heard of someone not being christened, unless they were Jewish. She pressed her lips together and said, 'What, none of you children?'

Vita smiled and shook her head. 'Nope. Not one. My father said we could decide for ourselves when we were older. He says the decision will be ours alone then.'

'I see.' The frown on Hilda's face continued to show her disapproval. 'Well, what about tomorrow? We shall be going to church and you are welcome to join us if you would like.'

Lucy listened uneasily to the edge of sarcasm in her mother's voice.

Vita shook her head. 'That's okay,' she said. 'I think I'll stay here and try to finish my book. I'm enjoying it so much, and I think it might be a bit hypocritical of me to go to church.'

Hilda went off to make the tea, muttering as she went that she doubted if Vita knew the meaning of the word hypocritical.

There was a curious incident that day when Lucy and Vita came into the house laughing and panting after racing each other through the nearby woods.

As the girls sat down at the kitchen table, Hilda reached over to Vita's head. 'You've got something in your hair,' she said.

As she said it, her hand raised to pick out the brown twig caught in Vita's thick black tresses, Vita jerked her head away suddenly and cringed from Hilda's hand, her right arm held up protectively before her face.

'Hey, I won't hurt you!' exclaimed Hilda. 'I'm just trying to get this twig from your hair.'

Vita stood up straight and gave her an embarrassed smile.

She recovered her composure quickly and laughed as if her exaggerated gesture had been deliberate.

Lucy watched intently. She was pretty sure why her friend had ducked away like that. Later that afternoon, she asked Vita about it.

The girls were out in the garden where Vita had just taught Lucy to catch grasshoppers, sweeping their feet through the long grass to make the insects leap before them and reveal themselves. Then the girls crept up, crouching down, two hands cupped together, ready to pounce and capture the creatures in their closed palms.

Quicker and more agile, Vita was much better at catching the grasshoppers than Lucy, though Lucy did not mind. It was not a competitive activity for, once a grasshopper was caught, it was released. 'The fun's in the catching,' explained Vita.

After a while, they stopped and threw themselves in the grass, rolling over on their backs to chew sweet blades of grass and stare up at the blue sky. Small dark swallows swooped and darted above them.

Remembering the earlier incident, Lucy turned over on her belly. 'Why did you shy away when my mother took the twig out of your hair?'

Vita did not respond. She chewed her grass and shut her eyes.

Lucy waited but Vita continued to ignore her.

'Don't you want to talk about it?'

Vita rolled over and smiled at her. 'You know, Lucy, a long time ago we talked about friends. You are my friend, I can see the point of having a friend, and that's nice.' She pushed herself to her feet. 'Come on, let's catch some more grasshoppers.'

The change of subject caught Lucy off guard. She smiled.

Vita owned her, had claimed her as a friend at last. And in her flush of pleasure, she forgot entirely that Vita had not answered her question.

On Sunday afternoon, when church was over and Hilda had served up a real Sunday roast in the cramped cottage kitchen, complaining constantly about the inadequate utensils, the girls went for a walk with Dr Butler.

They left Hilda behind to listen to the radio and Andrew to read the new book he had just started.

Dr Butler liked Vita. He found her a bright and inquisitive child and he liked to linger behind the two girls and eavesdrop on their charming conversations. He was struck by how sophisticated the Valentine girl appeared to be. Lucy seemed protected and naïve by comparison.

As they walked through the beech woods, Vita displayed an impressive knowledge of nature. She knew a lot about birds. She could identify the chaffinches and woodpeckers they saw, and identify their songs if she listened carefully enough. Some she could even imitate. Dr Butler raised his eyebrows in admiration as Vita mimicked the Great Tit – 'Tea Cher! Tea Cher!' and called to the wood pigeons in the trees with a 'Coo-roo-coo-coo!'.

But Vita also knew that all birds moult every feather at least once a year, and to prevent interference with flight, most moult slowly, shedding the feathers in orderly rotation.

Vita also knew about plants. She pointed out the vivid red berries of the lords and ladies and the pretty purple flowers of the monkshood, the waxy berries of the yew and the hanging fruit of the woody nightshade.

'You seem to know a great deal about plant life, young

lady,' remarked Dr Butler with amusement. He always enjoyed talking to children.

Vita smiled. 'My grandmother is terrified that one of us might eat poisonous berries by mistake so we have all been drilled from an early age, and taught what they looked like so we knew we should never touch them.

'It's interesting to think about the olden days, before there were books, when people discovered what was poisonous and what wasn't,' she said. 'Do you think a child would eat a yew berry and be very ill and then they'd know? Before books and pictures, how could anyone know about the dangers of some plants in advance?'

Dr Butler was stimulated by the child's chain of thought. 'Well, of course, in a village there would have been someone who knew a lot about plants and their medicinal value and they'd pass it on.

'And I'm sure you know, of course,' he continued, enjoying his role as teacher, 'that many poisonous plants can also be put to good use. Such poisons are often used in modern medicine.'

Vita looked up at him with her large dark appealing eyes. 'Really? Like what?'

'Well, take deadly nightshade, or belladonna. It produces something that is essential for ophthalmology, the study of the eye. It produces something called hyoscyamine, which changes into something called atropine. There's no substitute for atropine in treatment of the diseases of the eye. It is also an important antidote to a number of poisons, including lead and digitalis, or foxglove. It relieves muscle cramps and so it's also given for asthma. It's also used for gallstones and even sea sickness.'

The girls both looked impressed, so he continued. 'So you see that although many of our plants have great power to do harm, they also possess important medicinal properties that can do a great deal of good.'

Vita was pensive. Looking up, she asked, 'But how would a doctor know how much of a poison to give? How would he know how not to poison someone?'

'For a dangerous plant to become a remedy depends on the dosage, and it is then made weaker as a substance by dilution.'

'That's interesting,' murmured Vita, and she fell silent with her own thoughts.

They walked on. The only sound came from the little brook to their left and the occasional soft cooing of a wood pigeon in the trees.

Vita looked thoughtful, then a worried frown appeared between her eyes. 'Dr Butler,' she said quietly, 'can you tell me a little about leukaemia.'

Dr Butler smiled and looked quizzically at her. 'Of course! What do you want to know about leukaemia?'

'Well, what is it exactly and how do you know if you have it?'

'Leukaemia is a cancer of the blood. There are several types, and the symptoms vary but you would know if you had it. The symptoms are quite obvious and debilitating.'

They walked along side by side. Lucy trailed along behind.

'Why?' asked Dr Butler. 'Why do you ask? You don't think you have leukaemia, do you?'

Vita did not answer. She kicked the leaf mould with the toe of her brown sandal.

Dr Butler laughed gently. He did not want to mock her for her worries. 'I can assure you,' he said, 'If you are worried that you have leukaemia, that your worries are unfounded. You're as fit as a fiddle . . .'

Vita bit her lip and nodded but she said nothing.

Later that night, as the girls lay in their bunk beds in the dark, they referred back to that conversation.

'I like your father,' said Vita, staring up at the ceiling. There was a pause.

'Yes, I do, too,' replied Lucy. She would never actually admit to anyone except herself that she liked her father more than she liked her mother. But she knew it was true and Vita's remark confirmed that for her.

Vita turned over on her side. 'He made me feel much better about leukaemia.' She stopped and then started again. 'You see, I did think I had leukaemia but now he's made me think I probably haven't. I've been thinking about it a lot.'

Lucy smiled. 'I'm glad he's made you believe him. But why did you think you had leukaemia in the first place?'

She waited for her friend to reply but there was just silence in the room and the sound of a barn owl hooting outside. After a few minutes she stopped expecting an answer. Her breathing became steady and deep as she sank into sleep.

Vita lay awake in the dark, her eyes wide open, her mind ever-active as she thought about her life back home in the big house in Kentish Town.

Vita went home to London on the train. Seraphina Valentine had assured Hilda on the telephone that Vita would be perfectly safe on the train.

'She'll be met at the station in London. She's quite used to travelling on her own. She's often been on the train to Sussex by herself.

Hilda Butler was clearly surprised that Vita's parents should not drive up to collect their eldest daughter but she was not one to argue, and certainly not with intellectuals who did not baptise their children. Wherever could one start?

She did a final check with the child herself. 'Wouldn't you like someone to drive up and collect you from here?' she asked Vita.

Vita had shrugged. 'Not particularly,' she stated simply. 'I get to read a lot on the train and I like the peace and quiet. My home is very noisy most of the time,' she added with a spontaneous grin.

With her characteristic politeness, Vita thanked Mrs Butler for having her. 'I've had a wonderful time,' she said.

And on the train home she composed a beautifully written letter that would arrive a few days later.

'Well,' said Mrs Butler, reading it with approval. 'Whatever else those Valentine parents do, at least they've drummed some basic good manners into their children, which is more than you can say about a lot of people these days.'

CHAPTER 15

June, 1997

Reconciliation

Lucy paid her fare and got out of the cab around the corner from home. She did not want the whole street to see her returning at seven thirty in the morning dressed in her evening gown and high heels from the night before. It might have been something to flaunt and laugh about as a student, but she did not want the tongues wagging too much in their quiet west London street. She was particularly worried in case Mehmet, the friendly grocer, had seen her as he opened up his shop.

Lucy let herself into the house quietly and, taking a deep breath, braced herself for a confrontation with Simon. She squared her shoulders and held her head high. Although exhausted, she was still glowing inside from her adventure. Fired up, she was ready to meet Simon head on.

Having anticipated anger and recriminations, she was not at all prepared for what happened.

Simon was sitting in the kitchen, slumped miserably over a cup of coffee. His rumpled clothes and unshaven face made it clear that he had not been to bed at all. He had probably had even less sleep than Lucy.

He leaped up when Lucy came in. 'There you are! I've been so worried about you. Why didn't you ring and let me know where you were? I've been trying to get hold of Rosie. I assumed you'd have gone home with her but there was no answer, or only her answering machine. She never rang back.'

Simon's tired, bleary eyes looked pleadingly at her. 'I'm so sorry, Lucy.' Taking a step towards her, he held out a hesitant hand, unsure of how she was going to respond.

Looking at him standing there, so big and tall but so vulnerable and unhappy, Lucy gave in to the warm rush of affection which flowed through her.

'Oh, Simon,' she cried, moving towards him and placing her arms around his waist. She laid her head against his chest while Simon buried his face on her shoulder.

'I'm sorry,' he mumbled, giving way to his exhaustion. 'I'm sorry about what I did. I'm sorry about being unfaithful to you, and I'm sorry, so sorry, about lying to you.'

He paused and then stood back, his hands grasping her shoulders. 'I spent the whole night thinking about what was happening – what has happened and why. And then you didn't come home so I began to imagine all sorts of things – that you had left me, or something terrible had happened to you. I imagined that you had been murdered and I'd never know and it'd be all my fault.'

He was talking, gabbling so fast that he was almost incomprehensible. Lucy let out a sigh and reached for the kettle. 'I need some coffee,' she said. 'And then we should talk.'

They made a large pot of coffee and Simon rang his office to tell them he would be late. Then the two of them sat on opposite sides of the kitchen table and talked.

They talked about the strain of trying to have a baby and the pressure that had put on their relationship. They talked about how they had focused so much on that that they had forgotten about each other in their isolated obsessions. They talked about the miscarriage and what it had meant to them to lose the baby. They talked a lot about Andrew and the misery of watching him die while they were hoping to start a new life. And they talked about the strain of supporting Andrew and trying to bring about some sort of convincing reconciliation between Andrew and his parents. Finally, they talked about Vita.

'She means nothing to me,' said Simon.

Lucy was silent.

'And I know that I don't mean anything to her,' Simon continued. 'You shouldn't really blame her, either, Lucy. I initiated it and she responded. I asked her to come and see me at the paper to discuss the possibility of her doing a story for us. Then I invited her out for a drink. It went from there. She never once took the lead. It was all my doing and my fault.'

He promised never to see Vita again. 'At least, not without you knowing,' he added sheepishly.

Simon never once asked Lucy where she had been and she knew that he probably never would, either. That suited her fine.

After they had talked for three hours, they went to bed. Simon began to kiss her. 'I haven't even showered,' murmured Lucy.

But Simon was undeterred. It was as if he had to put his mark on his woman again. There was an urgency to his lovemaking that spread to Lucy. As they tussled and rolled on the bed, Lucy was fleetingly reminded of the time when Rosie had slept with three men in one day. But she knew that she was meant to be with Simon, that she loved him, and would continue to do so for a long time.

Exhausted, they finally dozed in each other's arms.

In the afternoon, refreshed and showered, Simon went in to work and Lucy went out for a walk.

Thinking about what had happened over the past few days, she realised that she was genuinely sanguine about Simon, and she knew that her relationship with him was solid and safe. When he promised that he would not see Vita again, she believed him.

She thought a lot, too, about Vita. Her feelings about Vita were much more complicated and she appreciated the fresh air to clear her thoughts.

She was surprised by what she thought about Vita Valentine. In spite of her rage and hurt, and her sense of betrayal, she was reluctant to sever all ties with her old-new friend Vita.

What Vita had done was wrong and certainly not the sort of behaviour you expect from a friend but, for some reason, Lucy knew that this whole affair was not really a moral issue. It was not even a serious matter. For some reason (and she did not know why) she knew that Vita, like the rest of her family, lacked a common sense of morality. She knew that Vita would not regard sleeping with Simon as particularly wrong. It just happened.

After all, Lucy herself had just slept with another woman's man the night before. She may not know Giles's girlfriend but she knew of her existence, and that had not stopped her sleeping with Giles. That was not very moral behaviour, either.

She walked into Holland Park and, as she walked, feeling the warm summer breeze on her face, Lucy was very aware of a primitive tug inside her for Vita's friendship. She valued her relationship with Vita, which stemmed from that long summer when they were nine. She valued it more than she was bothered by these recent events. She did not know why but she knew that Vita could not help herself, that in some odd way, she was not responsible for her actions.

Something had happened all those years ago that had made her understand this about Vita. Something linked them and bound them together. Lucy could not remember what it was; it was buried too deep inside her. But she knew that she had to forgive Vita, just as she had to forgive Simon.

The sun warmed her cheeks. Everything would be all right between her and Simon. They would go on holiday and get rejuvenated and start to try and have another baby.

They would not rush it. Even in her optimism, she had not forgotten that she had to wait for Andrew to die first. On holiday they would just try to relax and forget about trying.

As she turned for home, she decided that she would apply for the sub-editor's job on Rosie's magazine, after all. She needed a proper structure to her life, and some way to keep her thoughts off her own condition.

And it would tempt fate. If she was offered the job, she was bound to find herself pregnant!

The next morning the telephone rang at five o'clock. Lucy woke with an uncomfortable start and grabbed the phone, certain that something terrible had happened.

It was Andrew. His voice was rambling, almost incoherent. 'I just wanted to tell you, in case I suddenly don't get the opportunity, how much I love you,' he said. 'It's hard to get the opportunity to say important things any more, and I just wanted to let you know how I feel.'

Lucy was suddenly wide awake. Tears flooded her eyes.

She sniffed into the receiver. 'You know I feel the same about you, Andrew,' she said. 'I love you, too.'

Lucy and Simon went away to Provence for a week. The trip served its purpose. They went back to the place they were staying when they decided to get married. The weather was not too hot and they saw the sights of Orange, Avignon, Arles and Nîmes, and they ate and drank until they were bloated. They stayed in a small hotel in Beaumes de Venise and made love every night. It seemed like a new beginning to their relationship. Even Lucy's childmares seemed to subside.

'Perhaps we just needed this crisis to remind us of why we like each other,' Simon said one night after a particularly delicious and filling meal of crudités, chicken, and *marquise au chocolat*.

Lucy laughed and gave him a playful push. 'You sound like a therapist,' she teased.

'It's reading that magazine of Rosie's – according to that, if everyone "got in touch with their feelings" they'd all be a lot happier.'

Lucy poked him in the ribs. 'You laugh,' she joked, 'but even I think there's something to be said for that!'

They returned home several pounds heavier and much happier. Lucy had not felt so close to Simon since the early days of their courtship. It gave her strength to tackle what was awaiting her back in London.

She had interviewed for the job on Rosie's magazine and she had more or less been offered it on the spot. She knew the job was hers if she wanted it but she was beginning to wonder how wise it would be to work in the same place as Rosie. Much as she loved her as a friend, she was not sure what she would be like as a colleague.

But her uncertainty had more to do with her concern about Andrew, whose health was steadily deteriorating. He had had a couple more strokes since the last one, and although he had recovered completely each time, the gaps between them were shortening. In addition, the different drugs he took for his various conditions had debilitating side effects which were almost more unbearable than the condition they were meant to treat.

His eyesight was now failing. Although he was taking intravenous antibiotics every day, a recent examination had revealed that the blindness was advancing as the *cytomegalovirus* took hold.

Two days after Lucy returned from holiday, she had a call from Patrick to say that Andrew had been whisked into hospital again with suspected pneumonia.

'He's very down,' said Patrick. 'If you can manage to see him this evening, I know it'll mean a lot to him.'

Lucy cancelled her supper date with Rosie and took the underground to visit Andrew in the now familiar AIDS ward at the Middlesex Hospital.

Andrew was in the same bed he had occupied during his very first admission to hospital. He looked so thin and pale. His head looked too heavy to be held up by his thin neck.

Lucy took his hand and squeezed it gently. His fingers were just bones. She noticed that the purple-blue blotches of Kaposi's sarcoma were now on his chest and upper arms.

'This is it,' he said. His voice was cracked and tired. 'I've had enough.'

Lucy sat quietly next to his bed, not moving, not knowing how to respond.

A cheerful male nurse with a noticeably camp manner came round with the tea trolley. Lucy accepted his offer of a cup of tea but Andrew declined miserably.

'They're all so decent in here,' he said, 'but really I'm just a medical specimen. The doctors keep wanting to try out all sorts of tests and experimental drugs on me and they don't see that perhaps I don't want to fight for my life to the bitter end, regardless.'

He turned to Lucy and looked at her with his huge sunken eyes. He looked so sad a lump rose in her throat.

'The time has come now, Lucy, and you've got to help me.'

'Yes.' Lucy squeezed his hand again but she was puzzled. 'What do you want me to do?'

'I've got to do it.' Andrew was talking through his teeth with a frightening urgency. 'I've got to do it before it's too late, before I get too weak to carry it out. You must get me the pills, Lucy. You've got to get them to me quickly!'

Lucy frowned. 'But how, and where from?'

Andrew lay back on the pillow and closed his eyes. 'From Dad's drawer in his surgery. You know it's full of sleeping pills, all sorts of drugs. You have to get a large supply of sodium amytal . . .'

Lucy was puzzled. 'Surely you could write a prescription for yourself. You're a qualified doctor.'

Andrew shook his head. 'I'm not registered. I can't write prescriptions.'

Lucy stared at her brother. 'I don't know if I can do that. I'm not sure that I would even get the opportunity.'

Andrew frowned and looked annoyed. 'Of course you can,' he snapped back with a sudden strength to his voice.

Lucy looked quickly around her to see if anyone was listening. 'Look, Andrew.' She chose her words carefully. 'I have always been happy to support you and encourage you in every way I can but I never imagined that you expected me to provide you with the means to do away with yourself.

The very idea scares me for all sorts of reasons. It's illegal, for one thing.'

As she voiced her fears she could see Andrew growing angry. 'I've been banking on you helping me, Lucy. You're the only person I know with access to an untraceable supply of drugs – enough to make it work. I need your help now.'

His voice sounded bitter. 'I've been counting on you, Lucy.'

Lucy grimaced. 'I just feel a bit funny about stealing drugs from Dad.'

'Well, you didn't worry about that before,' he snapped impatiently.

Lucy stared at him in puzzlement. 'What are you talking about? What do you mean?'

'You must remember,' said Andrew, 'a long time ago. You got drugs out for those friends of yours. You didn't seem to be sorry about anything then. I'm your brother, Lucy, your only sibling, and I need your help.'

'I don't remember anything about getting any drugs, ever . . .'

'Well, you must have deliberately forgotten about what happened. Do you really not remember what you did? And what happened afterwards?

'I saw you. I came into Dad's surgery just as you were getting the drugs for your friends. You told me what you were doing. I was only seven but I remember the sequence of events. I remember those days as vividly as I remember yesterday.

'You are as responsible for what happened as your friends were. You may not have been in on the plans but you were instrumental to the plot.'

He laughed bitterly. 'I'm not surprised you've forgotten

about it. Your conscience would find it hard to tolerate something as bad as that.'

He raised himself on his elbow. 'Look, you got the drugs when you were asked to get them. Now you must do it for me. If you care about me, you'll do it.' He paused and looked at her, fixing her eyes with his gaze. 'Please . . .'

Lucy stumbled home with her head swimming with memories. Flashes of the past kept coming before her eyes, of the Valentine house, of a small boy in grey shorts. She could hear the tinkling sounds of children's voices, laughter and talking, and orders.

Gradually, something emerged, rising up from the dark caverns inside her, something she had forgotten long ago. Something that now was as familiar to her as the smell of her mother's shepherd's pie in the oven or Simon's warm body when he lay close to her.

Slowly the scenes unfolded. A massive piece of the jigsaw puzzle of her life slipped into place. She had completely forgotten that Andrew had known what she was up to. She knew he had been telling the truth and that she had to help him now.

She was shaking when she got home, shaking with dismay at the memories that now flooded her head, and with dread of the task which lay ahead of her.

CHAPTER 16

August, 1968

Right and Wrong

Home from their Norfolk holiday, Lucy went back to visiting the Valentine house every day. She was beginning to see something new in the family, something she had not noticed before. Lucy was beginning to realise that one of the things that made the Valentine children so different was their very odd idea of what was right and wrong. In fact, at times she thought that they did not think that anything was necessarily wrong at all; it merely depended on the circumstances. They thought nothing of cheating at games, of pinching from someone's stash of play money, for instance, when they went out of the room to go to the lavatory in the middle of a game of *Monopoly*. And she remembered being surprised by how often Achilles used to cheat when playing tennis on Parliament Hill. It seemed so unnecessary to lie about whether a ball was inside the court or out, when he was by far the best tennis player of the lot anyway. He had no qualms about it at all.

The first time Lucy became properly aware of this was when she found the five-pound note in the road.

One fine morning, Lucy was walking down Fortess Road with Vita and Perdita on the way to the public library, when she spotted a piece of grubby paper fluttering in the gutter. Something about it made her look again. She bent down and picked it up.

It was a five-pound note, crumpled and dirty.

'Five pounds! Look what I've just found.'

Vita and Perdita turned to look. Vita smiled. 'Let's spend it, quick!'

Lucy looked at her companions and stepped back, clutching the note in her raised fist. 'But we can't . . . it's not ours.'

For a moment, the Valentine sisters stared at her quizzically.

Lucy frowned. 'Surely we should hand it in . . .'

Perdita squared her shoulders. 'Hand it in? Where?' Her voice was sharp with disbelief.

Lucy could feel her neck reddening. Something was going wrong here. 'Well, the police station . . .'

Vita snorted, and tossed her head back dismissively. 'What's the point of that?'

Lucy's blush was creeping rapidly over her face. 'But if you hand something in and nobody claims it after three months, it gets given to the person who handed it in.'

Perdita was standing with her weight on one leg, a hand on her hip. 'Oh, yeah? Who told you that? The fairy godmother?'

Lucy bristled defensively. 'No, my mother . . .' Her voice tailed off.

'I think finders are keepers,' Vita said firmly.

'No, they're not.' Lucy was sure of her ground here. 'What if it belongs to an old lady who needs it? It's not finders keepers at all.' Her throat was tight and her voice came out rather squeaky.

Perdita took her hand off her hip and stood in front of Lucy. 'Look, even if you want to wait three months, if you go and hand that note in at the police station, the chances are the policeman will keep it for himself.'

Lucy was shocked. 'A policeman would never do that!' Again she felt she was on steady ground.

Perdita rolled her eyes impatiently. 'Oh, for goodness' sake, grow up. My father says a lot of policemen are worse than the criminals . . .'

The girls looked at each other for a long time, each one standing her ground on the corner of Leighton and Kentish Town Roads.

Finally Vita broke the silence. 'So, what are you going to do?' It was a direct challenge.

Lucy looked away and watched the cars crossing at the lights. Her heart was thumping uncomfortably. 'I suppose . . .' She started to speak and then she stopped. She swallowed back the hard lump in her throat. She tried again. 'I suppose . . .'

The Valentine girls were staring hard at her, their mouths set in identical straight lines.

Then Lucy knew she had to give in. She sighed. 'All right, we'll keep it,' she said quietly.

The moment she said the words, Perdita smiled and put her arm around her shoulders. She hugged her tight while Vita grinned and nodded approvingly.

'Good,' said Vita, 'that's settled, then. Now, let's go and buy a Wimpy. Then we'll have some money left over and we can buy some sweets.'

So the trio set off up the road to buy hamburgers and chips.

Lucy was quiet as they sat on the grass by the railway track and ate their food. She ate very little of it. What she

did consume of the greasy chips left the bitter taste of guilt
in her mouth.

A similar incident happened closer to the end of the
summer holidays.

Lucy had gone up, as usual, to play with the Valentines.
It was a hot day and Seraphina was sitting in a deckchair
in the garden, reading a book. She was wearing a flowery
ankle-length dress and a broad-brimmed hat to shield her
face from the sun. She had beautiful white skin, which she
carefully protected from the sun's rays.

The younger children were playing in the sandpit. Lucy
played a skipping game with Vita and Perdita for a while,
then the girls wandered into the house. It was quiet inside.
Olwyn was out shopping and the older twins had gone off
fishing somewhere. Anthony had driven a pile of books
over to Arnold and Dusky Wesker's house in Highgate.
The Weskers were collecting books to send to Cuba where,
because of the American blockade of the island, Vita
explained to Lucy, there was a terrible shortage of books.
Even the famous playwright John Osborne had sent a
complete collection of his works, Vita said.

The three girls went into the house. It was cool in the hall
and Perdita looked hurriedly around, as if to check that no
one was nearby. Then she turned to Vita and said, 'Let's
go see if Anthony's forgotten his change.'

Vita smiled and nodded, and the two Valentine girls ran
up the stairs. Lucy followed, taking the stairs at a slower
pace till she reached Anthony Valentine's book-lined study.
It was at the back of the house, overlooking the garden.
Perdita was already inside.

'Yes!' she exclaimed as Lucy entered the room. She
sounded triumphant. On the large wooden desk before
her was a pile of coins – pennies, threepenny pieces,

sixpences and a few shillings. Anthony Valentine had a habit of emptying his pockets every night before hanging up his trousers but he often forgot to put the change back the next day.

Lucy watched in amazement as Perdita's quick fingers picked up a couple of sixpences, three threepenny pieces, and one shilling.

'Do you think that's enough?' whispered Vita.

'I don't want to take too much,' replied Perdita. 'We don't want him to notice.'

Vita smirked. 'We usually get quite a bit,' she explained to Lucy.

Lucy looked at her tentatively, unsure of how she ought to respond.

Perdita laughed. 'Yes, we have to supplement our pocket money somehow. Come on, let's go and spend it.'

As they left the room they saw David dart across the corridor. Perdita sighed with irritation.

'Damn,' she spat. 'The Brat's been spying on us again.'

'Or trying to,' replied Vita. 'I don't think he could've seen us.' Nonetheless she glared at the sight of David scuttling down the hall.

The sisters looked at each other for a moment, clearly communicating something in that brief glance. It was as if they were confirming something that they had discussed and agreed earlier.

'Hey, David!' called Perdita.

The small boy stopped at the bottom of the stairs and turned around. 'What?' he asked in a small, frightened voice.

'Were you spying on us?'

'No, no I wasn't.'

'Well what's that you've got there in your hand?'

'Nothing.'

'Yes you have!' Perdita ran down to him and grabbed his arm. She twisted it hard to make him open his palm.

'Let go! Let go!' His voice was a terrified squeal, like the cry of a cornered animal.

'He's stolen something from Vita's room! He's taken your pear drops. You brat!' She grabbed at David's hand just as the boy threw the sweets on to the floor and ran off down the hall.

The girls picked up the scattered boiled sweets and stuffed them into their pockets. 'God, he's such a pain,' grumbled Vita.

'Come on,' said Perdita. 'Let's go spend the money before Olwyn comes back and goes through our pockets.'

Without telling anyone they ran out of the front door and down to the sweet shop round the corner. There they bought copies of *Bunty* and *Judy*, a couple of Kit-Kats and some sherbet lemons. Strolling to a nearby wall, they sat down and ate the chocolate wafers and sweets, swinging their legs and leafing through their comics.

Lucy felt troubled by what they had done. The chocolate tasted sour.

'It's not very good to take money like that, really,' she suggested in a quiet voice.

Perdita eyed her with raised eyebrows. 'What do you mean?' Her voice was both astonished and threatening.

Lucy began to stutter. 'Well . . . it's st-stealing, really. Isn't it?'

Vita shook her head. 'Not really. It's family money. And we're family.'

'But your father wouldn't like it if he knew, would he?'

Perdita shrugged. 'Probably not. But the point is, he *doesn't* know.'

'Don't you get enough pocket money?' asked Lucy.

Vita laughed. 'We get lots of pocket money.'

'Then why do you take more from your father?'

The sisters hesitated, Perdita rolling her eyes in exasperation.

'Because it's *fun*,' she said finally. 'Because it's not allowed.'

'Anyway,' added Vita, 'it's Anthony's own fault. He promised to take us up to the riding school in Barnet this morning, and then he couldn't. He had to take those stupid books over to go to Cuba. He's always saying he'll do something with us and then not doing it.' She paused. 'Taking his money somehow makes up for it. A bit.'

Vita leaned over and poked Lucy gently in the ribs. 'You're really quite the goody-goody, aren't you? I began to think it when you wanted to hand in that five-pound note to the police station, but now I know for sure.'

Lucy looked down at her shoes. She was hurt. Vita's remark had hurt her so much, she reddened with pain. 'No I'm not!' she protested.

Perdita jumped down from the wall. She squinted over at Parliament Hill where they could see people flying kites and sunbathing on the grass. 'You are a goody-goody, Lucy,' she said firmly. 'There's no getting around it, I'm afraid.'

Lucy went home that night feeling deeply wounded. She was angry with her parents for being so conventional, always sticking to the rules.

'Whatever's wrong with you?' her father asked, noticing his daughter's silent mood at supper.

'Nothing,' Lucy shrugged. 'I'm just tired.'

'Too much running around with those Valentine girls, if you ask me,' said Hilda.

But when Hilda chided Lucy for putting the milk bottle on the table instead of pouring the milk into a jug first, Lucy let out a cry of exasperation, and stormed out of the room, leaving her astonished parents open-mouthed and baffled by her uncharacteristic behaviour.

Only Andrew could guess what had triggered Lucy's rage. He did not know why his sister was in such a bad mood but he knew that it was stupid to care about whether milk was in a jug or a milk bottle.

The next day, Vita rang the doorbell at Falkland Road and asked if Lucy could come swimming with her and Perdita. Hilda was glad to let Lucy go, especially seeing how her gloomy daughter had lit up at the sight of the Valentine girl.

The girls went to the Lido where they swam and dived in the cold water. Lucy's swimming had improved a lot that summer. She had studied the way Vita and Perdita swam, and tried, with some success, to imitate them.

They went back for tea at the Valentines' house. And it was then, after tea, that Perdita came up with the challenge. They were in Perdita's room, playing rummy.

The top of the sash window was open. The curtains fluttered in the cool breeze. Lucy had been aware of the angry buzzing sound on the window as a fly tried to escape, banging pitifully against the glass.

Looking up from her hand of cards, Perdita frowned. 'That fly has been annoying me since early this morning.'

She placed her cards down on the floor and stood up. She stepped over to the window, crouched for a moment and then pounced. 'Got it!'

Under her cupped hands, the fly buzzed angrily.

Perdita rubbed her fingers together and manipulated the fly until it was held between her forefinger and thumb. Holding it against the sky, she pulled off one of its wings. Lucy flinched and watched with distaste as Perdita dropped the fly on the windowsill where it started buzzing furiously, turning round and round in circles like a stranded rower with one oar.

Lucy grimaced.

Perdita looked at her and grinned. 'I know what you're thinking, Lucy,' she said. 'You're thinking it's not nice to pull wings off flies.'

Lucy remained silent, afraid to agree. She was scared.

Perdita poked the fly which buzzed more angrily. 'Do you know what kind of fly this is?' She poked it again.

Lucy looked at the insect's large metallic-blue body. 'It's a bluebottle, I think,' she replied. She could feel both the sisters staring at her; the tension in the room frightened her even more.

Perdita nodded. 'That's right, it's a bluebottle. It's also called a blowfly.'

'Do you know what the dictionary says about the blowfly, Lucy?' Vita's voice was piercing. Vita reached up to the shelf and pulled down a dictionary. 'Let's see what it says.' She leafed through it nimbly. 'I'll read it to you: "blowfly: any of various flies (family *Calliphoridae*) that deposit their eggs or maggots especially on meat or wounds; especially a bluebottle . . ."' She laughed. 'The bluebottle's Latin name is *Calliphora vomitoria* – how appropriate! "Commonly found in houses and often carriers of disease."'

The iridescent blue fly was still moving in circles but the angry buzzing was no longer continuous; it stopped for a second or two before resuming.

Perdita studied it and then turned to Lucy with a laugh.

'I know it's cruel. I should put this household pest out of its misery.'

Crouching down, she positioned her forefinger above the fly and slowly brought it down to squash it on the woodensill.

The buzzing stopped.

'There!' Perdita smiled at Lucy. 'It's not suffering any more.'

Lucy looked away, perplexed. Vita shut the dictionary and replaced it on the shelf. She said nothing.

Perdita picked up the dead fly by the remaining wing and dropped it out of the window. She glanced at Vita, who gave her a quick nod.

'We wanted to talk to you about something, Lucy,' said Perdita. 'We like you a lot but we want to give you the chance to prove that you're not a goody-goody.'

Lucy looked at them both, from one sister to the other, puzzled. Her throat ached with fear and her heart was pounding.

Perdita was staring at her with a concentrated look in her eyes.

'Whatever do you mean?' asked Lucy in a faint voice.

Vita came up close and leaned towards her. Lucy could see her own reflection in her friend's dark eyes.

'We want you to do something for us,' she said. 'To get something we need.'

Lucy frowned, torn between relief that she could do something for her friends, that they needed her in some way, and a deep fear of what it was she was expected to do.

Perdita looked around as if to make sure that no one could hear her, then leaned forward to position her face just inches from Lucy's.

'We want you to get something from your father's surgery. You can prove you're not a goody-goody by bringing it to us tomorrow. At noon.'

'But I can't do that!' cried Lucy.

Perdita tossed her hair disdainfully. 'You don't even know what it is yet. Told you,' she mocked. 'We said you were a goody-goody.'

Lucy's heart was racing. She could not believe that this was happening. Suddenly her best friends were challenging her to prove to them that she was one of them.

Lucy hesitated. The trouble was that she *did* desperately want to be one of them. She felt a hardening inside her as she felt that she could do it. Narrowing her eyes, she turned to the sisters and faced Perdita defiantly.

'All right,' she said, looking Perdita straight in the eye. 'Tell me what I have to get, and I'll get it.'

Vita and Perdita glanced at each other again, smiling. Vita pulled a piece of paper from her pocket and said, 'It's a kind of medicine. I've written the name down here. Your dad has some in that drugs drawer of his, I've seen it. I'm sure I saw it when you were showing me round that day.'

Lucy took the paper in her hand but did not read what was written on it, even though she could see the blue ink in Vita's neat, confident writing.

As Lucy stood there, waiting, Perdita smiled sweetly. 'If you want to stay friends with us,' she said quietly, 'you'd better get this.'

'What's it for?' asked Lucy. Her voice sounded faint to her through the drumming of blood in her ears.

Vita frowned and snapped, 'It doesn't matter what it's for. Just get it. That's all you have to do, it's no big deal.'

Lucy bit her lip. 'Okay,' she said. 'I'll try and get it tomorrow.'

Vita put her arm around Lucy's shoulder and hugged her.
'That's the spirit,' she said. 'It'll be really easy for you,
I'm sure.'

Lucy went home that evening feeling shaken. What the
Valentine girls wanted her to do, to raid her father's surgery,
was wrong, but her desire to remain their friend was too
strong; she couldn't resist them. She did not know why she
wanted to remain friends with them when they tormented
her in these cruel and demanding ways. Even Vita, with
whom she shared so many interests, could be unpredictable
and suddenly turn on her savagely after a period of acting
like a best friend. What was the attraction that pulled her
back to them again and again?

Lucy did not know why she felt as she did. It was all
confusing. Yet she knew that even though the girls did not
always treat her in the way she would like, she would still
forgive them for it, in the hope, perhaps, that some day they
would accept her without question.

The Valentines were not like other people, and she would
do anything for them.

Lucy started to whistle as she walked down the road
thinking about the best way to slip into her father's surgery
and find the medicine for her friends.

CHAPTER 17

June, 1997

Criminal Acts

Her parents would be out shopping. They always were on Saturday mornings. Every week they climbed into their blue Ford Fiesta and drove to Sainsbury's in Streatham to do their shopping for the week. Dr Butler would drive his tense wife, stand next to her while she chose what she wanted, and wearily carry the shopping bags to the car for her. Then they would stop for lunch in the pub with the non-smoking area at Crystal Palace before returning home to unpack.

Letting herself into the house with her key, Lucy went straight to her father's surgery. It was almost identical to the one in Kentish Town she remembered from her childhood, with photos of her grandfather and great-grandfather on the wall, the huge bookcase with spellbinding medical textbooks down one side, the large mahogany desk and the locked cabinet behind it full of boxes and bottles of drugs.

As she sat down at the desk and opened the bottom right-hand drawer, a strange feeling came over her. She had done this before. She felt as though she were nine again, she could feel herself as a child, bending down like this to open her father's drawer. Indeed, the inside of the drawer was just as she remembered it, an untidy mess of letters and phials, boxes of samples and supplies handed in by patients or their families. It was her father's drug bin, that he was always meaning to clear out or lock up but never got round to doing.

Lucy walked over to the bookcase and pulled out a red catalogue. After a quick glance at the table of contents under INSOMNIA, she knew where to look for sleeping pills. Flicking through the pages she studied one page for a few minutes, then walked over to the drawer.

'Sodium amytal,' she murmured. 'Intractable insomnia. Blue capsule.' She knelt down and rummaged around in the drawer, picking up the plastic containers and reading their labels. *Norinyl. Buscopan monodral, Provera, Gestone* . . . They were all names that meant nothing to her.

'There must be some,' she murmured. Again a weird feeling of *déjà vu* enveloped her. She stood up to clear her head. She was all right; the peculiar feeling had gone.

Kneeling down again, she rummaged some more. 'Someone must use this stuff,' she murmured. Then she spotted a large grey plastic container with the name she was looking for.

'Yes!' she said aloud. Shaking the container she sensed that it was quite full, and opened it up. Blue capsules filled it nearly to the brim. She poured out a handful and counted roughly – there must be fifty in all, she thought. Lucy returned them to the container and carefully read the label: 'SODIUM AMYTAL 200 mg. One at night. Avoid alcohol.'

Lucy didn't know how many were needed, but surely there were enough there.

Her heart was thumping uncomfortably in her chest as she left the house, the container of pills tucked safely in one of the pockets of her handbag. She felt shifty as she left, fearful that the neighbours had seen her. If they did, would they report her presence to her parents when they came back? Not that it mattered any more. She had what Andrew needed now. But as she put her car into gear and drove off, she was troubled again by the old feeling of familiarity, of having behaved like this before, a long long time ago. Pushing these haunting feelings aside, she tried to concentrate on what Andrew was going to do with these pills. The events of the next few days were impossible to imagine.

Lucy drove straight to the hospital. Andrew lay listless in bed, his eyes half closed. Lucy smiled at him, proud that she could deliver what he wanted. She leaned over his bed and whispered to him, as quietly as she could, 'I've got them.' He opened his eyes and she spoke again.

'I've got what you wanted.'

Andrew's eyes lit up. He pushed himself painfully into a sitting position.

'Thank God,' he croaked. 'Thank God.' His eyes ran searchingly over Lucy's bag, as if seeking confirmation that she was telling the truth. Lucy reached into the bag and dug out the grey container, slipping it into Andrew's hand as casually as she could.

'There must be enough there,' she said. 'But you must make sure you get rid of the container, otherwise they may be able to trace them.'

Andrew nodded. 'Don't worry,' he said. 'No one's going to get into trouble for this.'

'I hope not,' replied Lucy. But she knew that the fear in her chest had nothing to do with being implicated in a crime. It had to do with what she knew the next step would be. She paused and then said, 'You will say goodbye, won't you? You won't just – just do it . . .'

Andrew looked down at his hands and picked at a fingernail. 'I don't know, Lucy.' His voice was very quiet, almost a whisper. 'I don't know if it'll be possible. I have to do what's easiest for me.'

'Yes.' Lucy could not argue with him.

Her head was still spinning with thoughts and memories stirred up by what she had just done. She longed to quiz Andrew, to ask him what he meant when he had talked about the Valentines and their father's surgery, but it seemed cruel to make him use up his precious energy thinking about something he was not concerned with. She would ask him one thing. She spoke softly.

'If you remember what happened, Andrew, years ago, why haven't you ever mentioned it?'

Andrew turned towards her with a look of surprise. 'Because I assumed you also knew what happened. You never spoke about it, so I assumed that you did not want to talk about it, and that it wasn't very important.'

Andrew reached over and took her hand. 'There's something else I need to talk to you about now, while I have the chance. I've been wanting to ask if you and Simon will organise my funeral. Patrick will be in too much of a state. Will you do that? I've chosen some tapes I want played and I've given Patrick five hundred pounds to be spent on a party afterwards. Loads of booze. I want my friends to have a spectacular time.'

Lucy fought back tears as she nodded. 'Yes.' Her voice came out as a croak. The opportunity had gone. She still did not know what Andrew knew, and she could not push him to spell it out. Now he was talking about life after his death.

'I know you'd do a really nice funeral: it won't be

impersonal like most of the ones I go to, where a priest who didn't even know "the deceased" pronounces his name wrong, and talks only in vague platitudes. And I've been to rather a lot of funerals like that in the last few years,' he added sadly. He sighed. 'But I've been to some good ones, and I want mine to be good.'

His head dropped back on the pillows. His eyes closed. 'By the way,' he said without opening his eyes, 'I've written my will. I've left almost everything to Patrick but the rest is left to you.'

'Thank you,' Lucy whispered faintly.

Brother and sister stayed in silence for a few minutes, hand in hand. Lucy knew it was time to go now, and she gave Andrew a kiss on the cheek before standing up and reaching for her bag. Impulsively, she knelt down again and gathered Andrew's thin shoulders in her arms.

'Please don't go without saying goodbye.'

Andrew pulled away, his head sagging when the emaciated neck muscles could support it no longer. He looked at Lucy with his huge, starving eyes and shook his head.

'I can't promise you that. Sorry. I'm really sorry.' He paused and smiled wryly. 'Look at it this way: George Eliot wrote somewhere that in every parting scene there is an image of death. So what difference does it make if it's real or imaginary?'

Lucy nodded, her eyes filling again with tears. There was nothing she could say.

'How long will you stay here in hospital?' she asked.

Andrew shrugged. 'It's Saturday today. I'll probably discharge myself tomorrow morning. I'm not sure . . .'

*   *   *

Lucy travelled home on the tube without noticing anything around her. She bought her ticket, took the escalator, boarded the train and sat in a seat all the way to Shepherd's Bush station staring blindly ahead of her, all thought shocked out of her. Was what she was living now real or imaginary? Were her feelings real or imaginary? What was real, if anything, ever?

When she got home, she found Simon lying on the sofa watching the cricket on television, his long legs stretched out and crossed in front of him.

Lucy slumped down next to him and stared at the television screen.

'What's up?' Simon looked over and saw Lucy's tear-swollen face. He sat up and reached over to hug her.

'I don't think I'll ever see Andrew again,' she said quietly.

She blew her nose noisily on the handkerchief she'd been clutching all the way home, then leaned wearily on Simon's broad chest and sobbed with a deep sadness.

Later that afternoon, Lucy felt she had to talk to Andrew again. Just one more time. She might never have another chance. She telephoned the hospital and asked for Andrew's ward. When she asked to speak to him, she had to identify herself as always: in the AIDS ward, every patient had a list of people from whom they would (and would not) accept calls. After the nurse checked his list, she was put through to Andrew on the ward's mobile phone.

'Andrew, hi. It's me. I was wondering . . . if you'd thought more about your plans.'

Andrew hesitated for a moment, then said: 'I've just discharged myself. I'm just on my way home now.'

'I thought you were going to wait till tomorrow,' replied Lucy with dismay. 'Tomorrow morning, you said.'

'I decided not to hang around. There's no point.'

Lucy sat in silence, shocked by the suddenness and inevitability of it all. Then Andrew spoke again, his voice weak but clear.

'Goodbye, Lucy.'

Lucy's voice cracked as she started to cry.

'Goodbye, Andrew. I love you.' She said the final words loudly, so he couldn't fail to hear them. Then the line clicked dead and she slammed down the phone, rising at once to run into her bedroom. Throwing herself on to the bed, she hugged the pillow, screwed herself into a foetal position, and sobbed.

Lucy and Simon went out to dinner that evening, to a new local restaurant off Shepherd's Bush Road. They ordered half a bottle of white wine to start with, and toasted Andrew. When that went, they ordered another half; then a full bottle of red with their main courses; then a glass of dessert wine with their puddings. Even as drunkenness came over her in slow waves, Lucy felt acutely self-conscious. She felt as if she were acting a part in a film and being watched by millions of people. 'I am someone whose brother is at this moment killing himself. He's swallowing pills I got for him. He is killing himself while I sit here eating rack of lamb like any other customer.' She imagined Andrew swallowing the capsules, one by one. Where was he doing it? What would he be washing them down with? What was he thinking? How did it feel? Would he know what was happening, or would he just go to sleep?

And at this time tomorrow, she thought, he will be dead. My little brother will be dead.

'And just think,' she said, slurring her words as she knocked back some more wine, 'what it must be like for poor Patrick . . . It's even worse for him.'

Back home, in bed, she and Simon made love in a fumbling, drunken sort of way. Though hardly up to it, they both felt – without discussing it – an urgency that was rare for them. They wanted to affirm that they were alive, while Andrew was dying.

Lucy woke up early the next day with a throbbing headache. It took a few moments for her head to clear, for her to remember what had happened the night before. When she did, a slow pain spread through her. Now she was wide awake. She wanted to ring Patrick immediately, but it was only seven o'clock. She had to make herself wait.

First she took a long, hot shower, then she put on the kettle and made a pot of coffee. She went out to Mehmet's shop to buy croissants and the newspapers, both of which the thoughtful shopkeeper sold on Sundays. She exchanged greetings with Mehmet, trying to sound as normal as she could. Mehmet could tell from the dazed look in her eyes that something was wrong, but it was not for him to comment.

Back home, Simon was still sleeping heavily. She flicked through the papers without registering any of their contents, and folded them up for Simon.

She noticed that the cooker needed cleaning, so she went at it with a Brillo pad and warm water. When that was done, she cleared out some clothes she'd been meaning for months to give to Oxfam. Anything to make herself busy, and to keep her hands away from the telephone.

Finally, at eleven thirty, just as Simon hauled himself out of bed and started to take a shower, she thought it was time. She could wait no longer. With her heart racing, she dialled

Andrew's number. The machine was on, his voice singing out as usual. Lucy hung up without leaving a message.

Two hours later she tried again. This time she left a message.

'Patrick, I, it's Lucy. I'm just . . .'

She was broken off in mid-sentence by a click, then by Patrick's voice on the line.

'Lucy,' he said. His voice was grave and heavy.

'He's dead, isn't he? Andrew's dead . . .'

'No he's not,' replied Patrick. He sounded worried. 'He took the pills last night, around eight o'clock. We had a wonderful evening together. We put candles all around the bedroom and put on some music. Then we drank some champagne and said our goodbyes. Then he took the pills. He took them all, one by one. I sat with him till he fell asleep, then I snuggled up beside him and fell asleep myself.

'But I don't think they've worked. When I woke up this morning, I expected to find him dead beside me, but he seemed the same. He just seems to be in a very deep sleep . . .'

'It probably takes a long time,' replied Lucy. But her words sounded false even to her. She could hardly believe that she was trying to act calm in these circumstances.

'I just don't understand it,' said Patrick. 'He took *thirty pills* – enough to kill a bloody horse! This is terrible, just terrible. He was so brave . . .'

'I don't think you should be there, Patrick. Just think what would happen if people knew you were with him after he'd taken the pills, and had done nothing about calling an ambulance or a doctor or anything. You could get into terrible trouble.'

'I don't care,' replied Patrick. 'What could be more

terrible than what we've been through already? I want to
be with him. I can't leave him.'

'But I really think you should,' said Lucy. 'At least go
out for a while. Go for a walk, stay away for a few hours.
Maybe when you come back, maybe then it will all be over.
Then you'll be able to say you found him like that. You
must, Patrick. Andrew doesn't want you to be in trouble.
And what you're doing now is definitely illegal.'

Patrick suddenly seemed worried. 'Do you think so?'

'I really do. Just go out for a few hours. Please. Then give
me a ring when you get back. It's bound to be over by then.'

At eight that evening, the phone rang again. When she
heard Patrick's voice, Lucy was frightened but relieved at
the same time. Now, she thought, she could collapse.

But the worry in Patrick's voice made her realise that
something was still wrong.

'I've just come in,' he said. 'Andrew's still breathing.
And I think, I think he's waking up. He's moving about
now, his legs and arms. Those fucking pills didn't work. I
can't believe it.'

'We're coming over,' said Lucy. She hung up the phone
and told Simon what was happening, and they got into the
car. Simon's hands were trembling as he steered through
the twilit streets.

Patrick answered the bell almost instantly, his face white
and drawn. They followed Patrick up the stairs to the
bedroom.

Andrew was lying on the bed, naked under a sheet. He
was in a deep sleep but breathing loudly, in great gasps.
His legs and arms twitched and his body and face were in
constant movement.

'Oh my God,' whispered Lucy. 'He's surfacing.'

Patrick started to cry. 'What shall we do?' he moaned.

'What if he's brain-damaged? Oh, what a cock-up. Oh, he was so brave. Jesus, what can we do? Perhaps we should stick a plastic bag over his head, before it's too late. He doesn't want to wake up. He doesn't want to live!' He was panicking.

Simon stepped forward. 'No, that would just make things worse. That would be murder.'

Lucy was relieved to see how readily Simon took charge, to make decisions, for she certainly could not. 'I think we should call the doctor,' continued Simon, 'just to cover ourselves. Otherwise we could all find ourselves in trouble.'

'But the doctor will want him back in hospital!' said Patrick. 'He'll want his stomach pumped. And we'll still get into trouble!'

'That's probably a risk we just have to take,' replied Simon. 'We'll just have to make something up.'

The doctor came out straightaway. He was a young GP who knew Patrick and Andrew well. At first they told him they had just discovered Andrew like this when they returned home after a drink in the pub, but then, after the doctor had given Andrew a brief examination, and picked up the telephone to call an ambulance, Patrick could not restrain himself.

'Oh, please don't call the ambulance,' he begged. 'He wants to die. He's taken a whole load of sleeping pills. He's in constant misery. He's going blind, he's got chronic diarrhoea, he's covered with KS, and he's had enough. It'd be cruel to send him back to hospital – he's just discharged himself, and he did this so he wouldn't have to die there. He wants to die before it gets any worse . . .'

The trio looked pleadingly at the doctor.

'Please,' Patrick begged. 'Please don't make him have to suffer any more.'

To their relief, the doctor relented. He had seen too many of his young patients die of AIDS to be unaware of how horrible the end could be.

'Well,' he said, 'let's make him as comfortable as we can. And hope there's no damage done as a result of the overdose. It looks as if he's close to surfacing anyway. I suspect that his body just didn't absorb the drug.'

Lucy and Simon stayed the night, dozing next door through the early hours of the morning as Andrew's body fought off the effects of the sodium amytal, attended to by the gentle doctor and Patrick. His soiled sheets confirmed the doctor's quiet guess that Andrew's chronic intestinal condition had caused the capsules to shoot through his body, giving it no chance to absorb toxic levels of the drug.

At six o'clock, Andrew became conscious. At first he was confused about where he was and what had happened, but gradually his head cleared and by eight o'clock, he had worked out what had happened. His suicide attempt had failed. He was overwhelmed by the thought, and deeply distraught. He wept uncontrollably.

Lucy felt so ashamed she could hardly bear to look at Andrew. She had let him down. He had put his life in her hands with the unquestioning faith of a little brother. And she had failed him.

Once the doctor had checked all Andrew's reflexes and made sure the drugs had caused no damage, he gave him a sedative to make him sleep.

Lucy went down to the kitchen. She stood at the counter making a pot of coffee, tears streaming down her face. On the kitchen table were three CDs and a scrap of paper with her name on it. She picked up the CDs – Mozart's *Requiem*, a Cat Stevens collection, and a band called the Gypsy Kings which she had heard once or twice. The note told her which tracks Andrew wanted played at his funeral, and which of his friends had said they would read poetry. He had written their telephone numbers next to the names but there was no other message.

Patrick sat on a chair by the window with his head in his hands. He was crying and kept shaking his head. 'I can't believe this has happened. Oh, God, we should have finished him off, for his own sake. Now he's got to go through it all again . . .

CHAPTER 18

August, 1968
The Task

By the time Lucy reached home, the words on the piece of paper Vita had handed her were ringing in her head like a chant: minims atropine, minims atropine, minims atropine.

She had no idea what kind of drug it was or what the girls could possibly want it for but she had the uncomfortable feeling that their purpose was not what their father would have called noble.

In spite of her concern and her hurt feelings at being doubted, she still so much wanted to prove that she was one of them, that she was as brave, as naughty, as fearless as any Valentine. She would find this drug and get it to them. She would show that they were wrong, that she could do it.

It had to be done that evening, too. Lucy knew she had to do it soon or she might miss the opportunity, and she had to do it fast because she could not bear even the thought of failure.

After supper her parents settled down to listen to a play on the radio in the sitting room upstairs. Confident that they would not be moving from their armchairs for at least half an hour, Lucy crept downstairs and let herself into her father's surgery.

It smelled, as it always did, of surgical spirit. The sharp smell made her nostrils curl. The door shut behind her with a soft click, and she walked straight over to her father's large desk.

'Minims atropine,' she muttered, pulling open the bottom drawer on the right.

The drawer was packed, as ever, with containers of all shapes and sizes. Many of them were unused pills handed in by patients, and many samples of amphetamines, sleeping pills, the contraceptive pill, anything and everything, sent to GPs by the drugs companies in the hope that they would prescribe them instead of the competition.

Lucy picked each one up, scrutinised the label, dropped it. She rummaged some more, looking, reading, scanning the labels, dropping and rummaging. Her heart was beating fast and she could feel a frightening panic rising up inside her. Time was running out. She could not find anything with the words 'minims atropine' on it. Her fingers moved with increasing urgency.

She was sweating. Her hands were clammy with perspiration as she became aware of the loud ticking of the clock on the mantelpiece. The ticking seemed to bore into her head. She tried to control the panic rising in her at the thought of the radio play drawing to an end. She had ten minutes left. This was ridiculous! Where was this drug? It had to be here somewhere. Vita said it was here, and her father could not have used it since Vita had looked inside the drawer. He never actually used any of the drugs in this drawer; the drugs he did administer, he kept in his black doctor's bag or in the locked drugs cabinet behind the desk. Perhaps she could find some there! The drugs were not in the bag. She had to look in the cabinet.

She knew where the key was. Pulling open the middle drawer of the desk, she lifted out a small key on a red cord.

Her fingers trembled as she slipped the key into the lock and opened the cupboard. In contrast to the muddle of the drugs in his drawer, the cupboard was, thanks to Hilda Butler, methodically organised, with all the drugs placed in alphabetical order with neat labels on the shelf beneath.

It took just a moment for her eyes to run along the names. She let out a gasp of relief as her gaze settled on the now familiar words, minims atropine. 'Yes!' she exclaimed. 'There it is!'

There were four bottles. One would not be missed. She grabbed one bottle and placed it on the desk while she swiftly shut and locked the doors to the cabinet.

As she turned the key in the lock, she gave a jump of fright as she heard the surgery door click open. She turned, and her heart thumped as the door began to open! Surely she was in big trouble now! The blood drained from her head as she stood, terrified, waiting to see who it was.

Then she dropped her shoulders and sniffed. 'Oh, it's you,' she said with annoyed relief as her little brother's tousled brown curls appeared around the door.

'What are you doing?' Andrew asked. 'What are you doing here, Lucy?'

Lucy turned her back on him. 'Never you mind. It's none of your business,' she snapped, in the sort of tone that Vita used when talking to the Brat. She dropped the key back into the middle drawer of the desk.

'I don't want you here,' she said bossily. 'Get out, quickly.

You know we're not allowed in here. You'll get us both into trouble.'

But Andrew was not going to be deterred. 'What are you doing?' He had spotted the bottle on the desk. He walked over to her. 'What's that? Why are you taking that?'

Lucy was feeling extremely agitated and annoyed. 'Stop asking questions!'

But Andrew persisted. 'Tell me what you're doing and I'll stop asking,' he said quietly. 'What are you going to do with this medicine?' He picked up the bottle and held it up to his face to examine the label.

Lucy snatched it from him. 'Stop it!' She hissed the words at him. 'Get out of here!'

'Just tell me what it's for.' Andrew paused and lowered his voice. 'Or I'll tell Mum and Dad what you're doing.'

He had trapped her.

Lucy hesitated as Andrew continued to stare at her through determined narrowed eyes. She could tell that he meant it. He would tell, not really out of malice but just to show that he would not tolerate being excluded from an interesting secret.

'Okay,' she said, giving in. 'I don't know what it's for. I've just been told to get it for Vita and Perdita.'

Andrew nodded. 'Oh,' he said. 'Okay.' He grinned and turned on his heels. 'I wonder what they want it for,' he mused.

He walked to the door and peered out. 'Okay, you're in the clear,' he whispered. As he walked out, he stopped and turned again. 'I won't say anything,' he said. 'Promise.'

Lucy forced a smile. She did trust her little brother to keep his word but she would rather that he had not caught her in the first place.

'Thanks, Andrew,' she said softly. 'I'll do the same for you someday.'

He nodded. 'I'll remember.' He pointed to the piece of paper lying on the desk. 'By the way,' he said with a conspiratorial grin, 'don't forget to destroy that note.'

Lucy quickly picked up the note and stuffed it into her pocket. Giving the room a quick check to see that everything was as it had been before, she followed Andrew out of the surgery and shut the door quietly.

Later, upstairs in her room, she tore the note into tiny pieces which she threw into the wastepaper basket.

The next morning, immediately after breakfast, Lucy ran as fast as she could up Lady Margaret Road to the Valentines'. Letting herself in through the side gate, she ran through to the back garden.

Vita was doing handstands on the grass.

Lucy laughed with proud glee as she announced her success to Vita. 'I've got it! I've got it!'

Vita landed gracefully on her feet and looked around warily. 'Good.' She spoke softly. 'But don't take it out now. We'll go inside. You can give it to me then.

'We're going to visit our aunt this morning, so you can't stay. Maybe you'd like to come and play tomorrow.'

Upstairs in Vita's bedroom, Lucy handed over the booty. She could hear Olwyn calling the children to hurry up and get ready as the taxis would be arriving at any moment to whisk them all off to Hampstead to see their aunt.

Lucy knew that she had to leave. She was not welcome in that chaotic frenzy. She saw Perdita run by excitedly. Perdita raised a thumb at Lucy as if to congratulate her on succeeding with her mission, but she did not stop to talk.

She was too busy brushing her sleek black hair while at the same time looking for a clean pair of socks.

Lucy let herself out of the house and walked slowly down the hill. She felt unwanted in that atmosphere and a sudden sadness dragged her down. If she could admit it, she was hurt that Vita and Perdita had not praised her more for her daring feat. They had barely thanked her, let alone congratulated her properly.

She frowned. Trying to push back the feelings of disappointment, she focused on her achievement. Tomorrow, when she went up to play, Vita and Perdita would praise her and thank her, and tell her that she was not, after all, a goody-goody. In their rush to visit their aunt, they just did not have the time today.

Lucy did not go to play at the Valentines' house the next day. The death in the night prevented that.

The Butlers were eating their supper. Dr Butler was entertaining his family telling them about an emergency call he had received that afternoon. A worried father, left on his own with his three-year-old while his wife was still in hospital after giving birth to a second child, had called Dr Butler out at tea time.

'He said his daughter had suddenly started to stagger about and fall over for no obvious reason. When I examined the little girl, I discovered that she had both legs through only one hole in her pants! The poor child could barely move. She'd been dressing and undressing herself all afternoon, and ended up behaving as if she had cerebral palsy.'

As he chuckled at the story, the telephone rang. It was for him. There was an emergency at the Valentine house.

'What's happened?' Lucy frowned anxiously at her father.

'I don't know yet.' Dr Butler pulled on his jacket. 'Someone's ill. A child. I have to leave immediately.'

Lucy tried to stay awake that night but at ten thirty, when her father had still not returned, her eyelids closed and she gave way to sleep.

The next morning Dr Butler was already up at breakfast when Lucy came downstairs. Her mother was clearing up. Andrew sat at the table reading the back of the cereal packets.

'What happened?' She was terrified that something bad had happened to her friends. 'Who's ill?'

Dr Butler buttered his toast and spread his wife's home-made marmalade on top.

'Everything's all right,' he said calmly. 'It's young David, the housekeeper's boy. He's had a nasty dose of scarlet fever. I thought he'd be all right at home but after a while I thought it safer to send him to hospital. I called an ambulance at about midnight.

'I'm about to telephone the hospital now to find out how he is.'

Lucy spread marmalade on her toast and took a bite. She heard her father in the hall, talking to someone at the hospital. The confident tone of his voice suddenly changed to one of alarm. The murmuring stopped. Lucy then heard a click as her father replaced the receiver on the hook. Then there was silence.

A few seconds later, her father walked back into the kitchen. His face was ashen.

Hilda dried her hands and ran over to him. 'Whatever's wrong? Has something happened?'

Dr Butler shook his head and sat down heavily at the table. He slumped down, his head in his hands.

'The boy's dead,' he said quietly, his voice cracking. 'He died on his way to hospital. He was dead on arrival.'

He stared at the table. His hands gripped his head. 'It seems that I made the wrong diagnosis. The boy probably did not have scarlet fever at all. They're doing a postmortem.'

'What's a postmortem?' Andrew sounded bright and cheerful in the gloomy atmosphere.

'It's when they look at a dead body to find out exactly why that person died,' Hilda replied impatiently.

Dr Butler's face was still white. He kept shaking his head in disbelief, and in his mind he went over and over the symptoms he had seen – the hot dry skin, the rash, the temperature, the quickened pulse, the reddened fauces. They were all the symptoms of scarlet fever. 'This can't be happening, it can't be . . .'

He turned to his wife. Lucy was shocked to see tears in her father's eyes. Never in her life had she seen a man cry.

'What's worse is that my diagnosis delayed matters. I should have sent him to hospital straight away instead of waiting. They might have been able to save him. I thought he had scarlet fever, I was sure of it. My delay made matters worse.'

Lucy's toast had formed a hard lump in her mouth. She was unable to swallow but she did not dare spit it out.

The next day, Vita Valentine rang Lucy. She sounded very cheerful on the telephone and did not say anything about David. 'Would you like to come to play this afternoon?' she chirruped. 'We've got some delicious biscuits for tea. Perdita and I made them this morning while Olwyn was out.'

The Valentine house was unusually quiet when Lucy got there.

'What's happened?' Lucy asked. 'What happened to David?'

Perdita looked at her with her large cool eyes. 'He died,' she said flatly.

'Yes, but do you know how?' Lucy was desperate for knowledge.

Perdita shrugged. 'No one seems to know,' she said airily. 'He was a pest, anyway.'

'Yes,' agreed Vita. 'A real brat.'

The Valentine girls made it clear to Lucy that even if they did know more than they let on, they would not divulge it to her. She did not feel at home and she did not stay long enough to eat the freshly baked biscuits. Her throat felt hot and dry. She felt a headache coming on and left the house feeling unhappy and excluded.

Her throat was getting more sore by the minute. She walked down the hill towards her house with her head down. The Valentine girls had not included her. In spite of what she had done for them, they would not share their secrets with her. She felt painfully shut out and used.

A postmortem a few days later revealed that David had died of atropine sulphate poisoning. There are few characteristics of atropine sulphate poisoning but what confirmed the diagnosis was the continued dilatation of the boy's pupils.

Dr Butler was required to attend the inquest. The coroner was told that the Valentine children had informed the police that David had been boasting of stealing medicine from the doctor's black bag when he had paid a home visit to Mrs Valentine a few weeks before. It seems that for several days the boy was experimenting with the eye drops to make his pupils dilate. Then somehow, the child managed to swallow a fatal dose of the drug and inadvertently poisoned himself.

It was a terrible tragedy that people spoke about in the pubs and shops of Kentish Town for weeks afterwards. Some talked with sympathy about the doctor's mistake, he was not to be blamed. Apparently, the symptoms of atropine poisoning are not dissimilar to those of scarlet fever. Others were not so generous. They changed their doctor and did not talk to Mrs Butler when they met in the butcher's.

Hilda was mortified. She knew that they had to move and urged her husband to look for another practice elsewhere. Dr Butler was glad to have a project to work on, to keep his thoughts away from the terrible thing he had done. But every now and then, at night as he lay in bed, trying to fight off the guilt and remorse, there would be something nagging him, something that made him know that the tragedy was linked to something else in his life. He had had a conversation at some point with someone, about atropine but he could not for the life of him remember when.

It would be many years before he did.

Lucy missed all these happenings. Her sore throat developed into tonsillitis which kept her in bed for a week. Then it was the end of the holidays and suddenly her parents were planning to move to south London. Lucy was taken for an interview at a school in Dulwich which took her on as a pupil that September.

When she rang up Vita to say goodbye, her friend was out. In spite of Lucy's message, Vita did not return the call. Lucy did not see the Valentine girls again.

CHAPTER 19

July, 1997

Paradise Lost

Slowly patches of memory filtered up to the surface. They were like dreams, uncontrollable thoughts, but they came in the day. They came while Lucy was lying in the bath or walking down the high street to do her shopping. They came as she cooked supper or watched the news or read the newspaper. Something would trigger the memories, new ones each time, and gradually a clear picture emerged.

Lucy began to remember details she had forgotten for years. She recalled the telephone ringing while they were sitting down to their supper that night, and her father being called out on an emergency at the Valentines'. She remembered trying to stay awake until her father came home but finally giving way to sleep, only to be told in the morning that it was the housekeeper's boy, David, who was ill. She remembered the sense of calm, of feeling proud that once again her father, the doctor, had made someone better.

Then there was a shift, a change in the atmosphere. It was all going wrong. Her father was talking in the hall. His face was ashen as he came back into the kitchen where they were having breakfast. Lucy was eating her toast and marmalade.

Andrew was reading the back of the Rice Krispies packet. Dr Butler appeared in the doorway and said that David was dead.

Lucy could see it all now, as if it were yesterday – her mother's look of alarm, the frightened eyes, the dropped jaw. Something terrible had happened. Something had gone wrong. Then there was the hushed conversation between the adults, her parents talking in tense voices behind closed doors.

There was also the silence in the Valentines' house the last time she went there, and the unhappy sense of exclusion she felt from the girls who were supposed to be her friends.

There was more that she remembered from a distance but which she would never be able to put into words. She recalled being ill with a high temperature and burning tonsils, and lying in bed for a week.

She was aware that what had happened to David was her father's mistake. It was his misdiagnosis that was the cause of David's death. And she recalled now that it was soon afterwards that the Butlers moved away from Kentish Town to what seemed a new life in Dulwich, south of the river. She could not remember talking to the Valentine girls again. The holidays were over, school took precedence, and the Butlers moved.

While his daughter could recall certain details about that incident, she did not, could not, know the true extent of Dr Butler's shame and mortification at his fatal misdiagnosis. He was crushed by a decision of his that had resulted in a child's death.

For her part, his wife was even more ashamed of her husband's failing. Until then she had idealised him, believing that his status as a doctor – and, consequently, her status too – would enjoy a relentless and splendid growth, like the march of progress through history. Then his error, his stupid error, had brought gossip and glances from the very people whose respect she craved.

Lucy did not know that that incident had changed for ever the balance within her parents' marriage. Hilda Butler had always been the stronger personality but she had admired her husband for the respect he commanded and for his medical knowledge. After David's death, she continued to be the dominant one in the relationship but she no longer felt admiration: she only felt shame and despair. And deep down, though she did not know it, she despised her husband.

For his part, Dr Butler accepted his wife's scorn and whipped himself with it. He was happy to go along with her decision to move away. He was lucky to be able to take over a small practice in Dulwich and start afresh, with patients who knew nothing about what had happened. He withdrew from family life and allowed Hilda to take over. He did not have any friends who could slap him on the back and say that everyone makes mistakes, that all doctors have memories of decisions they regret. He did not have anyone like that. All he had to go on was his wife's response and the curious looks from his patients for those strained weeks after the boy's death and the postmortem. It was not surprising that he was relieved to move away.

Lucy did not know then the extent of the damage done to her father and to her parents' marriage but she was aware of some of it now. She could see the link, she could see now what Andrew had always seen, she could see that she was responsible.

She could always remember that David had died – she had been reminded of that when she first met Perdita again – but it had never occurred to her that the drugs she had delivered so faithfully to her friends had been used to kill the child. She, Lucy, had thus been responsible for that boy's death. She had also been responsible for ruining her father's life.

Lucy did not say anything to Simon about these revelations and memories that haunted her. On their visits to Andrew, whose condition was deteriorating fast, they talked only about her brother.

Lucy wanted to talk about what she had done, and the consequences of her actions. She felt an urgent need to talk it all out, but it was not to be with Simon. She had to meet the memory head on, and the only way to do that was to talk about it with Vita herself. It was Vita who had caused Lucy to act as she did, Vita and her sister. Lucy had to pick up from where she had left their conversation all those years ago to confirm these terrible recollections.

Lucy telephoned a surprised and wary Vita and arranged to meet her that weekend.

They met on Hampstead Heath where, Vita said, her daughters liked to ride their bicycles. It was a blustery day and the wind whipped their hair around their faces as the women walked side by side along the tarmac path that cut across the green expanse.

The two girls rode ahead on their brightly coloured bicycles, laughing and shouting at each other.

Vita looked unworried. Her dark eyes gazed steadily off into the distance.

'I'm not here to talk about Simon,' Lucy said finally.

Vita looked at her quickly. 'I'm not interested in taking him from you,' she said hastily. 'You have to believe that.'

'I do,' replied Lucy. She stuck her hands in her pockets. Her jeans felt uncomfortably tight, as if she had put on weight recently. All this stress must be making her eat more than usual, she thought. And so preoccupied she had not even noticed.

'But I don't want to talk about that,' she repeated. 'It was a cruel and disloyal thing to do, particularly since you knew that we've been having trouble starting a family. But I'm prepared to believe that it wasn't a serious thing for you. I think that it was a one-off and I'm prepared to forget about it. Honestly.

'What I *do* want to talk about,' she went on, 'is David. Olwyn's son. The Brat, the boy who died. I want to talk to you about what happened to him.'

Vita nodded. What looked like a whimsical smile appeared on her lips, as if she had been expecting this to come up one day.

'I see.' They took a few more steps together, then Vita stopped and faced Lucy. 'What do you want to know?'

'I want to know what happened to him,' repeated Lucy. 'I want the truth. I think you and Perdita poisoned him. You made me get the drugs and then you poisoned him with them. Please tell me exactly how you did it. And—' she paused and drew a deep breath, 'I want to know why.' She looked at Vita challengingly, her heart beating hard in her chest. Was this going to work?

To Lucy's relief, after staring back at her for a moment or two, Vita dropped her gaze and nodded assent. She seemed happy to talk, and Lucy knew that she was going to tell the truth.

'I don't know if we really meant to kill him,' she said. 'It started out as kind of a joke, really. We thought we could play a good trick on him, just make him a bit ill. Then, somehow, it got serious . . .'

Lucy stared at her, her heart beating fast with anticipation. Vita was happy to talk about it.

'Once when I came round to tea,' Vita continued, 'you showed me your father's drawer where all the drugs were kept. It gave me an idea about something I had been thinking about anyway.

'Then another time I came over, I saw a copy of that drugs directory – what's it called – that your father had thrown away. Presumably he'd got a new copy and didn't need the old one any more. So I picked it up out of the bin and slipped it in my pocket while no one was looking.'

'You mean MIMS.'

'That's right. The Monthly Index for Medical Specialties, the prescribing guide for doctors. It was sent free to doctors once a month.

'Well, I took it home and we studied it, Perdita and I. Then one afternoon, we went down to Foyle's bookshop with Anthony. He often liked to spend Saturday afternoons browsing through bookshops. While he was looking at the history books, Perdita and I nipped downstairs to the medical books department, the toxicology section, to read some proper medical texts about poisons and their effects. It was a usefully spent two hours.

'Then, back home, with the MIMS, we were able to pick out a drug that contained atropine sulphate. It's a derivative of deadly nightshade – belladonna. All portions of the plant – the roots, seeds, leaves and fruit – are toxic. If put on the skin, atropine gets absorbed into the body very quickly. The best drug containing atropine, we decided, was one called minims atropine, which is used in drops to treat various eye conditions. If you take it on your eye it's harmless but if it gets into a cut, say, enough can be absorbed to cause death. So we knew that if it was swallowed in large doses, it could kill you. Not that we meant to kill the Brat. We just wanted to make him good and ill. Give him a shock.

'Anyway, we guessed that your father, being a family doctor, would probably have the eye drops in his surgery – possibly even in his drugs drawer. We didn't know for sure, but we thought it'd be worth trying to ask you to get it for us. We could hardly believe our luck when you actually turned up with it.

'That same evening we gave it to him. Olwyn was out. I can't remember what she was doing. Probably collecting one of the younger ones from a friend's house, or something. While she was out, we tricked the Brat into swallowing the whole lot in a glass of chocolate Nesquik – he was always drinking that stuff. We dared him to drink a huge glass, and made a joke that it was poisoned. But he wouldn't believe us. He drank the whole lot in about three gulps. And then,' she paused for a moment, 'he began to have convulsions, within minutes. It was weird. I'll never forget it, seeing the effects work so quickly. At first, he became cheerful and lively – I can still see all this so vividly in my head. He kept dancing around my bedroom and laughing hysterically. He got more and more excited until it was obvious that he was out of control. He was desperately thirsty and kept drinking out of the bath tap and falling about in uncontrollable fits of laughter. He had a sort of ghost-like energy which took him over.

'It was very frightening. Perdita and I did not know what to do. He began to hallucinate. He kept saying that the shape of the bed was changing and the colours were different. He seemed to go completely mad. We had no idea of what to do or what was going to happen, and at that point we were scared, really scared about what we had done.

'Luckily, by the time Olwyn came home, the Brat had calmed down and become quieter. But by then also he had a raging temperature and his skin had gone all red.

'We decided to run and tell Olwyn that David was ill, and she took one look at him and immediately telephoned for your father to come to the house. Olwyn hadn't seen David being delirious and we didn't say anything about it, so she had no idea about how serious it was. We thought the worst of it was over and that he'd recover.

'Your father didn't know about the delirium either, and we didn't tell him. By the time your father had arrived, the Brat was very calm. He had a bright red rash, his skin was hot and dry and his pulse rate had quickened. Not unreasonably, I gather – and luckily for us – your father decided that the boy was having an attack of scarlet fever. The symptoms are not dissimilar to what he was seeing. He made the fatal mistake of waiting to see what happened. He waited an hour, sitting downstairs having a cup of tea with Olwyn. When he saw him again, the Brat was beginning to get drowsy. Your father was uncertain at first but then he decided it would be safer to have him admitted to hospital. He called an ambulance and went home.

'Olwyn went in the ambulance with him. She said that it was on the way to hospital that it was obvious that David was dangerously ill. His temperature dropped and he slipped into a coma. By the time he got to hospital, he was dead.

'The cause of death came out in the postmortem afterwards. Your father had got it wrong, and the doctors knew that the Brat had died from poisoning.

'At first Perdita and I thought we'd be found out but we made up a story and stuck to it: we told everyone that the Brat had stolen the drugs from the doctor's black bag. We told them that he'd been experimenting with it and that he'd swallowed the stuff himself.'

Vita's children had reached the top of Parliament Hill. They stopped and waved to their mother. Vita waved back.

The two women climbed on up the steep hill after the girls. There was silence between them but Vita's words were ringing in Lucy's ears. The children turned and began to cycle off towards the green copse beyond. The women were puffing from the climb.

Lucy turned to Vita. 'You didn't have to tell me the whole truth, did you?'

Vita shrugged. 'No, I didn't.'

'So why did you, if you're incriminating yourself like this?'

Vita turned to look at her. 'Because you wanted to know the truth and I happen to know that you won't spill the beans. At least, that's what Perdita reckons.'

Lucy's thoughts were racing back all those years. She struggled to think straight as the underlying meaning of that last remark became clear. 'You didn't actually know if that particular drug was in my father's drawer, did you?'

'No.' Vita rubbed her eyes. 'That was just a lucky guess.' She paused and then added, 'If that's the right word.'

Lucy fell silent once again. She could not say now that she had not, in fact, found them in the drawer at all. She could not bring herself to say that she had opened up her father's locked drugs cupboard and taken the supply from there.

Now she felt even more implicated; she was as guilty as Vita and Perdita. This was what Andrew meant.

'You talk about it in a very matter-of-fact way,' she commented. 'The boy died. You and your sister killed him. Don't you think it was wrong? Don't you feel guilty?'

Vita turned to look at her. Her eyes were clear and steady. 'We didn't mean to kill him, I told you that. It just happened that way.' Her voice was flat and expressionless, as if she were describing a soufflé that had failed to rise or a business deal that had fallen through. 'Perhaps it was unfortunate that he died, I don't know. But I do know that I wasn't sorry then and I'm not sorry now. And neither is Perdita.

'I suppose,' she went on, 'the difference now is that I can see we weren't really angry with the Brat. It was Olwyn we hated. But we didn't dare admit that at the time, not even to ourselves. I suppose you could say that the Brat died for his mother's sins.

'But whether it was wrong – I don't know. Deep down, I feel that we did the right thing. After all, it had the right effect: we got rid of the Brat and of Olwyn, in the end. She left soon after the Brat died. Went back to Wales, and good riddance! She hated us and we hated her.'

Expression came into Vita's voice only as she spoke those final words.

'Why?' wailed Lucy. 'What did you do to make her hate you so much?'

Vita let out a scornful laugh, full of bitterness.

'What did *we* do? Christ, you don't know anything about what happened to us. Not a single goddamned thing.'

'Then tell me,' pleaded Lucy. 'Help me understand this.'

Vita looked straight at her and said, 'It's not what *we* did, it's what *she* did. That bitch Olwyn. What *didn't* she do to us? But you wouldn't believe it if I told you.' Her voice went soft for a moment but then she thrust out her chin and looked straight at Lucy. 'But it did happen,' she went on. 'Every bit of it.'

'Tell me,' Lucy ordered. 'What happened? Tell me now.'

Vita stared at her, her eyes wild, and shook her head fiercely. 'I can't tell you, I'm sorry. It's impossible for me to tell you.'

To her surprise, as Lucy looked at Vita she felt a great surge of rage build up inside her. Gritting her teeth, she gripped Vita by the arm and shook her. 'You *have* to tell me!' She shouted the words. 'You've ruined a lot of lives. You owe it to me to tell me, you bitch!'

Startled by her own outburst, Lucy let go of Vita's arm and stepped back. 'I'm sorry,' she said, dropping her voice. 'I didn't mean to be vicious.'

But to her surprise, Vita nodded her head. 'You're right, Lucy,' she said, 'I do owe it to you even if it's difficult for me. I shall suffer for weeks for stirring up the memories again, just when I had them under control.' Her voice was soft and sad. 'But I want you to understand everything now, so I don't have a choice.'

Vita turned away towards her children, waving to them cheerily. But Lucy could see that her shoulders were shaking, and the hand by her side was closed into a tight fist. She was silent for a moment, her mind swarming with questions and confusions. Finally she turned to Vita and put a hand gently on her shoulder.

'Tell me,' she said quietly. 'Tell me what happened. I'll believe you, I promise I will.'

They had reached the brow of the hill. Vita quickened her pace and strode on. They could see the girls in the distance, two small dots of colour against the grey-green of the wood.

'Only my siblings know about this. They all know it from their own perspectives, but the outside world is ignorant. We don't even talk about it among ourselves very much because it's so difficult to deal with the memories and to think about what they all mean.'

Then Vita began to talk about her childhood and, as she talked, in her low husky voice, Lucy felt a clammy chill settle over her skin. It was what she had known and what she had not known. It was what had a silent presence in that big Victorian villa all that time ago. Lucy had always been aware of it but did not know what it was until now.

The child is dreaming, unsettled dreams but not frightening. Then someone is shaking her.

'Wake up! Wake up!'

The child surfaces from her deep sleep. She can feel strong fingers clutching her upper arm, pulling her up from the bed.

'What's the matter? What's happened?' The child blinks in the bright light of the overhead bulb.

The voice is matter-of-fact. Sharp.

'The police are here. They've taken fingerprints on the boiler. They have discovered that they're yours. They know now that you keep turning up the boiler to a dangerous level. They've come to arrest you before you set fire to the house.'

The child shrinks back into the pillow. Her face crumples as she begins to cry. She clutches the woman's arm. 'I didn't do anything. Oh, please don't let them take me away . . .'

The woman shakes her head. 'It's no good. They know it's you. They've taken fingerprints.'

The child is panicking. She sobs and clutches the woman's clothes. 'Please, please don't let them take me away,' she begs.

The woman pauses. She disengages the child's hands and steps back.

'Let me go and talk to them. Wait a minute. I'll be back.'

The child sinks down under the covers and squeezes her eyes shut as she prays.

The woman is gone for ages. The child waits and waits. She can feel her heart thumping rapidly in her chest. Any minute now, she will know if she's going to prison or not.

Then the woman returns. She is smiling. The child sits up, anxious, hopeful.

'I've persuaded them to go away. They say they'll forget it this time. But if it happens again, they'll be back.'

The child leaps to her feet and cries with relief. 'Oh, thank you,' she cries, kissing the woman's hand in desperate gratitude. 'Thank you so much!'

The woman strokes the child's hair. 'That's all right, now,' she croons gently. 'Now get into bed or you'll be too tired for school tomorrow.'

The child snuggles down in bed. 'Good night,' she calls. 'And thank you for ever.'

'Olwyn had complete control over us,' Vita began. 'You see, our parents were too wrapped up in themselves and their work and their causes to notice what was going on behind the scenes at home. As far as they were concerned, so long as we didn't disturb their work we could do what we liked. What they didn't realise was that Olwyn came to control us so much that she did whatever she wanted. And she terrorised us.'

The child lies in the dark, unable to sleep. She thinks about her spelling test the next day and wonders whether the weather will be good enough for tennis. She listens to the sounds of the house. Her parents are out, as usual. The television is on downstairs in the den. Outside she hears a car door slam and a motorbike roar up the road. From her bed she can see the occasional flicker of her sister's torch as she reads her book under the bedclothes. It is an hour past lights-out. The house hums with familiar noises, the comforting screech of the water in the pipes, the gentle rattle of the wind against the windowpanes.

Then there is something else! The child holds her breath. Now she does hear the creak of the stairs. Is it the woman? The child tries to hold her breath more. She's trying to listen but all she can hear is the rush of blood in her ears.

Another creak. Silence. A long pause. There is nothing there. No, she always has time to warn her sister. The noises are something else.

But now she does hear quick steps on the stairs.

The child sits up in bed, startled. It is the woman. It's too late to call out a whispered warning. Too late . . .

She listens to the hurried steps, the sharp warnings, the thump, thump of a hard object on the bed. A hard object landing on bony knees under the covers.

Shrinking down under her own bedcovers, the child lays her head on the pillow and watches the woman pass her doorway, the brass poker glinting in her hand. Now she is gone. The child lies still, her open eyes sparkling with fear in the dark. No sound comes from her sister's room. The house is silent.

Vita's voice had dropped to a whisper. 'I can see now how Olwyn got so much power and how she abused that power. I can understand it as an adult, and be appalled, but at the time it just seemed normal for us children to be looked after by someone like that. This is the most awful thing about it – we thought everyone must be treated like that. It was nothing to make a fuss about.'

The child has a large piggy bank made of blue glass. She is saving up to buy a wicker basket for the bright red bicycle her parents gave her for Christmas. She has nearly got enough. She has three and sixpence saved up over the weeks from the pocket money she has not spent on sweets. It is made up of pennies and halfpennies, thrupences and sixpences, and sixpences collected from the tooth fairy. She likes having the money but she likes her piggy bank even more. It was given to her by her grandmother, who had had it as a child, so it's very old. She was given it because she is the eldest granddaughter.

The child comes home from school ready to count her money as she does every Friday. The piggy bank lies in shattered blue glass pieces on the floor of her room. The money is scattered about on the carpet.

She runs in tears to tell the woman, who is making pastry in the kitchen, sprinkling flour over the rolling pin which she pushes skilfully backwards and forwards across the table. The woman has no sympathy. She looks down at the crying child. 'It serves you right for leaving it in a place where it might get broken,' she says, and sprinkles more flour on the table.

Vita's eyes were dull with the pain of memory but she continued.

'Olwyn hit us regularly, with the back of the hairbrush, with wooden coat hangers, even the poker, if it happened to be nearby. If she couldn't find anything, she'd just use her hands and nails. She would creep up to our rooms at night, after the lights were supposed to be out, and if she caught one of us reading she would rush in and whack us on the knees – hard.'

'Surely there were bruises,' interrupted Lucy. 'Didn't anyone say something about the bruises?'

Vita made a snorting sound. 'Well, since Olwyn was the only person who gave us baths and put us to bed, no one else would have had the opportunity to see them. Besides, we were always climbing trees and mucking about, so it was not unusual for us to have bruises anyway.'

'But what about school? Didn't the teachers notice the bruises at school?'

'They may have noticed them but they certainly didn't comment. We were sent to middle-class schools. It would never have occurred to anyone that some of the pupils were being hit with pokers at home. All their pupils came from nice families,' Vita said in a voice loaded with sarcasm.

She smoothed her hair back on her scalp and continued. 'Olwyn particularly liked to hit me on my hands with the hairbrush. She used to hold it over my face as if to hit me there, so I'd hold my hands up to protect myself. Then she brought the brush down in short, sharp whacks on the tips of my fingers and my palms.'

The child is in a deep sleep and dreaming. She fell asleep as soon as she put her head on the pillow. The netball match after school has worn her out. She dreams of her mother and father, and of her brothers and sisters. They are laughing, first with her, then at her. But she is enjoying herself. She is at peace.

Suddenly the light is turned on, the harsh overhead light. The woman is standing by her bed, talking sharply to her in angry tones. Her face is twisted in a scowl.

The child sits up, confused. The woman pulls back the bedcovers and grabs the child by the wrist. She yanks the child off the mattress. 'I've got a crow to pluck with you . . . Get up and clear up that mess you left in the bathroom. How dare you leave your clothes like that, just lying on the floor!'

Blinking in the harsh light, the child crawls out of bed.

Unsteady on her feet, she stumbles to the bathroom and gathers up the piles of clothes in her arms. Her eyes are half closed. She says nothing.

'I'm not your servant, you know,' snarls the woman as she leans against the wall, her arms akimbo. 'Don't you dare do that again or I'll knock you into the middle of next week.'

The child's eyes are half closed as she walks slowly back to her room. She drops the clothes on to the chair in the corner and turns off the light. The child climbs back into the soft warm bed, and as she hears the woman's footsteps going down the landing, she hopes that she will be able to return to that nice dream which had engulfed her just before she was woken up.

As Vita talked, Lucy had to ask herself more than once whether she was dreaming. Vita's words were too unbelievable.

'I used to think that compared with the others, I had it easy,' said Vita. 'Olwyn would yank my little brothers and sisters across the room by the ear. She would literally bang our heads together if we were arguing. She was forever kicking the dog and breaking our belongings, and punishing us severely for the smallest misdemeanours. She killed our pets and told lies about us to our parents. She particularly liked throwing Perdita in the coat cupboard and leaving her there in the dark for half an hour or so. I think she had it in for Perdita more than the rest of us, probably because Perdita stood up to her more than the rest of us did, and Olwyn didn't like that. She wanted to break our spirits completely.'

The child is concentrating hard on her colouring in. She has made the clown's trousers and shirt red. She has given him yellow hair and blue shoes, a lovely deep blue like the sea.

The child smiles at her work. She is working very hard, like a grown-up.

Suddenly, the door opens. The woman walks in and marches straight to the child.

The child shrinks away. The woman is scowling at her.

'Don't take what isn't yours,' she yells. She reaches down to the child and yanks her by the ear to her feet.

The child yelps in pain, her feet barely touching the ground as the woman twists her ear and pulls her out of the playroom and into the hall.

'Oh, please, don't!'

The child cries out but the woman does not listen. She pulls open the door of the coat cupboard and pushes the child inside. Then she shuts the door fast.

The child breathes deeply. She has been in this darkness before. She knows she must fight the panic that creeps up inside her. Her big sister told her how. She is only six but she already knows that she must lie down on the pile of coats and try to think of wonderful things until the woman opens the door again to let in the light of the world.

Vita shuddered and wrapped her arms around herself. 'It gives me goose pimples even now to think about her hands on me. I can still feel her fingernails digging into the flesh of my upper arm.'

Lucy listened as goose pimples prickled on her own back.

'But how on earth could she do all this and get away with it? Where were your parents? Didn't you tell them what she was doing?'

Vita turned her head. The expression on her face was one of unbearable bitterness.

'I did try to tell them, very early on, when I was about

five. I complained to my mother that Olwyn had hurt me. She didn't do anything about it. I waited for things to get better but they didn't. Nothing changed, and I deduced, as only a five-year-old can, that my parents approved of what Olwyn did. I don't know if they really knew what was going on, but I do know that nobody believes the things that children say. They don't want to believe the word of a child.

'Whatever the case, I think my mother did not want to act on the word of a five-year-old, and perhaps waited to witness something herself, I don't know. All I do know is that pretty soon, being treated roughly and unkindly became so much the norm that we all thought there was nothing odd in it. I suppose I grew up believing that was how all adults treated children. We didn't talk about it ever, even among ourselves, because it was normal. There was nothing interesting about it.

The child runs home from school, eager to get back to the picture she has been working on with her new crayons. They are special crayons that become like paint when you dip them in water. She has been doing the picture for two days. It's of a special rainforest with lions and tigers and monkeys and goats, and colourful exotic birds among the green leaves on the trees. The picture is for her mother's birthday. Her mother is going to love it.

The child runs into the house and up to her room. The picture is on the bed. The paper is wrinkled and curling at the edges and the colours have run into each other so that you can hardly make out the animals any more.

The child is staring at it as the woman appears in the doorway.

'It was an accident,' says the woman. 'The flower jug was spilled on it.'

The child's eyes are filling with tears and her throat hurts. She turns away, partly to avoid seeing the light smile on the woman's face, but mainly to prevent the woman seeing how much she cares.

'And it wasn't just the physical side of things that was awful,' continued Vita. 'What Olwyn said did even more damage than her wallops with the hairbrush. Once I was looking at myself in the mirror and asked her about the veins I saw across my chest. She told me they were so big because I had leukaemia. I didn't know what that meant, so I asked her.

'"It means you'll be dead in five years," she told me.

'At first I didn't believe her and told her I was going to ask my parents. She smiled slyly, I can see her face now, and said: "There's no point in asking them. They don't want to upset you by telling you you're dying. So they'll just lie to you. They want you to enjoy the few years you have left without knowing that you're going to die young."'

'But that's incredible!' murmured Lucy.

'Incredible? I believed her for a few years. I used to look at myself in the mirror before bedtime and wonder if I would die that night in my sleep. It was your father who made me think that maybe I didn't have leukaemia, but even when I had the chance, I didn't dare ask him outright.

'She did the same to Perdita, too. Perdita had a hernia in her groin, a small bulge. She asked Olwyn what it was and Olwyn said it was cancer and that Perdita would be dead within a year. I didn't discover this until years later. Nice, eh.'

Lucy listened in horror. 'That's dreadful,' she said. 'I

don't believe that anyone could treat little children that way.'

Vita sniffed.

'Yes, that's the problem. It's really inconceivable. Unless you were there. And you know, the most ridiculous thing is that we deluded ourselves into thinking that we liked Olwyn – even loved her. I used to say that when I had children I would have Olwyn looking after them, just as my parents' nannies had looked after two generations of children. That's how deluded I was. For Christ's sake, when Olwyn left, after the Brat died, we all *cried*. I suppose that even though she was so cruel, she was all we had ever known. And we were afraid of who might replace her. We had lived with her long enough to judge her moods as far as possible. So we knew when to duck and dodge, and how to get around her as much as we could. For in the end, getting on with Olwyn became crucial for our survival. How could we break away and denounce her? It was dangerous, it could backfire, but it would also mean threatening the only solid base we had, however cruel it was. We could not denounce her because as children you don't know what's really right and wrong. And you cling to what you know, however bad.

'No, it was the Brat we all hated. I see now, of course, that we hated him because we couldn't risk hating Olwyn, since our survival depended on getting on with her. He was such a pain, such a sneak – always getting us into trouble. And he was incredibly lazy, never doing anything he was supposed to do while we all had to do our jobs in the rota. And he was a thief, always stealing our things.' She stopped and took a deep breath. 'And, of course, Olwyn never laid a hand on him. He would stand back and smirk while she walloped us.'

Vita paused, her eyes shut tight.

Then she opened them. 'But now . . . now that I'm a parent myself, I can see that he was just a sad, mixed-up eight-year-old who was desperate for attention. His only sense of worth stemmed from the fact that his mother had complete control over the rest of us.

'I suppose that at some level we all knew that attacking David was the one way we could get at Olwyn without her destroying us in retaliation. And we didn't mean to kill him, we really didn't. It just happened that way . . .'

Lucy ran her tongue uneasily over her lips.

'Don't you feel even a little bit sorry for Olwyn? After all, David was her only child, and she lost him.'

Vita frowned and spun round to face her. She was breathing heavily with rage.

'No, I don't feel sorry for her at all. And I never shall. What she did to us was criminal. It is only with my adult eyes that I can see just how criminal it was.'

'But there were other adults there,' Lucy said. 'Your parents were there. Why did they allow it to go on? Surely they're responsible in some way.'

Vita was silent. As she looked into the distance, Lucy could see a watery glint in her eyes. Then she turned, her upper lip quivering with barely contained emotion.

'Do you remember the trial of Rosemary West a few years ago? The woman who murdered those young women with her husband, and sexually tortured them? She and her husband had lots of children, and they were abused too. The ones who testified, or talked to the press afterwards, all said that at the time it seemed perfectly normal to be treated like that by their parents. They assumed that all families were like theirs, and they believed that for twenty years. They also said that they still loved their parents. Well, it was the same way for us.

'Yes, ultimately our parents were responsible. They employed Olwyn and they chose to keep her on, even after we had told them what she did. They chose to be blind and deaf about what went on because it suited them. They could get on with their lives and their children did not bother them. Which is what they wanted. They are selfish people. They always have been. They have always been wrapped up in each other and concentrated on their own careers and all their stupid causes. If it wasn't Cuba, it was the Vietnam War or battles with Camden Council, or some cause at the Camden Arts Centre. It was never us they thought about. They liked their public image as glamorous young parents of a vast family of brilliant and talented children, but they didn't really care about us as individuals. And they didn't want to put any effort into bringing us up.

'But I do love them, even if they don't really love us as parents should. And so I can almost forgive them in a way that I could never forgive Olwyn. If I saw Olwyn in the street today, I would attack her in some way. If I could poison her, I would. I'd like her to die a slow, painful death.

'And all my siblings feel the same way, particularly the younger ones. They suffered most in that monster's hands. You talk to them and see. They were all messed up by her. Not one of us has had a successful relationship: I think we're all incapable of getting close to anyone. Our parents were too remote to love us properly, and Olwyn was no substitute. All she taught us was how to survive. And to hate.

'And she succeeded: Perdita and I do not feel guilty at all about killing David. We were young, but we were all still old enough to know what we were doing when we tried to poison him – even if we didn't know how far it would go.'

*   *   *

The boy is on his hands and knees, his head close to the dog basket. The dog licks its lips and looks warily at him. The boy reaches out and pulls a thick whisker out of the dog's muzzle. The dog jerks its head away and growls gently. A warning. The boy laughs and pulls again, harder. The dog bares its teeth. The boy laughs. The dog snarls, then snaps its jaws, catching the boy's hand. The boy cries out and jumps to his feet. He runs crying to his mother who is ironing in the corner of the room. The boy holds out his hurt hand to her.

The boy's mother puts down the iron and walks across the room. The dog cringes into the far corner of the basket. The dog yelps as the boy's mother's foot kicks it hard. The boy's mother scoops up the loose skin at the back of the dog's neck and yanks the animal out of the basket. She carries the dog to the back door and throws it down the steps. The dog lands heavily. Its legs give way and its head crashes into a large garden tub filled with bright scarlet pelargoniums. The dog yelps loudly. It scrambles to its feet and limps painfully, its tail between its legs, to the bottom of the garden where it hides, trembling, under the blackcurrant bush, and licks its bruised body.

The women walked on round to Highgate ponds where the girls fed the ducks with the stale bread they had brought with them in a plastic bag. 'All my siblings are driven to do good, to protect the vulnerable in the world,' said Vita. 'You could say that's a good thing, but I think it's at the cost of any possible personal happiness.'

'What about you? You're the only one who is not in a profession, not a lawyer or doctor.'

Vita nodded. 'Yes. I am the odd one out in that way, but

I am also the only one with children. What happened to us makes it very difficult to be a parent . . .'

Her voice trailed off, and then cracked as she added softly, 'My children have suffered enough with the death of their father. But for me, every day they get older I ask myself how Olwyn could have got away with it for so long. And,' her voice cracked, 'I blame myself for not protecting the little ones, my younger siblings, more . . .'

The women said no more. Lucy had heard enough and Vita was drained. She was also now going to have to live with the revived horrors she had been forced to tell Lucy.

On the way home Lucy felt nauseous. Every time she imagined the scenes in the Valentine home, sour gorge rose in her throat. There were terrible, awful things going on in the house she had always thought was Paradise. She felt ashamed of herself for having been blinded by the glamour.

Lucy was shaken by the description of David's poisoning, and the cold clinical manner in which Vita had told her. Lucy now knew that she could never tell Vita the full impact of her and Perdita's deed. She could never tell her that the Valentine girls had not only murdered a child but they had also almost destroyed her own father. Certainly, they destroyed his career; his marriage and spirit had just about survived. She did not tell Vita because she knew that Vita would not care.

But beneath the shock of what she had just heard – both the details of Olwyn's cruelty and Vita's unrepentant hardness – Lucy felt a lightness springing up inside her. It was very strange, as if a voice inside her were singing – clear and loud – expressing an extraordinary elation.

Her talk with Vita seemed to have caused something to lift, something like a heavy dark blanket that had, for years, concealed some soft part of herself. She suddenly felt as if a wonderful space had opened up inside her, and around her, freeing her from something that had imprisoned her.

Now she could see what had happened. Andrew's request to get drugs from their father's drawer had forced her to confront something she had been running away from for nearly thirty years. Now she had turned and confronted it. She herself had done something wrong, something that had terrible consequences, and she had finally acknowledged it.

CHAPTER 20

August, 1997
The Cry of the Children

The days between Andrew's attempted suicide and his death took on a strange timeless quality. They were dreamlike, as though time were suspended. There were nine days in all. For those close to him it seemed like an eternity. Even when someone is seriously ill and obviously close to dying, he can linger on and on, waiting for the mystical moment when he finally slips from being a living person to a dead one.

Andrew's GP was heroic. He understood Andrew's terror of going back to hospital and of treatment that just kept him alive regardless of the quality of his life. He offered Andrew an alternative.

'You can declare that you want no more treatment, except that necessary to alleviate discomfort or pain. You can stay at home and be looked after by the palliative care doctor and his team.'

Andrew forced a wry grin. 'The palliative care doctor! You forget, I trained as a doctor myself. We used to call him the terminal consultant. I suppose that sounds too real.'

Thus Andrew came under the care of the local palliative care team, a group of doctors and nurses who specialised in the care of dying people. Andrew was put on a diamorphine drip which, at regular intervals, pumped its exquisite relief straight into his veins. The heroin made him sleepy and, for the most part, calm, as he lay in bed propped up against a high bank of soft pillows.

Every one of those nine days, as Lucy sat in her kitchen and drank a mug of morning coffee, she would look at the calendar on the wall. Would this be the day? Would this be the deathday that Andrew would never know and his family remember for ever?

Since Andrew could no longer be left alone, Patrick and Lucy divided up their days to look after him around the clock. Patrick obviously took the greatest share, looking after Andrew in the night as well as in the mornings before going to work in the afternoons.

Lucy took over at lunchtime and would take her work to do quietly while Andrew slept in the room upstairs.

The house was quiet for most of the day, except when the palliative care team came for their daily visit, or when friends came to sit upstairs next to the bed and whisper quietly to Andrew as his strength slipped away. Hilda and Dr Butler came every evening, driving up from south London in their car. They looked strained and subdued. They said very little on their visits, but always stayed for an hour, sitting on either sides of the bed, holding Andrew's hands.

Andrew went downhill rapidly. He gave up the fight. For the first few days he was capable of getting out of bed and coming downstairs. Once he even got dressed but it was upsetting to see how baggy his clothes were on his skeletal frame.

He had no appetite. His intestines were out of control. He ate very little and vomited up anything he did force down his throat. He became weaker and weaker.

Soon he was unable to go to the lavatory without help. He had become incontinent. The indignities grew every day. First there were the pads strategically placed to prevent him soiling the sheets. Then there was a catheter fixed to a condom pulled over his penis so he did not have to get out of bed to urinate. He had bed sores on his elbows and hips. His bottom was raw from the diarrhoea.

Lucy longed for the pneumonia to take over and kill him off. But, cruelly, it held off, refusing to come and put him out of his misery.

He talked to the doctor on the palliative care team and begged him to give him a massive dose of heroin and be done with it.

The doctor refused. 'I'm not in the business of killing my patients,' he said. And he said to Lucy later: 'I'm interested in making sure they have a good death.'

A good death! How could the death of a thirty-five-year-old, in any circumstances, be a good death? It made Lucy angry. There was nothing good about Andrew's dying. It was degrading and undignified. As she washed him down with a flannel, dressed his weeping pressure sores, changed the bed and tried not to retch if he soiled yet another set of sheets which required changing, she tried to keep her mind off the reality of it all. She tried to think of Andrew as the chubby-limbed little brother she used to wash in the bath, a little boy who needed his nappy changed, not this wizened creature who looked like a starving man of eighty, whose face was so wasted that it was impossible to read it or to decipher his expressions. Smiles could be grimaces, grimaces smiles. Her mental tricks did not work.

On the ninth day, Lucy could stand it no longer. When she arrived, she stood in the doorway of the bedroom and took a good look at her sleeping brother. She imagined coming to him afresh, trying to see him with the eyes of someone who had not seen him since he had become ill. And she was shocked. Andrew looked truly cadaverous. His body was completely emaciated so that his skin and remaining flesh hung from his long bones, his skull clearly defined with huge, sunken eyes and receding lips. When he slept, his eyelids did not close but remained half open constantly. Only the pulsating throb of his heart, faint but still visible under the thin skin stretched over his ribcage, indicated that Andrew was still alive.

For a while, Lucy tried to work at Andrew's bedside. She was copy-editing a novel, a fast-paced commercial thriller for which the publishers had high hopes. The vitality of the characters made her all the more aware of the heavy air and sickly-sweet smell of death that filled her brother's home.

Occasionally Andrew would surface into something like full consciousness. He mumbled in an incomprehensible rasping whisper. On the last day of his life, Lucy talked to him for a few minutes. He was thirsty and she lifted a beaker of water – one of the training cups that young children use when they are graduating from a bottle – to his parched lips.

'I'm so weak,' he said. His voice was raspy, like an old man's. He sank back against the pillows, his eyes half closed.

Lucy took his hand and squeezed it. 'What are you feeling, Andrew?'

He turned back to look at her. The fear in his eyes would haunt her for ever.

He struggled to lift his head and he made an obvious effort to talk so that his sister could hear. 'I'm terrified. I don't believe in an afterlife, but I'm so frightened . . .' His voice faded away.

Lucy winced and squeezed his hand again. 'Remember what Socrates said, it's just a dreamless sleep . . .'

But Andrew was frowning, his eyes shut, as if in pain. There was nothing she could say. She stared down and watched her brother as he dropped his head back on to the pillow. His breathing became steady and deep as he sank once again into sleep.

Lucy sat beside his bed for a long time. They were all so tired of this. It had been going on for too long now. She loved her brother and did not want to lose him, yet she also longed for him to be out of his misery. And there was no possibility that he could do anything other than deteriorate. His life could not get better. It could only get worse. Her sense of powerlessness made her angry.

As she sat there, she had a thought. She was not entirely powerless. She was in a position to end his suffering right then, if she wanted to. The opportunity was there. They were alone in the house. No one was expected for a couple of hours.

She glanced at the pillow on the floor and then up at her brother. Andrew's breathing was loud. His mouth lay open and a stream of saliva dribbled out of the corner to collect in a dark patch on the blue pillow.

The whir of the driver pumping more heroin into Andrew's bloodstream sounded like the roar of a train in Lucy's ears.

She knew she had to do it. As if in a trance, she lifted the pillow and clutched it to her breast for a second. Then she leaned over her brother's bed.

Andrew struggled only momentarily. He had no strength in his body left to fight. His arms flapped feebly for a few seconds. Then he managed to push himself up a few inches off the bed, his body rigid. For a horrible moment, Lucy thought that he would throw her off. She shut her eyes and pushed down harder.

Then it was over. He relaxed, peaceful at last.

Lucy's heart was pounding hard as she pushed the pillow behind Andrew's head. Leaning over, she gave Andrew a long kiss on the cheek. His eyes, still half closed, were dead and unseeing. Relaxed. At peace.

Lucy's head was clear as she rang the GP and told him that Andrew had stopped breathing. Then she rang Patrick, Simon and her parents. She went into the kitchen and put on the kettle to make some tea. She felt in complete control, breathing hard, proud of what she had done. Reaching into her handbag, she pulled out her diary. She flicked through the pages to reach the correct date. Then she wrote, 'Andrew died at four ten today.' The date was August 2nd. Andrew's deathday, the day he would never know. She measured out the tea and poured boiling water into the pot. Her eyes were dry.

It was only when Simon arrived thirty minutes later, having got a taxi from work, that she broke down and let herself cry.

She cried for the loss of her brother, both the little boy she had loved and cared for, and the adult man she had adored so much. She cried for her parents and for Patrick. She could never tell Patrick what she had done; his deep despair at not being at Andrew's bedside at the moment of death made her realise that. It had not occurred to her that he might have cared so much about such a thing. She was glad that she did not have enough room inside herself to accommodate the guilt about Patrick as well.

That evening, Andrew's family and friends gathered at the flat. Patrick was in control of himself for much of the time but every now and then he would break down and cry. Hilda and Dr Butler sat on the sofa, red-eyed and silent, while Simon held Lucy in his arms.

Lucy was relieved that there had been no suspicions about Andrew's death. The doctor filled out the death certificate. He wrote AIDS as the cause of death and gave it to Patrick so that he could register the death. If the doctor had suspected anything, he was not going to make a fuss about someone's life being ended a few hours or days before it would have ended anyway. Everyone had suffered enough. Besides, he had other patients to see. A few hours before Andrew had died, the doctor had attended the home birth of a baby girl just down the road. A nice balance that, a home death and a home birth both in one day. The balance of life, he thought as he drove home to his young family that night.

Rosie came round to the house on her way home from work. Like everyone else, she wanted to see Andrew's body. Lucy took her up to the bedroom and they stood together, staring at Andrew's face. The blood was draining away, so that his skin had begun to take on the waxy yellow look of the dead.

She touched his forehead. 'He's cold.'

'His body's still warm. It seems to go from head to toe.'

Rigor mortis was beginning to stiffen his hands.

'I suppose the virus is dead too, now,' said Rosie quietly. 'And good riddance.'

Lucy sighed. 'It's weird to think that I'm an only child now.'

The women continued to stare down at Andrew, now in silence. Rosie lifted the white sheet to look at the wasted body underneath. Andrew's penis lay curled against his thigh like a fat little worm. Rosie dropped the sheet and began to cry.

'You know I slept with Andrew once.' She sniffed loudly.

Lucy looked up in surprise. 'I didn't know that. When?'

Rosie smiled sheepishly and blew her nose. 'Yes, I seduced him when he was eighteen. I think he was hoping he would discover he was really attracted to women after all.'

She smiled ruefully. 'It failed, of course. It was hopeless all round, but we laughed about it afterwards. He still respected me in the morning!'

The two women laughed together. 'Now I understand why Andrew was so fond of you,' said Lucy. 'You were probably the only woman he ever slept with.'

'You're right,' laughed Rosie. 'I guess I should be proud of that, though maybe I put him off for ever . . .'

They stayed with Andrew's body for another fifteen minutes, saying nothing, just lost in their own thoughts and memories of Andrew when he was alive.

Lucy was tempted to tell Rosie what she had done but she decided not to. One day, perhaps, but not yet.

That night Lucy dreamed that she had given birth to twins, a boy and a girl. They were perfect. As she came out of the hospital, she held them up above her head for the crowd outside to see them. The crowd cheered loudly at her achievement and her GP presented her with a medal for her courage. It was a good dream. Lucy woke up feeling unusually refreshed and calm, and she had an uplifting sense that this dream marked the end of her childmares. Her night torments were over.

The next day Lucy rang the undertaker to arrange the funeral. She was glad to have such a responsibility. It helped to focus her thoughts during that stagnant period between the death and the formal farewell. There had to be a closing of the door, a final acknowledgement and acceptance of the end. She could suddenly understand how distressing it must be for people whose loved ones are blown to smithereens in a bomb explosion or lost in the bottom of the sea in a plane crash. It seemed to her that there was a basic need to know where a dead body was, and to have access to it, regardless of whether it finally ended up eaten by worms in a wooden coffin or burnt to grey ashes in the heat of the crematorium flames.

In many ways Andrew's death felt like a huge relief to Lucy. No longer did she have to babysit every afternoon – it had only been a couple of weeks but it felt like months – no longer did she have to feed him like a baby, help him to the lavatory, or clean his sheets. No longer did she have to carry his fear for him or have to assure him that he would be all right. She was aware of how steady she felt about his death. It was a relief because so much of the mourning had taken place as he was dying.

She did not know it yet but the missing of Andrew would not be felt for at least a year. The sharp pang of sorrow at the simple fact that he was not around to enjoy or share with her. She would think she could see him in the street, fleetingly, or hear his voice in a crowded train. She would turn in wonder and excitement before reason caught up with her and disappointment hit.

No, all that was to come. But what Lucy was aware of now was the fact that she would remember two Andrews, the healthy younger brother who was so quick and funny and handsome, and then the ill one, lying dying in his bed, his large sunken eyes looking at her with fear. Two different people, yet the same.

None of this was said to the undertaker. He was solemn

and sympathetic and arranged to come at lunchtime to take Andrew's body away.

Lucy and Simon went over in the morning to be with Patrick, and found him dressing Andrew's rigid body in his best clothes.

'He was so fond of these Paul Smith trousers,' Patrick said. 'There was a GAP shirt that went really well with them, but I can't find it. I'll have to iron another one.' And he disappeared to the laundry room. Lucy heard him rummaging around in the washing machine, then the swish-swish of the steam from the iron. Alongside the steam noise was another sound which Lucy couldn't identify at first. Then she realised that it was the sound of Patrick sniffling through his tears.

A few minutes later he came back with a perfectly ironed white cotton shirt. Lucy helped him lift Andrew's stiff body as he pulled the shirt over his wasted chest, buttoned it, and tucked the tails into his trousers. Andrew had once filled that shirt with gym-trained muscles. Now it hung loose and billowy on his torso.

The black-clad undertakers arrived promptly at twelve. They came in a black van which they had parked in the only available parking space, twenty yards down the road. They had a stretcher with them. Dressed in black, with slicked-down hair, they were dour and tight-lipped. They mumbled their respects and then asked the whereabouts of 'the deceased'.

They laid out the body and invited everyone to view Andrew before he went off. Patrick declined. Afterwards, Lucy wished she had too. It was a grotesque sight: Andrew dressed up in his oversized clothes, his eyes half shut and sunken in darkened sockets, his arms stiff across his chest, his skin grey against the brilliant white of the cotton shirt. She did not linger.

Then it was time for them to take Andrew away. The undertakers opened up the stretcher and unzipped a big black body bag. They placed the fashionably dressed corpse in it. Then they zipped it up, carried it carefully down the stairs and out of the house and down the road.

As Lucy, Simon and Patrick watched Andrew being loaded into the back of the van, they all broke down. Hugging each other clumsily and desperately, they wailed loud cries of anguish.

The morning of the funeral, Lucy went with Simon to buy food and paper plates for the gathering afterwards. The manager of the shop cheerily rang up the items – dozens of sandwiches and a stack of quiches and flans – and placed them in bags. He was a chirpy young man, no more than twenty-five years old and proud of his professional efficiency.

'Having a party, eh?'

Lucy and Simon exchanged uneasy looks.

'Er, well, sort of,' Lucy finally managed to say.

'Not going to eat them all yourselves, are you?' the young manager persisted. 'Looks like a right old beanfeast. Say, you're not getting married, are you?'

After another long, embarrassed pause, Lucy blurted out: 'Actually, it's for a funeral.'

The manager stopped dead in his tracks and looked at her with his jaw going. Words tried to come from his mouth, but he said nothing.

'Don't worry,' Lucy said. 'You weren't to know. I'll pay by Access if that's OK.'

*   *   *

The funeral was held at the crematorium in East Barnet. Lucy clutched the tape she had made from the CDs Andrew had left for her. It was a cold, overcast day with patches of drizzle.

Patrick was going to conduct the ceremony and had been holding himself together well. Rosie arrived dressed in a smart black Armani suit. Her face was puffy from crying; she had hardly stopped for the past few days.

Lucy's parents arrived in their little blue car. Dr Butler helped his wife out and escorted her into the building, holding her by the elbow as if he feared she might fall. And, indeed, Lucy thought that she had never seen her mother look so frail.

The service lasted forty minutes, which was all they had been allowed by the crematorium. Earlier in the morning Lucy had been worried that no one would come, but as the room filled up she saw that her fears had been groundless. They entered to the accompaniment of the Gypsy Kings, a mournful wail about the pain of lost love. By the time it had finished the room was packed with friends of Andrew's, several of them, Lucy noted grimly, showing signs of the same horrid disease. Nearly everyone in the room was crying.

The service was simple, with readings by friends from a selection of poems by A.E. Houseman, Walt Whitman, Mark Strand. Then the Cat Stevens song was played, with its plaintive protest against parental neglect.

Lucy glanced over at her parents to see how they reacted to this jibe from their dead son. But they either didn't listen or didn't understand. They sat staring glumly at the long coffin on the conveyor belt at the front of the room. The coffin was a spectacular sight, painted by a friend with brightly coloured scenes from the Sistine Chapel. The top was smothered with small white roses.

Lucy was beginning to feel ill. Her eyes drooped with exhaustion and she felt an overwhelming weakness coming over her. Surely she was not coming down with something, not now.

Trying to rouse herself for the final stages of the service, she rolled her head around to loosen up the stiff neck muscles. As she did so, she looked at the back of the room and was startled to see Vita and Perdita Valentine standing there together. Her mind went temporarily blank, her thoughts moving away from the service.

And then, suddenly, it was over. The blue curtains had opened and the lovingly painted coffin was being rolled into the furnace, with the ethereal music of Mozart's *Jesu Domine* soaring over the scene. As the curtain closed the music ended, and there was silence. Simon stood up to invite everyone back to Andrew's and Patrick's house, and the mourners started rising from their chairs. Everyone trooped out and stood around outside the crematorium, making small talk, lingering, some thinking about the coffin with its wasted contents burning in the fire, others thinking of the very different, healthy Andrew they had known.

Lucy stood to the side on her own. She breathed deeply, glad that the ritual was finally over and glad to get fresh air into her lungs.

She looked over at her parents who were standing together near the mass of flowers laid out carefully on the ground. They had spent a lot of time with Andrew in the end, but if only they had accepted his differences earlier, she thought. Everyone might have been a little happier.

The crowd had gathered around the sombre wreaths of flowers, scrutinising the cards to read the messages and to see who had said goodbye in this way. Lucy sighed and blew her nose and looked around for the Valentine sisters.

They had approached Dr Butler. Lucy watched them shake his hand, and then turn to Hilda and express their condolences with great respect. Then they backed away and stood a few yards away from the rest of the crowd. Lucy saw now that they were both wearing long flowing rain cloaks to protect them from the fine drizzle that had started to fall. It was chilly for August. She shivered.

The Valentine sisters were looking at her. Lucy nodded and walked over to them. She felt exhausted from the anxiety of the service. She realised how difficult the days between Andrew's death and his funeral had been. She could now see the point of a funeral, the final goodbye. It made her feel a little more settled now that it was over. Like the relief she used to feel after an important exam, she felt she could let go, if not collapse.

She felt quite light-headed.

'Well done,' said Vita with a light smile. 'It was a good service. It was personal and warm.'

Next to her Perdita looked at Lucy with her disturbingly pale eyes and nodded in agreement.

'Patrick and Simon did it all, really. And it's been hardest for Patrick, of course.'

Lucy looked at the sisters for a few moments. She had a longing to say something. The words were in her head. The women stared back at her. Lucy's eyes darted from one face to the other. She wanted to tell them what she had done. She wanted to tell them that she had killed Andrew, that she was as strong as they. She had had the courage to take away a life because it was necessary to do so. She was one of them, but there was a difference between them. What they did all those years ago had been wrong; what she did last weekend was right.

The three women stood there only for a few moments but in those moments, Lucy felt something give way. She was released from the hold these sisters had had over her for all her life. She had never realised it had been there until she cast it off.

'We must be going,' Perdita said quietly.

'You won't come back for some refreshments? You're very welcome.'

Vita shook her head. 'No, thank you. We won't stay . . .' She reached over and grasped Lucy's hand. She looked steadily at her. 'We'll see you . . .'

The sisters turned and walked away side by side. They walked in step, their long rain cloaks floating out gracefully behind them.

Lucy watched them walk down the gravel path between the gravestones towards their car. As she watched them go, she wondered if she would ever see them again. And she realised, as she wondered, that she did not care if she did or not.

She recalled vividly the deep longing to be like them, to be a Valentine child. Now she knew she no longer felt it. They were hard-hearted and cold. It was not their fault, perhaps, their childhood had made them that way. But Lucy was not like them at all, and she did not want to be, either. Not any more.

Her spirits lifted as she turned to walk back to the crowd of mourners by the flowers. Rosie came up to her. Her nose was red and she looked miserable. 'I won't come to the house,' she apologised. 'I have a lot of work to do but I also feel like being on my own for a bit.'

'I understand,' said Lucy. 'I wouldn't mind being on my own, too. Thank you for all your support – and I'll let you know what I decide about that job soon. I'm sorry I've taken so long to respond to the offer, but as you know I've been preoccupied.'

'Just so long as you tell us next week. We can't wait any longer than that because we'll have to find someone else if you say no.'

Lucy kissed Rosie on the cheek. 'Thanks a lot for your support in every way. You've been great.' She glanced at Rosie's suit. 'Nice bit of material there,' she commented.

Rosie chuckled. 'Yes, I bought it with my dress allowance. It's a perk. We're supposed to give back the designer clothes at the end of each year and they're sold in discount boutiques, or something.' She lowered her voice. 'The trick is to buy a Marks & Spencer version and swap the labels!' With that, she gave Lucy a strong hug, turned on her heels and walked off towards her car.

The gathering at the house was a mixed affair. Most of Andrew's friends were having a good time. They had been to too many friends' funerals over the past few years to be numbed by the pain any more. For Patrick, it was hard, and for the Butler family, it was grim.

Lucy longed to go home with Simon and shut herself away from the world. The buzz of conversation around her made her feel dizzy. The sip of wine had sent a wave of nausea through her.

Her father walked across the room to her. He looked tired. Lucy thought that he was looking much older than his years.

'I was surprised to see those Valentine girls,' he said. 'It was touching that they came along. I didn't know that Andrew meant anything to them.' He paused and looked thoughtful. 'Funny things, those girls. I was just thinking about the way they acted all those years ago when their housekeeper's son died.'

He stared into the distance, a puzzled expression on his face. 'I don't know why I've suddenly thought about it. I haven't thought about any of that business for a long time. Those girls were the two who were so adamant that they'd seen the boy take that medication out of my bag. I was always pretty certain that I didn't keep it in the bag at that time. Yet they were so sure of it . . .'

His voice trailed off, and he fell silent. Lucy stood beside him in silence. She owed it to him to release him from his torment. 'You were right, Daddy,' she said quietly. 'You remember correctly.'

Dr Butler glanced at her. 'What did you say?'

'I said that your memory is correct. The drugs were not in your bag.'

Her father turned to look at her, his face so tired and grey. 'You were too young. You don't know anything about what happened.'

Lucy looked deeply into her father's eyes. She was aware of some of Andrew's friends hovering behind her, waiting to offer their condolences to the old parents. She touched Gordon's forearm. 'I'll tell you about it when we meet next,' she said softly. 'This isn't the time, not now . . .'

There was no time to say more. The hovering couple engaged Gordon in conversation and Lucy moved off to talk to her mother, leaving her bewildered father in the corner.

Lucy joined her mother who was clutching a glass of orange juice, staring around the room.

'I still can't believe I'm here after the funeral of my own child,' she said quietly to her daughter. 'I can't believe that my son has predeceased me. It's just not natural.'

They stood against the wall watching the crowd of young people, Andrew's friends, talking, drinking and smoking, and laughing. They were all trying to have a good time, as they knew Andrew had wanted them to.

'They're all such nice, respectable, successful young people,' Hilda said, her voice choking. 'Every one of them has come up to your father and me to say wonderful things about Andrew. They obviously loved him a lot.'

Lucy watched the tears creep into her mother's eyes. 'It makes me sad to think of Andrew in the company of these friends,' continued Hilda. 'We've barely seen Andrew as an adult, and I know that's really been our fault.' She corrected herself. 'My fault. And now it's too late . . .' Her voice cracked again.

Lucy slipped her hand through the crook of her mother's arm. 'At least you've seen more of him over the past few months,' she said.

It occurred to her at that moment that she was so very different from her mother, and she wondered briefly if that fleeting acquaintance with the Valentines, the nonconformists, had saved her from such a fate. How could she know? But she wanted to believe that it was true.

Hilda nodded. 'Yes, and I'll cherish those moments with Andrew, and what I've learned from him in that time.' Her voice sounded wistful and sad. 'He taught me some good things, though, and I'm proud of him for that. He has made me think about things I've never questioned before, and he taught me that I can change – I hope for the better – even at the age of sixty.'

As she spoke, her husband came over to them. 'I think I'm ready to go home now, dear,' she said, turning to him. 'Let's leave these young people alone.'

Dr Butler was surprised by the gentleness in his wife's voice. She had not spoken to him like that for many, many years. Taking her by the arm, he pulled her gently to him and kissed her on the cheek. 'Let's go,' he said. 'I'm ready.' Then, turning to Lucy he touched her arm. 'We'll talk soon, yes?'

Lucy walked her parents to the front door to see them out. Simon came over to join her. They said their farewells, and as they shut the door, Simon placed an arm around Lucy and kissed the top of her head. 'I think it's going as well as it could.'

Lucy nodded. 'Andrew wouldn't be disappointed,' she said, pressing herself against him.

The day after the funeral, Lucy managed to get an appointment to see her doctor. She was certain that something was wrong. She was feeling nauseous and exhausted almost constantly. She expected the doctor to tell her that she was experiencing the normal symptoms of bereavement or anxiety, but she wanted reassurance, whatever it was.

Dr Kenny asked about her symptoms, then said she'd better have a look at her. The doctor listened to her heart and lungs and felt her neck and armpits for swollen glands. She looked down her throat and into her ears. Then she told her to lie down on the examination couch. She prodded and probed Lucy's breasts and then took a long time examining her belly, pushing it gently with her fingertips. Then she told Lucy to get dressed and sit down on the chair by the desk.

'Take a deep breath. I can tell you exactly why you're feeling the way you do . . .' She paused and smiled. 'It seems that you are pregnant. About sixteen weeks pregnant, I guess.'

Lucy felt her jaw go slack and her mouth open in amazement. For one ghastly minute she thought about her night with Giles. But that would be impossible if she was as much as sixteen weeks gone.

'Pregnant? How can I be so pregnant?' Lucy continued to stare at her in disbelief.

The doctor continued cheerfully, 'Judging from my examination I'd say you were well into the fourth month.' Dr Kenny ran her finger across a calendar. 'That means you conceived in early April.'

'But that was long before my miscarriage. It's impossible. How can that be?'

Dr Kenny nodded. 'It is possible. The likeliest explanation is that when you were diagnosed as pregnant earlier this year, you had actually conceived twins. When you miscarried, you lost one of them but the other continued to thrive.'

She looked down at Lucy's notes as she spoke, then continued: 'You had the miscarriage at home and, as I recall, you didn't come in for a follow-up examination or scan.'

'No,' Lucy said faintly. She hardly knew what to feel about this astonishing news.

'Well,' the doctor continued, 'it all looks okay to me. Chances are the baby is doing very well. It must be pretty tough to have survived the miscarriage of its twin. I'm sending you down to the hospital for a scan this afternoon and that'll confirm that everything's all right.'

Leaning forward, she touched Lucy lightly on the arm and gave her a friendly, maternal smile. 'I knew you'd get there in the end.'

Later that afternoon, Lucy lay on her back holding Simon's hand while the two of them looked at the flickering black-and-white monitor to their right. Simon was laughing and crying simultaneously at the sight of his embryonic child floating gently around in Lucy's uterus.

'It's going to be all right,' he said, hugging Lucy hard. 'Everything's going to be all right.'

Lucy laughed through her tears. Her throat was tight with emotion. 'I guess I'll have to tell Rosie that I won't be taking that job, not for the time being, anyway.'

'She'll understand,' said Simon.

'I'm not sure if Rosie will think a baby is a good reason for not taking a job, but she'll have to accept it. In fact, I was already having second thoughts about working at the same place as Rosie. Much as I love her, I think I'll love her more if I don't work with her.'

But Simon was not listening. His eyes were fixed again on the black-and-white image on the monitor. 'It's a miracle,' he whispered, 'just a miracle.'

Lucy squeezed his hand and lay back on the pillow. With a contented smile, she shut her eyes. Simon's exclamations of joy were drowned by the sound of happy children's voices echoing in her head.